THE BOOKSHOP ON ROSEMARY LANE

Ellen Berry is an author and magazine journalist. Originally from rural West Yorkshire, she has three teenage children and lives with her husband and their daughter in Glasgow.

When she's not writing, she loves to cook and browse her vast collection of cookbooks, which is how the idea for this story came about. However, she remains the world's worst baker but tends to blame her failures on 'the oven'.

By the same author, writing as Fiona Gibson:

Ellen Berry

the Bookshop on Rosemary Lane

avon

This novel is entirely a work of fiction.
The names, characters and incidents portrayed in it are
the work of the author's imagination. Any resemblance to
actual persons, living or dead, events or localities is
entirely coincidental.

AVON

A division of HarperCollins*Publishers*
1 London Bridge Street,
London SE1 9GF

www.harpercollins.co.uk
A Paperback Original 2016

3

First published in Great Britain by
HarperCollins*Publishers* 2016

A catalogue record for this book is
available from the British Library

ISBN-13: 978-0-00-815712-8

Typeset in Sabon LT Std by Palimpsest Book Production Ltd,
Falkirk, Stirlingshire

Printed and bound in Great Britain by Clays Ltd, St Ives plc

MIX
Paper from
responsible sources

FSC FSC™ C007454
www.fsc.org

Acknowledgements

Writing this book was made all the more mouthwatering, thanks to huge support from Caroline Sheldon, Helen Huthwaite and the wonderful Avon team. Cocktail stick nibbles to Jo Marino and Sabah Khan at Way To Blue. Lashings of wine and cheese for the amazing writing group I belonged to for 16 years – Tania, Vicki, Amanda, Pauline, Sam and Hilary, I miss you lots! Freshly baked vol-au-vents for Jen, Kath, Cathy, Liam, Michelle, Riggsy, Susan, Marie, Jan, John, Jennifer and Mickey. A truly 70s eggnog for Chris and Sue at my favourite bookshop, Atkinson Pryce in Biggar. Finally, to my family: because I love you dearly, I promise not to work my way through my own collection of raggedy 1970s cookbooks.

For Liam
Because I love the way you say *cookery book*

In The Beginning . . .

Of the hundreds of cookbooks in Kitty's collection, an extraordinary number were dedicated to cooking under difficult circumstances. *Meals With One Pan, Dinner For Pennies, The Frugal Hostess*, even *Cooking Without a Kitchen*. At ten years old, Della Cartwright was intimately familiar with her mother's personal library; she could instantly locate *Blancmanges, Jellies and Other Set Desserts*, and lay a finger upon *Rescuing Kitchen Disasters* with no problem at all. She knew, however, that there was no book in the house entitled *Rustling Up Dinner When Your Husband Has Left You For Another Woman*. Which was precisely what Kitty Cartwright needed right now.

Stillness had settled over the kitchen in Rosemary Cottage. Even the books, which entirely lined every inch of available wall space – promising infinite culinary adventures – looked forlorn. Usually the hub of the house, filled with delicious aromas as Kitty chopped and stirred, the room felt cold and uninviting now. A few shrivelled potatoes sat in the wire rack, and tiny flies drifted around them. The milk was sour in the fridge, and the Victoria

1

sponge Kitty had made over a week ago sat, hard and uninviting, beneath its fluted glass dome. Still in pyjamas at 2.30 p.m., Della skimmed her gaze over the books. They no longer promised treats. They *overwhelmed* her.

Della's stomach growled hollowly. Hunger had driven Jeff, her big brother, to his best friend Mick's house at the end of the lane, whilst Roxanne, the youngest, would occasionally emerge from her bedroom to snatch a Jacob's cracker or a handful of dry Sugar Puffs from the cupboard. Mostly, though, she remained in her room, styling the synthetic blonde hair of her army of Barbies.

Della, the middle child, had no interest in dolls. She owned a battered old Chopper bike – the one Jeff had outgrown – that she'd cycle through the mushy fallen leaves entirely covering the winding lanes of the small Yorkshire village of Burley Bridge. Mostly, though, she loved to stay indoors and cook. Kitty had never given the impression that she knew what to do with her children – it was as if they had been foisted upon her, forever requiring name tapes to be sewn into clothes, or to be driven en masse to Clark's in Heathfield for school shoes – but she did seem to appreciate a kitchen assistant. Della had made this her job. Together, mother and daughter would pore over the books. Whilst Kitty took charge in her rather flappy manner, Della would undertake menial tasks: peeling carrots, trimming green beans, and gathering up the eggshells her mother left strewn around in her wake. She felt useful then, as if she *belonged*.

Della ran her fingers along the spines of the books. *What to Cook Today* was where her hand stopped. Perhaps she hadn't known the whole collection after all. She didn't remember seeing that one before. She pulled it from the shelf and studied its plain brown fabric cover. It was slightly stained and smelled musty, its title almost faded away. There were no pictures inside: just tiny type on mottled yellowing pages and a few scribbled notes in the margins. Della fetched a notebook and pencil and, installed at the well-worn kitchen table, she started to flick through the book.

Potato Soup, she wrote in rounded childish lettering. *Roast Chicken. Semolina Pudding.* Warm, comforting foods to coax Jeff back from Mick's and Roxanne away from her Barbies and, most importantly, their mother away from her glass of gin. Della was sensible enough to know Kitty needed to eat, and that gin and tonic didn't count as real food, even with ice and lemon.

Getting up from the wobbly kitchen chair, Della took an elastic band from the rubbery ball which Kitty, frugal to the last, had made by collecting the ones dropped by the postman, and used it to secure her thick brown hair in a ponytail. Then she lifted her own navy blue apron from the hook on the kitchen door and, aware of the distant chink of ice cubes in a glass, turned back to the chapter entitled *Soups and Starters*.

And so she began.

Chapter One

It wasn't a train she was trying to catch but her mother's last breath. So Della *couldn't* be late. 'Start, dammit,' she muttered, repeatedly turning the ignition key: nothing. Her car appeared to be dead. Her mother could be too, very soon, if her brother was right. He'd called just a few moments ago.

'Della,' Jeff had barked, 'things aren't looking good. You'd better get yourself over here right away.' It was the phrase that had stung her: *get yourself over here,* implying that she'd spent the past three days lying prone on the sofa, posting chocolates into her mouth, rather than keeping an almost permanent vigil at their mother's bedside. In fact, even before Kitty had moved to the hospice, Della had done most of the caring, driving over to Rosemary Cottage every day after work, not to mention weekends. Jeff, who was based ninety minutes away in Manchester, was generally 'too tied up' to assist. As for Della's younger sister, Roxanne: despite their mother's decline, this was the first time she'd deigned to venture to Yorkshire from London in three weeks. And just when

Della had dared to pop home to catch up on a little sleep, it had started to happen.

Cursing under her breath, she turned the key over and over. It was as effective as repeatedly jabbing at the button to call a lift.

She scrambled out of her car – a scuffed red Fiat Punto – and glanced around the quiet residential street in panic. Running to the hospice wasn't an option. Della wasn't built for speed, and Perivale House – which sounded like a luxury spa rather than a place where people went to die – was a couple of miles away on the outskirts of the bustling market town. You couldn't just hail a taxi in Heathfield – they had to be booked in advance – and Della couldn't think of anyone she knew who'd be around, ready and willing to drive her, at 3.17 p.m. on a grubby-skied September afternoon.

Whilst pacing at the bus stop she tried Mark on his mobile, knowing he wouldn't pick up; his working days were filled with back-to-back patient consultations. Often he didn't even break for lunch. 'Going to the hospice,' she informed his voicemail. 'It doesn't sound good, love. Jeff and Rox are with her right now and, can you believe this, my bloody car won't start. I'll call you later, okay? Or call me. Yes, please call me, soon as you can. 'Bye.' She tried to calm her breathing before calling Sophie, their daughter, who didn't answer either. Not because she was working – she was probably in Starbucks hanging out with her best friend Evie, or perhaps Liam, the boyfriend who seemed to be fading from her affections – but because MUM had flashed up on her phone. These days, Della was always pleasantly surprised and faintly honoured when her daughter did answer a call.

Finally – *finally* – the bus crawled into view. Della

perched on the edge of the front seat, as if that would get her there faster as it trundled through the bustling market town. Her mother was dying, for goodness' sake, couldn't the driver put his foot down? Of course, it wasn't his fault that Heathfield was especially busy today, it being the first Wednesday in the month and therefore farmers' market day. Never mind a seventy-seven-year-old lady with terminal cancer: people needed their onion marmalades and artisan cheeses. And the driver had to let passengers on and off; it was his *job*, Della reminded herself, conscious of her thumping heart. And her job right now was to be with Kitty, to hold her bony hand as she slipped away to . . . where exactly? Although Della didn't believe in the afterlife, she hoped her mother might drift away to a place where pain, confusion and toxic chemicals would be replaced by a steady trickle of gin.

Come on, bus. Come ON! It had stopped, not at a bus stop but due to a van parked outside Greggs, hazard lights flashing, blocking the lane. Seven minutes, it took, for a man in unforgiving tight jeans to reappear and drive it away. Della felt herself ageing rapidly as the bus finally nudged its way along the tree-lined residential roads and out into the soft, rolling North Yorkshire countryside towards Perivale House. The turreted Victorian manor came into view. The bus doors opened and Della sprang off.

Roxanne and Jeff looked up from Kitty's bedside in the small private room. Jeff muttered something – it might have been '*Here* you are' – but Della couldn't hear properly. All she could do was look at the tiny old lady whose facial skin had settled into little folds around her jawline. A little downy fuzz was all that was left of her hair now.

'Oh, Mum,' Della whispered, kneeling down on the

rubbery floor and taking her mother's hand. Kitty's slim fingers were cold, her ring with its chunky emerald a little loose. 'I didn't get the chance to say goodbye. I'm so sorry.'

Roxanne reached down and squeezed her sister's arm. Apart from pinkish, sore-looking eyes, she was her usual immaculate self in a plain but clearly expensive black shift, plus an embroidered cream cardi and low, glossy black heels. Della was wearing the leggings and faded turquoise T-shirt she'd napped in. Jeff, the eldest of the three and something important in banking, fixed her with a resigned look across the bed. As her siblings were occupying the only two chairs, Della remained kneeling on the floor. 'When did it happen?' she murmured.

'About ten minutes ago,' Roxanne replied.

'Ten minutes! I can't believe it. That's when I was stuck outside Greggs . . .'

'You went to Greggs on your way here?' Jeff gasped,

'No, of course I didn't. I was on the bus, there was a lorry blocking the road.'

'The bus?' gasped Roxanne, who probably hadn't travelled on one since 1995. 'Why didn't you drive?'

Della let go of her mother's hand. 'My car wouldn't start.'

Jeff let out a heavy sigh. 'For God's sake, Dell, you're an adult woman. When are you going to get a proper car that's not held together with string?'

At first, it had seemed like a terrible idea: for the three of them to drive over to Kitty's house less than two hours since she had passed away. But then, the Cartwrights weren't one of those families who gathered purely to be together. They needed a purpose: a birth, a marriage, a significant birthday – or a death. And coming to Rosemary

8

Cottage – in which all three of them had grown up – felt like the right thing to do. They had things to attend to. They needed, as Jeff put it with his customary directness, to 'figure out what needs to be done'.

Mark arrived, still in his work attire of crisp striped blue shirt and dark grey trousers, with Sophie in tow. 'Oh, darling,' he exclaimed, 'I know how hard this is for you.' He gathered Della into his arms and kissed the top of her head where her haphazard top-knot was coming loose.

'Thanks, love,' she said, momentarily soothed by the embrace.

'I'm so sorry, Mum,' cried Sophie, her own tears setting off Della's. 'My phone was out of charge. I'd just got in when Dad came home and said Gran had—' She broke off with a sob.

'It's okay,' Della murmured, hugging her daughter. 'We knew it was going to happen. And, remember, it's been tough for Gran for such a long time . . .' She turned to Mark. 'It's just, I missed it, you know. I was too *late*.'

'It doesn't matter,' he insisted. 'You've done what you could. You've been amazing . . . looking after her, sitting with her for hours and hours.' She caught him throwing Jeff and Roxanne a glance of irritation.

'I just wish I'd seen her more,' Sophie said, blotting away tears on the cuff of her faded red sweatshirt. 'It's too late now. I should've made more effort. I should've gone every day . . .'

'Sweetheart,' Della said, 'you went often enough. Gran knew you loved her. She knew we *all* did.' She caught Roxanne's eye, and a flicker of acknowledgement passed between the sisters.

'What I feel bad about,' Jeff announced, looking around their mother's cluttered kitchen, 'is the state of this place.

9

How could she have lived like this? We really should have done something about it.' He cast a derisory glance over the floor-to-ceiling bookshelves crammed with ancient cookbooks.

'Mum liked it this way,' Della pointed out. 'You know that. She refused to throw anything away.'

'But there's so much *stuff*!' he exclaimed. 'It's oppressive, so dingy and dark. It can't have been good for her.'

'Clutter doesn't make people ill, Jeff,' Della countered, trying to soften the defensive edge to her voice. 'Books don't cause cancer. It was the way Mum wanted it, we couldn't just barge in and take over.'

He exhaled loudly and peered at the shelves, running a manicured nail along the books' spines. Their sheer volume lent Kitty's kitchen the air of a second-hand bookshop. Perhaps, Della figured, the peeling white-washed cottage did seem pretty chaotic when you visited so rarely. Like Jeff before her and Roxanne soon after, Della had been eager to escape Burley Bridge, the once-pretty, now rather shabby and beleaguered village which had formed the backdrop to their childhood. She had, too – albeit settling only seventeen miles away in the nearest sizeable town of Heathfield. However, as Kitty had become more dependent, she'd been the one to make frequent visits. To her, Rosemary Cottage with its vast collection of cookbooks and the enormous pine dresser crammed with chipped china knick-knacks, seemed *normal*.

Roxanne, too, was examining the books. 'I'd forgotten how many of these she had. What was the point? I don't ever remember her cooking much.'

'She did when we were young,' Della reminded her. 'Not so much in later years, after Dad left. But, you know,

10

they were important to her and for whatever reason she couldn't let them go.'

Roxanne smiled, her eerily unlined face looking drawn and pale. 'I'm sorry you've had to deal with all of this, Dell. You know I'd have come up more often if I could. It's just, I've had crazy deadlines lately.' Although Della knew nothing about the world of glossy fashion magazines – apart from the fact that they featured handbags covered in gold buckles and costing £3,000 – she did know that Roxanne's came out monthly, suggesting that she wasn't deluged by 'crazy deadlines' *all* the time.

Yet, while more support would have been appreciated, in some ways it was easier for Della just to get on with things on her own, without Jeff hectoring her and Roxanne fussing and dithering and never quite managing to get anything done. Living the closest to their mother, of course Della had been the one to step in. While Jeff could be patronising – making it plain it was a pity she worked in a shop rather than in the loftier professions of banking or journalism – he couldn't find fault with the way she had managed their mother's care. At least, he'd better not, Della thought darkly. Kitty's doctors' appointments had been dutifully marked on the wall chart in Della's kitchen. She had taken to batch-cooking meals for her mother and, as Kitty had come to rely upon her, Della had noticed her prickliness ebbing away.

They had settled into a comfortable pattern, chatting about nothing much: the weather, their preferred biscuits, an antiques show on TV. The once-formidable Kitty had softened and, for the first time, Della could figure out how to *be* with her: calm, reassuring – like a mother, really. As a child, Della had always been rather afraid of her mother's quick temper. However, towards the end of Kitty's

11

life, Della could tell that her mother liked her at last, or at least appreciated what she did. So did it really matter than the number 43 bus had been too slow today?

'So,' Jeff said, pacing around the kitchen, 'I suppose we'd better get started.'

Della stared up at him. 'What d'you mean, get started?'

He blinked at her. 'I mean, figure out what needs to be done. Isn't that why we're here?'

'Jeff,' Roxanne said sharply, 'Mum only passed away a few hours ago. Nothing needs to be done—'

'And we're here because . . .' Della cut in, before tailing off. How could she put it: that it now seemed *right* for them to have gathered here in the very place where they'd forever complained that there was nothing to do, yet had somehow found infinite ways in which to amuse themselves? Long, lazy summers had seen them roaming through the undulating fields and rather scary woods, summonsed back for tea by Kitty's shrill calls from the garden. Winters had featured endless games of Monopoly and copious reading by the crackling fire in the living room. Irritatingly, Jeff had had the best collection of books, all neatly ordered and catalogued in the floor-to-ceiling bookshelves in his bedroom. It looked – and indeed functioned – like a library. Frequently, Della had been fined twenty-five pence for a late return.

'Well, I'm glad we came here,' Sophie said firmly. 'What'll happen to this place now, Mum?'

Della grimaced. 'We'll sell it, I guess.'

'I'll help with that,' Roxanne cut in quickly, 'but with the funeral, well . . . I'm sorry, I just wouldn't know where to start.'

'It's okay,' Della found herself saying. In fact, she knew precisely what to do, having arranged her father's a decade

12

ago, when Jeff had been too caught up with his newborn twins to get involved, and Roxanne had been rendered helpless by grief.

Roxanne squeezed her hand. 'You're amazing, you know? The way you just . . . get on with things.' She swept back her long highlighted hair. 'I'm sorry, though, I'd better think about getting back. Early start tomorrow, and the weather's not looking too good tonight.' A little light rain, was what she meant.

'Me too,' Jeff said, 'but call me, okay, Dell? If there's anything at all I can help with. It's going to be a hell of a job, I'll do whatever I can.'

'Of course I will,' Della said unconvincingly. Minutes later Jeff was preparing to head back to his wife, their boys and fancy detached home in Manchester, while Roxanne was itching to return to London, to write about hemline lengths and the 'silhouette of the season', whatever that meant.

They hugged, the three of them, despite their differences, as they had never hugged before: the only ones who knew what Kitty was really like. But as he climbed into his gleaming BMW, Jeff cast Della a quick, disapproving look, as if he still suspected she had stopped off for a sly steak bake instead of catching their mother's last breath.

Chapter Two

In fact, it wasn't a hell of a job for Jeff or Roxanne because, despite their reassurances that they'd be readily available – 'I'm only a phone call away!' Roxanne had trilled before zooming away in her convertible – Della had organised everything. There had been a short service at the crematorium, then all back to Rosemary Cottage where the villagers had been invited for tea.

Mark hadn't involved himself in the preparations. 'You seemed to be handling everything so well yourself,' he remarked, when Della mentioned that a little help would have been appreciated. So she was immensely grateful to Freda when it came to sprucing up Kitty's place in readiness for the surge of guests. Della's friend since they had fallen into companionable chat while their daughters played together in Heathfield Park – the girls were still virtually inseparable – Freda had literally rolled up her sleeves and got stuck in. Together they had deep-cleaned Kitty's front room and dotted it with jam jars of late-flowering purple asters from the rampant cottage garden. They had gathered together all the china, sorting the chipped from the unchipped, and made vast quantities of dainty triangular sandwiches and a variety of cakes. (Freda was an excellent baker. Since her marriage broke up – amazingly amicably, Della had thought – she had been supplementing her part-time teacher's salary by supplying speciality breads to delicatessens all over North Yorkshire.)

'Well, I think we've done a pretty decent job here,' she murmured above the hubbub of the living room.

'We have,' Della agreed. 'Thanks so much. Honestly, I don't know what I'd have done without you.'

'Oh, don't be silly. I couldn't just sit back and do nothing while you grafted away.'

Della smiled gratefully, catching snatches of Mark's and Jeff's rather awkward conversation about their working lives. While Mark was capable of appearing intrigued by Jeff's corporate world, her brother clearly found it difficult even to feign interest in Mark's podiatry practice. 'So, um, how *is* the world of feet?' he boomed.

'Oh, you know, rich and varied.' Mark rubbed at the side of his nose.

'Anything new occurring? Anything I should be looking out for?' Jeff chortled, and both men stared down at his black lace-up shoes.

'You tend to know when things are going wrong,' Mark observed, trying to sip from his wine glass before realising it was empty.

'But I thought it was all about prevention these days?' Jeff turned to his sister. 'You know all about this, don't you, Rox? In magazine land?'

'Not about foot problems, no,' she remarked dryly.

Jeff laughed again, possibly forgetting that this was their mother's funeral gathering and perhaps he shouldn't be quite so jovial. 'Tell you what, Mark, you've got people like Rox to thank for all the cash you rake in.'

'How's that, Jeff?' Roxanne asked with a frown.

'Oh, come on, encouraging women to wear crippling heels that crush their feet and misshape their toes. Some of them look like – I don't know – Roman sandals with enormous platform soles! You see girls out in Manchester, hobbling around on a Saturday night . . .'

Della stopped tuning in. She offered sandwiches to the haberdashery sisters, as they were known in the village – Pattie and Christine ran a curiously old-fashioned store for anyone who needed an emergency zip or a spool of elastic – then continued her rounds with a tray of mini savoury tarts. 'Such a lovely idea to have tea here,' remarked Irene, who ran the general store-cum-post office and whose fluffy hair bore a curiously peachy hue. 'Kitty would have loved it, everyone gathered in her home to celebrate her life.'

'Yes, I know she would.' Della smiled. In fact, she wasn't entirely sure about that. Kitty had had an aversion to neighbours popping in, especially those who insisted on being helpful. *Irene Bagshott dropped by with a chicken and leek pie*, she'd exclaimed, just a few months ago. *What on earth would I want a pie for?* And she'd glared at the golden pastry lid as if suspecting that roadkill lay beneath. Today, though, the atmosphere was convivial, partly because Burley Bridge was that kind of place – a real, working village, where people actually cared about one another – and also, Della suspected with a twinge of guilt, because Kitty wasn't here.

'Such a terrible loss for you,' remarked Morna, a retired lollipop lady who lived in the next cottage down the lane, 'but what a full life she had.'

16

'Mum was in a good place, towards the end,' Della added. 'She was well looked after. The hospice staff couldn't have been more kind.'

'I'm glad. Such spirit, she had.'

'A real character,' added Len, who ran the local garage. 'One thing about your mother, Della, she knew what she wanted in life.' And so they went on: about how strong-minded she was, such a one-off. Ian the butcher agreed that 'things won't be the same around here without Kitty' – omitting to mention that she had once accused him of short-changing her for a rolled pork joint.

Della looked around the room. Pattie and Christine, who had run their shop together for forty-odd years, were clearly a couple of G&Ts down, while Tamsin, Jeff's nervy-looking wife, was admonishing their ten-year-old twins for repeatedly interrogating Sophie about her newly acquired wrist tattoo.

'Did your mum and dad let you get that?' bellowed Isaac, the bolder of the pair. 'Or did you just *get* it?'

'She just got it,' Mark announced tersely. 'No permission was sought.' Noah, Isaac's brother, laughed as if this were the funniest thing he'd ever heard.

'I'm eighteen,' Sophie said with a roll of her eyes, glancing at her boyfriend Liam, who merely shrugged in response.

'D'*you* like it?' Isaac asked him.

'Yeah, it's all right,' Liam replied.

'Wish she'd got one with your name on it?'

'No, 'course not.'

'Yeah, 'cause then if you split up, that'd be *so* embarrassing.'

'Isaac!' Tamsin snapped, causing him to totter back and shroud himself, like a toddler might, in the heavy velvet curtain.

Della caught Freda's eye and grimaced. In fact, she had been pretty dismayed about Sophie having her beautiful creamy skin indelibly inked, but then, what could she have done to prevent it? Seized her daughter's money or kept her under lock and key? Without prior consultation Sophie had taken herself off to Screaming Skulls, an insalubrious-sounding place in town – since boarded up, disconcertingly – and returned home with her wrist bandaged. The bandage was soon removed to reveal a wobbly line of scabs, which eventually fell away to reveal a daisy-chain design. 'My God, it looks so sore,' Della had exclaimed, examining the inflamed, puffy skin.

'It's fine,' Sophie insisted.

'Are you sure? It looks, I don't know, kind of angry.'

'You'd be angry,' Mark had muttered, 'if you'd been pierced with a needle thousands of times and pumped full of ink.'

Della glanced around the room, noticing that Terry and Val, Mark's parents, had just arrived, looking quite terrified as both twins twirled energetically in the curtains while neither Jeff nor Tamsin made a move to stop them.

'So sorry we're late,' Val explained as Della offered them their preferred cups of sweet, weak tea. 'The car broke down, we'd hardly been going five minutes . . .'

'Well, Val had put petrol in,' Terry admonished her.

'I thought it was diesel, dear.'

'But it wasn't.'

Della tried to placate them with mini tarts and fairy cakes, but no, they both had digestive issues at the moment – 'I couldn't stomach a thing,' Val whimpered – and they looked around Kitty's living room in awe, as if they had accidentally stumbled into a minor stately home. Everything seemed to intimidate them, Della

18

reflected. In fact, she had long been concerned about her in-laws, now in their late-seventies, living in their cottage on the North Yorkshire coast. Sparsely furnished and permanently cold, it had nothing of note nearby apart from a fume-belching refinery and an abattoir. Della worried about them, so stuck in their ways and rarely venturing out, but had long since given up on suggesting to Mark that they should invite them over more often. 'You know what it's like when they come,' he'd said, and Della did know; it was as if all their spirit had been directed into the raising of Mark, their only child whom they doted upon, leaving nothing left over for themselves. 'Excuse me, Della,' Val whispered now, 'could I possibly use your bathroom?'

Della escorted her to the antiquated loo upstairs and on her return gave Mark's hand a brief squeeze as she drifted by. He had escaped from Jeff only to be cornered by Nicola Crowther who ran the sole hair salon in Burley Bridge and who had only recently upgraded from the rubber cap method to foils. 'All these cookbooks,' she exclaimed, gesticulating towards the bookcases by the fireplace. 'I've never seen so many!'

'There are hundreds of them in the kitchen, too,' Mark murmured, '*and* in the bedrooms and bathroom. They're crammed into every room of the house.'

'Amazing,' she gasped as Roxanne strode past. 'Oh, look at you, Roxy Cartwright. I haven't seen you for years. Barely recognised you. You're so glamorous!'

'I don't know about that,' Roxanne said with a tight laugh. She had politely requested that no one should ever again call her Roxy before leaving for London.

'Seriously, are you planning to age at any point? You're putting us country people to shame . . .'

19

'You look great too, Nicola,' Roxanne murmured. Della saw the tendons tighten in her sister's long, slender neck.

'Thanks, but honestly, there must be something in that London water.' Nicola gazed at Roxanne reverentially as if she were a beautiful, unaffordable dress. 'You're only four years younger than Della, aren't you? Incredible! But then, you are very different physically, you with your lovely blue eyes and Della with brown.'

Something clenched in Della's chest. It was true, they barely looked like sisters at all, and at forty-six years old, Roxanne appeared eerily youthful: aided by whitened teeth, expensively honeyed hair plus, Della suspected, the occasional shot of Botox and a filler or two.

'Still working on that magazine?' Nicola wanted to know.

'Yep, still hanging on in there.'

'You must meet so many famous people! D'you get lots of free clothes?' While Roxanne insisted that she didn't – 'It's not nearly as glamorous as people think' – Della coaxed the twins out of the curtains with a plate of cookies, and caught snippets of village news from Len who, as well as running the garage, seemed to be the oracle of everything that happened in Burley Bridge. Virtually everyone else had gathered around Roxanne, as if hoping that a little of her London glitz might rub off on them. But no matter, Della decided: at least everyone was here to celebrate Kitty's life. That's why she had pulled out all the stops, having placed a notice – an open invitation really – in the window of Irene's shop. Virtually everyone had come, all the villagers who had known Kitty – for fifty-odd years, some of them – even though they hadn't been what you'd call close to her. Because *no one* was. Real friends had fallen away over the years, like dead-

20

headed flowers. There'd be some imagined slight, a hastily ended phone call, and their name would be angrily scribbled out of Kitty's address book.

Della nibbled a cucumber sandwich and wondered whether Morna, Kitty's nearest neighbour, had given any thought today to her run-in with Kitty over a visitor parking in 'her' space, even though the road outside Rosemary Cottage belonged to no one (maybe the council or the road department or something: Della had no idea. But she did know Kitty had no legal claim on it). She wondered, too, what Irene would have thought if she'd known that Kitty had scraped the chicken and leek pie into the bin, and whether Len was aware that she'd gone around complaining that he'd 'poisoned' her car by putting the wrong kind of oil in it.

The afternoon wore on, and then the villagers began to drift out amidst thank yous and hugs, leaving just Della's extended family – 'My tattoo,' Isaac announced, 'is going to be of a dog pooing' – plus Freda, who was rounding up glasses and crumb-strewn plates in the manner of an efficient waitress.

Reclining in an armchair while Tamsin admonished their sons, Jeff sipped his red wine. 'Well, I thought that went very well,' he said, his glow of satisfaction almost visible, as if he had fashioned those savoury tarts with his own, eerily baby-soft hands.

Chapter Three

The plan had been for the family to spend the night at Rosemary Cottage. Della had changed all the beds, opened the windows to let in a waft of fresh Yorkshire air and set vases of garden flowers on the bedside tables in the four low-ceilinged bedrooms. However Isaac and Noah had kicked up a stink about 'sleeping where someone's died': 'What if she *haunts* us?' Noah had exclaimed. 'What if she touches my face in the night?' No amount of persuasion – including Della reminding them that Grandma Kitty had actually ended her days at Perivale House – had changed their minds. Tamsin, too, had admitted that staying there might be 'a little creepy', and naturally Roxanne wasn't happy to sleep in her childhood bedroom alone. So here they all were in Della's lounge: far too many of them, arranged on the two facing sofas as if waiting for a train.

'So,' Jeff said, turning to Sophie, 'are you really sure about art college? I mean, is it the wisest choice?'

She picked at a burgundy-painted fingernail. 'Well, yes, Uncle Jeff. It's what I've always wanted to do. I've got my place, my accommodation, it's all sorted out.'

'Yes, but those childhood dreams, whims, whatever you want to call them . . .' Della glared at her brother, who was holding court whilst making inroads into a second bottle of red. 'I don't mean to rain on your parade,' he blustered on, 'but have you thought about the small matter of how you're going to make a living afterwards?'

'Jeff,' Della spluttered, 'Sophie's only eighteen. All that can come later.'

'And we've discussed it all with her,' Mark added, his cheeks flushed, either from the wine or annoyance or perhaps a combination of the two. 'It's all been carefully considered.'

'Dad, please don't talk about me as if I'm not here,' Sophie snapped.

Throughout this exchange Mark's parents had sat jammed close together on one of the stone-coloured sofas, as if they felt themselves unworthy of sitting on it. Val sipped her requested tap water and nibbled tentatively on a tortilla chip. 'Well,' Jeff boomed on, 'let's hope your parents are prepared to support you when you're starving in a garret.'

'Jeff!' Tamsin exclaimed, turning to pat Sophie's knee. 'He's only joking, darling.'

Sophie turned to her father. 'What's a garret?'

'An attic,' Mark said briskly.

'Not just an ordinary attic,' Della added, refilling her own wine glass. 'It's cold and miserable, probably with a bare bulb and a cracked window and the wind whistling through . . .'

'*Nice*,' Sophie retorted. 'Sounds perfect, Mum. When can I move in?'

Della forced a smile and touched her brow. It was sticky with perspiration. Actually, a draughty garret did sound appealing right now; it was terribly hot in here, or perhaps her internal thermostat had gone haywire. This had been happening lately – the sudden power surges to her face, and waking up in the night with the sheets clinging to her drenched body. Maybe that's why Mark had taken to sleeping at the very far edge of the bed. It couldn't be pleasant, lying entwined with someone bathed in sweat: a bit like sleeping with a fish. Della often tried to reassure herself that this was the case, rather than the possibility that he no longer found her remotely attractive. Anyway, was it realistic to expect a passionate relationship when they'd been together for over two decades?

Tamsin chuckled awkwardly and picked a bobble of fluff off her pink Boden cardi. 'I think what Jeff means' – why did she do this, as if an interpreter was needed? – 'is that maybe, I don't know, there are more *lucrative* routes you could take, Sophie. Like, er . . .'

'Like banking?' Sophie snorted.

'No, I mean like, er . . . packaging design.'

'What kind of packaging?'

'Well, everything needs designing,' Jeff said loftily. 'Washing-powder boxes, cereals, labels for jam . . .'

'But I don't want to design labels for jam!' Sophie exclaimed.

'What about websites?' Tamsin chipped in. 'Everyone needs a website these days, you could make a *fortune* that way.'

'But Sophie loves art,' Della said, more forcefully than she'd intended, 'and she's really good. Don't you believe in following your passion? I mean, isn't that what being young is all about? Why should she design marmalade labels when she wants to paint amazing landscapes and portraits?'

'Jeff only meant—' Tamsin started.

24

'Yes, well,' Della charged on, aware of her heartbeat quickening, 'there's the rest of her life for Sophie to grow old and cynical and, I don't know, worry about bills and drains and the garden fence blowing down and—'

'Our fence blew down?' Mark exclaimed. 'When did that happen?'

'No, no, that was just an example.'

'And what's wrong with our drains?'

'Nothing,' Della said sharply.

'If the shower's blocked again it'll be because of your hair. I had to hoick out a great wodge of it last time that happened.'

'There's nothing wrong with the drain, Mark!'

'No need to shout,' he muttered, glaring at her.

Della cleared her throat, aware of Isaac and Noah giving her foreboding stares, like two miniature policemen about to arrest her for breach of the peace. 'I'm sorry,' she said quietly. 'It's just been . . . quite a day, that's all.'

Tamsin smiled sympathetically. 'Of course it has, Dell, and you managed everything so beautifully.' She paused. 'And, you know, you're right about Sophie following her dreams. Passion is *great*, of course it is.' She turned and gave Jeff's earlobe a little tweak, a gesture that made Della's stomach swirl disconcertingly. She excused herself, heading for the kitchen where, a little fuzzy with wine now, she poured herself a large glass of water. 'For God's sake,' Sophie muttered, having followed her. 'All they care about is money, Mum.'

'That's probably why they have loads of it,' Della remarked.

Sophie smirked. 'Yeah, but what about creativity, doing something you love?' She shook her head in frustration. 'I mean, Aunt Tamsin doesn't even work.'

'Well, she's a full-time mum,' Della reminded her.

'Yeah, and the boys are, like, ten! They go to school . . . that's if a school will have them. What does she *do* all day?'

Della glanced at her daughter: so like Mark, with her sharply defined cheekbones and wide, generous mouth. Her wavy brown hair was dyed black at the moment, her brown eyes smudged with dark shadow, her red lipstick almost worn away. How Della would miss her fire and spark when she left for college in two weeks' time. It would be just her and Mark then; the phrase 'empty nesters' made her feel more than a little panicky.

'I'm sure she manages to fill her time, love.'

'What, with lunches and shopping?'

'Probably. I have no idea actually.'

'*And* they have a cleaner,' Sophie added. 'I'd hate that, Mum.'

'You mean, having someone come in and make your room all lovely and sweet-smelling?' This was Della's attempt to cheer her up.

Sophie frowned. 'No, I mean being completely dependent on a husband, doing what *he* wants, not having any independence at all . . .'

'You're right, of course you are. I know you'll never be like that.'

'I won't, Mum. God, they're like the, the . . . I don't know. People from the nineteen fifties!'

Della gulped her water. While she was impressed by her daughter's fiercely feminist streak, she couldn't help reflecting that, really, her own and Mark's marriage wasn't so different. They had remained in Heathfield because Mark's podiatry practice was here, as was Sophie's life – friends, school, the tennis and gymnastic clubs she had belonged to until sipping a caramel frappé in Starbucks with a gaggle of friends began to hold more appeal. However, while everything rolled along reasonably happily, Della had often caught herself thinking, is this *it*? She worked full-time in Heathfield Castle's gift shop and, whilst she didn't despise it exactly, never once had she thought, *This* is what I was made to do. It had never been her life's ambition to sell polyester tabards and chain-mail snoods.

Sophie swung morosely on the fridge door as Della made a pot of tea. 'Grab a tray, love,' she said. 'Hopefully this'll stop Uncle Jeff slugging down any more wine. And put out some more cookies, would you?' Sophie snorted in derision and selected the cheapest packet of biscuits from the cupboard, tipping them haphazardly onto a plate. As they made their way back to the living room, Della could hear Tamsin's shrill tones: 'What was that woman's name, the one with the awful peachy-coloured hair?'

'Oh, God, Irene Bagshott,' Jeff groaned, 'nosying into everyone's business.'

'Is her hair dyed that colour,' Tamsin mused, 'or is it naturally a sort of washed-out, faded ginger?'

'You mean the one with the hairy mole?' Isaac asked. For all their expensive education, the boys hadn't learned much in the way of manners.

'Er, yes, I did notice that,' his mother tittered.

'Could hardly miss it,' Jeff added.

'Is her hair a wig, Mum?' Noah wanted to know.

'Honestly, sweetheart, I have no idea,' Tamsin replied. 'I didn't examine her that closely.'

Isaac jabbed Jeff's arm. 'Dad, what's that little fruit, the furry one with a stone inside?'

'Peach, son.'

'Nah, nah, the other one.'

'You mean apricot?' Tamsin asked.

'Yeah!' Isaac spluttered. 'Apricot wig and a hairy mole!' Somehow, he managed to fit this instantly into a jaunty tune, reminiscent of an ice-cream van jingle, and now he and Noah were singing it in what felt like an endless loop.

Apricot wig and a hairy mole,
Hairy mole, hairy mole,
Apricot wig and a hairy mole . . .

Della felt as if a clamp was being applied to her skull. Let's run down the whole village while we're at it, she thought tersely, checking the wall clock and trying to calculate how long it might be before she could curl up on the blow-up mattress, which she planned to jam in between the two sofas, and go to sleep. When everyone else had gone to bed, she supposed.

Roxanne turned to her as Della set the tray down on the coffee table. 'So, what are we going to do, Dell?'

'You mean, tonight? Well, you're in the spare room and Mark and I are sleeping down here. Jeff, Tamsin and the boys can have our room . . .'

'*We're* not staying,' Terry cut in.

'No, that's fine, you did mention it,' Della said kindly.

'We can only sleep in our own bed,' Val added.

'Okay, Mum,' Mark said rather curtly. 'We're not going to force you to stay.'

Della threw him a quick glare and, as Terry and Val prepared to leave, she found them their coats from the pile in the spare room and escorted them, with Mark hovering distractedly at her side, to the hired Renault they had parked a little further down the street. She felt Mark emit a little sigh of relief as they drove away.

'I meant,' Roxanne said, as Della and Mark returned to the living room, 'what are we going to do about

28

Rosemary Cottage?' Silence settled around the room. The twins, mercifully with headphones plugged in now, munched absent-mindedly on the remaining biscuits.

'There's no rush, is there?' Sophie asked with a frown. 'I mean, we've only just had Grandma's funeral.'

'Yes, but there's no point in letting things drift on.' Ignoring the pot of tea Della had brought through, Jeff topped up his wine glass. 'When winter comes,' he continued, 'we'll be talking frozen pipes and slates falling off that godawful roof.'

'But it's only September,' Sophie countered.

'Actually,' Della remarked, 'Jeff's right. We might as well deal with it now, rather than putting it off.'

'I think you're right, darling,' Mark said.

'Yes,' Roxanne remarked, 'delaying things will only make it more horrible for all of us.'

Although Della nodded in agreement, it wasn't quite that. It was *this:* the gathering of the Cartwright clan, the way Jeff assumed authority as if he were still twelve years old and issuing library fines, and his wife's snidey remark about Irene's hair when she had been nothing but kind to their mother, making actual *pastry leaves* for the lid of that chicken and leek pie, for goodness' sake. It was as if all that kindness counted for nothing. And what about Len from Burley Bridge Garage who'd fixed Della's car for virtually no money? It made Della cringe, the way her brother and sister swept in and out of the village as if staying a moment longer would somehow taint them with its ugly, countryish ways. She couldn't bear the thought of endless meetings and wranglings as the Rosemary Cottage business rumbled on.

'You think we should put it on the market?' Roxanne ventured.

'Yes, I do,' Della replied firmly.

'We'll have to clear it out, of course,' Jeff added, glancing at Tamsin. 'There's nothing *we* need, is there?' Good lord, he was mentally divvying up their mother's possessions already. Della bit fiercely into a Rich Tea.

'No, no.' Tamsin shuddered visibly.

'What about the watercolour over the fireplace?'

'It's terribly drab, darling. It won't go in our place.' Tamsin turned to Roxanne. 'What about you, Rox?'

'I don't need anything,' she said, unsurprisingly: her tiny two-bedroomed Islington flat was a shrine to minimalism.

'Well, I can't imagine anyone would want all that hefty old furniture,' Jeff added, raking back his dark hair.

Mark put a hand on Della's knee. 'Isn't it a bit too soon to start thinking about clearing out all your mum's things?'

Della shook her head. 'No, we need to get on with it. There's that auction place in town, some of the furniture and paintings could go there.' She paused. 'And while we're all here together we should look through the smaller things – the mementoes – and decide what we'd like to remember Mum by.' She glanced at Sophie. 'You should have something of Gran's, love.'

Sophie nodded. 'I'd like that, Mum. Maybe just the plain gold chain she wore all the time.'

'Oh, the *jewellery*,' Tamsin exclaimed, eyes gleaming, then, colouring slightly, she added, 'Although I expect you'd like to have a rake through it first, Rox.' A rake through it, as if it were jumble! She turned to Della then. 'You're not really an accessories person, are you?'

Della choked on a fragment of biscuit. 'Well, I'd quite like—'

'I think we should look through it together tomorrow,' Roxanne said tersely. 'You, me and Sophie, I mean.'

'Good idea,' Della said, 'but you two can choose. And Tamsin, you should have a piece too.'

'Well, maybe those tiny gold earrings, if you're sure that's okay?'

Della nodded. 'No problem.'

'And the jet necklace? I mean, if no one else wants it?'

'Er, I don't think—' Roxanne started.

'And the opal ring,' Tamsin went on, flushing excitedly now. 'That is, unless it's particularly special to anyone.' At some point she must have compiled an inventory of Kitty's jewellery, Della realised.

'Actually, I don't want any of it,' she murmured.

'Why not?' Roxanne exclaimed.

'Because Tamsin's right, I'm not an accessories person.'

'It's not *accessories*, Mum,' Sophie admonished her. 'This is Gran's jewellery. You should have something personal.'

'But I will,' Della cut in. She stopped talking and stared around the room: at her brother and sister, who were regarding her intently, and at Mark, who still looked rather uneasy about the prospect of problems with the fence and the drains. She glanced at Isaac, who was now badgering Sophie to let them have a proper look at her tattoo again – the cuff of her outsized sweatshirt covered it – and at Tamsin, who was sitting bolt upright, eyes gleaming, as if in anticipation of taking possession of all that beautiful jewellery. 'I'll take Mum's cookbooks,' Della said carefully, 'if that's okay with everyone.'

Mark's eyes widened. 'The *cookbooks?*'

'Yes, if no one else wants them, of course.'

Roxanne shook her head. 'Well, I don't. When did you ever see me cook anything?'

'And we don't use them,' Tamsin added. 'Haven't for years. They just clutter the kitchen, get splattered with

31

food, so dirty and unhygienic.' She winced. 'So I got rid of them all, dumped them at the charity shop. Now I have this app. You just tap in whatever you have hanging around in the fridge – some pecorino, a bunch of kale, a few figs – and up comes a recipe to use everything up.'

Della tried to look suitably impressed. 'Amazing.'

'We never have pecorino or figs,' Mark said with a smirk. 'Maybe a bit of old Cheddar and some bendy celery if we're lucky.' He squeezed Della's hand. 'You don't need to decide about the books now, darling. I know you're upset, you've had so much on your plate.'

'No,' she said firmly, 'I *have* decided.'

'Let Mum have some, Dad,' Sophie cut in, turning to Della. 'I'll help you pick some out, Mum, if you like.'

'Thank you, love, but I'm having them all.' The living room fell silent. Della was aware of everyone's eyes upon her; even the twins were staring as if waiting for her to add, 'I'm joking of course.'

'All of them?' Mark gasped. 'But how many are there?'

'Nine hundred and sixty-two,' Della replied.

He let her hand drop. 'What? But that's just . . . that's insane!'

'It's how many there are, Mark.'

'So . . . you've counted them? When did you do that?'

'Years ago, when I was little girl.'

'But—' he started.

'And after Dad left, Mum stopped buying them,' she added.

Mark shook his head. 'We can't possibly keep them all, love. What on earth would we do with them?'

'Just *have* them,' Della said firmly.

He cleared his throat. 'Look, I know it's hard for you to let your mum go . . .'

'It's not about that,' she retorted, a tremor in her voice now. Her eyes were prickling too, perhaps due to it being the aftermath of the funeral, or maybe because the cookbooks seemed to matter so much. They were only books, filled with pictures of fondues and outlandish desserts slathered with cream and set alight at the table. How could they pose such a problem?

'But, Dell, they're worthless,' Jeff added. 'I doubt if a charity shop would even want them. Oh, they'd probably accept them just to be polite, then chuck them into the wheelie bins out the back.' Della could sense her heart rate accelerating. It was that tone he used. He really hadn't changed a bit. *I don't want to fine you but if I didn't, I'd never get my* Guinness Book of Records *back . . .* She glared at him, and then at Mark: two Alpha-males who always decided how things would be done. Well, not this time. She was the one who'd cooked with Kitty – and who, more recently, had held her hand tightly on numerous hospital visits – and, by rights, those were *her* books. No one else had given them so much as a perfunctory glance. Mark shook his head in exasperation and, as way of grabbing a few moments to herself, Della scampered upstairs to make up the futon for the boys.

'The cookbooks, Dad. Are you going to stop her or what?' Sophie's voice rang out from the living room.

'Yes, of course I am,' Mark replied.

'But she seems determined—'

'Well, it's just not happening,' he said firmly. 'No way are those ratty old books coming into *this* house.'

33

Chapter Four

They did, though – three days later – not because Mark and Sophie had granted permission but because Della had decided she didn't need anyone's approval to assume custody of her mother's books. They were hers by right, for goodness' sake. *Easy-As-Pie* was related to her by blood. *The Avocado Handbook* and *Elegant Catering* were moving into 57 Pickering Street and, short of armed security being installed at the front door, nothing was going to stop them.

So, post-funeral, Della had snapped into action. She hired a van and bought boxes, and she and Freda drove over to Rosemary Cottage to pack up the books. Jeff, Tamsin and Roxanne had visited the morning after Kitty's funeral, in the manner of ravenous magpies, to scoop up copious amounts of jewellery plus a bone china tea set and a set of engraved silver napkin rings. They hadn't wanted anything else, and Della had made sure Kitty's favourite plain gold chain went to Sophie as it was all she'd asked for.

Now Della gathered up the framed photos that were

dotted around in every room of her mother's house. Most were of the Cartwright children at differing ages: grinning in clammy swimwear or sand-dusted T-shirts and shorts at Morecambe Bay or on Scarborough Beach. It struck Della, as it always did when the three of them were pictured together, how different she was from Roxanne and Jeff: dark-eyed, with skin that easily turned honey-brown in the sun, against their fair colouring. 'Look at this,' Della said, showing Freda a small photograph in an Art Deco-style silver frame.

'Wow. Is that your mum and dad's wedding?'

'Yeah. Mum hadn't wanted a wedding dress. I mean, not a traditional one – said she couldn't be doing with all that fuss and nonsense. She was beautiful, though, wasn't she? Only about twenty-two then.'

They studied Kitty, a delicate slip of a thing, her make-up understated, her fair hair secured in a neat chignon. She was wearing a knee-length shift dress in white lace, teamed with pointed white sandals and a short fur throw. 'She looked so elegant,' Freda agreed.

'I know. I so wanted to wear that dress for my wedding – not that it would have fitted me, probably. Mum was tiny back then. Anyway, she'd lost it or thrown it away or something. She was always a bit vague about what happened to it.' Della smiled wryly. 'She probably tore it up when Dad left her.'

'Made it into rags,' Freda suggested.

'Yes, for cleaning the loo or something.' They both chuckled.

'Funny, isn't it,' Freda remarked, 'that she kept this photo on display even after they broke up? I mean, you'd have expected her to shove it in a drawer or something.'

Della nodded, glancing again at her parents who,

35

although standing close together on the registry office steps, were not touching. They'd had a small wedding, Della knew that, and a couple of friends – young, ridiculously good-looking, and dressed in a smart suit and a similarly fashionable dress respectively – loitered in the background of the photograph, as if not quite sure where to put themselves. Although a rather meek-looking William was gazing adoringly at his bride, Kitty's attention seemed to be somewhere else. Throughout their marriage, she had always behaved as if William had slightly disappointed her. Perhaps she had felt that a little even on their wedding day.

Having filled the van, Della and Freda drove back to Della's red-brick terraced house in the quiet residential area of Heathfield. She hadn't warned Mark or Sophie about the imminent arrival of the books. Mark was having drinks at the golf club, and Sophie was just 'out': Della found it virtually impossible to track her movements these days. With impressive speed – and an air of stealth – Della and Freda unpacked the boxes in the hallway, stacking books along one entire wall.

'They're amazing,' Freda breathed, leafing through *Venison Cookery,* which, disconcertingly, featured a wide-eyed, distinctly Bambi-like deer on the cover. 'Of course you had to have them, Dell. It was obviously a real passion for her. She must've been a brilliant cook.'

Della considered this. 'It's hard to say. Dad liked everything plain – big joints of meat, a splash of gravy if he was feeling wild. He was suspicious of vegetables, apart from potatoes and frozen peas. Jeff was the same.'

'What about Roxanne, though? Can't imagine she was exactly a meat-and-potatoes kind of girl.'

Della laughed. 'Well, you know what she's like now with her juices and spiralised veg and all those intolerances.

36

As a kid, she was terribly picky, so I suspect Mum felt there wasn't much point in being too adventurous.'

'So why all these books?'

'Oh, they'd have dinner parties when she and Dad were still together – they were lively affairs – with prawn cocktail starters and proper napkins folded into swans.' Freda chuckled. 'And occasionally she'd push the boat out and try something wild, just for us.' Della flicked through a lavishly photographed volume entitled *Be the Perfect Hostess*. 'She made this – Hungarian goulash – and this salmon in aspic. Look at it, perched there under its little blanket of jelly . . .'

'Ugh! I can imagine what you all made of that.'

'Well, I was willing to try, it was new and different, but the others . . .' Della's eyes lit upon a luridly coloured picture of a fondue. 'And this! Oh, I remember this. Cubes of raw meat we had to dip in bubbling oil . . .'

'Health and Safety,' Freda sniggered.

'Yes, Mark would have a heart attack.' Della chuckled. 'But mostly, I think Mum's books were a way into another world – you know, where people ate veal and set fire to their desserts instead of ripping open a packet of Angel Delight. You know what Burley Bridge is like, such a sleepy, tucked-away little place. Maybe the books were a sort of escape from all of that.' The door opened then and Sophie flopped in.

'Hi, love,' Della said.

'Er . . . hi.' Her gaze fell upon the teetering piles. 'What are these?'

'Grandma's cookbooks, darling.'

'Look, Sophie.' Freda grinned, waving the fondue page at her. 'How d'you fancy this for dinner tomorrow? Little bits of raw beef deep dunked in boiling oil?'

'I'm vegetarian!' she exclaimed. 'Mum, these books, they're not . . . staying here, are they?'

Della nodded. 'Well, yes, for now.'

'But . . .' Sophie pushed a strand of hair from her face. 'But they can't.'

'I'm sorry love, but they are.'

'But they're old and falling to bits and they smell . . .'

'No, they don't,' Della protested, although in truth Sophie was right: a rather musty, old papery aroma had filled the hall, plus something else: a hint of dinners from days gone by. Sunday roasts, rich gravy, a steamed pudding slathered in bright yellow custard . . . It wasn't unpleasant – it was familiar, almost comforting – but it was definitely *there*.

Sophie wrinkled her nose. 'They do. They smell of . . . old things, old people.'

Della looked at her. 'But you like old things, love. You love vintage shops, you hardly ever buy anything new.'

'Clothes are different,' she exclaimed.

'Are they, though? They're unique, you're always saying. They have a history, a story to tell. It's the same with cookbooks.'

Sophie picked up *The Fine Art of Margarine Cookery* and shuddered. 'Who the hell eats margarine?'

Della swung round as the front door opened and Mark strolled in. His fine-boned face was a little flushed around the nose and cheeks.

'Hi, darling.' Della pecked his cheek, but he didn't seem to register the kiss as he too was staring down at the books. He hadn't acknowledged Freda either.

'What are these doing here?'

Della cleared her throat. 'They're just sitting quietly, in piles.'

'For how long, though?'

'I don't know exactly.'

By now, Sophie was leafing through another book. 'There's a whole chapter on dripping. What's that?'

'It's just the fat that comes out of meat,' Freda explained.

'Ugh!' gasped Sophie.

'People used to have bread and dripping,' Della added, at which her daughter mimed vomiting.

'This is crazy, Dell,' Mark cut in. 'Tell me they're not staying here. Please tell me it's only temporary.'

'I don't know yet,' Della replied as Sophie snatched a book and waved it in front of him.

'Look, Dad. A whole book on margarine!'

'I *hate* margarine,' he declared, as if someone were about to force it upon him.

'They're not all about margarine,' Freda said, laughing.

'And people used to have it, Sophie,' Della added, 'when they couldn't afford butter.'

'Yeah,' Mark cut in, 'people used to have all sorts, didn't they? Diphtheria, scurvy, Bubonic Plague . . .'

'Oh, for God's sake,' Della spluttered. 'Don't be like this.'

'. . . consumption,' he went on, cheeks reddening further. 'Rickets, smallpox . . .'

Della laughed in disbelief and turned to her friend. 'He's a ray of sunshine tonight, isn't he?'

'They're just books, Mark,' Freda added with a smirk. 'Not a contagious, olden-days disease.'

He grunted, and Della accompanied Freda to the front door. 'Thanks so much for helping, and sorry about Mark.'

'They're just not his kind of thing,' she observed.

'Well, they're *my* thing,' Della said with a defiant smile.

Freda paused on the doorstep. 'What are you going to do with them, though?'

'You know, I haven't the faintest idea.' They laughed and hugged, and as she stepped back inside Della reflected that Freda was right: Mark simply didn't enjoy being surrounded by old things. Eight years ago, when they had upgraded from their flat to the then rather dilapidated end-of-terrace house in Pickering Street, he had set about hiring builders to remove internal walls and plaster the whole place so there wasn't a bump or a crack to be seen. The place milled with joiners, electricians and tilers, all managed by Mark who seemed to relish his role as Director of Operations. Della would never have imagined a 120-year-old house could appear so unblemished and pristine. The kitchen – original sixties, which she had thought rather charming – had been flung into a skip, to be replaced by glossy white units and sleek granite worktops. She had found one of the original pistachio green Bakelite drawer knobs lying in the gutter and had wiped it down and stuffed it into her pocket.

When the work was complete, Della had been seized by an urge to fill their home with dazzling colour, of the kind their daughter used to love to daub onto rolls of lining paper before progressing to canvasses at the easel in her room. 'This place should be bright and cheerful,' Della had announced, 'like a butterfly.' The fiery dashes on a Red Admiral's wings, she meant, or the beautiful azure of a Common Blue. While Mark started to pore over the sleek, modern furniture offered by high-end stores, she dabbled around on Gumtree, hoping to source more interesting items to add a dash of character to their newly renovated home.

'Hey,' Della said now, finding Mark reading the five-day-old Sunday paper in the living room. She perched beside him on the unyielding sofa. 'Look, darling, I know

I've been a bit rash. You're right, we don't have space for them. But they're important to me, okay?'

'Mmm.' His gaze remained on the newspaper. 'You could have left them in their boxes, though. At least then I'd have been reassured that they're not a permanent fixture.'

'But that'd look awful, as if we'd just moved in.'

'And it looks *great* with them all piled up, hardly any room to move, stinking the place out?' As if she had lugged a crate of rotting fish into the house!

She glared at him, deciding not to explain that unpacking was just an excuse to go through the books, to handle and pore over them, as she had done as a child. She had wanted to feel the pages, to study her mother's rather ill-tempered scribbled notes. *Pie far too tart. Jeff refused to eat. 2 oz more sugar needed . . . Took TWICE as long to bake as says here . . . Unpleasant cheese sauce. Waste of ingredients. Avoid!!!*

'Okay,' Della went on, aware of tightness in her chest now, 'I accept that they can't sit there piled up in the hall forever. I mean, I know it makes us look like the crazy family, and no one'll want to visit us.'

She glanced at him. Not that Mark was a huge fan of gatherings in the house anyway, lest a drink be spilled, heaven forbid. 'I'll find somewhere else to store them,' she added, feeling like a child, summonsed to the head teacher's office to give an explanation for some minor misdemeanour.

Was *this* how marriage was meant to be? It wasn't as if Mark was unkind. Yet somehow, without Della even noticing it happening, *he'd* become the one who decided pretty much everything. It made her feel faintly ashamed and bewildered – why had she allowed it to happen? She had raised Sophie to be confident and strong and to go

41

for whatever she wanted in life. Yet here Della was, pandering to a man who barely seemed to care or even notice what she did, unless it involved 962 cookbooks.

He turned to her. 'Okay, have your books. Keep them wherever you like. That's not really the issue.'

'What *is* the issue then?' She frowned.

He flared his nostrils in a rather equine way, Della thought. 'You and Freda, in cahoots . . .'

'She's my friend,' Della retorted. 'We weren't *in cahoots*. She was only helping me out. She's been a huge help, actually, these past few weeks.'

'What I mean is,' he cut in, 'the two of you hatched a plan, hiring that bloody great van that's parked outside . . .'

'It's the smallest one they had!'

'And bringing them all here without even consulting . . .'

'Consulting?' she spluttered.

'I mean, without even discussing it with me.'

Della stared at him, and all the words she wanted to say – *I don't have to consult you about everything* – faded away in her mind. Instead of defending her actions, which would have led to a row, and which Sophie would have heard from her room, she sat still and stared around their living room. It was a shrine to neutrals, a study in muted good taste. That's what Della felt like too sometimes: muted, as if all the sparkle in her had been dimmed down so low as to be barely noticeable anymore. She hadn't got her way in the decorating scheme for their home. Mark had vetoed any vintage furniture she'd found on Gumtree. Without any discussion – and certainly no *prior consultation* – he had taken himself off to Homebase and returned with several cans of Farrow & Ball's Cabbage White.

*

In fact, Mark was only pretending to be engrossed in the newspaper. He couldn't read right now; he could barely think, since it had become apparent that Della was determined to keep those darned books. She couldn't let her mother go – *that* was the real issue. She had spent weeks looking after and visiting her, and now Kitty had gone, leaving a gaping hole that Della had no idea how to fill. Mark hadn't really considered how he would feel when his own mother and father passed away, but he was pretty certain he wouldn't want to pack up their possessions and haul them all to this house.

In fact, books in great numbers had always made him feel decidedly uneasy. His parents owned perhaps a dozen between them, and he had never been a great reader himself. It had always pained him slightly, the feeling of being hemmed in by all those cookbooks whenever they had visited Kitty at Rosemary Cottage. And now – he could hardly believe it was true – the books had damn' well migrated here.

He couldn't bear it. *Hemmed in:* that was precisely how he felt right now. Why, he wondered, as he made his way through to the kitchen in search of wine, couldn't Della have chosen one of Kitty's necklaces instead?

Chapter Five

Della could forgive Mark's air of mild grumpiness because that was just *him*: a hardworking fifty-two-year-old man who tended towards jadedness but was still capable of small acts of kindness, like the way he had started to bring her coffee in bed every Saturday and Sunday morning.

'Thanks, darling,' she said, registering the time on the bedside clock – 7.47 a.m. – as he handed her her favourite mug. 'You golfing today?'

'Yep, leaving in a minute. Lovely morning so we're having an early start before the riff-raff show up.' He chuckled. 'You have a lie in. You've had an exhausting time lately, you look really tired . . .' *Gee, thanks*, Della thought, suppressing a smirk.

'I can't today. I'm working.'

'Oh, I thought you'd finished doing Saturdays?'

'So did I,' she said with a shrug, 'but Liliana's gone back to Poland so we're short-staffed.' In fact, she had already told him this, but clearly the information hadn't sunk in.

She sat up and sipped from her mug. Although Della

44

appreciated the gesture, the weekend coffee delivery had only started a few weeks ago, and after nineteen years of marriage it had been a surprising turn of events. Mark was so *particular* about it, too, deciding to abandon their cafetière for an Italian espresso maker that sat on the hob. 'Richer flavour,' he'd explained. Ground coffee had been swapped for beans, requiring the purchase of an electric grinder that Della was forbidden from using for spices. 'How good can coffee be?' she'd laughed, when, having decided their perfectly acceptable Yorkshire tap water wasn't up to scratch, he'd brought home a jug filter in which to purify it for her morning brew.

'If you're going to have coffee,' Mark replied, 'it should be as enjoyable as possible.' Della smiled, knowing this was what made him so respected as a podiatrist: he cared about details. She'd lost count of the times his patients had stopped her in town and told her how *fantastic* he'd been, taking time to discuss their lifestyle and footwear choices instead of giving their cracked heel a perfunctory poke and sending them out with a tube of cream.

Like the morning coffee, golf was a relatively new thing too. He had mooted the idea in late spring and, before she knew it, he was off to the course every Saturday. Della could understand the appeal of certain aspects: being outdoors on a bright, breezy morning in the company of friends. But the actual game seemed lacking in action, in her opinion. The ones she enjoyed were of the fast, shouty type: quizzes and board games played at Christmas, with dishes of nuts and crisps, and a glass of chilled white wine to hand. The kind of games that didn't require a whacking great bag of clubs to be dragged around on wet grass for four hours. Fifteen clubs, Mark had amassed, at the last count. Couldn't he make do with three or four? (Although

Della knew she could hardly quiz him about this, now that she owned 962 cookbooks.) He had also bought golf shoes, a visor, a peaked cap, an umbrella and a special towel for cleaning his clubs. Where hobbies were concerned, Mark *was* an accessories person.

She swung out of bed and caught him glancing at her body as if it were somehow inappropriate for her to stroll naked across their bedroom. When had he started looking at her that way? At some point, without her really noticing at the time, he seemed to have started regarding her like a mildly irritating housemate. She couldn't remember the last time they had been out to dinner together – or kissed properly, like lovers – and now, with Sophie about to leave home, this was something she had to address. Of course it was possible to feel close again; they would soon be undisturbed, completely free to do whatever they wanted. She pulled on her towelling dressing gown and belted it tightly, lest it should flap open and, God forbid, some flesh should be exposed.

Mark's newest acquisition – a gleaming putter, for practising his shots on their bedroom carpet – was propped up beside the door. It was wearing a little black leather hat. 'Very saucy,' Della had remarked when she'd first seen it.

'It's to protect the head,' Mark replied, deliberately missing her attempt at a joke.She padded to the bathroom. Of course he needed an outlet, she decided under the shower's invigorating blast, being faced with gnarly old feet every day of his working life. All those verrucas, calluses and fungal toenails: no one consulted Mark Sturgess if they had perfectly pretty, well-functioning feet. And never mind the visual aspect: the smell, she imagined, must bother him sometimes. 'You get used to it,' he'd said, soon after they'd met when, rather immaturely, she'd asked whether particularly stinky feet ever made him feel ill.

Della glanced down at her own feet in the shower. They were well tended, although by her and not Mark. If anything, he seemed *averse* to hers – although perhaps that wasn't so surprising. Expecting him to lavish attention upon her recurring corn would be like being married to a chef and demanding that he rustle up dinner for her after a gruelling shift at his restaurant. When she'd experienced a more serious problem – plantar faciitis, a painful inflammation of the sole and heel – he'd merely told her to rest it, adding, 'For God's sake, Dell, don't go running anymore. It's not for you. You're not built for speed.'

Ouch, that terrible phrase! As if she were an ageing carthorse ready to be shunted off to a sanctuary to spend the rest of her days munching oats. She surveyed her pillowy stomach as water cascaded down it, and told herself she was merely voluptuous, like those luscious ladies in Renaissance paintings – not fat. A few months ago she had taken up running with Freda, who was enviably lithe and supple and only accompanying Della for moral support. Della had been determined to lose weight, to fit into the dress she had in mind for her fiftieth birthday party: foxy, drapey, in a brilliant cobalt blue. She had already bought it, confident that by the time she shed a few pounds, it would fit her perfectly.

Buying a dress to slim into: by her age, she should have known better. The plantar issue had soon put paid to running and the dress had still been too tight; now, three months after her raucous party in the King's Arms, Della was a generous size 16. She turned off the shower. 'I'm off in a minute, okay?' Mark called out from the landing.

'Okay, love.' By the time she had briskly dried herself

47

and stepped back into their bedroom, the shiny new putter – and Mark – had gone.

The sky was pale grey, and it was drizzling, but poor weather never put him off a Saturday game. With Sophie still to emerge from her room, the house felt still and quiet as Della dressed in the semi-uniform of cream shirt and knee-length black skirt that she was encouraged to wear for work. Four days since Kitty's funeral, it was her first day back at the shop. She was ready for it, for catching up with her colleagues and putting on her public face, and while she wasn't too keen on her rather staid outfit, Della strongly believed in the transformative power of make-up. At seventeen, she had discovered how a little colour could bring her rather nondescript face to life, and even now she still experienced a glow of pleasure on applying her customary flicks of black eyeliner, plus two coats of mascara to give her naturally lavish lashes an extra boost. Della's eyes were startling – a deep choco-latey-brown, like Sophie's. She twisted up her favourite lipstick – Estee Lauder, a gorgeous red. Della loved its name: *Impassioned*. Ha, she thought, carefully outlining her lips with pencil before slicking it on: that was a joke. She pictured Mark glancing at her naked body just twenty minutes ago, as if he dearly wished she still wore her fleecy PJs, buttoned up to the neck.

Anyway, *Impassioned* was now perfectly in place and Della was ready, if not for passion, certainly for selling plastic jewel-encrusted swords to excitable children in the castle shop.

'You awake, darling?' she called through Sophie's closed bedroom door.

'Mmmuh,' came the muttered reply.

Della gave the door a polite knock and pushed it open.

Sophie was in bed, dark hair fanned across her pale cheek. 'I'm off to work, love. Back just after five.' Della paused. 'Actually, no, I think I'll pop down to Gran's after work, just check everything's okay.'

'Mmm, all right . . .' Sophie said sleepily.

'Dad's golfing, but he should be home early afternoon. There's fresh pasta and a pot of sauce in the fridge. Could the two of you have that for dinner?'

'Yeah, no problem.' A pause, then Sophie turned slowly towards her, as if the movement required gargantuan effort. 'Are those books still there?'

Della frowned. 'You mean Gran's cookbooks?'

'Yeah.'

'They are, love, unless we've been burgled during the night, and Dad probably would've mentioned that on his way out.'

Sophie chuckled. ''Cause obviously, they're the first thing a burglar would take.'

'You might be surprised. We could be sitting on a gold-mine, you know.'

'Yeah, well, better keep them for me then, for when I'm living in a garret with nothing but bread and . . . what was that stuff again?'

'Margarine?'

'No, the meat grease.'

'Oh, you mean dripping.' Della laughed.

'Yeah, dripping in a garret. I'm really looking forward to that.' Della glanced once more at her sleepy daughter, then around the messy bedroom with its bold magenta walls. Mark had conceded that Sophie could choose her own paint colour, probably as he was so rarely in the room. In fact, most of the magenta was concealed by wonkily Blu-tacked posters depicting bands Della knew only vaguely, plus an arty one (a scratchy illustration of a girl's head with crosses for eyes).

'Mum?'

Della turned back to her daughter. 'What, love?'

'Stop pulling that face. I know what you're thinking. Evie says her mum's the same.' She smiled cheekily, and Della felt something twisting inside her.

'What am I thinking?'

'*You* know. You're doing that face again. Leeds isn't that far away, you know.'

'No, I know where Leeds is, honey.' She couldn't resist padding over to Sophie's bed and giving her a hug.

Sophie rubbed at an eye and grinned. 'It's not as if I'm going to China.'

Della laughed. 'Well, if you were, I'd be stowing away in your suitcase. You wouldn't be able to get rid of me that easily.' She kissed the top of her daughter's head, then straightened up and checked her watch. 'I'd better go. What are you up to today?'

Sophie shrugged. 'Aw, I dunno.'

'Seeing Liam?'

'Mmmm . . . maybe.' Ah, so Della's hunch had been right. She knew better than to ask Sophie how her boyfriend felt about her leaving Heathfield in three days' time. Whereas her girlfriends were heading off to uni or college – desperate to 'live somewhere where things happen,' as Sophie had put it – Liam seemed set to stay put, assisting his father in his joinery business. 'I'll probably just hang out with Evie,' Sophie added. *Just hang out*. How lovely to enjoy these last few days together just dawdling around, Della reflected as she drove through steady rain – it was too wet to walk – towards the castle. She had never had much time for just hanging out with

50

her friends. Even as a child, Della been the one Kitty had sent out on errands, because Burley Bridge was that sort of place: familiar and safe for children to wander, clutching their mothers' shopping lists, which entailed visiting several shops (butcher's, greengrocer's, newsagent's, haberdasher's – in those days the village even had a fishmonger and an ice cream shop). Jeff was deemed too important to be sent out to buy butter and Roxanne tended to come home with the wrong kind of flour. After leaving school, Della had been cajoled by Kitty into doing a secretarial course: 'Because you might not be the brightest button in the box, darling, but you're extremely good at getting things done.' Jeff had already left home and Roxanne, whose bedroom was by now papered with pages ripped out of *Vogue*, was set on a career in fashion. Della was still waiting, as if her true calling might flash before her in a dream.

She suspected Kitty had hoped that, once endowed with secretarial prowess, her eldest daughter would attract the attention of some wealthy businessman, and be safely off her hands. 'You have the *figure* to be a secretary,' she once remarked, as if large breasts and slender legs were all that was required.

Colin, Della's first boss, had festooned her with illegible hand-written correspondence, which she was expected to type up immaculately. This was pre-computers, even pre-electric typewriters, at least at Belling & Doyle Lift Installations: 'The dark ages,' as Sophie laughingly referred to it, whenever Della described office life in the early 1980s. It was also pre-men realising that perhaps it wasn't quite right to pat a secretary's bottom as she walked by. When Della complained – actually, no, she merely barked, 'What are you *doing*?' – Colin scratched at his beer gut

51

and said, 'If you don't like it, you shouldn't go around looking like that.'

Della had rushed to the ladies' where she surveyed her reflection in her neat grey pinafore dress and cried all her mascara off. Then she strode back to her desk, typed out GOING HOME WON'T BE BACK and, leaving the sheet of paper still wedged in her typewriter, did just that.

Afterwards Della had worked mainly with women, though not through any conscious choice; it had just happened that way. She was drawn to Heathfield's sole veggie cafe due to her love of cooking, and after waitressing there for a year she ended up managing the place. When the owners sold up, she took a job at a florist's and that's where she met Mark, a dashing young man with a big, bright smile who needed an emergency bouquet for his mother's birthday. 'I forgot,' he said, catching his breath as if he'd been running, 'and it's too late to post anything. Don't suppose you could deliver to Tambury today?'

'Of course we can,' Della replied. 'What kind of thing would you like?'

He looked at her for a few moments longer than necessary – time actually seemed to stand still – and she was conscious of every beat of her heart. 'Er, anything really,' he blustered. 'Whatever you can, um, throw together. Um, I don't mean *throw*, I mean carefully arrange, I'm sure you'll do a lovely job . . .' Feeling as if she had regressed to being sixteen years old – she was twenty-nine at the time – she assured him that she would indeed do her best.

In fact, Della reflected now, she would have somehow managed to find him fifty blue tulips – which don't even exist in the natural world – so eager was she to help out the flustered stranger who had left her with a fistful of tenners and her head in a spin.

She pulled up into the castle car park, telling herself it was natural for things to become rather humdrum after over two decades together. But occasionally she wondered what had happened to the eager young man who'd come back to Fresh and Wild the next day and asked her out. She supposed he'd just grown up.

Had *she*, though? As she climbed out of her car and the castle came into view, Della supposed she had. She went to work, she was a mother – at least, as much as Sophie would allow it these days – and cheerfully handled the hordes of schoolchildren who hurled themselves into the castle shop, so grateful were they to have reached the end of their history lesson and be allowed to *buy stuff*. Two stout stone towers flanked the castle's main entrance. The imposing archway led to a courtyard, the entrance to the grand hall and the obligatory tearoom and gift shop. Della waved to Georgia, who was manning the ticket office, and to Harry, who was brushing up copper beech leaves in the stone-flagged courtyard.

'How are you, love?' Angie greeted Della with a hug as she entered the shop.

'I'm fine, honestly.' Della pulled off her jacket and hung it on a hook in the back room. 'I miss her, of course,' she added. 'It's like, I don't know . . .' She shrugged. 'A big gap, I suppose. I mean, we spent so much time together towards the end.' Della cleared her throat. 'But I'm just glad it all went smoothly, and it was good to see everyone together – all the people I knew from growing up, I mean.'

Angie nodded. 'You must be shattered, being left to organise the whole thing.'

'It was simpler that way,' Della said truthfully.

Angie squeezed her hand. 'Your poor mum.'

'I know. All her life, not a single thing wrong with her.

53

She'd never been to a hospital, not even to give birth – she had the three of us at home.'

'Stoical,' Angie laughed.

'Yes, I guess she was. But I suspect she also wanted to do things precisely her way.' It was true, Della decided; at home, Kitty could manage her births, barking commands to William and even the beleaguered midwife on duty ('Your mother was very forthright in her wishes,' William had told Della, when she had asked about the circumstances of her own birth). Only now did she realise how hard it must have been for Kitty to succumb to the routines of the hospice.

As no visitors had arrived yet, Della started to unpack a box of bendy plastic shields that would be as much use as floppy tortilla wraps in even the most mild-mannered battle. It seemed wrong that, while Heathfield Castle had stood for over nine hundred years, most of the souvenirs would barely last the car journey home. 'Authentic' tunics – fashioned from something like potato sacking, dyed silver – disintegrated at the first hint of energetic play. (Della knew this, having sent Isaac and Noah one each several birthdays ago.) Generic notebooks, rubbers and chocolate bars were emblazoned with the castle's logo: a rather shabby drawing of the North Tower. But at least business was brisk as visitors began to drift in, which helped to take Della's mind off Mark's ill humour and Sophie's imminent departure and, of course, what the heck she was going to do with her mother's books.

By late morning the shop was milling with parents and grandparents and boisterous children. Two little girls launched into a full-scale scrap by the colouring books, and a mournful-looking boy seemed bitterly disappointed when his mother wouldn't buy him an amethyst the size of a human head. 'You can have this instead,' she said, radiating fatigue as she brandished a bouncy ball that was supposed to resemble an eyeball (nothing medieval about that, as far as Della could make out).

'So I guess you'll be clearing out your mum's house,' Angie ventured, as the shop quietened down towards the end of the afternoon. 'That's going to be hard for you, Dell.'

She nodded. 'I'm going to pop over after work and try to get my head around what needs to be done. It was tricky, with Roxanne, Jeff and Tamsin there.'

Angie pulled a sympathetic face. 'I hope there's no wrangling over your mum's stuff? It's just awful when that happens.'

'No, I don't think there will be. My sister-in-law's bagged most of the jewellery already.'

'No, that's terrible!'

'It's fine,' Della said firmly. 'To be honest, Mum didn't wear it much – at least, not after Dad left because he'd given her most of it.' She paused. 'I *have* taken her cookbook collection though.'

'Oh, you can never have too many of those,' Angie remarked, breaking off as a rather dishevelled man in a rain-speckled jacket tumbled into the shop, clutching the hand of a grumpy-looking boy of around eight years old.

'Eddie, please stop moaning,' the man exclaimed, throwing Angie and Della a quick look.

'I wanted to go in the castle,' the boy muttered. 'You said the dungeons are haunted. Why can't we just have a quick look?'

'We will next time, okay?' The man exhaled and raked back his light brown hair. Everything about him – the Toy Heaven carrier bag, the sadness in his soft grey eyes that

55

suggested that today wasn't turning out as he had hoped – said *weekend dad*.

'You promised,' the boy said crossly.

Della stepped towards them. 'I'm sorry, the castle closes in five minutes.'

'Yes, I realise that now,' the man said with a rueful smile. 'I've messed up my timings today.'

Della fixed Eddie with a bright smile. 'The dungeon's great, but you really need plenty of time to enjoy it properly. There are tours, you know. They turn the lights off and it's really creepy.'

With his grumpiness subsiding, Eddie rubbed at his eyes. 'Cool,' he murmured.

'So you should come back when there's a tour on. That way, you'll have a better chance of seeing a ghost.'

He regarded her intently. 'Are there *really* ghosts here?'

Della paused. 'Well, no one knows for sure. But there are plenty of stories about them.'

'Who were they? The ghosts, I mean?'

'Eddie, we really should be going,' the man said, resting a hand on his shoulder. 'These ladies will be closing the shop.'

'We've got a few minutes,' Angie called over from the till.

'Who are the ghosts?' Eddie repeated, eyes gleaming with rapt interest.

'Um, well, some people think they're prisoners who died in the dungeons hundreds of years ago.'

'Why did they die?' he asked eagerly.

Della glanced at Eddie's father, wondering whether this line of questioning was okay. As a young child, Sophie had enjoyed the more gruesome aspects of history: floggings and hangings and witches being burned. She had devoured *Horrible Histories* books and, during one particularly fervent period, had insisted on visiting the castle's dungeons every weekend for months on end. 'They weren't well looked after,' Della explained, 'so I think they probably died of starvation.'

Eddie seemed pretty thrilled by this as he turned to his dad. 'Can we come back tomorrow?'

Della saw the man's face relax for the first time since they had blundered in. 'That might be tricky. It's Milo's party, remember?'

'Can we come next weekend then? *Please?*'

'I don't see why not.' The man smiled at Della. 'Thank you,' he added.

'You're welcome,' she said, although she wasn't quite sure what he was thanking her for. What she did know, though, as the man and boy left, was that she felt *different*: lighter somehow, as if the weight of her mother's funeral, and Mark's grumblings about the cookbooks, had simply floated away. Even more startling was the fact that, when she climbed into her car and glimpsed her reflection in the rear-view mirror, she saw that her red lipstick – *Impassioned* – was still perfectly in place.

Chapter Six

Without the cookbooks lining the walls, Rosemary Cottage seemed different too. It was as if a vital part of its fabric had been stripped away, leaving empty shelves stretching from floor to ceiling in every room of the house. The place looked ransacked, but then, what else could Della have done? Anyway, soon the whole place would be empty and someone else – perhaps a young couple keen to move from town to country – would look around and think, *Hmm, well, it needs renovating, of course, and that antiquated kitchen and bathroom need to come out. But it has lots of potential . . .*

Della ran a finger along an empty bookshelf. It came away fuzzy with dust. Striding from room to room – the cottage already felt rather chilly and stale – she assessed what needed to be done. It wasn't that she relished the thought of sending the polished mahogany dining table or Kitty's glass-topped dressing table to the auction house; more that, the sooner it was all dealt with, the sooner she could move on from all of this.

In the rickety utility room she found a wicker basket into which she packed hand-printed silk scarves, elegant handbags and a slim box containing a set of mother-of-pearl-handled butter knives. These, plus Kitty's handmade wooden sewing box, were just the obvious things to take home for safe-keeping: clearly, Della would be making numerous trips back to the house. She continued to flit through the rooms, gathering up small mementoes along the way. Photograph albums were packed into a faded tartan suitcase, along with reams of paperwork to be sorted through later. Perhaps it was for the best that her siblings weren't exactly clamouring to help. Without Jeff, Roxanne and Tamsin sticking their oars in, Della felt clear-headed and purposeful.

As she investigated the contents of Kitty's dressing table, thoughts of that man and his son who'd wanted to see ghosts filtered into her mind. With a smile, she realised now what she'd done: overly sympathised, just because he was a dad in charge of his own child. How many mothers had she seen trying to control screaming toddlers and cheer up sullen kids over the years? And how much notice had she paid, really? That was the thing with fathers, Della decided: they didn't have to do very much to be hailed as superheroes by starry-eyed women. 'Some woman came up to me in the park,' Mark announced, when Sophie was a baby, 'and said I deserved a medal.' A medal, for taking his own daughter out in her pram for fifteen minutes! It hadn't even been raining. Della had dragged the buggy through the park in all weathers – driving hail, four inches of snow – and she couldn't recall ever being festooned with praise. The woman had probably just wanted an excuse to talk to him, Della had decided, aware of how the presence of a small child – like a puppy – heightened a man's allure.

Satisfied that she'd gathered up everything she needed at the moment, Della locked up the cottage, placed the basket and suitcase on the back seat of her car and, ravenously hungry now, decided to stroll along Rosemary Lane to the chippy. Another shower of rain had given the solid, stone-built shops and cottages a rather huddled appearance. The tang of vinegary chips tickled Della's nostrils. Rather than grabbing a take-away to eat in the car, she ordered at the counter and took a seat in the cafe at the back. It was warm and bustling with a large family who had perhaps stopped to break up a journey; despite the chippy having been here since her childhood, Della had never ventured beyond the counter before. Kitty didn't approve of eating out: 'Why would I pay those prices,' she'd declared more than once, 'when I can make it so much better at home?' Sitting at a red Formica-topped table with a plate of battered cod and chips hardly counted as eating out, Della thought with a smile, liberally sprinkling everything with vinegar and tucking in.

'Della? We thought that was you!'

She had almost finished as Pattie and Christine, the haberdashery sisters, made their way towards her. 'Oh, hello. Having dinner here too?'

'Yes, we thought we would,' Christine replied as they took seats at the next table. 'Far too busy to cook today.'

Della speared a chip, marvelling as she often had how two siblings could exist in such close harmony. She and Jeff or Roxanne would manage twenty-four hours at most. Yet, when the sisters' husbands had died within six months of each other, they had each sold their home and moved in together into the tiny flat above their shop.

'You did yourself proud,' Pattie remarked. 'At Kitty's funeral, I mean.'

'Oh, thank you. It was lovely, actually, so many people turning up.' She paused. The sisters, who were in their

60

early seventies at a guess, kept glancing at each other, as if barely able to suppress their excitement about something. Della suspected it wasn't about the imminent arrival of their fish and chips. 'So, how are things around here?' she asked casually.

'Much the same,' Christine said, peeling off her beige raincoat to reveal a murky green sweater.

'Nothing ever changes,' Pattie added. She, too, was wearing a turtle-neck sweater in a dingy hue. 'In fact, we're leaving.'

'Leaving? You mean leaving Burley Bridge? Oh, I'm sorry to hear that, I always loved coming into your shop . . .' Della stopped abruptly. Perhaps they were selling up due to necessity. Surely, in modern times, a haberdashery shop in a sleepy village would struggle to survive, and of course the sisters might not wish to keep peddling embroidery threads forever.

'We loved seeing you too,' Christine said warmly, 'and Kitty was always a wonderful customer.'

'But we thought it was time for a change,' Pattie ventured.

'So, um . . . are you selling up?'

'Oh, it's not ours to sell. We rent, dear. Always have. No, you see, we moved into the flat above the shop to . . . er . . .' She looked at her sister and smiled. 'To make our plans and, you know, put a bit of money aside.'

'What kind of plans?' Della asked, intrigued.

Christine grinned. 'We didn't like to mention it at Kitty's, erm, gathering . . .'

'The day was about her, not us,' Pattie cut in. She paused, as if about to disclose a salacious secret. Their platefuls of fish and chips arrived, although neither sister seemed terribly interested in tucking in.

'We've been planning this for years,' Christine added. 'You see, we've always loved Majorca. The four of us went together, year after year, when Phillip and Freddie were still with us, and we've finally bought a little place . . .'

'You've bought a place in Majorca?' Della gasped.

Pattie nodded. 'That's why we're here. It's our last supper of sorts. The flat's all packed up, we couldn't be doing with cooking tonight.'

'Well, I'm so happy for you,' Della said as the waitress placed her bill on the table. 'So is it, um, a timeshare or something?'

Christine chuckled. 'No, nothing like that. It's a little place up in the mountains.'

'Wow,' Della breathed.

'A rather tumbledown cottage,' Christine added with a smile. 'But it's beautiful, with incredible views, and they're loveliest, friendliest people in the world.' She met Della's gaze. 'We've been taking Spanish lessons.'

'It's lovely to hear of someone having an adventure.' In fact, Della was ashamed now of being so surprised that these women – who had resolutely stuck with their old-fashioned cash register and wrapped purchases in brown paper, tied with string – could not only negotiate the internet but were actually moving to another country. Why shouldn't they, after decades of running the shop? She hugged the sisters goodbye before paying at the counter, and stepped out into the soft Yorkshire rain.

Della strolled past Len's garage, with its faded shopfront – offering little more than cartons of screenwash and out-of-date packets of Maltesers – and Ian's immaculate butcher's shop with its row of gleaming empty metal trays. Next came Nicola's salon – A Cut Above – and the haberdashery, Sew 'n' Sew's, empty now, its interior dark and looking a little forlorn. It had been months since she'd strolled down to this end of the village. She peered into the shop, almost envious of the sisters upping and leaving for a new adventure. Seven years Della had worked in Heathfield Castle's shop. It alarmed her, how quickly the time had sped by. She, too, should think about doing something thrilling and new, especially with Sophie about to leave for art college. But what would that be? She felt a tightness in her chest, a sense of panic that nothing would change, that she would continue to potter about at weekends while Mark nipped off to golf, and that would be that.

Della strode back along the lane to Rosemary Cottage, climbed into her car and set off for home. The rain had stopped and the sky lifted; the trees were ablaze with copper leaves as if shined up by the recent dowsing. As a change from her usual direct route, she turned off the main road and took the twisting single-track lane that climbed high into the lush rolling hills, offering a breathtaking view of the valley. Della loved autumn, the gentle shift into cooler days, with great swathes of forest turning ochre and burnished gold.

She switched on the radio: she liked bluesy jazz, smoky voices reminiscent of late nights in cosy bars. She wished she and Mark went out more often together, on proper 'dates', as they were always referred to in women's magazines: *Rekindle your relationship! Schedule regular dates!* But then, she had glimpsed his jam-packed diary on the computer in his consultancy room and couldn't blame him for being reluctant to schedule his down-time too. The road led Della back down the valley towards Heathfield. The Norman spire of St Cuthbert's came into view, and the fortified castle was just visible behind the town centre. Della was approaching the golf course where

63

Mark played; an unremarkable one, she had always thought, rather scrubby and not particularly well tended. It looked particularly desolate today. She slowed down to 30 m.p.h. in order to get a proper look, and couldn't see a single golfer. She doubted it was due to the rain earlier; Mark's new-found golfing buddies never seemed to be deterred by poor weather. No, she realised now, the sign attached to the padlocked gate made it clear why the place was deserted: HEATHFIELD GOLF COURSE CLOSED UNTIL FURTHER NOTICE.

She frowned and drove on, on autopilot now, as the lane took her down into town, past the market square and along the high street with its rather bland, generic shops, then along the residential roads of almost identical red-brick terraced houses that led her to Pickering Street.

Della parked in front of her house at the end of the road and took a moment to compose herself.

Of course, there were lots of possible explanations. The course had closed at the end of today, or Mark and his friends had been so keen to whack a few balls about that they'd clambered over the rather flimsy fence with those ruddy great golf bags and played anyway. The thought of grown men *breaking into* a golf course rather tickled her. Of course, what had probably happened was less amusing; on discovering that the course was shut, they had simply driven on and played somewhere else. Della climbed out of her car, unloaded the bits and pieces from Rosemary Cottage and, still with a sense of unease, let herself into her house.

'Hey, Sophe,' she called out, dumping the suitcase and wicker basket in the hall. 'Have a good day?'

Sophie appeared on the landing. 'Yeah, just started a painting.'

'Ah, your favourite part.' Della smiled.

'Yeah, the beginning bit before it all goes horribly wrong.'

Della chuckled. Sophie didn't mean this; she was an excellent painter, possessing a creative streak that seemed to come from nowhere, as Della had never been particularly artistic, and Mark – a science type through and through – reckoned he couldn't even draw stickmen. 'Where's Dad?' she asked. 'Isn't he home yet?'

'No, he called to say they're having a few drinks at the club.'

Della's heart jolted. A few drinks at the club, which was closed.

'Did he say which club?' she asked lightly.

Sophie shrugged. 'No – the usual, I suppose.' Della nodded. Maybe it was just the course that was out of action, although she hadn't noticed any lights on in the rather bleak, pebble-dashed clubhouse, which seemed to hold such allure for him these days. 'Want to see what I've done so far?'

Della flinched. 'Sorry?'

'My painting, Mum!'

'Oh, yes, of course. I'd love to.'

She trotted upstairs, honoured to be shown a work in its initial stages. When she stepped towards Sophie's easel she marvelled at how much progress had been made. Sophie had captured a September landscape with confident brushstrokes, the sky heavy with pewter clouds over vigorous splashes of copper and pink. It was a stunning work. 'Oh, love, that's fantastic. It already looks finished to me.'

Sophie's face broke into a wide smile. 'It's a long way from that. But thanks, Mum. It just seems to be coming together, you know?'

'It really is. You're going to love college, aren't you?'

'Yeah, even if Uncle Jeff thinks I've made a terrible

mistake, and that I should be designing washing-powder packaging . . .'

Della laughed, turning as she heard the front door opening. 'Hi, honey, I'm home!' Mark seemed unusually perky as he lapsed into a jokey American sitcom voice.

She headed downstairs, deciding not to comment as he propped his bag of clubs against a wobbly pile of cookbooks. 'Hi, darling. Good game?'

'Yes, great, thanks.'

'Did you win?'

'Did I *what*?'

'Did you win? I mean, it is a competitive sport, isn't it?'

He peered at her as if she were asking a silly question. 'Yes, it is, but that's not really the point, Dell.'

So what is the point? she wanted to ask, knowing she was being prickly as she waited for him to mention Heathfield course being closed. But he said nothing. She watched as he pulled off his shoes, and when he wandered through to the living room she repositioned his clubs so they weren't propped up against her precious books.

Irritation niggled away at her as she made a pot of tea, then carried it through to the living room and curled up in an armchair. Of course, the simplest course of action would have been to ask, 'Mark, where did you play today?' But she had never questioned him about his whereabouts, never endured a moment's suspicion of where he might be. And it felt all wrong to quiz him now.

There would be a simple explanation, she decided, and she would find a way of asking him without sounding accusatory. She *would* ask, she fully intended to – but she needed to choose her moment, which clearly, with Mark already snoring softly on the sofa, wasn't now.

Chapter Seven

Della couldn't sleep. This had been happening a lot lately: dozing briefly, then waking up simmering hot, her chest slick with sweat, hence sleeping naked these days. This time, though, it was clear to her that it wasn't just due to her internal thermostat going haywire, but the *thing,* still swirling around in her mind at 2.17 a.m.: *Mark's whole day and evening at a golf course that was damn well closed.*

She turned in bed and glanced at the back of his head as he slept. In all the years they'd been together, he had barely had a broken night's sleep. She envied this, resented it, even: the way men's bodies just carried on doing their thing so efficiently without so much as a single hot flush. It wasn't that she wished a temperature, or even mild discomfort, on him. It just seemed unfair that, after pregnancy and childbirth along came facial sproutings, a thickening waist and irrational mood swings ('I am not being irrational!' she told herself, silently). Not his fault, of course. He'd got lucky when it came to ageing, too. 'Are you planning to age any time soon?' Nicola Crowther had asked Roxanne during their mother's funeral tea. She might as well have asked Mark the same question.

Some men became rather pouchy as the years rolled by: a cosy, unthreatening look which, as an enthusiastic eater herself, Della certainly had no problem with. But that hadn't happened to Mark. While he no longer had the long, lithe frame of the young man she had fallen in love with, he was in extremely good shape, nicely toned with the kind of body that still looked good in the Levis he favoured when gardening or lounging around the house.

The thing is, she decided now, staring up at the ceiling rose in the shadowy room, he *exercised*. Every Saturday, after bringing her coffee, he was off. The question was, what sort of exercise was he participating in exactly? Oh, what a ridiculous thought. The course was closed and now Della's imagination was running riot. That was the trouble with lying awake in the small hours: there was a tendency to churn things over and over, to let minor concerns blow up out of all proportion.

She was careful not to wake Mark as she slipped quietly out of bed, pulled on her dressing gown and padded downstairs. In the hallway now, she clicked on the light and crouched down to examine the cookbooks. She plucked out *Microwave Cakes*, remembering begging her mother to let her make one, and what a joyless thing it was too: a turd in a cup. 'Told you so,' Kitty had said with a shake of her head (right up until the end, she had regarded her microwave with deep suspicion, still labelling it 'newfangled').

Della scanned the numerous piles and wondered if perhaps she should try to whittle down the collection just a little. There were fat, meaty tomes devoted entirely to roasts and offal, which she was confident she would never use. Della opened *The Boiled Beef Bible*, certain that she caught a whiff of testosterone as she flicked through the pages. She picked up an outsized book entitled *Entertaining With Flair*. Della remembered her parents' dinner parties, before her father upped and offed with Jane Ribble from the insurance company where he worked: the house filled with tipsy laughter, and cigarette smoke filtering up to her little bedroom in the eaves. She missed those parties, even though she had never actually been invited to them – or perhaps it was her calm, quiet father she had really yearned for. Contact with him was sporadic after the split. Della got the impression that he was too wrapped up with Jane to pay much attention to the family he'd left, and although he always remembered his children's birthdays, soon a fiver began to replace presents, until eventually it would just be a card.

Della flicked through slim specialist books on olives, lemons – even salt. There were lavishly photographed volumes devoted to cooking with butter and cream: saturated fat virtually oozed from the pages. She could sense her arteries furring just by looking at the pictures. No one seemed to shun dairy or gluten in those days. The only intolerances Della could remember her mother having was when she or Roxanne took a biscuit without asking. Jeff was allowed to help himself to whatever he wanted.

Now, at nearly 3 a.m., Della sat cross-legged on the polished floorboards of the hall, reading about tender stews for the elderly and infirm, and being transported back to a world of chopping and stirring in her mother's kitchen, a place that always felt comforting and right. She pored over elaborate picnic menus and remembered the Burley Bridge kids all congregating by the river where they built a fire and cooked sausages. She studied cocktail recipes – almost able to taste a stolen sip of her mother's G&T – and sensed herself hurtling rapidly towards type-2 diabetes whilst immersed in *Sugarcraft Delights*. From its pages fell a small sheet of thin blue paper, folded over several times. Della opened it carefully and studied it. Typed on a manual typewriter, it read:

The Recipe Sharing Society
Meeting held 16 August, 1971

Della frowned. She would only have been six then, and couldn't remember her mother being a member of any sort of society. Kitty had never been the 'joining in' sort. She read on.

Members present:
Barbara Jackson
Kitty Cartwright
Monica Jones
Celia Fassett
Moira Wallbank
Dorothy Nixon

And that was it, plus a typed note at the foot of the memo: 'Recipes Are For Sharing'. There were no minutes of what had been discussed at the meeting, no matters arising or action points to be followed up. And, apart from her mother's, none of these names were familiar to Della, suggesting that the society wasn't based in Burley Bridge. Even as a child she had known pretty much everyone in the village, at least by name. She studied the list, trying to dredge up some long-ago memory of these women

70

being mentioned, intrigued by the possibility of Kitty having had a circle of women friends whom she had kept strictly separate, gathering together only for meetings. Or maybe – and this was perhaps the most likely explanation – Kitty had attended one meeting and decided it wasn't her thing?

Della turned the piece of paper over, hoping for more information. It was blank, apart from a faint pencil-written note she had to squint to read: *Such a delightful evening, Kitty, yours affectionately, R.*

R? She checked the typed names again: no R there. She folded up the piece of paper and slipped it back into *Sugarcraft Delights,* then eased the book into its pile.

Not remotely tired now, Della flicked through other books for notes hidden inside, but found nothing. Checking all of them would take days and, in any case, she didn't really know what she expected to find. She gathered herself up and examined Mark's golf clubs. Like the putter upstairs, these wore little black leather hats too. One by one, she removed them and inspected their heads. A couple were flecked with dried mud, suggesting . . . what exactly? That somehow she had changed from being a woman who went about her business in a reasonably cheery manner to the type who crept downstairs in the night to examine her husband's sports equipment? She shuddered and made her way to the living room where she perched on the sofa and flipped open her laptop. It was wrong, of course; downright stupid even. Della knew, as she Googled Heathfield Golf Club, that she had tipped into paranoia and should be in the kitchen right now, making a mug of chamomile tea before heading straight back to bed.

The website looked as if it had been designed by a ten

year old. Maybe Jeff was right and Sophie should consider website design, at least as a lucrative sideline. The colours jarred and the text – light blue on a sage green background – was barely legible. Still, she clicked on the news page and stared at a photo of the golf course dotted with small dark mounds.

Course Closed Due To Mole Invasion read the headline. *As our members may be aware, Heathfield Golf Course has suffered an influx of tunnelling moles, which has caused considerable damage to the greens* . . .

She frowned. Of course, a few moles burrowing about didn't mean that the clubhouse was closed. Mark could still have met Peter and Ivan and Rory, or any of the others he'd mentioned in passing occasionally. Apparently, Peter had been the one to invite Mark to join the club in the first place, when he'd come to have his feet seen to and it had transpired that Mark had dabbled a little as a teenager. Della had thought it quite sweet, two middle-aged men chatting about golf while Mark treated Peter's crumbling toenail with his laser machine. But the whole place had looked shut and, even if the clubhouse were still serving drinks, would Mark really have whiled away his entire Saturday there? She couldn't imagine many worse ways to spend a day.

Perhaps he'd been studying the moles?

Della turned at the sound of footsteps in the hallway. She heard Mark stumble, then curse, 'Christ, these damn books!'

'Are you okay?' she called through.

'Yeah, fine. Nearly broke my neck, that's all, tripped over that bloody margarine book . . . can't we put them somewhere else?'

'Like where?' she asked vaguely.

'I don't know. Like a storage facility or something.' He stomped through to the living room. 'Anyway, why are you up at this time of night?'

'Oh, I couldn't sleep, that's all.'

His face softened as he sat beside her on the sofa. 'Something worrying you?'

'No, not really.' He lifted her laptop from her, rested it on his own lap and flipped it open. Heathfield Golf Club appeared.

'The *golf club*?' Della's heart quickened as he blinked at her. 'Why were you looking at this?'

'I was just, er, curious,' she murmured.

Mark gave her a bewildered look. 'Thinking of joining, are you?'

'No, of course not.'

'Because there is a ladies' section, you know, although I'm not sure it'd be your sort of thing . . .'

'Oh, I don't know about that, with it being such a slow, sedate game and me not being built for speed.' She broke off, aware of Mark gawping at her.

'What *are* you on about?'

'Anyway, I can't imagine belonging to anything that has a ladies' section . . .'

'Dell, what on earth's got into you tonight?'

'Nothing! It just sounds like it's stuck in 1972, that's all. The *ladies' section*.' She shuddered and glared at him, knowing she sounded bitter and out of sorts. Mark was studying the screen now. For such small creatures, moles couldn't half wreak havoc on a course. In certain areas the piles of earth had all joined together, almost obliterating the grass.

'Della . . .' He paused. 'You weren't . . . checking up on me, were you?'

73

'No, of course not.'

She looked around the room, at the study in neutrals. Even the abstract painting above the fireplace was a homage to beige, a series of perfect circles that might have been drawn around a coffee mug.

'Yes, you were. What on earth made you do that?'

Della looked back at her husband, wondering how a fifty-two-year-old man could still look so attractive in rather old-mannish checked M&S pyjamas at 3.20 a.m. 'I just wondered,' she muttered, 'when I was coming back from Mum's and drove past the course and saw it was closed.'

'Oh, right.' His tone lightened. 'Well, yes, you've read about it now. Mole invasion. Completely out of control these past couple of weeks.' She watched his shoulders relaxing, and glanced at the wisps of dark hair on his chest. 'Started when Gordon – he's the new green keeper – took over,' Mark added. 'Bit of an environmentalist.'

'What d'you mean?'

'Well, the guy before used poison and there was barely any problem at all.'

'Poison? That sounds pretty extreme.'

'You can't just chase them away, Dell,' he chuckled.

'And what does this Gordon do?'

'Nothing,' Mark remarked with a wry laugh. 'That's the problem. He's tried humane traps where you catch the buggers, then take them off for a drive and release them so they can wreak havoc somewhere else. And when that didn't work he had some mole whisperer guy come round . . .'

'A mole whisperer?' Della spluttered. 'Is that really a thing?'

'Apparently so,' Mark replied, closing her laptop. 'He

74

was supposed to be able to coax them out of their tunnels by, I don't know, whispering sweet nothings, I guess.'

Despite everything, Della laughed. 'I wonder what he whispered?'

Mark leaned closer and breathed into her ear. 'Come out, little moley. Stop wrecking our course. There are so many more fun places you can go.'

She turned to him and smiled. After all these years, she still noticed how lovely his eyes were, a soft greeny-blue, outlined with the dark, silky lashes she'd once pronounced wasted on a man. 'So, where have you been playing, then? Since the mole thing, I mean?'

'Cragham. It's actually a much better course.'

'Why didn't you say?'

He gave her a curious look. 'Since when have you been interested in golf, Dell?'

'Well, it's just not my kind of— '

'I mean, d'you really want me to come home and give you a detailed report on the game?'

Della frowned. 'Of course not.'

He smirked. 'D'you want to know how I broke eighty for the first time, but it all went to pot and I tried to grind it out with a wedge?'

'I beg your pardon?' she asked, sniggering now.

'You want to know about my *swing*, honey?' She smiled, overwhelmed by a desire to kiss him. But he was already on his feet, tugging her up by the hand too. 'Come on, let's get back to bed.'

'God, yes, it's so late.'

He held her hand as they made their way upstairs, and it was still wrapped around hers, warm and comforting, as they lay side by side in bed. 'Is there something else, Dell?' he ventured.

'No, no, there's nothing.' She felt ridiculous now, petty and jealous, no better than the kind of woman who rummages through a partner's emails and finds precisely nothing untoward.

'Is all this about Sophie leaving? I mean, is that why you seem so tense?'

She turned this over in her mind. 'Maybe. I mean, I know it's great for her, a whole a new adventure . . .' She broke off. 'I ran into Pattie and Christine today after I'd been to Mum's. Popped into the chippy for tea.'

'Pattie and Christine?'

'Yes, you remember, the ladies from the haberdashery shop, they were at Mum's funeral tea.'

'Oh, yes, the weirdos!'

She pulled her hand away from his. 'They're not weird, Mark. They're really kind. I've known them practically all my life.'

'Yes, I'm sure they are, but don't you think it's a bit, I don't know, *sad* to spend your whole life running a dismal little shop in the back of beyond?'

She considered this. 'Not really. I've never thought about it like that.'

'What would you think if that was the sum total of Sophie's ambitions? To sit behind a shop counter for years on end?'

Like I have, you mean? The words hovered on her tongue. 'That's different.'

'How is it different?'

'Because . . . she's young, she's talented and ambitious.'

'And she's *ours*,' he added gently.

'Yes, exactly. Anyway, what I was *trying* to say is that they've closed the shop . . .'

Mark chuckled softly. 'Front-page news: haberdashery

76

shop in Burley Bridge shuts down. Where will old ladies get their zips?'

'Yes, well, they've been saving up and now they've bought a place in Majorca.'

'You mean a holiday apartment or something?'

'No, a cottage in the mountains.'

A beat's silence. 'And they're going together? The two sisters, you mean?'

'Yep, that's right.'

'Now, that *is* weird.' He sniggered in wonderment.

Was it, though? Della wondered. It didn't seem remotely weird to her. She imagined the sisters were as thrilled to be packing up their belongings as Sophie had been when the two of them had selected her student's starter kit. Together they had trawled IKEA, choosing a new duvet and pillows, cutlery, a set of pans and a colander. It was all sitting in its gigantic blue bag in the cupboard under the stairs. It had been months since they had done something together, just the two of them. These past couple of years Sophie had preferred going to the cinema with Liam, Evie or a big pack of friends, and Della had found herself grateful, like a dog being offered scraps, when her daughter deigned to watch TV with her. Gone were the days when they'd spend a whole afternoon at a vintage fair together, choosing a gilt-framed mirror for Sophie's room. But there in IKEA they had chatted and laughed and deliberated over wine glasses and tea towels, and even stopped for lunch. Sophie had virtually shimmered with excitement over her plate of curious little veggie balls, like a little girl compiling her Christmas list.

Della's thoughts drifted back to the haberdashery sisters, who had probably shed their possessions rather than acquiring new ones. Now *that* was appealing, the clearing of clutter and starting afresh. Jeff had been right about Kitty's hoarding tendencies, and Della certainly didn't want to turn into her mother. As Mark mumbled in his sleep and edged further away from her, she pictured the cookbooks in their hallway, towering in piles, hemming them in. Then she visualised Sew 'n' Sew's, which she had so loved popping into as a child, now slowly dulling with dust.

When she woke up next morning Della knew exactly what she needed to do.

Chapter Eight

Della was rarely up at 7 a.m. on a Sunday but today she slipped quietly out of bed, leaving Mark dead to the world, and pulled on jeans and a faded T-shirt, and padded softly downstairs. The house was pleasingly quiet as she settled at the kitchen table with her laptop.

Despite being awake half the night, she felt fresh and ready for action. She Googled 'Sew 'n' Sew's', trying many different apostrophe variations, plus commercial property/shop to let, with zero result. Perhaps the shop wasn't available for letting yet, or the owner – whoever that was – believed advertising online to be far too modern and convenient, and had opted for a note in the window of Irene Bagshott's general store instead. Keeping her ears pricked for the sound of movement upstairs, as if she were engaging in something rather sleazy, Della switched to Googling 'Burley Bridge to let'. And there it was, on Gumtree, of all places, 'purveyor of old tat,' as Mark had put it:

SHOP TO LET
74 Rosemary Lane, Burley Bridge
Formerly a haberdasher's
Comprising shop unit plus bathroom facilities and
small storage room
Front display window looking directly onto main
thoroughfare . . .

And that was it – apart from the rent, which seemed ridiculously low, although Della had no knowledge of such matters – plus two rather grim photographs. The exterior shot had clearly been taken on a gloomy day. The sky was leaden, the painted sign faded and peeling. The interior shot was no more inviting. There was a ragged crack in the ceiling and the pinky-beige walls, bare now that the racks of multicoloured zips and embroidery threads had gone, looked mottled and bleak. It was hard to picture it as the welcoming shop it once was, crammed with wools and ribbons and bales of fabric, which Della had so loved. The fact that the owner hadn't even bothered to use any flowery descriptions about the quaintness of Burley Bridge, or how the shop offered huge potential, suggested that they didn't really care whether the place was let or not.

The thought of it lying empty, slowly decaying, was just too sad for words.

But it needn't be like that. The place could be hers; Della could open a bookshop – not an ordinary bookshop, but a dedicated second-hand cookbook shop. Her mother's books would go to good homes and be cherished by her food-loving customers; and, more importantly, they'd be *used*. They would be well thumbed and splattered with sauces and cake mixture. That's what she loved about Kitty's collection: the fact that the books bore the evidence of the once-busy kitchen from which numerous meals for a family of five were turned out.

Della looked around at the plain white units of her own kitchen, in which everything was stored out of sight. It was a bit rich, she reflected, for Mark to insist on designing it when he had rarely ventured beyond boiling up a pot of pasta in here. Perhaps that's why her own interest in cooking had waned over the years: at least the everyday, 'What's for dinner tonight?' kind. She had never felt entirely at home here – not like in the kitchen at Rosemary Cottage – and besides, Mark rarely commented on her meals and Sophie favoured the plainest possible vegetarian food. It was hardly inspiring. But *this* was – the thought of setting up her own shop, and doing everything her way. Della's heart quickened.

She turned back to the screen and re-read the details. Of course it was a risky venture, and possibly even quite insane – but at some point she would have her share of the inheritance from Kitty. It seemed absolutely right to use the cookbook collection to kick-start a new life for herself. Just like Pattie and Christine – and her own daughter, in fact – Della could do something thrilling and new. She realised what a rut she had fallen into, trotting off to the castle five days a week and accepting the fact that she and Mark did virtually nothing together. This wasn't about her husband, or even Sophie. It was about *her*.

Della closed her laptop and pictured the shop fitted out with floor-to-ceiling shelves filled neatly with the cookbooks. She knew, instinctively, that such a shop would be talked about for miles around. She could paint the interior a vivid cornflower blue – no, a rich red would be more welcoming, encouraging customers to browse and settle on a deep, squashy sofa. She imagined herself, not bagging up yet another set of Heathfield Castle highlighter pens or packets of authentic Norman fudge, but instead sitting serenely behind the counter, welcoming customers and falling into easy conversations about food and cooking and what they might possibly be looking for. She'd have music playing – something low-key and jazzy – and fresh coffee brewing, perhaps little cakes for customers to nibble on. And although the shop would be filled with books, there'd be room too for some interesting objects; perhaps a display of the well-worn utensils from Kitty's kitchen. There would be art too. She could commission Sophie to create evocative paintings of memorable meals . . .

Della's stomach growled: all this fantasising was making her hungry. She made a pot of coffee and toast and took it, with two mugs, on a tray upstairs to Mark. 'Hey,' he said, 'this is lovely, thanks. You're up early.'

'Yes, I just felt, you know . . .' *Excited. Energised. As if anything is possible* . . . Della could barely keep the grin off her face.

He rearranged the pillows and gave her a curious look. 'What's got into you this morning?'

'Nothing.' She poured two mugs of coffee – not freshly ground, but who cared when she had a thrilling plan to share? – and scampered back downstairs, where she extracted the Recipe Sharing Society memo from between the pages of *Sugarcraft Delights*. Then, tucking her laptop under her arm, she hurried back upstairs and snuggled next to Mark in bed.

'You're all hyper,' he observed, biting into his toast.

'Oh, I know. I've just been thinking, that's all.' She sipped her coffee and opened her laptop.

Mark raised an eyebrow. 'What's this? Moles again?'

She grinned. 'No, it's not moles, darling, although I'd

like you to keep me posted on their activities.' She brought up the ad for the shop on her screen.

Registering the Gumtree logo, Mark leaned closer. 'Thinking of selling something?' His face broke into a relieved smile. 'Oh, you're selling the cookbooks! That's a brilliant idea. Someone'll want them if they're cheap enough . . .'

'Mark, I'm not—'

'. . . just offer them all as a job lot, nine-hundred-and-odd books for, I don't know, fifty quid or something? To get them off our hands.'

'Listen,' she said, more forcefully now, 'I'm not selling the books. At least, not on Gumtree. Look, this is Sew 'n' Sew's, the haberdashery shop in Burley.' She swivelled her laptop towards him and jabbed at the exterior shot.

'Oh.' He frowned. 'So it is.'

She glanced at him. 'Remember I told you about Pattie and Christine giving it all up for a new life in Majorca?'

'Ha, yes,' he chuckled. 'Giving it all up . . . we're talking a poky little shop selling . . . well, whatever it is they sold. They were hardly joint CEOs of ICI.'

Della frowned at him, wondering when this mild peevishness had begun to creep in. 'No, they weren't,' she said coolly. 'But I still think it's pretty amazing.'

'It's *retiring*, Dell. That's what people do when they get to seventy-whatever.'

'Yes,' she said, with a trace of impatience, 'but that tends to imply just stopping work, and doing lots of pottering, and they're doing something bold and adventurous.' As Mark shrugged in a *yeah, whatever* sort of way, it struck her again that in just a couple of days' time Sophie's room would be Sophie-less and it would be just the two of them. Instead of thinking, Hey, we can do whatever we like, Della felt a jolt of alarm. 'Well, *I* want to do something bold,' she added.

He blinked at her. 'When you retire, you mean?'

'No, I mean *now!*' Della sensed him edge away a little, as if she might pounce and demand that they make passionate love, despite that happening with a similar frequency to a lunar eclipse these days.

'Er, what d'you have in mind then?' He drained the last of his coffee as if to fortify himself.

'This,' she exclaimed. 'The haberdashery shop. It's empty and available and the rent's so cheap . . .'

He smirked infuriatingly. 'Hmm, wonder why?'

'Well, yes, it's pretty scruffy and definitely needs cheering up. But that can be fixed, Mark. I'd like to – well, I'd like to view it at least.'

'View it? Why?'

'Because . . .' She paused. 'Because I think I might like to take it on.' Mark looked at her, without speaking at first, as if considering how best to handle the issue. She could virtually hear him formulating a diagnosis and appropriate treatment: *patient has clearly spent too long trundling back and forth to a gift shop. She would benefit from variety in her life. Perhaps she could try a new hobby or, seeing as we didn't go away this summer, a weekend trip might offer a cure.*

'Dell.' He placed a hand over hers. 'Look, I know you've had an awful time lately with your mum and the funeral, and Jeff and Rox being hopeless as usual. You've had such a lot on your plate. But . . .' He exhaled heavily. 'I really don't think opening a haberdashery shop makes any sense at all.'

She spluttered with laughter. 'Oh, I don't mean I'd keep it as a haberdasher's. I haven't a clue about sewing and, to be honest, I don't know how it survived all those years.'

'Well, *that's* a relief!'

She glanced back at the screen. 'No, look – it's an empty shell. Just a building. It could be *anything*.'

'Like what?'

She paused. It felt important to describe the inside of the shop and her dream for it: the books, naturally, plus the mellow music, the low lighting, the coffee and cakes and art on the walls. 'I want to open a bookshop, Mark. A bookshop that only sells . . . *cookbooks*.'

He blinked slowly at her. 'What? Is this a joke, Dell?'

'No, it's not a joke. Look, I know we can't keep Mum's books. They're always toppling over, scattering all over the floor . . .'

'Ah, so you've noticed,' he remarked dryly.

'And it'd be amazing,' she charged on. 'The sort of place where people would want to hang around and browse for hours.'

'So that's your business model, is it?' He chuckled infuriatingly. 'It's pretty flawed, darling. It's just not viable. Browsing doesn't put any money in the till.'

'No, no, *listen*. What I mean is, it'd draw people in. It would be like a cosy living room full of, oh, I don't know . . . ideas and memories and inspiration.' Aware of him staring at her, as if anticipating a punchline, Della pulled out the Recipe Sharing Society memo from her pyjama pocket.

'Right, so cooking with lard and dripping and refined sugar, that's really what people want these days, is it? Inspiration for heart disease and type-2 diabetes.'

'No, Mark,' she snapped. 'Customers would *love* the nostalgia aspect. I mean, everyone has memories of being with their mums or grandmas in the kitchen, weighing out ingredients, baking, licking out bowls . . .' He threw her a blank look. 'I found this,' she added, handing him the memo, 'tucked inside one of Mum's books.'

He unfolded it and frowned at the text. 'The Recipe Sharing Society. What is this?'

'I don't know exactly but it must be something she belonged to.' Della pointed at the last typewritten line. 'Look: "Recipes are for sharing." It's true, Mark. They are!'

'Yes, but you can't start a business because of some scrap of paper you found stuffed in an ancient book.'

'I'm not. It's not just because of that. I wanted to show you the whole *point* of it, what it's all about for me. You were right, the books shouldn't be sitting there in our hallway. I could never use them all, I couldn't even use a tenth of them. They should find new homes and be used and enjoyed . . .' Her voice tailed off.

'Don't you think there's a small problem with this?'

Della looked down at her hands and picked at a nail. 'Well, I know it's a risk, and the place needs a ton of work – I don't think Pattie and Christine had got a paint-brush out for decades. But, you know, it has charm.'

'No,' he cut in, 'what I mean is, you have a full-time job.'

'Yes, of course, but—'

'So I'm assuming,' he went on, 'if you really want to go ahead with this, you're talking about employing someone to run it, which surely would wipe out any tiny profit you managed to make? I mean, how many cook-books do people actually need?'

Lots, Della wanted to snap back as she climbed out of bed. As many as possible, unless, of course, that moment came when you needed just one, your very own version of *What to Cook Today,* filled with soothing dishes to make everything feel a little better than it had before. She was conscious of her eyes filling with tears as she strode towards their bedroom door.

'Della? Don't be like that. Come on, love, you must admit it's a bit, I don't know . . . impetuous.'

Stopping in the doorway, the memo stuffed back into her pyjama pocket, she glared back at her husband. 'I'm not being like anything. I just wanted to talk to you. Why is it so hard for us to talk these days?'

'Oh, come on, don't be all emotional . . .'

And don't tell me how to be! she fumed silently, marching out onto the landing, aware of him flouncing out of bed and scurrying after her. 'I'm just thinking *viability,* darling. Listen, I didn't mean to upset you . . .'

'It's fine,' she snapped back.

'I was just saying, if you want to take that place on and hire staff . . .'

She paused at the top of the stairs. 'I wouldn't take on staff. Not at first anyway. I'd do it all by myself.'

'*But you already have a job*!'

Della stared at him. Sophie's bedroom door opened and their daughter stepped out, bare-footed, hair mussed up, wearing her outsized Miffy T-shirt and washed-out pale pink pyjama bottoms. 'Why are you shouting?'

'*I'm* not shouting,' Mark muttered.

Sophie peered at her parents in turn. 'Mum, what's going on?'

'Erm . . . I'm thinking of opening a bookshop,' she said levelly. 'Remember the haberdashery shop in Burley Bridge? Well, it's vacant at the moment and up for let.'

Sophie's eyes widened. 'Your own bookshop? That'd be amazing!'

'Mum means a cookbook shop,' Mark explained. '*Only* cookbooks. Nothing else.'

'Really?' Sophie frowned. 'You mean no novels, no travel or anything else?'

'No, darling,' she murmured. 'That would be the whole point.'

Sophie nodded, clearly mulling this over. 'Well, I s'pose that'd make it unique. I mean, if it got known, and you needed a cookbook, then you'd be better going to a specialist place than any ordinary old shop.'

'Well, that's what I think.' Della wanted to hug her. That was the thing she loved about her daughter: the way she saw possibilities rather than obstacles. Of course studying fine art probably wasn't the safest option; website or packaging design, as Jeff had been keen to point out, would probably be more lucrative. But Sophie was doing what she wanted in life, the very thing that compelled her. What was so wrong with that?

'It's far too niche,' Mark muttered.

Della fixed him with a cool stare. 'I don't think food is particularly niche, Mark. I mean, we all have to eat.'

'So you'd leave the castle shop?' Sophie asked.

'Yes, darling, I would.'

'But it's a regular income,' Mark huffed. 'You can't just walk out on a perfectly good job.'

'Yes, I can,' she said firmly. 'Look, I know it's impetuous but it all feels, I don't know, like the right thing to do. Mum's books, the note . . . and in a few months, when it's all sorted out, there'll be my share of the inheritance from Mum. It won't be huge but it'll tide me over if business is quiet to start with.'

'Yes,' Mark said, 'but we could use that for other things.'

'Like what? Doesn't this seem like the right thing?' She

studied his face, which was clearly telling her, *no, it isn't, it's completely ridiculous*. He just shook his head and, registering the disappointment on her face, stepped forward and tried to hug her. Della turned away.

'Mum?' Sophie murmured. 'Are you okay?'

'No, she's not okay,' Mark mumbled, which was Sophie's cue to disappear back into her room.

What did he mean by that? That she was clearly upset, or had actually lost her mind? *'You're not right in the head!'* Kitty had cried when Della broke the news that she had walked out of Belling & Doyle Lift Installations and wouldn't be going back. *'But you can't just throw away a good job like that! What will everyone think?'* Never mind that. What about the fact that Colin Stone had groped her? *'Oh, men in his position do that. He was probably just being friendly.'* What, squeezing her bottom as if testing market stall fruit?

Della stomped downstairs, relieved that Mark hadn't followed her. Much as she craved affection sometimes, she didn't want to be hugged right now. Annoyingly, too, she had left her laptop in their bedroom, which she couldn't retrieve because Mark was still up there and would lecture her, throwing around words like *impetuous* and *viability*, words she didn't want to hear because this was something else, something she absolutely felt she must do, and she refused to accept that he might be right.

Chapter Nine

Cooking had always offered comfort. Weighing and measuring, chopping and stirring: these simple acts somehow lifted the spirits and, luckily, Della had plenty to occupy her that day. She set to immediately, her enthusiasm reignited as she gathered together her ingredients and ran through a mental checklist of what needed to be done. Mark had presumably sloped back off to bed – he enjoyed a lie in on Sundays, being *golf-free* – even though there was a small party to cater for this afternoon. Della had suggested to Sophie that she could invite a bunch of friends over before they began to disperse to colleges and universities all over the country during the following week.

She spent the next couple of hours making mini savoury tarts and samosas, without Sophie's help – her daughter wasn't a cook, she could barely peel the foil off a yoghurt pot without slopping it everywhere – and anyway, Della preferred to get on with the job alone. Mark remained upstairs as she chopped onions and peppers, and she couldn't help but feel relieved. Negativity seemed to ooze from his pores these days; he wore it like a particularly unpleasant aftershave, and she wondered whether he had begun to carry it with him to his consulting room. *Sorry, Mrs Fletcher, it's a particular vicious strain of fungal infection. This toenail is no longer viable . . .*

He did have a point, though, about the whole viability thing. After all, it wasn't as if Della had bookshop experience, or any kind of proper grown-up business plan. She had been a shoddy typist, worked in a cafe and a florist's, and spent the past seven years selling Heathfield Castle perfumed soaps and build-your-own balsa wood castles (with working drawbridges). She wasn't even terrible gifted in the practical department. When she had brought a castle kit home, hoping to entertain Isaac and Noah on a visit, she had got a splinter in her finger and been unable to fit the pieces together in any kind of castle-resembling way. 'Looks derelict,' Jeff had snorted from his spectator's position on the sofa, sipping his wine. *It's meant to look derelict. It's not a Barratt house. It's supposed to be nine hundred years old!* Plus, how many cookbooks would she need to stock this hypothetical bookstore of hers? It occurred to Della that, while 962 were clearly far too many for the narrow hallway of a terraced house, they might not be enough for a shop.

Jane Ribble, the woman for whom Della's father had left Kitty, had opened a shop in Ambleside in the Lake District: a boutique of the mother-of-the-bride variety, selling jewel-encrusted dresses and stiff little pastel-coloured suits. 'A vanity project,' Kitty had sneered, and she was probably right. On the rare occasions Della had visited her father, the shop had seemed rather bare, as if the flouncy frocks and lilac net fascinators were only on display temporarily, and would soon be whisked away to make way for the kind of shop people really wanted.

91

And what kind of shop was that? As she placed her tarts and samosas in the oven, Della tried to conjure up the image she had already painted in her own mind. Deep red walls, glowing lamps, a velvet sofa to sink into . . . but now all she could think of was Jane Ribble, a terribly gushy woman, the Cartwright children had decided – well-meaning and kind, in the way that she cooked for them whenever they stayed for weekends. However, they did wish she wouldn't try so hard, serving up uneasy parings of meat and fruit (pork with prunes, a ham salad with slices of blood orange weeping slowly into the iceberg lettuce), as if driven by a desire to impress them. With no children of her own, Jane had seemed bewildered by the Cartwright trio. She hadn't realised they'd have all been far happier with Alphabetti Spaghetti on toast. Della had visited Jane only a couple of times after her father's funeral, and only because she happened to be in the area. She couldn't help feeling sorry that, as Jane's shop had failed, she had had to sell their semi-detached home and move into a poky flat above a photocopier repair shop from which a sharp chemical odour seeped at all hours of the day and night.

Stopping for a coffee now, Della flipped through *Entertaining with Flair,* deciding that canapés would be fun for Sophie and her friends. Actually, here they were called hors d'oeuvres, which sounded pleasingly quaint. She could have a section for hors d'oeuvres cookbooks in the shop – an entire shelf dedicated to things on sticks. That would be fun; in fact, she could have a bookshop opening party, inviting all the villagers who had so kindly turned up for Kitty's funeral tea. She would pick out her favourite canapé recipes and have a retro theme . . .

Turning her attention back to the matter in hand, Della

decided to rustle up a batch of vol au vents. Adults were coming, as well as Sophie's gang: Freda, of course, plus Charlotte and Tricia, fellow mothers she had known since their children were friends at primary school.

At around eleven Mark finally put in an appearance, requiring Della to negotiate her way around him with floury hands and a scalding tray of just-baked tarts. 'Sausages,' he observed as she slid another tray into the oven.

'Honey and chilli-glazed chipolatas,' she corrected him, trying to lighten the atmosphere between them. 'Both veggie *and* pork.'

'What is it about teenage girls and vegetarianism?'

'Oh, I don't know – I think it's sort of obligatory. Here, try one of these.' She thrust a plate of samosas at him.

'Mmm, these look great.' He bit into one. 'They're delicious, Dell. Can't believe you've managed to make all of these. They look so professional.' He glanced appreciatively at her morning's baking all set out on the kitchen table.

'It was fun, actually.'

Mark smiled. 'Nice to see you enjoying cooking again.'

'But I *do* enjoy it.'

'Yes, but you know what I mean – being creative about it, the way you used to be.' He meant this as a compliment, Della decided as she started to load the dishwasher. 'You're so good at it,' Mark went on. 'Look, if your heart's set on leaving the gift shop – and I really don't blame you for that – maybe you should think about doing something with catering?'

'Maybe,' she said lightly, not wishing to discuss the folly of her bookshop idea now.

'I mean, surely it'd make more sense than opening a

93

shop? You could work from home, there'd be no overheads really.' She nodded, pretending to consider this. 'And this kind of thing,' he continued, 'top-quality party food . . . people would love that, wouldn't they? I mean, it's a bit of a step-up from crisps! And you have tons of experience from running that veggie cafe.'

'I'll think about it,' she said, pecking his cheek and pulling on the old fisherman's cardi she had plucked out of Sophie's ready-for-charity bag. 'I'm off to buy drinks, okay? I'll take my car.'

'Fine,' he said, as if rather hurt by her lack of enthusiasm over his suggestion for what she might want to do with her life.

In the supermarket Della roamed the booze aisle, plonking wine into her trolley, plus beer, cider and soft drinks for the teens, and a couple of packets of puff pastry for the vol au vents. Although she knew Sophie and her friends favoured vodka with mixers, she couldn't quite bring herself to buy spirits: silly, really, as what was the difference? They were all over eighteen and if they wanted vodka, they would simply bring their own.

She was making her way to the checkout when she saw them: the man and his boy who had arrived at the castle just as it was about to close. Della stopped and watched them. Eddie, that was the boy's name. She didn't know the father's. They were debating what to buy at the fish counter; the supermarket had a proper one, with a range of catches displayed on crushed ice. 'I don't want anything with a face,' Eddie retorted, and Della smiled.

'What are those, Dad?'

'They're scallops, a kind of shellfish.'

'What are *they*?'

94

'Sardines, Eddie.'

'No, they're not!'

'They are, look, the sign says so.'

'But sardines are in tins . . .'

Della stood for a moment, hoping she looked casual rather than weirdly stalkery, gripping the handle of a trolley laden with booze. She wanted to go over and say hi. Although she wasn't sure why, it seemed important to remind them where they'd met, and to say she hoped they'd come back to the castle sometime.

The man turned and caught her eye. He was tall and rangy, with kind eyes, and still had the slightly harassed air of a weekend father. Della smiled and, perhaps a little too eagerly, pushed her trolley towards them. 'Hi,' she said.

'Hi,' the man said distractedly. He took his son's hand – she was surprised that Eddie allowed it – and turned back to the counter. 'How about salmon, Eddie? You liked it last time.' Eddie gave Della a blank look and muttered something to his dad.

Feeling foolish now, she stared hard at the fish. She had planned to say something funny about sardines, about them having a life outside tins before they were canned, but what kind of lunatic eavesdropped on father-and-son conversations in supermarkets? Anyway, it was clear now that neither the man nor his son recognised her and that, on a score of one to ten, the risk of her seeming like some batty middle-aged stranger probably hovered at around a nine.

They ambled off together with their bag of salmon, and Della found herself buying two trout fillets she didn't even want (Mark was funny about fish). No wonder they'd had no recollection of ever having met her before. Although she planned to spruce herself up later, to apply the full whack of make-up and dig out her most flattering dress, right now she was wearing the lumpen old fisherman's cardi she'd plucked out of Sophie's charity bag. Beneath this, clearly visible, was a faded T-shirt which, she realised now, had a daub of eggy mixture – the filling for her savoury tarts – on the chest. She hadn't even showered yet.

'We need to get Milo's birthday card, Eddie.' The man's voice floated over from the pickles aisle. It shouldn't have mattered that this attractive, clearly kind man and his son – with whom she'd had a proper conversation about the terrible fate of prisoners in the dungeon – didn't even recognise her. But it *did* matter, because she clearly remembered them.

In the car park she loaded her purchases into the boot of her car, noticing the man and his boy pulling away in a rather scruffy blue Mini. She watched them leave. Occasionally, Della wondered if she was starting to fade, like the botanical illustrations on the tea towels Kitty used to buy from National Trust properties, and would use for years until the flowers and their exotic Latin names were barely visible.

Whatever Mark thought, she decided, slamming the boot shut, she had to do something – something that *thrilled* her – before she completely faded away.

He shrugged. 'Okay, fine, if you want to do something different . . .'

'Yes, I do.' She glanced at the stubbly borders and wished, as she did every year, that he would just leave them be. However, while Della loved the twiggy stems and seed heads, Mark preferred everything chopped down to size. 'I'd like to do something for myself,' she added, 'especially with Soph about to leave home.'

'Of course. That's totally understandable.'

He turned and resumed snipping away, and she headed back to the kitchen where, once the puff pastry had defrosted, she rolled it out – such a soothing process – and cut neat circular shapes with her frilly-edged cutter, just as she had as a child at Rosemary Cottage. When they had baked and cooled, she filled them with mascarpone and sautéed mushrooms; then, with Sophie's help, she spruced up the house, setting out plates and glasses.

With everything ready for the party, Della showered quickly and tried on the clingy blue dress again, taking in the sight of her squishy tummy and ample hips: areas she rarely regarded as problematic until she saw herself encased in unforgiving jersey fabric. If anything, she had gained weight since her fiftieth birthday, back in June, probably due to the stress of caring for her mother, driving to Rosemary Cottage – and latterly the hospice – every day after work. She would arrive home shattered, after Mark and Sophie had eaten, and tear ravenously into any odd bits of pie and creamy dips and whatever else she found lurking in the fridge, all washed down with a large glass of wine, which was basically sugar in liquid form. As a regime, it certainly wasn't recommended in Roxanne's glossy fashion magazine. Occasionally, she packaged some up and sent them to Della, who found it unsettling, being faced with all those clearly airbrushed pictures of Hollywood actresses whose bodies had 'snapped back' to perfection – breasts pert, tummies taut – seemingly hours after childbirth.

Her daughter was eighteen now and Della's body still hadn't snapped back. It was soft around the edges, pillowy and comfy, and she really should do something to try and get herself on track.

She pulled off the dress, threw it onto the bed and selected a plain black shift instead, plus low heels. She blow-dried her abundant dark hair so it fell in soft, bouncy waves, and by the time she had applied her make-up – eyeliner and customary *Impassioned* lips – her spirits had risen. As her friends began to arrive – cheerful women who tied back their hair with Scrunchies, and who wouldn't dream of denying themselves carbs – Della had forgotten about the man in the supermarket failing to recognise her, or Mark's lack of enthusiasm over her probably utterly bonkers project.

Freda had brought her a bunch of pale lemon roses, and Charlotte and Tricia were laden with edible gifts. Liam ambled in – Sophie hugged him, briefly, although she soon drifted out to the garden to join her girlfriends – and Della found him a little later, hovering uncertainly by the fridge. 'How are things, Liam?' she asked.

'Yeah, all right, thanks.' He shuffled awkwardly from foot to foot.

She looked at him, wondering whether she should try and make him feel more at home or just leave well alone. It was hard to know how to handle a morose teenager who wasn't hers. Sophie had seemed super-keen on Liam until a few months ago, when she'd left school and the summer, then art college, hovered in front of her like a gift she couldn't wait to take in her hands. Liam had finished school the previous year to work with his carpenter father. Sophie wouldn't be drawn on the subject; in fact, Della detected distinct 'I don't want to talk about Liam' vibes.

'So,' she ventured, feeling obliged to chat as there were only the two of them in the kitchen, 'Sophie's off on Tuesday.'

'Um, yeah,' he muttered.

'But Leeds isn't that far away.'

He looked down at his battered trainers. Was that patronising? Della wondered. The boy was nineteen, of course he knew where Leeds was. 'What are you up to these days – still working with your dad?'

He nodded, and Della understood how Sophie viewed him: as the boy who had no intention of leaving Heathfield, while she was embarking on a thrilling new stage in her life. 'I'm sure she'll be back home a lot,' added Della, feeling desperately sorry for him now. After all, he had dutifully visited Kitty, both at home and at the hospice. He had taken her After Eights, a bunch of carnations from the garage and a Get Well card; perhaps that wasn't quite right, as by that stage Kitty clearly wouldn't be getting well at all. But at least he had tried to do the right thing.

Sophie appeared, grabbed a plate of samosas and swished off out to the garden again, with Liam following limply behind. Della arranged Freda's impressive home-made cupcakes and truffles on the table next to her own savoury creations. Mark busied himself with serving drinks – Della was relieved by this, that he was joining in, but then why wouldn't he? He wasn't an awkward thirteen year old at a school dance.

'All those books in the hallway!' Tricia exclaimed, when

Della joined her friends in the living room. 'Thinking of opening a library, Dell?'

'No, a bookshop,' Mark cut in quickly. 'A bookshop that only sells . . . *cookbooks*.'

'Really?' Charlotte gasped. 'That's amazing! When did this happen?'

'I, um, only decided a few days ago.' She caught Mark giving her a resigned look. 'They're Mum's cookbooks,' she added, willing him not to start carping on about viability and the fact that she had officially lost her mind. 'I'm going to view an empty shop in Burley Bridge.'

'You're actually going to look at it?' Mark gasped.

She threw him a sharp look. 'Well, yes, if it's still available.' Della and Freda exchanged a quick glance.

'No harm in looking, is there?' remarked Charlotte, a brisk and infinitely capable woman, who ran her own marketing consultancy. 'I've always loved Burley Bridge but, I hope you don't mind me saying, Dell, it does need an injection of life.'

'Yes, I realise that.'

'Something to put it on the map,' agreed Tricia.

'That's the problem,' Mark pointed out. 'The place is dead half the year. On a wet winter's afternoon there's hardly a soul on the streets, so there'd be no passing trade . . .' Della clamped her back teeth together, willing him to stop. She felt oddly possessive about Burley Bridge, and it irked her to hear it described in this way. Yes, she had yearned to escape as a young woman, but now it felt like the perfect home for the books. Perhaps a shop like hers could breathe some new life into the place, and make it more like the vibrant village she remembered as a child.

'D'you have any retail experience, Mark?' Charlotte

101

asked, adjusting her tortoiseshell glasses. *No, he bloody doesn't!* Della wanted to shout.

'Er, no, not exactly.'

Charlotte's mouth twitched. 'Well, with a specialist business like Della's – ' Della loved it that she was describing it as an actual thing, as if it already existed ' – you don't get much custom through passing trade. Let's face it, the average person wandering along Burley Bridge High Street probably isn't looking for a cookbook.'

'That's my point precisely!' Mark cut in, and Della was seized by an urge to stuff a gruyère and broccoli tart into his mouth.

Charlotte frowned and turned back to Della. 'Yes, so with a shop like this it's all about word of mouth, reputation, and building a story around your business that'll capture people's imaginations. That's how it happens. You could be halfway up a mountain and people would still come.'

'You really think so?' Della was trying to suppress a huge grin.

'Yes, absolutely. So long as they know you're there – through social media, PR . . .'

'I'll need to do some PR?' Della cut in.

'Yes, but it's not difficult with something so unique. You're bound to be featured in the *Heathfield Gazette* and on local radio, maybe even national press, specialist food magazines . . .'

'Maybe Roxanne could help,' Freda suggested.

'She works on a *fashion* magazine,' Mark pointed out.

'That doesn't matter,' declared Charlotte. 'She'll know people. She'll have contacts. I'd imagine that's not the only magazine her company publishes?'

Della sipped her wine, her heart racing now, not with

nerves but the thrill of it all. 'Yes, there are lots, I'm not exactly sure what kind . . .'

'They'll be falling over themselves to feature you,' Charlotte said with a grin. 'I mean, how often d'you hear of something so unique, so niche?'

'It's *too* niche!' Mark exclaimed, rather too loudly. Freda shot him a quick look.

'What I'm saying,' Charlotte continued with exaggerated patience, 'is that your customers will make the effort to come to you. It'll be like a day out for them – to visit this amazing shop in a little tucked-away Yorkshire village, spend an hour or two there, then a wander around, stop off for . . . um, what else is there in Burley Bridge?'

'Nothing,' Mark said witheringly, and now Della was seized by an urge to pelt him with chipolatas.

'Sorry, Mark, but I *do* think it's a brilliant idea,' Tricia said firmly. He gave her a resigned look as if to say, *You would, wouldn't you? Being Della's friend . . .*

Della stood up to refill glasses, keen now to veer the conversation away from the bookshop, at least while Mark was around. The day had turned into one of those golden September afternoons with an unblemished blue sky. They all drifted outside where the teenagers had gathered on a rug on the lawn, and Freda and Della ferried out more food and drinks to set out on the table. 'These vol au vents are amazing,' exclaimed Tricia, biting into her third.

'Don't think I've had one since 1979!' Freda quipped.

'It's all completely delicious, Dell,' Charlotte agreed, and even Mark murmured his appreciation. Della glanced at Sophie and her friends, who were all huddled together and laughing hysterically, and started to feel a little better about her leaving home in two days' time – because she wasn't the only one. All of these bright, sparky kids – that is, all apart from Liam – would be heading off for college or university this week. And so the afternoon turned to evening, with no one seeming in any hurry to rush off home. The sky darkened, and Della brought out speakers so Sophie could play music. 'Would you like to join us, Norma?' Della asked, when their next-door neighbour appeared and glanced over the fence.

'No, thank you, I'm a little tired,' she remarked.

Della smiled, pleasantly fuzzy with wine now, as Norma – a short, sturdy woman in her sixties, who seemed to be on an unfeasible amount of committees – peered at Sophie and her friends. 'We'll try not to disturb you then,' Della added.

'Oh, don't mind *me*,' Norma said, clearly meaning, *Yes, please don't*. But it didn't irk Della, and nor did her husband being so negative earlier because Mark was just being Mark: cynical, yes, but sensible too. Perhaps it was just as well she had someone around to bring her back down to earth.

At around ten, she and Mark said their goodbyes to the adults and, leaving Sophie and her friends in the garden – with strict instructions not to annoy Norma – they started to clear up. Della was gathering empty wine bottles in the kitchen when her husband took her hand. With a jolt, she looked round at him.

'Have fun today?' he asked.

'Yes, it was lovely, wasn't it?' She was still clutching a smeared bottle with her free hand.

Mark smiled. 'It really was. You did everyone proud, as usual.' He paused. 'You know, I really think you should set up your own catering business. You'd be perfect for it, Dell. You're such a grafter, you really get things done. Wasn't that what your mum always said about you?'

'Hmmm,' Della said wryly. 'She also said I wasn't the brightest button in the box.'

He chuckled. 'Well, she was wrong about that. Would you just think about it, at least? There'd be none of the risk of taking on premises, paying rent, business rates and all that.'

'It's a good idea,' she cut in, 'but it's not what I want.'

'So what *do* you want?'

'*You* know, Mark. A cookbook shop.'

He shook his head and let her hand go. 'Look, all I'm saying is, please think about it carefully. It's a huge decision to make.'

She nodded. Buoyed up by the company of friends, and no longer feeling like an invisible woman lurking by the fish counter, she stretched up and kissed her husband on the lips. 'Yes, I know that,' she said.

'You won't rush in?'

'Of course I won't, this is far too big a thing to just dive into.'

He gave her a dubious look, as a headmaster might when not completely convinced by a promise of further good behaviour. 'You really mean that, Dell? Because I'd hate to see you make a terrible mistake.'

Chapter Eleven

Della meant to keep to her word because she knew, as a bona fide adult, that they had a mortgage to pay and their daughter to see through three years of college. Although Mark was by far the main breadwinner – Jeff had been right, feet were pretty lucrative – it felt important to Della to play her part. *But there's no harm in looking,* she kept reminding herself all day at work. She was just putting out feelers, that was all. Certainly no decision would be made today. She strode out of the gift shop at just gone 5 p.m. and through the castle courtyard, where a few straggling visitors were photographing the ornately carved crest above the arched entrance.

In fact, Della had niggling doubts herself as she pulled out of the car park. Perhaps Mark was right, and Burley Bridge was just too sleepy a place to set up any kind of business. Would anyone seriously drive miles to browse through faded old books about suet puddings? Still, she would meet the man from the letting agency as arranged – actually, it sounded like a one-man operation – and just get a feel for the place.

Della drove along the winding country lanes through insistent rain and pulled up outside Sew 'n' Sew's. Since she was fifteen minutes early, she decided to check on Rosemary Cottage to make sure all was okay. Although Morna from along the lane was popping in regularly, it still felt important to keep an eye on the place.

Kitty's garden had grown wild during these past few months. Della had tried to keep on top of it, ripping up that wretched convolvulus that spiralled its way up the lupins and the tarnished iron railings. Yet still it had grown – there was no beating it back – and as Kitty's cancer had spread, seemingly unstoppable despite radiotherapy and chemo, Della had given up on the garden and ceased to notice the herbaceous borders becoming shrouded by weeds.

Now the leafless forms looked starkly beautiful, the lupins thickly coated with velvety pods, the alliums spindly cages you could crush with a breath. She turned away and let herself into the house.

In the stillness of the kitchen, Della shuddered. With its bare bookshelves and a stale odour hanging in the air, she knew without doubt that the house must be put up for sale as quickly as possible. As a little girl, Della had loved the cottage's numerous nooks and crannies and its fire crackling in the living room for half of the year. Despite her mother's chilliness, the place had always felt cosy and comforting. However, it had never seemed quite the same after her father had left, and when Jeff headed off to university the house had felt emptier still. Now it was hard to believe that a family had played hide and seek here in the currently dusty, spider-populated cupboards, and gathered around the gnarled old oak table for vast Sunday dinners. It took all of Della's powers of recollection to picture the huge cooked breakfasts, and the times Kitty had veered off piste and presented something rather more exotic: a kedgeree, filling the kitchen with its delicious smoky aroma, or, on one occasion, a curious dish called a salmon loaf ('For breakfast?' William had exclaimed, before dutifully tucking in).

Morna had left a neat pile of junk mail – seed catalogues, charity mail-outs – on the kitchen table. Della inspected the bedrooms – her old room was tiny, hidden under the eaves – then the ancient bathroom with its roll-top bath, which bore a dark metallic streak where the dripping cold tap had worn the enamel away.

In the living room now, Della wondering if the Recipe Sharing Society had ever met here and, if they had, how she had been unaware of it.

Yours affectionately, R. It was probably friendly affection rather than the romantic sort, Della decided. In 1971 Kitty and William were most definitely together, albeit amidst perpetual low-level bickering and the occasional Not Speaking phase. She remembered one Christmas when, using the muddy brown wool Della had been asked to fetch from Sew 'n' Sew's, Kitty had knitted him a sweater. On Christmas Day he'd tried to force the too-small neck hole over his head. He'd laughed – not unkindly, Della had thought – and Kitty had refused to speak to him for a whole month.

Della locked up the cottage and walked briskly down Rosemary Lane towards the shops. A besuited man was already standing outside Sew 'n' Sew's, and he raised a hand in greeting. 'Della? I'm Nathan. Come in, let me show you around.'

'Great, thank you.' He had messy dark-blond hair and dark shadows beneath his eyes, hinting at a hangover. She glanced up at the hand-painted sign, peeling gold lettering with rather amateurishly painted haberdashery items – scissors, a tape measure and a spool of thread – floating around it. 'Lot of potential, this place,' Nathan said briskly, bringing with him a powerful whiff of cheap spicy after-shave as they stepped inside.

'Yes, I can see that.' She glanced around the room. The laminate flooring was beginning to curl up in various places, and the bleak centre light buzzed intermittently. She paced around, trying to conjure up her vision for the shop: red walls, glowing lamps, a deep, squashy sofa, perhaps in purple velvet. But with Nathan hovering by the scuffed counter it was impossible.

'So, um, there's a little storage room out back,' he added, 'and bathroom facilities and . . . er, well that's about it, really.' He flashed a wide, teeth-baring smile.

'Who actually owns it?' she asked.

'My uncle.' Nathan paused. 'To be honest, I can't under-stand why he doesn't just stick it on the market and get rid of it.' He chuckled. 'Shouldn't say that really but, y'know, the rent he's charging, it hardly seems worth hanging on to. All the years he's had it, and now those two old biddies have gone, I'd have thought it'd be a great opportunity to get shot of the place.' He smirked. His suit had given way to shininess, and his light blue eyes never quite met hers. 'So, what d'you think?' He raised one eyebrow.

'Um . . . I'm not sure,' she said. 'So what's happening with the flat upstairs? Does your uncle own that too?'

'Yeah, that's being let too, separately. You interested?'

'No, no, just the shop,' she said quickly.

'And what line of business are you in, if you don't mind me asking?'

'I'm thinking of opening up a bookshop,' she replied.

He peered at her. 'Really? So you think that'd work around here?'

She blinked at him. 'Well, um, it's just at the idea stage at the moment. I'm only starting to look at possible premises. Why, d'you think it's a bad idea?'

'Oh, I'm probably the wrong person to ask. Haven't read a book since the *Beano Annual*. More of a movie person myself, so long as it's not some weird subtitled rubbish . . . I mean, who goes to the cinema to *read*?' She laughed politely. 'But it's all e-readers these days, isn't it? You can see why. Middle aged-women secretly reading their saucy novels on the train, nobody any the wiser.' He chuckled throatily.

'But there's still a place for real bookshops,' Della remarked.

'Yeah, well, I can see the appeal of having a little business like that. For someone like you, I mean.'

She frowned at him. 'What d'you mean, someone like me?'

'Uh, you know, a woman of . . . er . . .' Della stared, waiting for him to continue. 'I mean a woman,' he blundered on, 'who's looking for a little, uh, thing to do on the side, that whole bookshop-florist's-cupcake-bakery thing.'

Della gawped at him in disbelief. 'What d'you mean, a thing? Is a bookshop a *thing*?'

'Oh, come on,' he chortled. 'I mean those fantasy shops, the fluffy little businesses women dream about having when they're bored at work, sick of the office job. Life's dreary, they're unfulfilled . . .'

'That's a bit of a leap, isn't it?' Della exclaimed, deciding not to mention that, actually, she had worked at a florist's.

110

'Oh, no, I'm sure *you're* not,' he added quickly, flushing a little. 'You seem very, er, together. But, y'know, there's a time in a woman's life, kids flown the nest . . .' Della bristled '. . . and they're thinking, I need something else, some *excitement* . . .' She started to make for the door.

'Yes, well, thank you, Nathan. I think I've seen all I need to see.'

He scuttled after her and they both stepped outside. 'Are you rushing off?'

'Sorry?'

'I mean, if you're not, I know a nice little pub near here.'

Della looked at him, confused. 'I . . . I'm just going to head home actually.'

Nathan looked taken aback. 'Are you sure? I thought, y'know, we could have a drink, you and me? Just a chat, somewhere local.'

Why? she thought crossly. *So you can patronise me some more about my silly little fantasy shop?* He did a thing with his eyes then, sort of narrowing them at her – although it came across as more of a squint – probably something he'd seen a male model do in a shaving-cream ad. 'Just a drink,' he added, with a shrug. 'No strings.'

Della laughed. 'Really? No strings at all?'

'Well, I just thought you might like—'

'A drink with you.' She smirked. 'You thought it might bring a little flurry of excitement into my terribly dull, dreary existence?'

Nathan flushed. 'Aw, look, I'm sorry if I offended you.'

'It's okay,' she said briskly, climbing into her car. 'I'm not at all offended. Look, I'll call you when I've thought it over. About the shop, I mean.' He nodded and looked disgruntled as she pulled away.

111

It wasn't quite true, Della decided as she drove back to Heathfield under a heavy grey sky. Although the offer of a drink was hilarious, and she'd enjoy sniggering over it with Freda ('Still got it!'), she couldn't shake off her annoyance at Nathan's suggestion that bookshops came under the florist's/cupcake-bakery/namby-pamby-little-enterprises-for-ladies umbrella. For one thing, it implied that she had the air of the terribly unfulfilled middle-aged woman. (Now why would *that* be?) Plus, he wouldn't have made that remark if she'd been a man, or if she'd said, 'I'm thinking of setting up an electrical shop.' How dare he write her off as a silly, fluffy type!

Della didn't feel remotely fluffy. She had her daughter to see off to college, without dissolving into a weeping wreck; she absolutely refused to be the only parent sobbing outside the student halls tomorrow when they'd settled Sophie in. She had Rosemary Cottage to clear out and sell, and a shop – a proper bona fide business – to get started. She was a capable woman, a working mother who had run their home with reasonable efficiency and made a decent job of being a parent. No one had starved, or had to venture out in dirty clothing due to laundry services being suspended; and now here she was, half a century old with the parenting part (at least, the hands-on part) almost done. And rather than it symbolising the end of something, it could be the start of something new.

Oh, stuff him, she thought, deciding not to dwell on Nathan's belittling remarks a second longer. She turned up her antiquated car stereo, replaying his clumsy offer of a no-strings drink – whatever *that* meant – and chuckled all the way home.

Chapter Twelve

'So, how was it?' Mark asked, looking up from his laptop at the kitchen table.

'Kind of how I expected,' she replied. 'I mean, I know the shop so well, I must've been in hundreds of times.' She paused and dropped her car key into the bowl on the worktop. 'It looked pretty dismal actually. Scruffy, gloomy, bit depressing.'

'Ah, that's a real shame,' Mark said without conviction.

'The guy who showed me around was a bit of a creep,' she added as Mark turned his attention back to his emails. 'Can you believe this? He actually asked me out for a drink.'

'Really?' Mark spluttered and swung round.

'Yes, I know.' She grinned. 'First time it's happened since we've had decimal currency.'

He chuckled. 'So what did you say?'

'No, of course! I told you – he was a creep.'

'Oh, right, so you'd have gone if he'd been a roguish charmer . . .'

'Naturally,' she said with a smile, pulling off her jacket

and heading upstairs where Sophie was packing the last of her things.

Together, they had already filled six cardboard boxes. Della had kept herself under control during the process, pretending that Sophie was preparing for some kind of trip: a quaint French exchange, perhaps, during which she would need clothes for all weathers. Now she found her daughter in her room, sitting cross-legged on the rug as if waiting for inspiration to strike on what to do next.

'Hey, sweetheart, how's it going?'

'Um . . . nearly done, I think.'

Della glanced around the room. The explosion of clothes and underwear suggested that this wasn't the case. 'Are you sure?'

'Well, I thought so. It's just hard, y'know, deciding what to take.'

'Come on, let me help you. Are all these to go?' Della indicated the toiletries strewn on Sophie's bed.

'Er, yeah.'

Della started to pack the products into a zip-up bag, marvelling at the sheer volume of shine treatments and heat-protection sprays her daughter required. When Della was her age, a can of Elnett did the job. 'I've just been over to Burley Bridge,' she added, 'to view a shop.'

'A shop? What for?'

'For *me*,' Della said with a grin.

'Really?' Sophie's eyes widened.

'Yes, darling, for the bookshop.'

'Oh, the *bookshop*! You mean it's an actual thing now? God, Mum, how exciting!'

'Well, yes, I suppose it is. It's also probably quite mad and pretty terrifying . . .'

'No, it's not. It's a great idea. I mean, what is there to lose?'

Della smiled. She loved the way everything seemed possible to teenagers; tedious details such as viability just didn't feature. At what point, she wondered, did human beings lose their wild enthusiasm and start to see only obstacles and risk? 'Well, I'll have to give up my job so if it fails . . .' She shrugged. 'I'll be jobless, obviously, and I'm far too ancient ever to find anything else.'

'Don't be so negative!' Sophie exclaimed. 'Honestly, Mum, I don't know how you've stood it, working at the castle all these years.'

'It hasn't been that bad,' she said, a trace defensively.

'Yeah, but you're hardly using your brain, are you? So, what about this shop? Did you like it?'

'Well . . .' Della hesitated. 'It's pretty uninspiring at the moment, and the guy who showed me around – not that there was much to see – he kind of . . . well, he made assumptions about what I'm planning to do.'

Sophie frowned. 'What kind of assumptions?'

'He said, "Oh, *that bookshop thing*," as if – I don't know – it was typical for a woman of my age to want to do something like that.'

'How patronising. He wouldn't have said it if you were a man.'

'No, darling, that's exactly what I thought. But it did set me thinking.'

'*Please* don't let some idiot man's comments put you off.' Sophie gathered herself up off the floor and carefully unhooked her gilt-framed mirror from above the dressing table.

'What are you doing?' Della asked.

'I'm just packing.'

'Yes, but you're not taking that, are you?'

115

''Course I am,' Sophie retorted. 'I love this mirror.'

'So do I, sweetheart. And you won't need it. I mean, it might get damaged in student halls . . .'

'How will it get damaged?' Sophie laughed. 'It'll be on my wall, Mum. Perfectly safe. And I'll need a mirror, won't I?'

'Won't there be one in the bathroom?'

Sophie stared at her. 'Mum! I'd like my own mirror in my room, okay? Why is that a problem?'

'It's not,' Della muttered, although of course it was: because the mirror wasn't just a thing. It wasn't a can of hair detangler or a ragged old copy of *The Catcher in the Rye*. It was a prominent feature of Sophie's bedroom, and Della wanted the room to remain just as it was. 'So,' she went on, 'are you sure you know where you're supposed to go tomorrow?'

'*Yes,* Mum, we've already been, remember?'

'No, I don't mean the halls,' Della said, recalling the open day when she and Sophie had inspected the student flat in the vast modern block. Mark hadn't come. He hadn't been able to take time off work, and golf had meant that the Saturday viewing day was tricky too. *I'm sure it'll be fine,* he'd said blithely.

'I mean, d'you know where you're supposed to pick up your keys?'

'Yeah, I just need to go to some office.'

Della glanced at her daughter, who was now trying to wrap the mirror in a bath towel secured with poorly applied brown tape. 'Let me do that for you. So, um, I just wanted to say . . .' Their eyes met, and there was so much Della wanted to say, she didn't know where to start. She cleared her throat. 'You do know you can always come back, don't you, love?'

'Mum, I'm not coming back. I'm moving out!'

'No, I mean just if you're feeling unsure or lonely or homesick . . .'

'I won't get homesick.'

'. . . or if you're ill or even a bit under the weather.' Della glanced at the ghostly circle on the magenta wall where Sophie's mirror had been.

'I'll be fine. Stop worrying.'

Della could hear Mark on his mobile downstairs, muttering away, his voice too indistinct for her to make anything out. How could he go about his business, conducting conversations with friends, as if nothing untoward was happening? *Avoidance tactic,* she decided. *He's finding this as hard as I am.* At least Della could keep busy, and be useful; Mark rarely ventured into the mysterious territory of Sophie's boudoir.

'I know you'll be fine, darling,' she murmured as her daughter carefully peeled her posters from the walls, then plonked her wind-up alarm clock into an already overfilled box. 'You won't need that, will you?'

Sophie peered at her through her fringe. 'It's my clock. Of course I'll need it.'

'But no one uses clocks these days. You've got your phone.'

'I want my clock! Why are you trying to stop me taking things?'

'I'm not,' Della protested as Sophie unplugged her desk lamp and coiled the wire around its base. *But you won't need all this,* she wanted to protest. *I thought you'd just be taking a few things – essentials – not your mirror and clock and lamp and . . . oh, God, now you're packing your owl cushion, couldn't you leave that? I didn't think you'd be emptying your whole damn room.* She caught herself

117

and vowed not to go on like this, not to be the clinging, pathetic mother, acting like someone bereaved. Tomorrow was a new beginning, she reminded herself: a blank canvas. All those possibilities . . . She glanced at the dramatic landscape, painted in acrylics, which Sophie had propped up against the wall. 'Oh, you finished your painting.'

'Yeah, just in time.'

'It's really wonderful. Are you taking that with you too?' Della swallowed hard and distracted herself by straightening Sophie's duvet.

Sophie shook her head. 'No, it's for you, Mum. You and Dad.'

'I really love it,' Della said truthfully. 'Thank you, darling.'

'Okay. Great. So, will you stop pulling that face and help me pack the rest of my stuff?'

Mark did appear, eventually, peering cautiously around Sophie's bedroom door. He cleared his throat. 'So, um . . . what's to go downstairs?'

'This lot here.' Della indicated the stacked boxes and crammed bin liners. Together the three of them carried Sophie's possessions down and dumped them in the hallway, where Mark made a big show of stumbling over the piles of cookbooks.

'All done?' he asked brightly, meaning, Can I get back to my important emailing now?

'Yes, I think so.' Della turned to Sophie. 'We'll make an early start tomorrow . . . is Liam coming too?'

Sophie frowned. 'No, Mum.'

'It's just, I wondered if he'd want to see you off.'

'I really don't want this to be a big thing,' she said briskly.

'No, love, I know.' Della felt something twist inside her, not because Sophie didn't want her boyfriend to come – of course, a teary farewell would be mortifying, especially with her parents hovering about. It was more that this *was* a big thing, of course it was.

'Can I take some food with me?' Sophie asked.

'There *are* shops in Leeds, Sophie,' Mark said with a chuckle.

'Yes,' Della said, 'of course you can.' In the kitchen, as if amassing provisions in preparation for a siege, Sophie snatched tins of tomatoes and chickpeas, jars of pesto and honey and packets of dried lentils and pasta. 'Okay if I have these?'

'Yes, yes, just take what you like.'

'And these?' Now she had grabbed two types of vinegar (cider and malt), plus Della's posh almond chocolate and a bottle of white wine. Della watched in silence, feeling as if her heart would break: not because she would miss the food – or even the wine — but because this was all happening too fast.

Hold it together, she instructed herself. Why on earth was she getting all emotional over a packet of tagliatelle? Sophie was rummaging about in the fridge now, grabbing squeezy tubes of mayonnaise and ketchup – 'Okay if I take these?' – while Della busied herself with finding a box in which to pack everything. And all the while, Mark tap-tapped at his laptop at the kitchen table, as if in agreement with Sophie that this really wasn't a big deal at all.

In fact, it was a relief to Mark when his wife and daughter drifted back upstairs to conduct the umpteenth discussion about what Sophie should leave and what she could take,

119

and would she need extra blankets and a hot water bottle . . . as if Leeds was in Northern Finland. How about a colander, a mug tree, a toast rack? *Why would she need one of those?* he'd wanted to shout, feeling utterly wrung out by it all. *As a family, we have functioned pretty well by just having our toast off a plate.*

The endless deliberating, the expectation that he should join in with these discussions – and actually have an opinion – was causing him more grief than anyone would ever know. His daughter, his only child, was leaving home. In some ways, not because he was a callous man – he loved Sophie to distraction – he would be relieved when tomorrow was over and he could set about getting on with the rest of his life.

After Sophie had turned three, Mark had been keen to try for another child – a boy ideally, an ally, although of course you couldn't choose. Babies weren't sweets at the Pick 'n' Mix counter, and anyway it just hadn't happened. Month after month Della's period had arrived, and she'd always seemed pretty relaxed about it. To Mark, although he knew he was being ridiculous, it almost seemed as if she wasn't trying hard enough.

Maybe it was for the best, he'd decided finally, when Della had shunned the idea of trying at least one round of IVF. 'Let's just see what happens,' she'd said. 'Let's leave it to fate.' Typical Della, drifting along without any kind of coherent plan. But then, his practice was doing well, and he was starting to be invited to speak at podiatry conferences, which he enjoyed immensely. Mark had consulted on a new pioneering treatment for wart removal, and enjoyed delivering his PowerPoint presentation and fielding questions after a talk. He loved wearing his best clothes, the only bespoke suit he had ever owned, and standing on a slightly elevated platform, holding forth on a subject he knew a great deal about. This flurry of attention had inspired him to broaden his knowledge, to investigate ground-breaking treatments for hammer toes and persistent athlete's foot; he didn't want to be known as The Wart Man, after all. And so, as his reputation had grown, he had let go of the idea of fathering another child. Della was right. How could they feel anything was lacking in their lives when they had their beautiful, talented Sophie?

He could hear the two of them now, chatting and laughing upstairs, and sensed a small twinge of envy. That was silly, he decided. He had to stop thinking that way, as if he were an outsider within his own small family. Of course Della had been the one to accompany Sophie to vintage fairs and the cinema; old things and quirky romantic movies weren't his cup of tea. What mattered now was how they were going to move on when it was just the two of them. These things took careful planning and Mark wasn't one to rush in. He'd spent three months deliberating over paint colours for this place, all for Della to complain, 'It's just cream!' when he'd returned home with the pots. No, it wasn't cream, it was *Cabbage White* – subtle and beautifully calming. Della could paint the bookshop whatever colour she wanted, he thought, sensing his irritation over her little project beginning to bubble up again.

Had anyone ever had a more bonkers idea? Okay, so the castle gift shop paid a pittance, and was no doubt mind-numbingly dull – so why not just find a more lucrative job? Della could dust down her secretarial skills, bone up on the new software packages. She was attractive and personable and reasonably bright – he was confident that someone would take her on. He could understand that she needed a change. With Sophie leaving tomorrow, he and Della were moving into a new chapter, which implied choice and freedom: words that made Mark, at fifty-two years old, feel almost giddy with delight.

He dashed off an email – just a couple of hasty lines – then went into his sent mail folder and erased it. At the sound of Sophie's music starting up – and Della singing loudly, embarrassingly – he closed his laptop and reassured himself that no one would blame him for the choice he was about to make.

Chapter Thirteen

Sophie was moving into a student village, although it wasn't a village in the Burley Bridge sense of the word. Having never been to college or university – Della's first independent home had been a flatshare with an air stewardess, when she worked at Belling & Doyle – she had expected the student accommodation to be a charming muddle of turrets and twisty stone staircases. In fact, Darley Court consisted of three vast beige modern blocks set in gently undulating grounds. As Mark pulled into one of the few remaining parking spaces, Della skimmed her gaze over the scattering of parents and their teenage offspring all busily unloading car boots. 'I'll go and pick up my keys,' Sophie announced, jumping out of the car and scampering off.

'D'you want me to come with you?' Della called after her, but she was gone. Della undid her seatbelt in the passenger seat and looked at Mark. At least he had taken the day off work. He may not have looked around the accommodation with them but he was here now, doing this part with her, and that's what mattered.

'Does she know where to go?' he murmured.

'I hope so. She can ask someone, I guess.' As they fell into silence, Della watched a mother and daughter carefully manoeuvring an enormous cheese plant out of a BMW boot. 'We didn't get Sophie a plant,' she murmured, to zero response. Now out came suitcases, a cool box, a wine rack . . . 'Should we have bought her a wine rack?'

'Of course not.' Mark exhaled loudly. 'What would she need one of those for? Students don't store wine. They just tip it down their necks straight away.'

'Yes, of course,' Della murmured, wondering what kind of rock her husband's heart might be made of: granite, perhaps, or quartz? That was it: he had a jagged little heart of quartz.

To break the silence, she remarked, 'What was it like when you left home for uni?'

'Well, you know I stayed at home the first year.'

'Oh, yes, I'd forgotten. Poor you.' She meant this genuinely. She couldn't imagine that living with Val and Terry as a student would have been terribly joyful.

'It was fine, really. It made sense, you know? Financially, I mean, and uni was only an hour away by train.'

'But what about all the fun?' She gazed around at the chattering groups, almost able to taste the sense of anticipation quivering in the air.

'I still had a good time,' he remarked as Sophie reappeared, flung open the passenger door and waved a small brown envelope at them.

'Got them!' she yelped. 'I've got my keys!'

So off they went, with Sophie striding ahead in her stripy sweatshirt and ripped skinny jeans, literally distancing herself from them in case they might try to hug her, or make some kind of fuss. While Sophie's embarrassment at being seen in public with her parents had peaked at around fifteen years old, there were still traces of it occasionally, usually when she was nervous or unsure. Della glanced at Mark, hoping to see a flicker of empathy, but now he too was marching ahead, as if this was any old ordinary day.

All around them, teenagers were checking each other out; the odd smile, a quick glance at the contents of a transparent carrier bag (fluffy slippers, a music case of some kind, a fluffy blanket). Sophie pushed open the main door of her block and zoomed in. Della and Mark strode in behind her and clattered up the concrete stairs, and by the time they reached the top landing the door to Sophie's flat had already been opened by an impossibly beautiful auburn-haired girl.

'Hi, I'm Sophie.'

'Luella.'

The girls grinned at each other. Della and Mark hung back, and when it became apparent that they weren't about to be introduced – there was no need, of course, they were Sophie's mum and dad, the whole place was milling with parents who didn't quite know where to put themselves – Della cleared her throat and said, 'Shall we and go and fetch your stuff, Soph?'

Sophie swung round as if only just remembering her parents were there. 'Oh. Yeah, sure.'

'I'll help,' Luella said brightly. 'I'm all unpacked, arrived a couple of hours ago.' And so the four of them trooped back to the car to fetch Sophie's belongings, with the girls opting for the lighter loads (a biscuit tin containing jewellery, a pillow stuffed into a carrier bag) while Della and Mark lugged boxes of books like a couple of packhorses. In the hallway of Sophie's flat, other students emerged from their rooms: a boy with Clark Kent specs and a possibly ironic (and certainly unseasonal) reindeer sweater, then another boy, startlingly ginger with bright blue eyes and a sweet, eager face.

'Hi, I'm Cameron,' offered the reindeer boy.

'Nice to meet you, Cameron, I'm Sophie.' How confident she sounded now, clearly well able to survive without Della reminding her to consume the occasional green vegetable.

'I'm Josh, can I help you with that?' The ginger boy gallantly relieved Sophie of a bag containing a dressing down.

'Oh, thanks! That's so kind of you . . .' Still no introductions, as if Della and Mark had ceased to be of significance the moment they had stepped out of the car. They were removal people now, dutifully striding back to the car umpteen times to collect the rest of Sophie's things while the students started to bond, a little shyly at first but not, Della suspected, for very long: she had spotted a box of cheap Bulgarian red wine sitting in the hallway. The moment she and Mark left – begone, gnarly old parents! – it would be opened and sloshed into brand new IKEA glasses, and they'd chat and drink and realise the wine was almost gone, and someone would have the bright idea of opening the box to get at the foil udder inside, which they'd squeeze to milk out the last drops. Della had done just this, when she had first left home.

'Your room's lovely,' she remarked as they hugged their daughter goodbye.

'Yeah, I really like it.' Sophie shuffled her feet and glanced around distractedly.

'Er . . . d'you want us to help you unpack?' Mark asked, casting a derisory glance around the bare cell with its navy blue curtain and flimsy-looking desk.

'No, it's okay, Dad.' A gale of laughter filtered down the corridor from the shared kitchen.

Della touched Mark's arm. 'I think we should go, darling.' He nodded, looking relieved. 'So, um, we'll leave you to it, love,' she added.

'Yeah, okay, Mum.'

Della bit her lip. 'They seem nice, your flatmates.'

'Yeah!' A small, awkward laugh.

'Friendly, the boys. Luella seems lovely too. Good of her to help you move in . . .'

'Yeah-yeah.' *Please go,* said Sophie's wide-eyed expression.

'Would you like us to hang up your mirror before we leave?'

'No thanks. I am capable of bashing a nail in.'

'Bashing it in?' Della exclaimed. 'But you could hit an electrical cable or a water pipe . . .'

'Mum, *please*.' Sophie rolled her eyes.

Sophie exhaled and glanced at Mark, as if willing him to usher her mother off the premises before she started running a bath for her and making tea. 'You don't have a hammer,' Della added, horrified to sense tears beginning to tingle at the back of her eyes.

'It's all right, I'll use a rolling pin or something.'

You don't have one of those either! Della wanted to shriek, but of course Sophie was joking, and Della really needed to gather herself together and get the hell out of Darley Court before she started to cry.

'Okay, sweetheart.' Della forced a big smile and hugged Sophie tightly, then off they went; down the bleak concrete stairs and past more parents and teenagers brandishing enormous bags as they made their way back to Mark's car.

Something was missing, Della realised. Other parents seemed to be emitting a sense of jollity, if only to mask their anxieties and offer each other a little mutual support.

127

She glimpsed a dad in a maroon tracksuit putting an arm around a slim blonde woman and giving her a reassuring squeeze. Other couples were holding hands, and exchanging glances that might have said, *It's okay, I'm here for you.* All around her were couples, couples, couples, doing this thing together.

Della glanced at Mark who, once again, was striding ahead as if eager to send off a parcel before the post office shut. She caught her breath, willing him to slow down and take her hand too, or at least to ask, 'Are you okay, darling? Doesn't this feel weird?' But clearly, he wasn't thinking about her at all. As she watched him from behind, tall and long-legged with his purposeful stride, she couldn't remember ever feeling quite so alone.

Which was why, across the grassy mound between the blocks of student residences, Frank Nicholson made the assumption that the dark-haired woman from the castle gift shop was, like him, a single parent. Clearly, she had just dropped off her child and was trying to breeze through it as he was. Or maybe it wasn't such a big deal to her? Her son or daughter might have been in second or third year, so she'd have done this – the dropping off thing – many times before. It wasn't like that for Frank. It had been a new and deeply unsettling experience, leaving his daughter Becca, who was studying graphic design, in that poky little room – all the more so because Jill, Becca's mother, had announced that she 'couldn't bear it', and that he'd have to do it alone. Frank reckoned that plenty of divorced couples would have managed to see their children off together today. It just seemed decent and right.

He watched Della striding towards the car park and, for a moment, wondered how she'd react if he caught up with her and asked about whoever she'd dropped off. He would also apologise for being unable to place her when she'd come over and said hello in the supermarket. But he'd been distracted on Sunday, his head filled with Eddie's friend's birthday party where his ex-wife, Jill – mother of his two children – was helping out.

When he'd arrived home, and was cooking his salmon, he'd pictured Della standing there with her trolley full of booze – plus, he'd happened to notice, two packets of frozen puff pastry perched on top. Like an idiot, he'd thought about what he could have said: *Having a party?* Well, obviously she was, she didn't strike him as someone who'd be heading home to guzzle half a dozen bottles of wine all by herself.

She seemed to be alone now, though, and he wondered about catching up with her – but what if she had no recollection of him?

Making his way towards his own unreliable Mini, Frank noticed with surprise that she was climbing into the passenger side of a car. Someone must have given her a lift. Maybe she didn't drive. The man in the driving seat must be a friend, Frank decided, who'd done her a favour on this, the most momentous of days. And he'd stayed in the car so she and her son and daughter could do the big goodbye thing without him hovering, getting in the way.

Yes, that was probably it. Frank now wished he had a friend with him, someone just to be here to reassure him that it was normal for Becca barely to speak, and to snatch her bags and suitcases from him with a curt ''Bye then', as if he were a hotel porter. If he was a porter, he thought wryly as he turned the ignition key, he might at least have been given a tip.

129

Chapter Fourteen

Della closed the passenger door and looked at Mark. They sat for a moment, not because they were too choked to speak but, she suspected, because neither of them could think of anything to say. Mark's face was set, expressionless, as he pulled out of the car park and indicated left. Cars were still arriving, the student village thronging with activity and a palpable sense of excitement. 'Well, I thought that went okay,' he ventured finally, as if they were returning from a trip to B&Q.

'Yes, me too.' Della cleared her throat. Having been unable to face breakfast, she should have been ravenous by now. But she wasn't. The hollowness she felt inside had nothing to do with lack of food, despite it being nearly noon. 'I thought she might've wanted us to hang around for a bit,' she added.

'Yes, well, I suppose they all want to get to know each other without us muscling in.' Ah, that was better: a proper opinion. Della took this as her cue to salvage the rest of the day.

'So what d'you fancy doing now?'

'Um . . . I don't know really.' His gaze was fixed on the road ahead. These days, when the two of them were together, Mark always drove. It didn't usually bother Della; she enjoyed being a passenger, being able to relax and take in her surroundings. But now she wanted to be in control, to whisk them off somewhere exciting to take their minds off the fact that their only child simply didn't need them anymore.

A mystery trip, now that would be fun. In their early days she'd instruct Mark to dress warmly and not ask any questions, and off they'd set, with Della at the wheel, crying out, 'I cannot divulge any information!' every time he tried to probe her, until they arrived at the white-sand cove she'd heard about, or an inviting pub nestling in the Yorkshire Dales. Sometimes they'd even stay over, on the spur of the moment, if they liked the look of a cosy hotel or a guesthouse on the seafront, and they'd drink a little too much and make their way, giggling, up to their room. Spontaneity, that's what she missed most from the old days: when time spent together didn't require a schedule, and would merely unfold in a delightful way.

What she *didn't* want to do was go home to Pickering Street with no Sophie.

'Mark,' she ventured, 'you've got the day off. Let's make the most of it.'

'Well, I took the day off to bring Sophie here,' he pointed out.

'Yes, I know, darling, and we've done that now. So let's *do* something, just the two of us. We hardly ever find the time these days.'

He gave her a quick look. 'Like what?'

She glanced out of the passenger window. The sky was blue, the September day sharp and invigorating. 'Oh, I

131

don't know. Shall we spend the day in Leeds? We could see a film, find a nice restaurant . . .'

'I'm not really sure, Dell.' With no further comment Mark drove on, and as the city streets faded into the suburbs, Della felt her own brief flash of enthusiasm ebbing away too. She looked out at smart red-brick semis with bay windows, their front lawns strewn with leaves. 'We could stop off for a pub lunch,' she offered, despite still not being remotely hungry.

'Aw, I'm not really in the mood.' For what? she wondered. For eating, or simply spending time with her? 'I don't mind rustling us up a bit of lunch at home,' he added, as if to placate her.

It's not that I don't want to make lunch, Della fumed silently; *it's that I don't want to have it at our kitchen table.* 'Come on, Mark. Let's turn around and go to a gallery or something.'

He threw her a curious look. 'But we're out of town now.'

'Well, we could turn back.' *We are not robots programmed to return to Heathfield.* She shifted irritably in her seat.

'I'm not sure there's much on.'

No, of course there isn't, she thought bitterly. In a huge, multicultural city like this, there wouldn't be a damn thing to do. She racked her brain for other ideas, but realised she couldn't think of anything else they would enjoy together. 'You don't mind if we just head back, do you?' he asked lightly. *Yes, I do mind. I mind very much.* 'Plenty of stuff to get on with,' he added, and she knew precisely what that meant: tapping away at his laptop, firing off emails about whatever happened to be the current hot topic in Foot World. She glared at him, which he appeared not to notice, and felt hysteria rising inside her.

'Mark, I'm sorry, but this has been a really big deal for me today.'

He gave her a quick look. 'What d'you mean?'

'Seeing Sophie off! For God's sake, don't you feel *anything*?'

He emitted a gasp of irritation, as if she were child who had just announced that she desperately needed a wee just after they'd pulled away from the service station. 'Of course I feel something. I *am* her father.'

'I mean, you're not really showing it.'

'What d'you want me to show exactly?'

Her vision blurred as she stared determinedly ahead. 'Nothing,' she growled.

'Would you be happier if I'd crumbled back there, if I'd begged her to come home with us and hauled her into the car?'

'Don't be ridiculous.' Della's throat was dry, and her eyes were watering alarmingly. *Don't cry now, idiot. You managed to leave Sophie standing there surrounded by bags and boxes without dissolving into tears, so you can hold yourself together now.* 'All I mean,' she added, as levelly as she could manage, 'is that it would be nice to have a sense of . . . togetherness today.'

He shook his head in bewilderment. 'We *are* together, aren't we? I mean, you're here and I'm here, in the car.' Della glowered at him, aware that Mark knew perfectly well that wasn't what she meant. She wasn't referring to physical closeness. A couple could be mere millimetres apart – even naked together, having sex – and not be together at all. She knew this was possible because that's how it had felt, on the rare occasions it had happened

133

these past few months. Della had initiated it, and Mark's response had been rather grudgingly to take part, as if she had dragged him onto the dance floor when he'd have preferred to be left sitting in a corner sipping his drink. And afterwards, she'd felt even lonelier than ever. 'It's just normal,' Freda had reassured her when Della had confided how dismal things had become. 'That's how it is after years together. Imagine how it'd be if you were still all over each other, spending whole days in bed . . .'

'It'd be *lovely!*' Della had exclaimed.

'No, it wouldn't. It'd be exhausting.'

'Exhausting, yes, and I'd weigh about nine stone.' They'd laughed and Della had convinced herself that Freda was right, and that no couple acted that way after nineteen years of marriage.

'Okay then,' Mark said, jolting her back to the present, 'let's do something today. What d'you fancy?'

Della glanced out at neatly trimmed hedges. 'Oh, it doesn't matter. We're nearly home now.' She knew she was being petulant.

'Come on, if you want to do something, let's do it. Where d'you want to go?'

She blinked rapidly as her vision blurred again, willing the tears that were wobbling on her lower eyelids to seep miraculously back into her eyes.

'Where d'you want to go?' he repeated sharply.

She cleared her throat. Speaking now would cause the tears to spill and, anyway, what would they do? Sit morosely opposite each other at a greasy pub table whilst picking at steak and chips? She could picture them now: one of those tragic middle-aged couples you saw out having lunch together, with nothing to say. 'I don't want to go anywhere,' she said quietly.

Mark tutted. 'Dell, I don't want to make a big thing of this. You're obviously upset . . .'

Ah, so the quartz-hearted one had actually noticed. She clicked on the radio and smoothed back her hair, breathing slowly and deeply. 'It's all right,' she added, 'and I'm not upset. I think we should just go home.'

So that's what they did, and as predicted Mark zoomed straight to his laptop as if it were a vital life-support device, while Della went upstairs and retrieved the number she'd saved on her phone for No-strings-Nathan.

'Ah, Della!' he gushed as if she were an old friend. 'Good to hear from you. So, um, did you have any further thoughts?'

'I did,' she replied, 'and I think it's just the kind of place I'm looking for.'

'Oh, that's great!' he exclaimed with a note of surprise. There was a small pause, during which Della wondered if Mark was listening in, and how he'd react if he was. *I don't care*, she thought defiantly. *I needed him today, and he wasn't there. Wherever he was during that awful car journey home, it was miles away from me.*

'So what happens now?' Della prompted Nathan.

'It's all pretty straightforward. There's a two-year minimum lease agreement . . . I should have explained that when I showed you around. Why not pop over to my office and I can go through it all with you?'

'Great. Can I come over now?'

'No time like the present,' he said with a chuckle, just as Mark called out something from downstairs, something Della didn't catch because Nathan was babbling away now, obviously amazed that she had even called back. 'I mean, I was pretty surprised when you said it was a bookshop you were opening but, hey, you never

135

get anywhere in life by dwelling on the negatives, do you?'

'I'm a firm believer in that,' Della said, the gloom of the day lifting as she pictured herself behind that counter in the glow of a lamp, with deep red walls and books – hundreds of books, from floor to ceiling – all around.

'I'm in Casper's Lane,' Nathan added. 'Number sixteen. Green door next to the off licence. Bell doesn't work but the door's open – just give it a firm shove, it tends to stick a bit.'

'See you soon then,' Della said with a smile, heading downstairs and realising that Mark – and his golf clubs – had already gone.

Chapter Fifteen

Nathan's office was a dismal affair up a narrow flight of stairs above Beer World. 'Ah, *here* you are,' he exclaimed, leaping up from his desk with an eager grin. He was wearing the same navy blue shiny suit, and his greasy blond hair was swept back this time, grooved as if styled with a wide-toothed comb. 'I'll pour us a coffee,' he added, scuttling towards a percolator perched by a small sink.

'Thank you,' said Della.

'How d'you take it?'

'White, one sugar, please.' She glanced around. There was a grubby low-slung chair in the corner, which Della suspected folded out into a futon. The magnolia walls were adorned with amateurish laminated A4 adverts for various companies: CosyGlow Electric Radiators, Cuddle-Me Personalised Teddies, and some kind of solution to paint on your furniture to give it 'that authentic weathered driftwood appearance'. She smiled, imagining Mark's face if she suggested they slapped such a product onto the sleek unit he'd had built at great expense to house the six coffee-table books he owned.

'My various business interests,' Nathan said proudly, catching her surveying the room. He handed her a chipped mug of weak coffee.

'So you're not just involved in property letting?'

'God, no. It's the only way to do business these days – to have a *portfolio* career.' He took a seat behind the cluttered desk and motioned for her to sit on the stained padded chair opposite.

'What does that mean?'

'Having fingers in lots of pies. Show me a pie and I'll put my finger in it, ha-ha!' He guffawed, and Della smiled uneasily. 'The property letting thing,' he went on, 'is just a side-line really. My uncle bought up loads of ropy old places in the seventies, got them for pennies . . .' He broke off. 'I mean, the Burley Bridge shop, it's an excellent property but he's getting on, you know, so he has me taking care of the contracts, the legalities, that kind of thing.'

Della nodded and glanced around again. 'So these are all your businesses too? The teddies, I mean, and the weathering furniture stuff?'

'Yep, keeps things ticking along. So, um, a bookshop, eh?' He leaned forward, simulating interest.

'Yes, that's right.' She sipped her muddy coffee – it wasn't a patch on Mark's perfect brew – eager now to get on with business, to sign whatever needed to be signed and get out of this drab little room. 'So, um, what do I need to do?'

'Right. Okay. So here's the lease agreement . . .' He handed her a wad of papers. 'You're welcome to take it away, or you can read through it now.'

'I'll read it now, thank you.' She was aware of him pretending to study something crucial on his laptop while she read. It was eerily simple: monthly rent to be paid in advance; insurance, repairs and business rates to be dealt with by the tenant. She re-read it to check for no sneaky clauses, no hidden pitfalls to trip her up. 'So I'm taking the shop on for two years?'

'Two years minimum,' he replied. 'Like I said, if you need time to think it over . . .'

'No, I don't need time, thanks. It all seems fine to me.'

'Great. So, rent is payable, um, now, really, and from then on at the start of the month . . .'

'I'll put through the first payment later today.' She had enough in her account to pay the first couple of months – *just*.

'Okay,' said Nathan, beaming at her. 'Well, congratulations! It all seems very, er, exciting, Della.'

'Yes, it really does.' He passed her a Cuddle-Me pen with a plastic teddy on the end, and she signed her name, thrilled and also alarmed at the prospect of potentially selling Kitty's legacy. With a flourish, Nathan signed as a witness, then delved into a desk drawer and handed her a set of keys.

'So that's all there is, is it?'

'Yep, all done. The business part anyway!'

She laughed involuntarily. 'What other part is there?'

'Well, you know.' He flushed. 'You can always call or drop by – any time you like – to, er, let me know how things are going . . .'

'I'm sure I'll be fine, thank you,' she said, unable to keep the smile off her face as she slipped the lease and keys into her bag.

'Well, maybe I'll drop by the shop sometime. See what you've done to the old place.'

'Please do,' Della said, her stomach fluttering with

excitement as she got up and made her way down the narrow stairs, stepping out into the alley and wondering now what she'd done, and how Mark would react when she told him. Naturally, there'd be some muttering and sulking and a suggestion that she had lost her mind. Yet she was certain that he'd come round eventually, and understand that she *needed* to do this, not simply to purge their hallway of cookbooks but to embark on a thrilling adventure all of her own, just as Sophie had.

She needed to catch him at the right moment, butter him up with a glass of wine. She stepped into Beer World, a morose little shop with much of the beer and wine sitting in boxes on the floor. A rather tired-looking woman with lank burgundy hair looked up from her crossword book on the counter. 'Can I help you?'

Della glanced at the meagre selection of bottles on the shelf behind her. 'Erm, do you have any champagne?'

The woman looked bemused. 'No, we've got prosecco. It's not chilled, though.'

'Oh, that's fine. I'll have a bottle please.' Della paused. 'Actually, no, better make that two.'

When Della had gone, Nathan Sanderson sat in the high-backed leather swivel chair he had bought in the hope that it would lend him an air of importance, and looked at the coffee cup sitting on his desk. There was an imprint of lipstick on it, bright red against the cream and blue livery of CosyGlow Electric Radiators. It was a particularly unappealing mug, he thought and, worse still, cracked. What had he been thinking, giving her coffee in that when the Cuddle-Me Teddies one, with its garland of bears around the rim, was far more attractive? But maybe she wasn't the teddy sort either. Come to think of it now, he was sure she wasn't, and he was still squirming about that stupid remark he'd made when he showed her around the shop – about assuming she was embarking on a fluffy little bookshop-florist's-cupcake bakery kind of enterprise. How patronising it must have sounded. He wasn't used to being around attractive women, that was the problem. He hadn't been in a relationship since . . . well, it felt like about 1997 but of course it was a bit more recent than that.

Ruthie-Jane, his last proper girlfriend, had loved teddies more than anything else in the world. That's where it had come from, this notion of fluffy businesses for ladies, and indeed his own foray into Cuddle-Me Bears; Ruthie-Jane's sole ambition had been to open a teddy hospital for the care and convalescence of injured bears. Their bed had been strewn with such a vast menagerie of soft toys that sometimes he'd felt as if she only grudgingly made room for him. He would wake in the night to find himself curled up in the foetal position perilously close to the edge, whilst Ruthie-Jane slept soundly with an outsized fluffy gorilla clamped to her chest.

Nathan got up to refill his coffee – at least he had a proper percolator, none of that instant rubbish – and pondered about Della's home situation, and what had made her sign the lease on a clapped-out shop, in a dead-end village, seemingly without so much as a flicker of doubt. He admired her courage, but assumed there was a wealthy husband in the background – he'd registered the wedding ring – who was willing to fund the venture, or at least pick up the pieces if it went wrong, as Nathan regrettably expected it to. A bookshop! Maybe he just didn't get it. Why had he said that, when he'd shown her the place, about not having read anything since the *Beano*

Annual? What a dough-brain he'd sounded. And maybe there were enough people who enjoyed cookbooks to make it tick over. He really couldn't tell.

Nathan used to pride himself on his business acumen but now he'd had to admit that his 'portfolio career' was faltering a little. The bottom had fallen out of the personalised teddy bear market, and he wasn't sensing much enthusiasm for CosyGlow radiators either, despite his mate Mikey assuring him that it was a sure-fire route to success. No costly plumbing bills! Instant heat, whenever you needed it! Nathan shivered and switched on the fan heater that he tried not to use too much as it cost a fortune to run, then opened up the futon and tugged out the duvet which lay bunched up beneath it. He would get himself a proper flat, when he could afford it. But right now, this grim little office was home.

Although it was only 3.15 p.m. Nathan had nothing much to do that afternoon. The phone was unlikely to ring – he suspected Uncle Tony only asked him to help out with leasing contracts because he felt sorry for him – and he couldn't face hammering out a chirpy press release about how to weather a perfectly good coffee table with Shabby Chic Glaze. Shabby Chic was over. Nathan feared that he was too. With a clear imagine of Della's beautiful face shimmering in his mind – that creamy skin, those chocolatey eyes and sensuous red lips – he pulled the thin duvet around him and closed his eyes. As the sun slid lower a sort of peacefulness settled over him and he decided that, at forty-seven years old, it wasn't too late for him to cultivate an interest in cookbooks. And he might not be in too much of a hurry to wash that coffee cup.

Chapter Sixteen

Della virtually skipped to the high street with her Beer World carrier bag. She had a shop, an actual *shop*. It was hers to do whatever she wanted with. No trying – and failing – to negotiate over paint colours. Now all she had to do was scrub it out, fit shelves, paint the place, install some decent lighting and fill it with the books . . . which now, actually, felt like rather a lot. But she was a capable woman, adept at juggling tasks. It was how she had managed to cook for her mother and rather ungrateful siblings from the age of ten; how she'd managed being pretty much in charge of anything Sophie-related – home-work, dentist's appointments, the organising of her myriad of activities – plus the funerals of both of her parents. She strode home in the weak afternoon sunshine, formulating how she'd tell Mark when he returned from golf.

Ravenous now, Della fixed herself a late lunch from odds and ends in the fridge and called Freda. 'You've done it?' she exclaimed. 'Oh, that's fantastic! What did Mark say?'

'He doesn't know yet. He's at golf.

'Really? But it's not Saturday,' Freda chuckled.

'No, but he had the day off, we took Sophie to college . . .'

'How did that go?'

'Fine, sort of. Weird, you know. How was Evie?'

Freda laughed. 'Oh, fine. Couldn't wait to get rid of me, virtually marched me off the premises . . .' Della perched on the kitchen table, grateful to have Freda as a friend. 'I'd thought she might like us to spend the day together,' she added. 'Get to know the delights of Hull with me.'

'Not a chance,' Della empathised.

'So, your first day as empty nesters . . . and Mark's at golf?'

'That's right,' Della replied dryly.

'Hmm. And you went and signed the lease on a shop?'

Della glanced down at the remains of the cheese, cole-slaw and crackers she'd assembled for herself. 'I know how it sounds – that I only did it because I was annoyed.'

'Of course you didn't,' Freda exclaimed. 'I'm only teasing.'

'But, you know, there's probably some truth in that. I just thought, oh, stuff it then, which perhaps isn't the best way to go about setting up a business.'

'It's probably as good as any. So, when can I see it?'

'How about now,' Della suggested, 'if you're not busy?'

'Great, I'll come over right away.'

Half an hour later they were driving along the back road – the prettier route, past the golf course – on a golden September afternoon. 'I've figured out the golf thing,' Della remarked.

'What d'you mean, you've figured it out? You want to start playing?'

'God, no. No, what I mean is . . . why it's so appealing to Mark.'

'Dell, it's a bloke thing. It's what they do when they hang out together. There has to be a *thing*.'

Della smiled briefly. 'Well, maybe that's true, but mainly I think . . . it's his way of getting away from me.'

'Why would he want to do that?'

'No idea,' Della said with a dry laugh. 'But when you think about it, it's ideal. Takes hours and hours, and there's not the slightest chance I'd ever want to try it, to join in, be a member of the ladies' section . . .'

Freda chuckled. 'You could, you know. You could give it a go.'

'Not me. I'm not the sporting type.'

'But you *could* be,' her friend teased. 'You could buy all the kit in secret and turn up, surprise him.'

'He'd have a heart attack,' snorted Della as the road dipped down towards the village. 'Anyway, never mind that. Here we are. You don't think the shop, this thing of mine, is just a reaction to Sophie leaving, do you?'

Freda frowned. 'No, I don't actually, but what would it matter if it was? It doesn't matter why you're doing it. The fact is, you want to, you're passionate about it and you're going to make it work.'

'Well, if it doesn't, it's not as if I'm tied to the lease for a hundred years.'

'Don't think that way,' Freda chastised her. 'You're not going to fail.'

Della held this thought in her mind as Burley Bridge came into view, looking pretty in the late-afternoon sun. She parked outside the shop, and kept checking Freda's reaction as she climbed out and surveyed the rather faded exterior.

'Oh, I love this place,' she exclaimed as Della let them in. 'It's perfect!'

145

'Well, it does need a heck of a lot of work,' Della remarked.

'Yes, of course it does, but that's what makes it so great. You can make it whatever you want it to be.'

Della looked at the friend who had been by her side throughout all the years of mothering, when the tiniest thing – the baby running a temperature, or throwing up her lunch during the music and movement class – seemed like a disaster of epic proportions. Freda's gung-ho attitude shrank worries down to a manageable size, and made anything seem possible. 'So when are you going to start?' she asked.

'This weekend, I think. I don't see why not.'

'Need some help?'

'That would be fantastic, thank you.'

Freda grinned, looking as excited as Della felt. 'And you're definitely going to give up your job?'

'Yep, it's time I left anyway. I'm on a month's notice. If I get the chance, I'll tell them tomorrow.' She glanced around the empty shop again. What had seemed rather dreary in the company of Nathan now felt full of possibilities. 'Oh, you're right, it *is* perfect,' she added. 'It's just the right size for plenty of stock, but small enough to feel intimate and cosy.'

'It really is. So, what are you going to call it?'

'You know,' Della said, laughing, 'I haven't the faintest idea.'

They stood outside, looking up at the old, weather-worn sign: Sew 'n' Sew's, whose proprietors were now – Della liked to think – enjoying a gin and tonic in their rosemary-filled garden in the Majorcan hills. 'The Delicious Bookshop?' she ventured.

'Hmmm . . . The *Scrumptious* Bookshop?'

146

'Yes, that's better.' Della paused, her attention caught momentarily by Len who was locking up the garage over the road. He waved, and she waved back. His shop was terribly basic: no filter coffee, no sandwiches or array of glossy magazines, just a few cartons of oil and screen-wash and some out-of-date Mars Bars, everything rung up on an antiquated till.

'The Burley Bookshop?' Freda suggested.

'Um, maybe . . .' Della glanced down the lane where she just could make out the outline of her mother's house. She didn't plan to pop into Rosemary Cottage today; it was a day for looking forward, not back. But the cottage – or, rather, Kitty – was the sole reason this was happening. Without her love of bustling around in her kitchen when Della was a little girl – and possibly the Recipe Sharing Society – there would be no bookshop at all. 'I know,' she murmured. 'I'm going to keep it simple. I'll call it The Bookshop on Rosemary Lane.'

A grin spread across Freda's face. 'That's the one.'

'Yes, it is,' Della said, and she knew it was right: it was simple. It just fitted. Oh, she'd probably have to add another line, to make it clear that this wasn't any old bookshop: *An Emporium of Books for Cooks,* or something along those lines. She could fix that later. They climbed into her car, and Della's heart quickened with excitement as the miles flew by, because Mark would be home now, and she could talk him round into believing in the shop – and believing in *her.* Not even he could play golf in the dusk.

However, when she unlocked the front door, having dropped Freda at home, there was no sign of her husband. 'Mark?' she called out from the hallway. No reply. Just to make sure, Della checked their bedroom, in case he'd

147

sloped off for an early-evening nap. When she'd once had the audacity to suggest that golf wasn't that strenuous – how could it be when it amounted to strolling slowly, whist chatting to friends? – he'd protested that it was exhausting, actually, all that marching up and down hills and vigorous swinging of clubs, not to mention the fierce concentration required. 'It's the only sport that offers a full cardiovascular and mental workout,' he'd said tersely.

Hmm, maybe that's why he always seemed to retreat into himself after a game – because his *brain* was tired?

No Mark in the bedroom. She tried his mobile, which was either out of charge or switched off. Pacing the living room now, Della willed him to come home. He *would* be pleased, when she told him. He'd admire her courage and vision and perhaps even apologise for being so grumpy and negative about it. She cleared her throat anxiously and turned on the TV, flicking between a documentary about compulsive hoarders, and a gritty thriller in which a severed human ear had been found sitting on the bonnet of a car.

She turned off the TV and tried Sophie's mobile. 'Hey, Mum,' her daughter squawked amidst pounding music and people shouting. What kind of place was this noisy on a Tuesday night at 7.20 p.m.?

'Hi, darling. Just wanted to make sure you're all settled into your room.'

'Yeah, yeah, it's great.'

'Did you unpack your desk lamp?'

'Yeah . . .'

'Did you make up your bed? I wish you'd let me stay and help you.'

'Mum, I am capable of putting a duvet cover on!'

Della felt as if she had been delivered a small punch to

148

the ribs. Clearly, now wasn't the right moment to ask if her daughter had managed to hang up her mirror without severing an electrical cable. 'I know you are, love. I was only wondering—'

'Sorry, signal's breaking up . . .' No, it wasn't. This was what Sophie said when she didn't want to talk – the signal never broke up whenever she called to ask for a lift home from a party – but then, of course, she didn't want to be fussed over by her mother on her first night out with her new friends.

The call ended abruptly. Della glared at her phone, as if the device itself were to blame for Sophie's brusqueness and the fact that Mark's game seemed to have somehow drifted well into the evening. She tried him again, to no avail, and reassured herself that he'd be having a perfectly pleasant time in the clubhouse with Peter and 'the guys', *on the very day that their only child had left home*. Well, fine! She stomped through to the hallway and crouched down by her mother's books, hoping that browsing through them might soothe her.

Whereas Kitty's collection had seemed vast when she and Freda had unpacked it, Della wondered now if there were enough books here to stock an entire shop. Without seeing them there, neatly arranged and categorised on the shelves – shelves which did not, as yet, exist – it was impossible to tell. And what if there was a stampede when she opened, with all the best ones snatched, leaving gaping holes of nothingness? This thought cheered her immensely. She must source some more, even if only to have some stock in reserve. Della fetched her laptop, curled up on the stone-coloured sofa and Googled 'cookbooks for sale'.

This led her to mostly bookstores and antiquarian shops. She tried eBay, where numerous individual books were up for auction – but where were the people like Tamsin, her sister-in-law, who believed cookbooks to be unhygienic and passé, and were selling off entire collections for next to nothing?

She moved over to Gumtree, momentarily distracted by alluring lamps, sixties and seventies style with elegant opaque glass shades, and then rugs and throws – deep reds, burnt oranges and turquoises, just asking to be scattered about in the shop . . . Hauling herself back to the matter in hand, she entered 'cookbooks' into Gumtree's search box, selecting a ten-mile radius. And up it popped:

Cookbooks for free. Three large boxes full. Many used but all good condition. Must collect.

Her heart racing now, she tried the mobile number – it went straight to voicemail, must be the day for it – and, rather than leaving a message, she tapped out an email: *Really interested in your cookbooks, could I come over and look at them, please? Thanks, Della.* She paused, added her mobile number, and pressed send.

At a loss for what to do now, she closed her laptop and delved into the cupboard under the stairs, starting to pull out the boxes she'd flattened after unpacking Kitty's collection. She found brown tape in Mark's Drawer of Important Things – he excelled at that, putting stuff where you could find it – and made the boxes up, before starting to fill them with books.

He'd be pleased by this, she decided, wondering not for the first time why it seemed so important to get on the good side of the man she was married to. Into the box they went: *Suet Cookery For Girls* – she could imagine what Sophie would make of that – and an intimidating six-volume *Encyclopaedia of Culinary Matters,* which was so dense with text, she wondered if her mother had ever read a word of it.

With one box filled, Della pulled her phone from her pocket to check that she hadn't missed a call from Mark, just to see if she was okay, and to ask whether she felt sad about Sophie, and to ruddy well tell her where he was. Oh, he was probably holed up in the Cragham club-house for the evening now, maybe for some impromptu celebration. While she wanted him here, urgently – she was desperate now to show him the contract for the shop – she refused to be the kind of woman who demanded that her husband came home.

She fetched a large glass of wine and continued to pack up the books, still discovering volumes she barely remembered from childhood. Now, this one wasn't a cookbook, nestling beneath *101 Freeze-Ahead Meals.* It was a slim ring-bound notebook: Kitty's address book, Della remembered it well, with its Monet water lilies cover. Kitty had never made the leap to storing contacts on a mobile phone (although she had finally given in and acquired one, in a small act of defiance she had refused ever to switch it on). Perhaps the other members of the Recipe Sharing Society were listed in here, and Della could contact them to find out what it was all about? Picking up *Sugarcraft Delights* from its pile, she extracted the neatly folded memo:

Barbara Jackson
Kitty Cartwright
Monica Jones
Celia Fassett
Moira Wallbank
Dorothy Nixon

Della leafed through the address book, skimming her mother's handwriting. She had favoured cheap biros – pages were dotted with inky blobs and smears – and there were many scribblings out: either a single line or, in several cases, furious scrawlings, as if the very presence of a seemingly benign name – *Maisie Waters* – had enraged her to the point at which it must be almost obliterated. What had Maisie Waters done? Della wondered. She hadn't died – at least, not at the time of the scribbling. Della noticed that her mother had written DECEASED beside the names of friends lost.

None of the names from the memo appeared to feature in Kitty's address book. Della turned the piece of paper over and studied the neatly written note. *Such a delightful evening, Kitty. Yours affectionately, R.*

Probably just a passing acquaintance, she decided, and no big deal at all. Just as it was no big deal that Mark seemed to have gone AWOL, and that by 10.20 p.m., with her mother's collection neatly boxed up, she still hadn't received so much as a text.

A golfing injury? she pondered half an hour later, as she sank into a deep, sudsy bath. What could possibly go wrong during golf? It was hardly rugby. But perhaps he'd been whacked in the head with a club when one of his friends had taken a swing? Or he'd tumbled into a bunker and sprained an ankle, or been savaged by a rabid mole . . . she wallowed in the bath until it started to cool, then pulled on her cosiest pyjamas and tried to banish all visions of Mark lying bleeding and broken, surrounded by concerned-looking men in diamond-patterned sweaters, as she settled into bed to read.

Della must have dozed off with the book in her hand because when she woke, at 2.09 a.m., her bedside lamp was on and the book had tumbled to the floor. She looked at the space in the bed where her husband should have been and, registering it vacant, wandered blearily downstairs. And there he was, splayed out on the pale grey sofa, fully clothed as far as she could make out, with the Norman-style hairy grey blanket – a range which hadn't sold at the gift shop, and were given away to staff – strewn over his lower half. He was snoring throatily, and his brown brogues had been kicked off haphazardly on the living-room floor.

So this was what it had come to. On the day their daughter had left home Mark had chosen to spend the night on their wildly expensive but not particularly comfortable sofa. She supposed she could wake him and try to coax him upstairs but, in a surge of annoyance, decided to leave him be and talk about it in the morning. His switched-off phone, the shop lease, his decision to spend the night downstairs . . . There was a lot to discuss, and Della wasn't sure she felt good about any of it.

Chapter Seventeen

However, in the morning there was no discussion at all, because Della woke up to find herself still alone, and by the time she came downstairs at 7.35 a.m. Mark had gone. The blanket had been put away and the sofa bore no sign of being slept on. For a moment Della wondered whether she had conjured up Mark's presence in a dream and never been downstairs in the night after all.

She straightened the cushions unnecessarily and spotted a note, with a freesia-scented candle plonked on it, on the coffee table:

Della, I'm so sorry, M.

Sorry for what? What on earth had he done? His handwriting didn't look right either: it was sort of wobbly, as if written with his left hand. She retrieved her phone from the kitchen and called him, taken aback when he answered immediately. 'Hi, Dell.' His voice had acquired an unfamiliar hoarseness.

'Mark, where *are* you? What on earth's going on?'

'I'm at work, had to come in early, tons to sort out.' A throaty tickle morphed into a substantial cough, which took a few moments to die away.

'Why did you sleep downstairs last night?'

'Oh, God,' he groaned. 'Look, I'm sorry, I didn't plan for it to happen. The night sort of ran away with itself. I feel completely stupid . . .'

'What did you do?' she exclaimed, grateful, for the first time, that Sophie was safely installed in her student halls.

Mark sighed heavily. 'It was just meant to be a game, okay? Only it was Peter's birthday, and his wife's away for work, so we had a few in the clubhouse, which turned into a few more . . .'

'So Peter was off work yesterday too?'

'Yeah, yeah. Well, he's freelance, remember?' Della probably should have remembered, but Mark's new coterie had been described to her in such a hurry that she had been unable to store the crucial details about any of them.

'So you got drunk,' she said levelly, relieved now that that was all it was. Unusual, though – and on a Tuesday night too. As a moderate drinker, Mark tended to avoid hangovers and be irritatingly smug on the rare mornings when she had over-indulged with Freda and her other friends.

'Yep, and it was late when I got in – after one. Didn't want to disturb you . . .'

Well, that was considerate, she supposed. 'You didn't drive home in that state, did you?'

'No, one of the guys dropped me off, my car's still up at the course.'

'So you're at work now.'

'Yes, needed to come in and get some papers together for this seminar.'

'Seminar? What seminar?' Della frowned.

'The one I'm speaking at, remember?'

'Mark, I'm sorry, you might have told me but I don't have any recollection . . .'

'The one in Weston-super-Mare? The three-day thing, the really important one I've told you all about, which starts – Christ! – three hours from now.'

'Oh. Erm, you probably did mention that . . .' Although she tried to dredge up some recollection of a conversation they'd had, nothing came. Head too full of Sophie leaving home, and her dreams for the bookshop, which she couldn't talk about now – not on the phone, and *especially* not with Mark being hungover and on the verge of going away. Face to face, when they had time to discuss things properly, was the only way to do it.

'. . . pretty big deal,' he went on, sounding huffy now. 'Been preparing for weeks, two hundred delegates, you *do* remember me saying . . .'

'Yes, yes, of course I do,' Della fibbed. 'Erm, so how long are you away for again?'

'Just two nights, some Godawful faceless hotel. Look, I'm sorry I didn't say 'bye this morning. I was in a bit of a rush and I still don't feel too good, to be honest.'

'Poor darling,' she said flatly.

'Nauseous,' he went on. 'But I'll be okay. I'll get a taxi to Cragham, pick up my car and I'll be right as rain by then.'

Della pushed her mussed-up hair out of her eyes. 'Are you sure you'll be okay to drive?'

'Of course,' he said firmly, which she fully accepted: Mark was not a risk-taker, where driving was concerned.

'Take care then, darling,' she said, feeling a little warmer towards him now. Getting accidentally drunk after a game? Well, at least he'd had fun, let his hair down, and done

156

something spontaneous for a change. 'Hope the seminar goes well,' she added. 'I'm sure you'll be brilliant.'

'Huh, well, let's hope so. See you Friday then, Dell.' With that, he finished the call.

So that was when she'd tell him: when he returned, bolstered by three days of talks, which she was sure he'd handle magnificently. He would come home feeling revived and important, and she'd cook them a sumptuous meal to celebrate his success. It was just the two of them now, with Mark's career in fine shape and her own life about to take a thrilling new turn. They had much to celebrate, she decided, and in the meantime she would make use of every minute while Mark was impressing the pants off his podiatrist colleagues in some faceless hotel in Weston-super-Mare.

Della arrived early at work, and fetched a coffee from the tearoom before giving the gift shop a quick, unnecessary tidy. Even though she'd wanted to confide in Angie first, her friend was away on a short break to Crete and it felt important to Della to hand in her resignation as soon as possible. In fact she felt that, if she didn't do it today, she might actually explode.

All morning she manned the shop with Rosie, a new staff member who was fresh out of school and only planning to work there until she headed off on her travels to India in January. Della knew Julia, the manager, was due in today, but so far there had been no sign of her. She found herself refolding the commemorative tea towels with extreme precision and almost willed customers to ruck them up again, to give her something to do.

At lunchtime, while she tucked into a smoked salmon bagel on a bench in the courtyard, she used her phone to browse house-clearance companies. It wasn't that she relished the thought of emptying Kitty's house and putting it up for sale. However, if she was about to throw herself into transforming Sew 'n' Sew's into a beautiful shop, then she might as well snap into action on the Rosemary Cottage front too. She just wished the clearance companies didn't have such insensitive names. Who would honestly entrust the emptying of their childhood home to an outfit called AnyJunk or Dump-It? They hardly suggested a thoughtful approach. But then, to anyone else's eyes – even Roxanne's and Jeff's, given the lack of interest they had shown in dealing with things since Kitty's death – the contents of Rosemary Cottage had amounted to a load of junk.

Della bit into her slice of carrot cake and checked the clearance companies' websites again. Admittedly, some of them mentioned recycling, which seemed a little less callous than mere 'disposal'. As she finished off her cake she wondered what she could rescue, recycle or whatever, before she let the clearance guys loose.

Her mother's numerous bookshelves, perhaps? Could they be carefully taken out of Rosemary Cottage without wrecking the walls, and somehow remodelled to fit out the shop? It was worth looking into and it seemed fitting to re-use the shelves from the cookbooks' original home.

As a school party snaked its way into the castle's recon-structed kitchens, Della mulled over who to call for advice. Would Liam be willing to help? He was only starting out in joinery – but then, she needed someone who would listen to what she wanted, and not talk down to her in a silly-middle-aged-woman-with-your-fluffy-shop kind of way. And young men were, she felt certain, less likely to think like that.

She called Sophie. 'Mum, hi,' she said sleepily.

'Hi, darling. I didn't just wake you, did I?' *It's nearly one o'clock,* was what Della meant.

'Uhhh . . . yeah, sort of. Had a bit of a night . . .'

Della smirked. It seemed as if everyone had had a bit of a night apart from her. 'So you had fun, then? Was it a pub you were in?'

'Yes, Mum.' *Where else would it be?* her tone seemed to say.

'Okay, well, there was just something I wanted to ask you . . .' Della paused. 'It's about the bookshop. I looked at that shop in Burley Bridge – remember I told you I was interested?'

'Yeah, of course I remember . . .'

'Well, it seemed perfect so I've signed the lease.'

'What?' Sophie exclaimed. 'You mean you've bought it?'

'No, just renting. But it's mine, sort of.'

'That's brilliant, Mum! So what does Dad think?'

Della scrunched up her cake wrapper. 'Er, he's away at a conference until Friday so I haven't been able to tell him yet.'

'He'll be fine. He'll come round to it.'

Della could sense her daughter's attention wavering already. 'Anyway,' she added hastily, 'I need someone – a joiner – to take the bookshelves out of Gran's house and fit them into the bookshop, if it's possible to do that . . .'

'Uh-huh,' Sophie grunted, all interest evaporated now.

'So, um, d'you think Liam might be up for doing it?'

She sensed a shrug. 'Dunno. Maybe. You could ask him, I s'pose.'

'You think he'd be, you know . . . capable of doing a job like that?'

Sophie sighed impatiently. 'Mum, I have no idea about his joinery skills . . .'

'Okay, okay . . . and it wouldn't be, you know, awkward for you in any way?'

'Why would it be awkward?'

'I just . . . thought it might be difficult for him. And for you.'

She could sense Sophie's bafflement radiating through the airwaves. ''Course not. Why would it be? I'll text you his number, okay?'

Della thanked her, holding back the urge to ask what she was planning to do that afternoon, and the following days before college started properly next week. They finished the call and, moments later, Liam's number popped up. Della's lunch break was over and, apart from an elderly couple who were taking enormous care to select Heathfield Castle pin badges for their seemingly numerous grand-children, the shop was deathly quiet. Della busied herself by rearranging the entire children's books section and pinning up an embroidered cot bumper, as if Norman babies had had such thing.

'Wow, this is looking *great*.' Julia, Della's boss, had swept in and was glancing around in admiration.

'Thanks,' Della said. 'Erm, d'you have a minute, please? There's something I need to talk to you about.'

Julia grimaced. 'Can it possibly wait? Lunch with the Friends, you know how it is . . .' Ah, yes, the Friends of Heathfield Castle, whose donations went a long way to funding the special events they ran throughout the year: the jousting tournaments and ghost tours and murder mystery nights.

'Maybe later, then,' Della started, and Julia rushed out saying *yes, yes, of course, got to dash* . . . And for the

160

rest of the day, Della tried to keep herself as busy as possible when a mere dozen or so customers wandered in, all the while willing Julia to remember that she needed to talk to her. It was just gone 5 p.m. and Della was pulling on her jacket when she finally reappeared.

Julia adjusted her gold-rimmed spectacles. 'So sorry, you know how these things go on and on, and there's always someone who insists on holding court about how things should be done around here . . .'

'Yes, I can imagine. Erm, d'you mind if we grab a quick coffee?'

'Of course, I'm in no hurry.' They adjourned to the tearoom, which had closed to visitors now, and took a seat by the window. 'So,' Julia prompted her, 'everything okay, I hope?'

'Yes, everything's great, but I, um . . .' Della sensed her cheeks blazing, as if she were embarrassed about handing in her notice for a job that had only been meant to tide her over until something more challenging came along. 'I, um . . . I've done this thing.' Julie peered at her. Come on, Della chided herself, you can do better than that. It's a thrilling new adventure – not a *thing*. 'I've taken on the lease of a shop,' she explained, still incredulous to hear herself say it out loud. 'I'm opening a bookshop. A cook-book shop, actually. You see, I inherited Mum's huge collection of books, and I thought . . . well, I'm convinced . . . it could really catch on for foodie types, people who love old things, old food – I mean, not *old* food, I'm talking about that whole nostalgic cooking thing . . .' She babbled on, apologetically, until she realised that Julia wasn't looking incredulous, as if Della had taken leave of her senses, but delighted for her.

'Oh, I think that's a brilliant idea. I'm so happy for you.'

161

She was up on her feet now, hugging Della, even though Julia wasn't usually the hugging kind. She sat down and squeezed Della's arm. 'I'll be sorry to lose you, of course. You're such an asset here, always doing way more than what's expected of you. Please promise to drop in and visit.'

'Of course I will.'

'But this . . . well, it's such a bold move, so exciting.' Julia's crystal bracelet tinkled as she clasped her hands together. 'I wish I had the nerve to do something like that. You know, open my own business, a little gift shop perhaps, I think I'd have a good eye for that kind of thing . . .'

Della smiled. 'Well, maybe you should.'

'Oh, I don't know. I'm nearly sixty, too old to make that leap.'

'No one's ever too old for change,' Della protested.

Julia shook her head. 'Maybe not, but Gordon would think I'd gone completely mad . . . not that I think you're mad, of course!'

'I probably am,' Della laughed, flooded with relief.

'We all are, a little bit, and that's no bad thing. So . . . when are you hoping to finish here?'

'Well,' Della ventured, 'I know I'm on a month's notice but I wondered if there's any way I could, you know . . . it's just, I'm keen to get the shop fitted out.'

'Oh, we won't tie you to that,' Julia cut in quickly. 'With something like this it's important to get started, keep the momentum going. I wouldn't dream of letting a few nylon princess outfits get in your way.'

'Thank you,' Della said, smiling. 'I really appreciate that.'

'And you must have plenty of holiday entitlement left? Even with your mum – everything you were going through – you've hardly been off at all this year.'

Tell me about it, Della thought: all those days saved for the family holiday she had hoped for, before Sophie spread her wings. Sophie and Evie had gone Inter-railing around Europe together instead. Della could have pressed for Mark to come away with her, but as Kitty's health had declined, she couldn't shake off the fear that her mother would die the very moment they stepped onto a plane.

'Right then,' Julie said briskly, 'so how about you make Friday your last day?'

'This Friday?' Della exclaimed. 'You mean, two days away?'

Her boss smiled. 'Yes. Not that I'm trying to get rid of you or anything.'

'No, no, that would be . . . fantastic,' she said, feeling a little choked.

'Great. Then I'll see you tomorrow.' Julia smiled indulgently like a proud aunt. 'What an exciting new chapter for you, Della. I hope that doesn't sound patronising. It's just, you know . . . I've always felt you were rather wasted around here.'

Back home, and with no Mark around, Della snapped into action. It was rare for him to stay away on a conference and, she had to admit, she quite enjoyed the space. Although he didn't exactly expect dinner on the table – he prided himself on being a modern man, who ironed his own shirts and certainly did his share around the house – Mark's working day often stretched into the evening and Della felt it was only fair that she should cook. However, right now she was experiencing a heady wave of pleasure that she could spend this evening – and tomorrow night, too – doing exactly as she pleased.

She rustled up a speedy stir fry and forked it straight

into her mouth from the pan. For dessert she feasted on the bar of dark chocolate with almonds she had stashed away for such an occasion. She checked her phone; no missed calls from Mark, but then, they weren't the types to keep in constant touch. Next, she called Liam. ''Lo?' he said gruffly.

'Liam, it's Della.' Small pause. 'Sophie's mum,' she added, as if to distinguish herself from all the other Dellas he might know. 'Look, erm, I wondered, if you had the time, whether you'd mind checking out a job I need doing? It's a shop-fitting thing. I've taken on this place, just a small shop in Burley Bridge. It's simple shelving, really.' She cleared her throat, wondering if the line had gone dead. 'Liam?'

'Er, yeah?'

'Would you mind having a look, seeing what you think?'

'Er . . . yeah.' He didn't sound enthralled, but Della pressed on anyway.

'How about tomorrow evening? I finish work at five so I could pick you up straight afterwards and drive us down there.'

'Um . . . okay.'

Della frowned. 'Are you sure? I don't want you to feel pressurised just because it's, well . . . me.' The mother of your girlfriend who seems to have dropped you, is what she meant.

'No, no, it's fine, I was just wondering, uh . . .'

'Why don't you figure out how long you think it'll take, and then we can talk about a price? And, of course, if it turns out to be more fiddly than you thought, then I'm happy to pay you whatever you think's fair.'

'Yeah, okay,' he cut in quickly. 'I just wondered, um . . . have you heard from Sophie?'

She paused. 'Only briefly. I think she was pretty busy settling in.'

'Hmm,' he mumbled. Have *you* heard from her? Della wanted to ask, but could guess what the answer would be.

'She's only been gone a couple of days,' she added unnecessarily. 'So, er, shall I pick you up tomorrow?'

'Yeah, great,' he said, sounding for all the world like a boy who had very little else going on in his life.

To shake off any niggling doubts that she should have called him at all, Della dug out a blank sketchbook and a box of coloured pencils from Sophie's room and settled at the kitchen table to draw. Who would her customers be? Both women and men, so it shouldn't be overly girlie: more cosy, comfortable, luxurious, but faded around the edges. Della knew she was no artist – Roxanne, who sketched the collections at fashion shows, had been the creative one of the Cartwright children – and her own attempt at sketching out the bookshop looked rather childlike. But no matter, no one was going to see it but her, so she carried on drawing the counter and shelves, with a suggestion of gauzy curtains at the window, then she added glowing lamps and twinkling fairy lights along the tops of the shelves.

Colours came next: a deep, rich red for the walls, rugs in azure blue and burnt orange. She smiled, realising she was going a bit bonkers with her colour scheme, but enjoying herself hugely. She added a deep purple sofa and an armchair in emerald green, as absorbed as a child with a colouring book. By now she had forgotten about Mark, lapping up the attention in Weston-super-Mare. Instead, she pictured bookshelves thoughtfully arranged into sections: meat cookery, vegetarian, family meals, plus all

165

the regional cuisines – French, Italian, Spanish, Indian, Moroccan . . . She paused. Where would the quirky books go? *Sensational Soufflés, The Lard Handbook, The Fine Art of Margarine Cookery?* There'd be a delightfully retro section, she decided. Fondues would go there, plus anything featuring seventies housewives merrily setting their desserts alight. Flambé-ing – there would be lots of that. She could even host special events in the evenings with dishes sloshed with alcohol and set alight . . . or would that be too hazardous? Burning booze, highly flammable books . . . perhaps better to host a wine-tasting evening instead.

Oh yes, there'd be a section for books about drinks too, and others for baking, cake decorating, children's party food, not to mention seasonal cookery (Christmas, summer picnics, barbecues). There would be a 'Cooking In Difficult Circumstances' shelf, books to save your bacon if you had only one pan, or not even a kitchen . . . Della's heart quickened as she drew elegant signs on the shelves to denote the sections. The shop would be organised – for customers who were searching for that elusive book on Tuscan cookery, or vegetarian Thai – whilst still feeling pleasingly ramshackle, filled with hidden delights.

So what if people just wanted to enjoy a pleasant hour or two of browsing? Surely that was the whole point of bookshops. It no longer seemed to matter that Della's 'business model' was flawed – as Mark had put it – because she didn't have one. Della wasn't a business-model type. She would be led by her instincts, by what made *her* feel happy – and although her drawing looked a little crazy now, she would damn well paint her shop in butterfly brights if the mood took her. It would be anti-Cabbage White.

She stopped drawing. She wanted to call or at least text

Sophie to share her plans, but sensed that she should give her a little space. 'I'm sure she's fine,' Mark said when he called, just after eight.

'Yes, I know she is. I just keep thinking about her and how quickly it's all gone. Her childhood, I mean. I can't believe it's over, Mark.'

'I feel that too,' he said gently.

'I mean, it seems like one minute it was all about routine, routine, routine. Her bathtime, storytime, bedtime . . .'

Mark chuckled and it struck her that perhaps this might be good for them, a couple of nights apart. A twinge of missing him took her by surprise. 'It was always a some-thing-time,' he added, and she knew he was smiling.

'Yes.' Della smiled too. 'Anyway, how did your day go?'

'Oh, really good!' he said brightly.

'Bet you impressed the pants off them.'

'Don't know about that,' he said with a bashful laugh, 'but I hope I came across as at least *slightly* knowing what I was on about.'

'Come on,' she chided him, 'all those talks to deliver in front of hundreds of people. I'd be petrified! And you didn't even practise, as far as I know. If it was me, I'd have tied you to the sofa and forced you to be my audi-ence while I went over and over my speech.'

Another chuckle. 'Well, maybe it's not your forte.'

'No, it's definitely not.' She was more of a background person, she reflected; sitting there behind the counter, surrounded by books would suit her just fine. She yearned to tell him now about signing the lease, and her plan to drive Liam over to Burley Bridge tomorrow to see what could be done. But she knew it wouldn't be right. Mark sounded jovial and happy, all traces of grumpiness gone. She didn't want to dampen the mood.

'Well, I'd better go,' he said. 'It's been a full-on day and a few guys are waiting for me in the bar . . .'

'Poor you,' she chuckled, 'trapped in that faceless hotel.'

'Yeah. Guess I'm quite lucky really.'

Lucky in what way? she wondered. To have a talented daughter, and a wife whom he still loved? Or did he mean having a comfy hotel room and a glass of wine waiting for him at the bar? 'Have fun then,' she said, hoping he would still be as perky and chipper when she made her big announcement on Friday night.

Chapter Eighteen

Thursday saw the castle flooded with school parties. They snaked their way through the courtyard and photographed each other pulling grotesque faces by the gargoyles. Clearly delighted to be released from their classrooms for a few hours – even if they didn't nurture a deep love of history – they gathered on the lawn to tuck into their packed lunches, seeming not to mind that it was too chilly really for picnicking.

The till in the gift shop rang virtually non-stop. The pocket-money display – usually resplendent with rubbers, keyrings and kaleidoscopes – was vastly depleted, and Della was replenishing it when Angie strolled in. 'Hey,' said Della, 'I thought you weren't due back till next week.'

'Got home last night and Julia texted me,' she said with a grin. 'So just thought I'd drop by . . .'

'You've heard then! Look, I wanted to tell you first.'

'Oh, it's so exciting, Dell.' Angie pulled her in for a fierce hug. 'I take a few days off and look what happens!'

Della laughed. 'Well, it all kind of ran away with itself. I viewed the shop and signed the lease, and you know what it's like when you just want to get on with something . . .' She paused. 'Julia was here yesterday and it just seemed like the right moment to tell her.'

Angie beamed. 'I'm so happy for you – and jealous. Is it okay to say that? Your own shop! Not flogging this old tat.' She lowered her voice as a gaggle of schoolchildren wandered in. 'I mean, doing things your way,' she added. 'So, how does it feel?'

Della shrugged. 'Honestly? Exciting, terrifying . . .'

'What on earth is there to be terrified about?'

'Well, I haven't even told Mark yet. He knows I *want* to do it, of course. But he's away on a conference so, er, he isn't quite up speed with the details.'

'He'll be fine, won't he?'

'Of course! Anyway, he'll have to be now.'

'That's my girl. So when's your last day?'

'Tomorrow.'

Angie laughed. 'No hanging about then. Good for you, Dell. I'm going to miss you so much, though.'

'But I'll be popping in . . .'

''Course you will. The lure of the synthetic tabards will be just too much to resist.' They laughed, and Della left the shop at the end of the day feeling lighter than she could ever remember. It was as if the years – and all the responsibilities that came along with them – were floating away, leaving her feeling like her old self, the younger Della who had had the courage to walk out of her job due to inappropriate groping and would never look back.

She walked home briskly and let herself in. In the kitchen, the red light was blinking on the answerphone. Probably a cold call; none of her friends called the landline, and neither did Sophie or Mark.

She played the message. 'Hello, Mark?' It was Val, his

170

mother. There followed a pause, plus some nervy throat-clearing, as if she were mustering up the courage to talk to the terrifying machine. 'I, er . . . well, your dad and I . . . I mean, it's not a *big* thing, it's not *terribly* important . . .' Cough-cough. 'We're just a bit worried, dear.' There was a clunk as the message ended abruptly.

Della's stomach tightened as she called back. 'Oh, it's nothing, Della,' Val said quickly. 'I'm sorry, we didn't realise Mark was away.'

'Val, has something happened? You sounded quite upset on the message.'

'Erm, when will he be home?'

For goodness' sake, why couldn't Val just talk to *her*? Even though she might not always act like one, Della was a bona fide adult too, just like Val's darling son. 'Not until tomorrow night. Please tell me what's wrong.'

She detected Terry's rumbling tones in the background. 'It's just – it was our anniversary yesterday,' Val muttered apologetically.

'Not so much as a card,' Terry barked.

'Oh, I'm so sorry!' Della blustered. 'I, er, we've had a lot going on. Sophie started college on Tuesday and he's had this conference to prepare for . . .' Della realised she was babbling, and cursed herself for having taken on the responsibility for remembering the occasion in the first place. Her in laws' anniversary was a big deal to them, Della knew that, although she could never quite understand why; she and Mark barely acknowledged their own.

'Oh, I know you're both busy,' Val said, as if Sophie's departure hadn't even been mentioned.

'Well, you must come round again soon,' Della murmured.

'That would be lovely. So, where *is* Mark?'

'In Weston-super-Mare.'

'Ah, at the seaside. That's nice.' He hasn't exactly taken a bucket and spade, Della thought wryly. 'He's done ever so well, hasn't he?' Val added as if he were eleven years old.

'He really has,' Della replied with exaggerated warmth.

'Worked so hard. So talented. So dedicated!'

'Yes, he really is amazing,' Della remarked, feeling as if someone was rubbing tin foil against her fillings now.

Val emitted a little sigh. 'Well, don't bother him with this when he comes home.'

I shall, Della mused, enjoying the thought. *I shall roundly punish him the minute he walks in through the door.* 'No, but we should have sent you a card, Val.'

'Oh, you know us, we're simple people, we don't like a fuss.' It needled her every time, this 'we're simple people' line, as if she and Mark – but Della especially – were living some rarefied life that his parents couldn't begin to comprehend. 'I work in a shop!' she wanted to remind them every time it came up. 'My dad was an accountant, my mum was a dressmaker, and I went to a normal comprehensive school.' It made her feel immensely uncomfortable, as if she should apologise for buying so much as a new toaster.

Phone call over, she slugged down a coffee without even taking off her jacket, grabbed her car keys and stepped back out into the cool evening. Laden with shopping, her next-door neighbour was letting herself into her house. 'Can I help you in with those, Norma?' asked Della.

'No, I'm fine, thanks. But I was going to ask, would Mark like to borrow my blower sometime?'

Della frowned. 'Your *blower*?'

'You know, the little machine I use to tidy up the leaves

172

in the garden. It's just, I have noticed there are quite a few on your lawn . . .'

'Are there?' Della genuinely hadn't noticed.

'. . . and they seem to be blowing over to mine.'

Della suppressed a smirk. 'Mark's away until tomorrow evening, but I'll mention it to him as soon as he gets back.'

'I'd appreciate that,' Norma said with a tight smile, and Della climbed into her car and drove away, reflecting that she now had two urgent conversational topics for when he came home: the forgetting of Val and Terry's anniversary, and the fact that they were bringing the neighbourhood down by leaving the odd sycamore leaf flapping about. Perhaps she'd pour him a drink first to soften the blow. She chuckled to herself as she drove through town, and out past the castle to the small 1970s estate where Liam lived with his parents.

She pulled up behind his father's blue van with *Dennis Bracken Bespoke Joinery Service* painted on the sides. It occurred to her that Dennis might be a little put out that she hadn't gone to him instead – but then, it was up to her who she hired. Since signing the lease, Della had become aware of a surge of bravery rising within her – not the urge to abseil down buildings or indeed stretch herself physically in any way, but to follow her own instincts on the way things should be done. She was, she realised with a flutter of pride, feeling in charge of her own life, for the first time in years.

Liam shambled out of the neat semi-detached house before she had even opened her car door. 'All right?' he asked, seeming not entirely comfortable as he climbed into the passenger seat.

'I'm good, thanks, Liam, are you?'

'Yeah, yeah, great,' he replied unconvincingly.

173

She pulled away and an awkward silence settled around them. 'So, been busy lately?' she enquired.

'Yeah, this and that.'

'Still working with your dad?'

'Uh, kinda.'

She nodded, deciding to leave it for now. Forcing the poor boy to communicate all the way to Burley Bridge seemed rather unfair, and besides, their common link – Sophie – hung awkwardly in the air. Worryingly, too, Liam didn't seem to have anything with him (she had expected a notebook at least, on which he would sketch out his plans for the shop). He was hardly giving the impression that he was on the way to assess a potential job.

'Aren't you cold?' she asked.

'Nah, I'm fine.' She glanced at him and frowned. He was dressed entirely unsuitably for the chilly afternoon in a rumpled white T-shirt and ripped jeans.

'Are you sure? D'you want to go back and get a jumper?'

'No, I'm okay, thanks.'

'Or a jacket?'

'Honestly, I'm fine!' *Oh, for goodness' sake, stop this,* Della chided herself. *You're not his mother.* Still, as the winding lanes took them up into the hills, she wondered what it was about teenagers that made them so allergic to wearing proper warm clothing.

They pulled up just down the street from the shop. Liam remained silent, his tall, lanky frame slightly hunched, fringe flopping forward over his dark eyes, as she fiddled to unlock the door. They stepped inside and she clicked on the light.

'Well,' she said, 'this is it.'

Liam nodded. While she didn't expect him to enthuse wildly about the possibilities, she willed him to say *some-*

thing. 'I know it's just a shell at the moment,' she added, running a finger through the velvety dust on the counter.

'Yeah.' He thrust his hands into his jeans pockets.

'So what I'm thinking,' she continued, wondering why the poor boy wasn't shivering – it seemed even chillier in the shop than outside – 'is that I'd like as many shelves as possible. I mean, I'd like it *all* to be shelved, if you can manage that?' Liam looked rather baffled as he glanced around. 'You know, *bookshelves*,' she continued, 'like the ones my mum had, I mean *has* – what I mean is, they're still in the cottage.'

He chewed at his lip. She wished he'd say something, even if it meant politely explaining that this wasn't his kind of thing. Della started pacing now, trying to visualise the fitted-out shop with customers browsing, sipping their coffee, nibbling on a slices of Freda's heavenly lemon drizzle cake. 'I was wondering,' she went on, 'how tall the shelves could be? I mean, they can be fairly high, don't you think? I'll have stools so shorter people can reach the top shelves . . .' She was babbling now, so as not to let silence creep in. 'So!' she said with a forced grin. 'That's it. Not much to see, is there? But I think that's a good thing. Sometimes it's nice, isn't it, to start afresh, a sort of blank canvas thing? Sophie always says that, when she starts a new painting . . .' Agh, now she had uttered the S-word. She looked at Liam, whose expression was unreadable. 'I mean the excitement of something new, all those possibilities . . .' And now she was making it even worse. Despite the chill in the air Della was starting to sweat, her underarms prickling against the cream cotton shirt she had worn for work. 'So!' she said again. 'Shall we go to Mum's cottage so you can see what you can salvage from there?'

'Yeah, sure,' Liam replied.

Della's enthusiasm waned even further as they marched, heads bent against the rain, towards Rosemary Cottage together. She could see as they approached that the garden needed serious attention, perhaps even the slash-it-all-down approach favoured by Mark. The small windows looked dark and bleak and the gable end bore a rusty brown stain, suggesting guttering trouble. *Salvage,* Della thought. That was the word for what she needed to do now: salvage this toe-curling situation. Poor, dejected, *rejected* Liam. The last thing he needed was a middle-aged woman trying to force him to be part of her hare-brained scheme.

Chapter Nineteen

If Sophie's bedroom was beginning to show signs of being uninhabited, Rosemary Cottage now felt as if nothing of note had happened here for several years. It was hard to believe that, just over a week ago, the chintzy living room had been filled with the family and villagers for Kitty's funeral tea. Apart from a couple of brief conversations, there had been no significant contact since from Jeff or Roxanne. Della had checked their Facebook pages, wondering if they had been insanely busy, and had spotted a photo of Tamsin wearing Kitty's jet necklace at a dinner party. Not that Della minded, really. She pictured Sophie wearing her gran's simple gold chain on the day she left home, and her heart filled with longing, not for jewellery but for her daughter who, naturally – healthily, really – wouldn't be giving her parents, or mundane Heathfield, a second's thought.

'Okay, so most of the shelves are in here,' Della told Liam as she flicked on the kitchen light.

He nodded. 'Yeah, I remember.'

'And there are lots more, here and here.' She guided

him around the ground floor and then Jeff's bedroom, which still had the floor-to-ceiling bookshelves he'd used for his library, making her smile at the recollection. 'So, what d'you think?' Della asked. *And why aren't you measuring things and writing stuff down?*

'I think . . . yeah.' He nodded. Please give me more than that, she willed him.

'D'you think you could use all of these to fit out the shop?'

Liam's face set as they looked at each other on the landing. 'Well, the thing is, it's just . . .' His voice tailed off.

'I know it's quite a fiddly job, Liam. Please say if you'd rather not do it.'

He nodded. 'Actually, it's not that fiddly. I mean, it's moving shelves and making the walls good again, bit of plastering and fitting, I could do that.' She nodded eagerly. 'They're all different shapes and sizes, bit wonky, bit worn . . .'

'I like wonky and worn,' she cut in.

'Yeah, and maybe that's good if you want your shop to look, I dunno . . .' He shrugged. 'A bit . . .'

'Wonky?' she said with a smile.

'Yeah.' He dropped his gaze to the floor.

'So . . . could you do this for me? I mean, could you give me a quote? I'd like to get started soon.' Her heart-rate quickened with excitement.

'Er, I'm sorry. I'm not sure . . .'

She looked at him, Sophie's first boyfriend whom she had clearly left behind now, like the band posters and red duffel coat she had grown out of, and who could blame her? A new start, a fresh canvas, all that. Della took in Liam's deflated expression. 'I think this is too weird for you, isn't it?' she said gently.

'What d'you mean?' He looked startled.

'I don't know . . . working for me, I suppose, when you and Sophie . . .' She stopped, wondering if she had overstepped the mark. It was so easy to accidentally patronise teenagers; demanding to know precisely *why* they needed a mirror or an alarm clock, and fretting about whether they were capable of boiling up pasta without scalding themselves.

'No, it's not that,' he muttered. 'It's just . . . er . . . look, this is a bit embarrassing. I'm just . . . not really working at the moment.'

'Oh, why's that?' She caught herself. 'You don't have to tell me, of course. And it's fine, Liam, honestly. I can call John Hartley, the guy who renovated our place . . .'

'You see, I left Dad's van unlocked,' he cut in, cheeks reddening now. 'We were doing this thing—'

'A job?' She frowned.

'Yeah, a job, this church renovation, and he left me to finish things up. It was easy,' Liam added. 'I mean, I knew I could do it. All I had to do was finish some beading, bit of sanding and tidying up. And it looked really good.' He flushed even deeper, as if ashamed of boasting. 'I was so pleased, y'know, so I packed up the tools in the van, and then I went back inside . . . you know St Cuthbert's by the market?'

'Yes, of course.'

Liam laughed awkwardly. Della had never heard him utter so many words in one go and studied him with rapt attention. 'It was the first time I'd been in a church when there wasn't a wedding, full of people and *different*, y'know?' A small smile played on his lips. 'Yeah, so I sat on a pew and looked at it – at the stage me and Dad had built, or whatever you call it, where the priest stands when church is on . . .'

179

Della suppressed a smile. *When church is on,* as if it were the movies with popcorn. 'So . . . what happened?' she asked cautiously, wondering how she'd react if this gangly boy in ripped jeans confided that he'd experienced some sort of religious epiphany.

Liam raked back his fringe and started to amble downstairs. 'Don't know how long I was in there. Lost all track of time really. I'd never realised what the windows were like from the inside. I mean, I hadn't even noticed when we'd been working in there 'cause me and Dad were so busy. But it was dead nice, you know, just to sit and think about stuff, about me and Sophie, about her going away . . .'

Della blinked. Ridiculously, she wanted to hug him right there in Kitty's gloomy hallway, but knew it would terrify the poor boy. 'It really is a beautiful church,' she murmured.

Liam looked at her, his eyes dark and solemn. 'Then I went back outside and realised I'd left the van doors open, and everything – I mean, all Dad's tools, the lot – was gone.'

'You mean they'd been stolen?' she gasped.

He nodded. 'Yeah.'

'Oh, Liam.' She reached out to touch his arm. 'And your dad was furious, I'm guessing.'

''Course he was. He went mental . . . hit me. He's never done that before.'

'That's terrible!' she exclaimed.

He shrugged. 'Yeah, well, it meant he couldn't work and, y'know, earn money.'

'I know, but . . .' She shook her head, trying to think of something – *anything* – to say to make this poor boy feel better. She barely knew him, that was the problem. He had always seemed a little awkward around Mark –

who, granted, had made virtually no effort to get to know the boy – and even with Della herself, despite her attempts to make him feel at home with her offers of dinner and rather ineffectual conversational openers. Liam wasn't blessed with the knack of charming girlfriends' mothers, as some boys his age were.

'Look, I think I'll just take us home,' she murmured.

'Yeah, I'm really sorry.'

'You don't need to be. It was an awful thing that happened. I mean, I don't suppose there's any chance of tracking the stuff down, putting up ads somewhere – you know, in case someone tries to sell it on?' She locked up Rosemary Cottage and they made their way back to her car.

'Dad says there's no point.'

'Were his tools insured?'

'Nah, he says insurance companies are rip-offs.'

She sighed as they climbed into her car and pulled away from Burley Bridge's deserted high street. 'So . . . you mean that's why you can't do this job? Because you don't have the tools?'

'Yep,' he replied curtly. *You could have said at the start,* she decided, but then, for a nineteen year old perhaps that would have been far too obvious an option.

'Well, Mark has tools,' she ventured as the road took them high into the hills. 'Power saws, drills, the lot. Not that they've ever been used. They're just the kind of thing that men – especially dads – think they should own to show that they're in the club.'

'What club?' Liam frowned.

'The proper grown-up man club.' Della glanced at Liam, hoping to see a small smile of understanding, but there was none. Of course, he was some way off from even being considered for that club himself; that is, if he ever wanted to join. 'Anyway,' she went on, 'you could have a look at what he has, I'm sure he won't mind, we could do that now if you like?' She paused then asked, 'Would you consider doing it then?'

'Oh, yeah,' Liam exclaimed, and the fug of gloom seemed to lift as they followed the winding lane that led them back down to Heathfield. So that was the problem – the stolen tools – and not the fact that Liam was traumatised over the departure of his girlfriend.

Back at her house, she lifted Mark's power tools and pristine toolbox from the cupboard under the stairs. Liam started to assess them, placing them one by one in front of him on the hall floor, as if laying out the equipment required to perform an operation. 'Yeah, everything's here.'

'Great.' She smiled hopefully. 'So, you'll have a think about the job and get back to me?'

He nodded. 'No problem.' Then, shunning her offer of a lift home, he shambled out into the cool September evening. She watched him wandering past Norma's house.

'Liam?' she called after him.

He turned and gave her a quizzical look. 'Yeah?'

She stepped out towards him. 'Why didn't you just tell me that at the start? About your dad's tools, I mean?'

He exhaled through his nose, his dark hair flopping around his brown eyes. 'I didn't want to sound like an idiot.'

She smiled. 'You're not an idiot. It was a mistake, that's all, and everyone makes those.' He nodded, and Della felt a surge of maternal concern as he sloped off down the road. It was all she could do not to remind him that he really should be wearing a jumper on a night like this.

*

Hope you had a good day, love, Della texted. *Can't wait to see you tomorrow. Really missing you.* It was true, sort of. It was only just gone nine, and she felt the rest of the evening stretching emptily ahead of her. Gathering a selection of cookbooks, she curled up on the sofa, deciding to greet Mark's homecoming with a special dinner, a proper grown-up evening with wine and delicious things to eat. She could sense her love of cooking beginning to stir again in her and wished she could fast-forward to tomorrow night.

That's what they needed, she decided. Mark hadn't wanted a day out in Leeds, not because he was allergic to her company, but because they had simply lost the habit of having fun together. Eschewing the more bizarre books – now wasn't the time to dabble with *The Margarine Bible,* or *Stuffed Peppers And Other Stories* – she leafed through *A Guide to Tuscan Cookery,* sensing herself transported to the beautiful farmhouse of their honeymoon.

Before the trip, Della had never been to Tuscany – she wasn't even entirely sure she could have pointed it out on a map – and Mark hadn't either. But his career was on the up, and honeymooning there seemed exotic and thrilling. Plus, Della knew from Kitty's culinary library that the Italians knew a thing or two about food.

When they arrived, as overly excited newly-weds, they couldn't believe their luck. The photos in the brochure really hadn't done the place justice. Perched on a hilltop, the terracotta-tiled cottage looked out over great swathes of vineyard and olive groves with dense forests beyond. The charmingly overgrown garden was filled with sprawling bushes of rosemary and thyme, and the warm air carried their scents as she and Mark tucked into the lamb she had barbecued on the terrace. There'd been a deliciously soft, almost sweet loaf – Della had discovered that the local bread was made without salt – plus a hand-painted bowl of sautéed potatoes, which managed to be both crispy and melting. While Mark had swum a few lengths of their private pool, Della had dressed a simple green salad with sharp lemon juice and locally produced olive oil. She hadn't minded preparing the meal while he did his own thing, because food was *her* thing: that had been clear from the off. In fact, she could think of few things more pleasurable than preparing dinner in that thirteenth-century cottage, having just married the man she loved. She couldn't remember their dessert now. Had they even had one, or had they been too eager to sneak back into their little bedroom with its rough, white-painted stone walls, to think about pudding?

She had been about two dress sizes slimmer then, Della reflected, now browsing the recipes and deciding on a simple roasted pork dish with sides of green beans and tiny roasted potatoes. Nothing too complicated. The last thing she wanted was to be darting to and from the kitchen with a sweaty face and things burning. Now definitely wasn't the time for flambé-ing. She wanted to be serene, as she had been nineteen years ago, her waist defined, her face unlined and honey-tanned.

Out of the three Cartwright siblings Della was the only one who turned golden-brown in the sun. It had always been a source of consternation to Roxanne that even Della's *legs* tanned, at the first whiff of sunshine. She'd had what Mark had described as 'superb legs' – Della had laughed at his choice of word – her toenails painted deep red, her hair worn a little longer than it was now. On their honeymoon she had eaten whatever she fancied – even the soup, *ribollita*, had bread in it – and not gained an ounce. Carb soup! Della smiled at the concept, imagining Roxanne and her colleges recoiling in horror. Della and Mark had made love every night and during long, lazy mornings, and they had made a baby too.

Maybe, she thought, placing the book beside her, she could bring something of that mood back when her husband came home to her tomorrow. She would woo him with food and flickering candles and she wouldn't even mention Norma's leaf-blower machine, or his parents' forgotten anniversary, until the next day. She might not even mention the bookshop, if the moment didn't seem quite right. Contentious matters could wait. One thing she could say about Mark was that he always appreciated being cooked for, especially when she went the extra mile. In fact, she suspected that was partly why he had fallen in love with her in the first place. He had been intrigued by her when he'd first met her in the florist's, and after they had started dating she had seduced him with food.

As she pulled on her pyjamas, Della allowed herself the small hope that tomorrow evening might evoke a little of that long-ago honeymoon. Good food and wine, with Sophie away now . . . just the two of them again. She checked her phone – no reply to her text. He was in the bar, probably. Or maybe the signal was iffy in Weston-super-Mare. She replaced the cookbooks in the hall, the water-lily cover of Kitty's address book catching her eye once more.

She flipped through it and a name caught her eye, one that she had missed the first time she'd looked through it: Monica Jones, a member of the Recipe Sharing Society. Della read the entire address book again. No other names from the memo were noted down. She checked her watch:

9.37 p.m. Not too late, she decided, to call a stranger. She tapped out the number on the landline.

'Hello?' An elderly man's voice, deep and rumbling.

'Oh, er, hello, I'm sorry to bother you. Is there a Monica there, please?'

Small pause. 'Who is this?'

'My name's Della – Della Sturgess, although it used to be Della Cartwright. I'm Kitty Cartwright's daughter and . . .' She broke off, wondering whether or not to mention that Kitty had died – but, of course, Monica might have passed away too. In fact, it was highly likely that someone totally unrelated had taken over the landline number. 'I'm really sorry to bother you,' Della repeated. 'It's just, I'm, er, trying to track down some old friends of Mum's and there's a Monica Jones, with this number, listed in her address book . . .'

The man cleared his throat, and his voice had softened when he spoke again, in a murmur this time. 'Erm, I'm very sorry I can't be of any help, but there's no Monica here.'

Chapter Twenty

Next morning, instead of grabbing her usual lunch to eat in the grounds, Della had been instructed by Julia to be at the tearoom by noon. There were cheers as she walked in. Everyone was assembled there – the café ladies, tour guides and ticket-office girls, even the gardeners and maintenance guys, plus a few bewildered-looking visitors – and it struck Della that perhaps she was taking an almighty risk in leaving. As Kitty had once said to a twenty-one-year-old Della: *Are you out of your mind, walking out on a perfectly good job?*

'Thank you,' she said now, cheeks blazing as Julia handed her a glass of prosecco. Angie, who had come in on the last day of her holiday, pulled Della in for a hug.

'So this is it, then,' she said. 'Your new adventure!'

'I guess so. I can't actually believe it's happening.'

'Are you having an opening party?' asked Morag, the senior guide.

Della smiled. 'I plan to, yes, and you'll all be invited, of course.' She paused. 'So, everyone knows what I'm planning to do?'

187

'Of course we do,' remarked David, one of the gardeners, as Julia caught Della's eye and mouthed: *'Sorry.'*

'Not supposed to be secret, is it?' she asked aloud.

'No, no, of course not.' Della laughed, dismissing the little snag of worry that it seemed as if her husband would be the last person to know. Even Liam knew about it. He was probably drawing up plans for the shelving right now. But it would be okay, Della told herself, when she'd presented Mark with a sumptuous Tuscan feast.

'So,' Angie prompted her, 'the opening party . . . ?'

'Oh, we'll do the food if you like,' remarked Meg, the tearoom manager. 'We could do canapés or maybe tapas, whatever you fancy really.'

'That would be great,' Della enthused, draining her glass and aware of bemused glances from customers sitting by the windows. Her spirits soared. The Bookshop on Rosemary Lane now felt as if it was real and not just a pipe dream. While Rosie manned the shop, Della was quizzed and congratulated, and it struck her then that she *was* lucky, and that she hadn't felt that way for a very long time. Cassie, one of the waitresses, appeared before her with a goodbye cake: a rich chocolate affair, with *Good Luck Della!* beautifully piped within the castle crest. She cut into it and shared it amongst her colleagues. 'This is from all of us,' Julia announced, handing Della a silver envelope. She opened it, and grinned at the voucher for Iris, the boutique just off the high street that she had only ever peered into lustfully. 'This is too much!' she exclaimed. 'But thank you, I really wasn't expecting anything.'

'Well,' Angie teased her, 'if you need some help spending it . . .' Della laughed, and as everyone started to drift back to work, she and Angie and Julia made their way back to the gift shop together.

'Are you and Mark out celebrating tonight?' Angie asked.

'No, he's been away for work for a couple of days so I'd thought I'd pull out all the stops, cook a special dinner at home.' In fact, she was already itching to head to the shops, to gather the ingredients she needed for a perfect evening.

'That sounds lovely,' Julia remarked. 'Look, why don't you head off now?'

'But it's only just gone three,' Della pointed out.

'Come on, you want to get home and prepare, don't you?'

'Well, yes.' Della felt quite overwhelmed as she pulled on her jacket. ''Bye, then . . .'

'Do pop by,' Julia added.

'Of course I will.'

'With our invitations,' Angie added.

'As soon as I've set the date,' Della promised, casting a last glance at the plastic shields and chain mail. She'd miss this place, the cosy routine of it, but now, as she gave Julia and Angie a quick, final hug, she felt the sense of lightness return. Yes, something had ended today, but Della had far more pressing matters on her mind to feel any regret.

Pork loin, green beans, rosemary . . . Della loaded her provisions into her basket and wondered now if a starter might be fun. She would just do bruschetta, she decided, something to nibble over drinks. She grabbed sweet vine-ripened tomatoes, plus pungent fresh basil and thyme, pausing then before the fresh raspberries: perfectly plump Scottish specimens. She inhaled their scent – it seeped out, even through their clear plastic container – thinking dessert would be nice . . .

She remembered a tart they'd had in a hillside cafe in Tuscany, with sweet, crisp pastry that dissolved on the tongue, filled with a light vanilla cream and topped with ripe berries. A recipe from *A Guide to Tuscan Cookery* floated into her mind – *crostata di frutta*, a simple fruit tart – and she grabbed a pot of double cream. Was it over the top, to welcome Mark with a three-course homecoming dinner? It wasn't as if he had spent six months trekking through China. He'd only been talking about bunions in Weston-super-Mare. In fact, as she selected a couple of bottles of decent chianti she wondered now if she was trying to cajole him into being happy about her decisions to sign the lease and leave her job, all without prior consultation.

Della strode briskly along the high street, clutching her carrier bags and formulating a mental plan of everything she needed to do to make the evening perfect. Oven on, bake pastry shell, prep everything else . . . They would eat outside, she decided, as it promised to be a warm, mellow autumn evening. She would make the garden look lovely, and dress up a little, blow-drying her hair, *Impassioned* in place . . . She stopped at the arched entrance to the cobbled lane which lead to a small selection of upmarket shops. There was a silversmith's, an art gallery and Iris, the boutique. Della had often wondered how the shop managed to survive, being tucked away like that, but maybe it was its very exclusivity that drew customers in.

Filled with excitement now, she decided to spend her voucher right away. Iris's door opened with the sound of a bell ringing as Della stepped in.

A waif-like girl with a curtain of fine, fair hair glanced up from the counter. 'Hi,' she said.

'Hi,' Della replied with a smile as she began to peruse the rails.

'Can I help you with anything?'

'Just browsing, thanks,' she replied, aware that she should be at home, sawing up the baguette for bruschetta rather than flicking through the elegant dresses. They were lovely, the clothes, but tended towards the muted: they said grown-up, refined. And right now, with her clinking carrier bag – and feeling pleasantly dreamy from the lunchtime prosecco – Della wasn't sure if she was capable of fitting either of those descriptions, even in the right clothes.

She moved on to the crushed velvet scarves and soft tan leather handbags, then found herself browsing the small selection of lingerie: exquisite bras and knickers in ice blue or black lace, plus satin camisoles and a slip . . . now *that* was a thing of beauty, dangling all on its own by its fine ribbon straps.

Della placed her carrier bags at her feet and held up the slip by its hanger. Could she ever wear such a thing? No reason why not, she decided rashly, but when would there ever be a suitable occasion?

'It's lovely, isn't it?' The girl smiled, exposing perfect white teeth. 'It's really special. Silk georgette, and the trim's French lace.'

'Oh, I love it. It's so glamorous.'

'It's a real siren slip,' the girl added. Della smiled – a *siren slip* – and examined the price tag. It was hugely expensive for underwear – for anything-wear, come to that – and even if she could squeeze herself into it, she couldn't justify the expense. She dipped a hand into her shoulder bag and felt a corner of the envelope containing her voucher. 'Would you like to try it on?' the girl prompted

191

her. 'It's the only one we have left, I'm afraid, but it looks about your size and it's incredibly flattering on.'

'Okay, I'll try it.' Leaving her bags dumped on the floor, Della disappeared into the tiny curtained cubicle, deciding that she could choose to interpret the girl's comment to mean, 'It'll make you look thinner and God knows you need that.' But no – as soon as she had stripped off and pulled on the scrap of slippery silk, she understood what she'd meant.

In fact, it didn't just flatter; it was nothing short of a miracle. The fine ribbon straps enhanced her shoulders, and the subtly supportive cups gave her just enough lift to create a sumptuous cleavage. The slip finished mid-thigh, and seemed to have an almost uncanny leg-lengthening effect. *Superb legs,* Mark had told her, what felt like a hundred years ago. *God, Dell, you should show them off more often.* Would he think that now? On top of all that, it hung so beautifully that her wobbly tummy and bottom seemed to have melted away, shrouded as they were in the shimmering silk.

She stared at her full-length reflection, allowing herself a few moments to take in the sight of herself, Della Sturgess, fifty year-old former shop assistant and currently unemployed – no, not unemployed, *in between projects* – who right now looked every inch the very best version of herself that she could possibly be.

Her heart raced as she hurried home, thrilled by the act of having paid more for the slip than she had for anything else she had worn in her whole life. But what the hell? It really was the most delicious thing, and she couldn't wait to see the expression on Mark's face when he saw it.

Chapter Twenty-One

Della realised the house was already showing signs of deterioration since Mark's departure. Although it was not quite a hovel, the bed was unmade, with clothes, cookbooks and her make-up bag strewn across it, spilling its contents. She gathered everything up and smoothed down the duvet, then decided a fresh bed was necessary: their best linen, a White Company set from Mark's parents last Christmas (a lovely gift, although Val's comment – 'We know you only like the best!' – had made Della squirm a little).

Downstairs, she gathered up the mugs and plates she'd left dotted around from her husband-free grazing, and noticed the winking red light on the answerphone. She pressed play. *Hello, Della?* The voice was female, elderly but not tentative like Val's. It was rather forceful, Della thought. Forceful and posh. *I think you might have called last night. I'm sorry, I was here, it was just rather . . . difficult. So I kept your number . . .* A small pause. *I'm Monica Jones. I knew your mother. Kitty and I were sort of . . . er . . . anyway, you can call me again, if you like.* There was a sharp clunk as the message ended abruptly.

Della stared at the answerphone, as if Monica Jones's face might shimmer before it, like a hologram. How strange, the man she'd spoken to saying there was no Monica there. Still, Della would call back later. Tonight wasn't about Kitty or her mysterious group of friends. It was about Della and Mark and she was determined to make everything perfect.

In the living room, her pencils and sketches of her fantasy shop littered the sofa. Della collected everything together and found a shoebox in which to hide it all until the time was right to reveal her grand plan. It reminded her, disconcertingly, of madly tidying up her first shared flat before her mother had dropped in for a visit. She checked the time – 4.20 p.m. – and fired off a text to Mark. *What time home you think? Dx*.

In the meantime, she bashed together garlic and rosemary, then stabbed incisions into the pork loin into which she stuffed the garlicky paste, leaving it to stand for a little while. She rolled out ready-made pastry and eased it carefully into a fluted glass dish, pricking it with a fork 'So it doesn't rear up at you!' as Mrs Gillespie, her home economics teacher, had always instructed. The tart was put to bake blind in the top oven.

Glugging oil into a pot, Della heated it and dropped in the pork, browning it before placing it in the lower oven to roast. This was the kind of cooking she enjoyed most. So simple, yet just what was wanted sometimes. She had made this discovery – that food didn't have to be tricky or stressful or involve plunging things into bubbling oil – when she'd made that roast chicken at ten years old, and carved it herself, ignoring Jeff as he hectored her on the right way to use a knife. Even her mother, still parked in the living room with her glass of gin, had said it was 'not too bad at all, for a first attempt'.

On to the vegetables now: spuds to be peeled, beans topped and tailed, tomatoes and herbs to be slowly softened in olive oil and set aside for the bruschetta. There'd be a chance later to whip up a sumptuous filling of cream and fruit for the tart.

And talking of sumptuous . . . the siren slip was waiting upstairs, still in its tissue wrapping and rope-handled paper bag. With a flurry of excitement, Della lifted her tart shell from the oven and, while it cooled, scampered upstairs to the bathroom where she pulled off her smart cream shirt and straight black skirt, those work clothes she would probably never wear again because running a bookshop meant being herself and wearing whatever she wanted.

She pictured herself chatting to customers, finding out what they were planning to cook that night. She imagined the swapping of ideas – perhaps even a Recipe Sharing Society of her own – then pulled on her toweling robe. Back downstairs she stepped out into the garden to see what transformation she could bring about there.

Della glanced at the hacked-down borders. She wondered if next year Mark might be persuaded to leave the tangle of twiggy stems and fragile seed heads alone instead of chopping them to the ground. It was too late to pretend that Sophie needed them for an art project; Della would just have to be more assertive. Her phone pinged with an incoming text, and she snatched it from her pocket. Not Mark, but Liam.

Good about shop. Been thinking. Liam. Ah, the economic prose of the nineteen-year-old boy.

She replied: *That's great to hear, could I poss have a quote and when do you think you can start?* Then she fetched a cloth to wipe down the garden table, and searched the house for something to use as tablecloth, to add a little siren glamour to the garden.

There was nothing to be found in the kitchen – they weren't a tablecloth kind of family – and Della had almost given up hope when she wandered into Sophie's room, which seemed so still now, so empty. Funny, she mused, how you could tell if a room had been devoid of human activity for a while. It had only been three days, but already it felt like weeks. The smell of acrylic paint and cinnamon candles had faded and now it just had a spare-room smell, unused and slightly stale. Della opened the cupboard in which Sophie had stored all her half-finished projects. There it was, the perfect thing: a length of silky azure fabric, embellished with gold spirals, which Sophie had bought from an Asian shop in Bradford when she'd been crazy about all things Indian. Surely she wouldn't mind Della borrowing it?

She draped it over the banister, then showered quickly and pulled the dressing gown back on so as to avoid any food-related splatterings when she was properly dolled up. Dressing for a date, she thought with a smile: that's what this was, an actual *date,* like the magazines always said long-term couples should schedule. *Synchronise your diaries,* she'd read in Roxanne's magazine, which at the time had sounded like arranging a business meeting. Well, maybe there was something in that, she decided as she mixed cream, sugar and vanilla for the tart's filling and spooned it into the pastry shell, then placed raspberries on top with precision.

In her bedroom now, Della selected her best underwear – black lace French knickers, matching bra – and pulled on the siren slip. She had feared that the cubicle in Iris might have had weirdly flattering lighting, or that the mirror had distorted her reflection to make it seem more appealing than it really as. But no: the slip still looked fabulous. Shimmery, sexy . . . totally unnecessary, of course, as underwear went. Then, having wriggled into her favourite print dress – the one that draped flatteringly over her hips and created the illusion of a reasonably slender waist – Della installed herself at her dressing table and turned her attention to her face.

Always blessed with decent skin, she noted with pleasure that she seemed to have a certain glow about her today. Her dark eyes looked bright and alive, enhanced by the creamy shadow and slick of liner she was applying now. With a sweep of blusher and *Impassioned* in place, she pulled on low, strappy heels and, armed with the sari fabric and a selection of scented candles, stepped gingerly out into the garden.

The fabric looked wonderful, sparkly and glowing, on the garden table. She lit candles in jars, and dotted more in the pots containing the rosemary and thyme she had tried to grow, and which had failed to burst forth in the way that she'd hoped. She placed yet more candles on the back step, then stood back and admired the scene in front of her.

At 7.25 p.m. the sky was already beginning to darken to a purplish hue, and the setting – no longer a rather dull rectangular back garden – seemed magical in the flickering lights. Della allowed herself the luxury of admiring it for a few moments more. Back into the kitchen now, she peered at the pork in the oven, which was looking wonderfully tender, and checked her phone – still no texts. She considered firing off another message to Mark, realising that perhaps he'd be home too late for dinner, and she'd be left with a heap of bruschetta and roast pork and a whole darned tart all to herself. But then, surely he'd have let her know? Gathering up plates and glasses and cutlery, she stepped back outside where the garden was now filled by an insistent drone.

Over the fence, Norma was beavering away with her leaf-blowing machine. 'Got to keep on top of these,' she shouted over the din, registering the beautifully set table. 'Ooh, someone's birthday, is it?' She switched the machine off.

'No,' Della said, wondering now if all of this might seem a little over the top. 'It's just, Mark's been away for a couple of days and I thought, you know, I'd make it a bit special.'

Norma smiled briefly. 'Ah, lovely. It's nice to make an effort.'

'Yes, it is,' Della remarked, vowing now to do this more often, to make every Friday like this . . . why not? It would be their chance to catch up, to reconnect, at the end of each week.

'I won't spoil it then,' Norma added, 'with my blower machine.'

Della laughed. 'Thanks, Norma.'

As her neighbour glanced past her, at the table set with candles, Della thought she saw a flicker of something else in her face: of envy, perhaps. 'Della?' Mark's voice rang out from the kitchen.

She turned towards the house. 'Oh, Mark's home . . .'

'Enjoy your evening,' Norma called after her as Della, feeling as excited as if this was a first date, scampered inside.

He was standing in the middle of the kitchen, surveying dishes at various stages of preparation: the finished tart, the glass bowl of bruschetta topping, the pot of green beans ready to be simmered. 'Hi, love!' Della reached up and planted a kiss on his lips.

'Hi,' he said stiffly.

198

Della took a step back. If he had noticed her blow dry, her make-up and dress and heels, he was failing to register anything. 'So, how did it go?' she asked.

'Great, thanks,' he said flatly.

'Are you tired after the drive? D'you want a drink?'

'Yes, that'd be great.' He shrugged off his jacket and draped it over the back of a chair. Della went to pour him a glass of wine, her heels clacking on the slate kitchen floor, deciding that perhaps he was bemused to find her somehow propelled into fifties housewife mode, like the perfectly coiffed women on the covers of the oldest books in Kitty's collection: done hair, red lips, tending to his needs. All she lacked, she thought wryly, was a pinny. Might there be room for a selection of charming retro aprons in the bookshop?

'I'll go and get changed,' Mark muttered. As he trudged upstairs she checked on the pork dish again, and the potatoes slowly roasting and wafting their rosemary scent. She heard him running a shower as she sliced up the baguette and fussed and fiddled with unnecessary tasks – rearranging the spice jars, polishing the apples in the bowl – as she waited for him to reappear.

He wandered into the kitchen in jeans and a navy blue sweater, with his hair still damp. 'Smells nice in here,' he offered.

Della grinned. 'I'm making us a special dinner. Hope you didn't stop off for something on the way home?'

'No, of course not.' He assumed a distinctly queasy look.

'Are you sure? Because if you have . . . well, it's okay. I just wish I'd known.'

'I haven't eaten,' he protested. As he took a big sip from his wine glass she decided to tell him now, to blurt it all out about leaving her job, and signing the lease – get it

199

out in the open so they could talk it all through over dinner. Della took a deep breath as she picked up the lease from the table. 'Er, Mark . . . while you were away I signed an agreement on that shop.'

He frowned and took it from her. 'What shop?'

'You know. Sew 'n' Sew's in Burley Bridge. I'm sorry, I wanted to talk it over with you but—'

'You did this while I was away?'

Della nodded. 'Yes. I didn't want to wait in case someone else snapped it up. It's *mine*, Mark.'

She watched him flicking through the pages. Any moment now he'd stop and say, *Wow, it's a bit sudden, but . . . great!* He'd hug her, maybe. Make some barbed remark along the lines of, *Thank goodness, I'm sick of tripping over those damn books*. Instead he shook his head and placed the lease back on the kitchen table.

'Well?' Della said.

Mark lowered himself onto a kitchen chair and laced his fingers together. 'I don't really know what to say.'

She cleared her throat and sat down opposite him. 'How about, "Great." or "How exciting."?' She fixed her gaze upon his face. He wouldn't meet her eyes.

'I'm just amazed,' he started, 'that you went ahead and did this without talking it over with me.'

'I've tried,' insisted Della, 'but you were so negative about it there really wasn't much point.'

He snatched the document from the table and waved it at her. 'But you signed it! You didn't even ask me to look over it first.'

'I'm not an idiot, Mark. I read through it all twice. It's fine, very straightforward.'

'But what if you're saddled with it for years and it's a complete flop?'

Della glared at him, her heart rattling in her chest. 'I won't be saddled with it for years. It's a two-year contract.'

'Two years!' he exclaimed. 'So you're stuck with paying rent for two years even if you close after three months?'

She blinked, unable to believe what she was hearing. 'It won't close after three months.'

'How can you be sure? You haven't the first idea what you're doing!'

She opened her mouth to speak, wishing now that she had taken the time to create a business plan, littered with graphs and spreadsheets and columns of figures, if only to prove to Mark that she did realise the enormity of what she was taking on. She should have *scheduled a meeting* to run through it all with him. 'It just feels like the right thing to do,' she said, fiddling with the pepper grinder.

Mark was studying her across the table. With a clatter he pushed back his chair and started pacing back and forth across the kitchen. 'I've resigned from the shop,' she added.

'Great. Fine. Just do whatever it is you need to do.'

Out of the corner of her eye, though the kitchen window, she could see the glow of the candles on the garden table. She felt idiotic now, having created a date setting and dressed up simply to eat roast pork in their back garden. She had even curled her eyelashes, for crying out loud. Mark clearly wouldn't have noticed if she'd greeted him in a boiler suit with three days' worth of grease in her hair. 'Look,' she started, 'I'm just going by my instincts here. Everyone I've told thinks it's a great idea.'

'So, everyone knows but me?'

She squirmed in her seat. 'Well, er, Freda knows.' *And Sophie, and everyone at the castle . . .*

201

'Oh, well, so long as Freda thinks it's a good idea!'

She glared at him. 'Why are you being like this?'

'Like what?' He shrugged dismissively. 'I'm just being sensible, Dell. You've given no thought to the financial implications.'

'Yes, I have! Look, Mum's will should be settled in a few weeks so I'll have money from that, then Rosemary Cottage will be sold.'

'But what if it doesn't sell?'

She stared at him, wondering now if he had always been this negative but had managed to conceal it under a veneer of pleasantness during their early years together. 'It *will* sell. Of course it will. Why wouldn't it?'

'Because it's a wreck,' Mark countered.

'It's not a wreck. It's fine, it just needs a bit of upgrading.'

'Now you're talking like an estate agent. Anyway, you shouldn't be planning to live off your inheritance . . .'

'God, Mark, you make it sound like I'm some kind of socialite. Of course I'm not planning to live off it. You don't have any faith in me, that's the trouble.'

'I just think it's totally the wrong time . . .'

'When *is* the right time to do something like this?'

He seemed to pale then, and she wondered now if he *had* stopped off for dinner on the drive home, eaten something greasy and horrible that had disagreed with him. He wasn't one for service station food usually but maybe he'd been exhausted after three days of foot talk and had needed refuelling for the rest of the drive home . . . She glimpsed her fruit tart sitting there on the worktop, picture perfect, like something from a cookbook if she said so herself. Right now, she wasn't sure she would be able to manage a single slice.

'I don't know when the right time is,' Mark replied.

'But it's not when our daughter's just started college, and we're paying her rent – *supporting* her – and everything's in such a state of flux.'

Della blinked at him. He was leaning against the baby blue fridge he'd chosen, his face an unhealthy chalk-white colour. 'What d'you mean?'

'Oh, nothing.'

She stared, now seeing a man who was not merely tired. Instead he looked like someone who wished he'd never had to come home at all. 'Mark,' she said shakily, '*what's* in a state of flux? What are you talking about?

He met her gaze finally, and the fear in his eyes told her that this wasn't about the shop, or her leaving her job; it was something else, something so huge and terrifying that he didn't even want to say it aloud. And she knew then that she'd been foolish to set the table outside with candles and a tiny vase containing the very last of the garden flowers. He didn't want a date night; he didn't want her in red lipstick and a siren slip. He inhaled and rubbed at his tired-looking face, and his guarded eyes and tightly set mouth told Della everything she needed to know.

Something had happened at that conference in Weston-super-Mare and soon she would find out exactly what it was. But she couldn't ask him. She couldn't bear to hear what he'd really been doing when she'd assumed he was just strutting around, sharing his expertise. Right now, all she could do was sit and stare as her husband said, 'Della, I'm so sorry to tell you this but I'm leaving you.'

Chapter Twenty-Two

She was up on her feet somehow, her heart pounding hard and fast. 'What d'you mean?' she cried, already deciding: This is some sort of terrible, cruel joke. He's only saying it because of the bookshop. He's just angry, that's all.

'Della, *please*.' He negotiated his way awkwardly around her as if she were a confused shopper blocking a supermarket aisle. She froze, incapable of speech, as her husband made his way across the kitchen. Della stared at the back of his head as he took his jacket from the back of the chair and pulled it on, then felt in the pockets – for his wallet and keys, probably, as if he were popping out for milk. Only when he reached for the front door handle, with Della scuttling after him, could she find her voice.

'Mark! What are you doing?' She was shaking, her breath coming in rapid bursts.

'I'm sorry, I just have to go.' He wouldn't look at her.

'*Where* are you going? What d'you mean?'

His mouth seemed to crumple as he glanced at the door. 'I don't want to be here anymore.'

She was overcome by a swell of nausea. 'You mean, you don't want to be in the house, or with me?'

'With you. I just . . .' He broke off and looked as if he might cry. She wanted to hurl herself at him, to tell him that it was okay, they could figure things out, but couldn't bear the possibility that he might push her away. 'I've wanted to say for a while,' he muttered, although she wasn't hearing the words properly.

'Mark, please, just come back. Sit with me. We can talk about anything you like.' She looked at him, and a sliver of hope flickered in her chest, like a tiny glinting fish.

He shook his head. 'What's this all about? Don't you love me?' How pathetic it sounded, but she had to ask.

'Della, I'm sorry, I can't do this anymore.'

Tears were pouring down her cheeks. It felt as if they might never stop. 'Is . . . there someone else?' she croaked.

'No, of course not.'

'Is it me, then? Is it something I've done?' She felt a lurching sensation in her stomach and dropped her gaze to the neat stacks of boxes containing her mother's cook-books. 'Is it the books? Because if it's that much of a problem – the shop, I mean, the whole stupid idea . . .' She wiped her face with the sleeve of her dress. 'I mean, if you're planning to leave me because of some ratty old books about fondues . . .'

'No, it's *not* about fondues.'

She stared at him, her heart hammering against her ribs. 'Please, Mark. It's been such a strange time. Sophie's gone, it's bound to feel weird but it needn't be a bad thing, you know? I mean, there's just us two now. It could be really good . . . couldn't it?'

'I don't think so, Dell,' he said quietly.

'*I* do,' she insisted. 'Okay, we don't do much together,

we've probably got stale, but let's try and look at it positively, see it as an opportunity to start afresh . . .' Why was she speaking like a women's magazine?

'We can't,' Mark said quietly. 'I'm really sorry, Dell, but it's not what I want.' His mouth had firmed and now he had assumed a neutral expression, as if he were merely heading off to work.

'What do you want, then?' she yelled.

'I can't talk about that right now, okay?' She glowered at him, furious now that he could remain so calm and unflinching when she was still quaking inside, feeling dizzy and sick and having to mop at her nose with the sleeve of the lovely print dress she'd chosen so carefully to minimise her 'faults'.

'All right,' she murmured, 'but can I ask you something?' Mark nodded. 'Were you waiting for Mum to die so you could do this?'

He gawped at her. 'For Christ's sake, Della. Wasn't I supportive, all those months she was ill, looking after things here, trying to take care of everything?'

'Sophie, then. Were you waiting until Sophie had gone?'

'It's nothing to do with Sophie. She's only gone to college, although you're acting like you're bereaved . . .'

Fury whirled inside her at his use of that word. 'I meant, were you waiting for Sophie to move out so you could leave me?'

He blinked at her. 'Well, sort of. I thought it would probably be best.'

With that, he turned and opened the front door, and stepped out into the street. She watched him striding towards his car parked a few doors down, the one he kept factory fresh and wouldn't allow anyone to eat or even drink in – apart from maybe a small bottle of Evian in exceptional circumstances, if you were about to *expire* from thirst.

'Come back!' she bellowed, not caring that Norma might come out and start going on about rogue leaves blowing into her garden. Without turning back, Mark unlocked his car and climbed in. Della watched, aghast, as he smoothed back his short, neat hair and pulled out of the space. With his gaze fixed ahead he drove past her and down to the end of the street, where he indicated left and disappeared from sight.

She stood there, on her own doorstep, staring ahead. It occurred to her that she could drive after him in some crazy car-chase scenario, raging like a lunatic. But the state she was in, she would probably crash. Instead, she stepped back into the house and shut the door, then wandered into the kitchen and blinked at the chair where his jacket had been.

It was the only possession he'd taken. Surely that meant he was just planning to drive around for a bit then come home and apologise, explaining that he'd had a mad turn and everything was going to be okay? Her phone bleeped, and she snatched it from the worktop. *Hi, Mum, just wanted to say am so happy here!! Love Sxx.* It was the only time she had been disappointed to receive a text from Sophie in her whole life. It occurred to Della that she would have to be the one to tell her that her father had walked out. Another text pinged in: *All ok with u?*

Della started at it. She just couldn't do it. She couldn't crush the excitement of an eighteen-year-old girl; in fact, she wouldn't have to, because Mark would come home, and they'd fix things, and Sophie would never know.

As she tapped out a quick reply – *All fine here darling, love you xxx* – it struck Della that at the start of the week there had been three of them here, and now there was just one.

In times of stress – like when Sophie was a baby, wailing for breast milk that Della seemed unable to produce in sufficient quantities – she had always turned to food. There was, she had always believed, very little in life that couldn't be fixed with a hunk of tangy Cheddar, or a thick slice of crusty white bread slathered with butter. This time, though, the thought of eating didn't even occur to her. Instead, she sat gingerly on the edge of the sofa as if half-expecting bailiffs to barge in and tip her off it before carrying it away. Without the radio or TV on – or, crucially, Mark pottering about – the house felt eerily still.

Della glanced at the bookshelves which housed a small selection of books about art, architecture and interior design – chosen by Mark as a sort of set dressing. They might as well have been vases, for all the attention he'd paid them. There was a chessboard too, its onyx and ebony pieces set out with precision. Ridiculously, she wanted to mess it all up, put the knights in the squares where the king and queen were meant to go, as if *that would show him*. They'd never even played chess so why the hell was it sitting there?

Her mobile rang, and Freda's name appeared, but Della didn't pick up the call. She couldn't talk to anyone, not even her best friend – at least not yet. She wasn't sure she would even be capable of saying anything comprehensible. She sat feeling stunned and shivery, and when the shaking got too much she ran a bath and peeled off her dress and underwear. The siren slip – in effect, her leaving present for seven years' service at the gift shop – lay in a shiny heap on the floor.

Della soaked in the bathwater until it was tepid, then dried herself and wandered down to the kitchen in her dressing gown. She picked up the rental agreement for the shop and glared at it. She must have been out of her mind.

She tried Mark's mobile, but it went to voicemail. 'It's me,' she said dully. 'Look, I have no idea where you are, or what's going on, but I have to talk to you. You can't just . . . disappear like this. It's not fair. You owe me more than that.' She ended the call, feeling hollow and stupid. She stuffed her mobile into her dressing gown pocket and decided he could damn well phone *her* next, as she wouldn't be calling again. Would he have gone to Terry and Val's? she wondered. Surely not. While his doting parents would be kind and concerned, she couldn't imagine them being his first port of call.

Della clicked on the kettle for a cup of tea and noticed that the oven was still on. She opened it and reeled back as the smoky heat hit her in the face. The pork sat, looking wizened and sorry for itself. The potatoes were brown and gnarly, like lumps of bark. She grabbed a bin liner and tipped the meat into it; the sizzling joint melted straight through the thin plastic. She gathered up the mess and threw it all in the sink, then hacked the potatoes off the bottom of their roasting tin, and dumped those in too.

A Guide to Tuscan Cookery was still sitting there, mocking her from the worktop. Fat lot of use that had been, transporting her as it had back to the blissful, sun-filled days of their honeymoon. More tears came, dribbling down her hot, pink cheeks, and she blotted her face on a tea towel. It had been idiotic, really, to hope that some rustic food and chianti might have brought her and Mark somehow closer again. All the while, as she had topped and tailed beans and rustled up the bruschetta topping – feeling proud again of her culinary skills – he had been driving home and planning how to announce that he wanted to leave her.

Those cooking under duress books were useless, she decided, sloshing boiling water into a mug. No one wanted to prepare a meal when their heart had been stamped on. Now, she understood precisely how her mother must have felt when William had announced he was in love with that woman from work. No wonder Kitty had merely picked at the roast chicken Della had presented her with, in the hope of restoring normality to their shattered home. It was a wonder she had managed to choke down anything at all.

Belatedly dropping a tea bag into her mug, Della carried it up to her bedroom. It was just gone 9.30 p.m. and too early to sleep, but she needed the cosiness of bed. Only it wasn't cosy – it was as vast and chilly as the Atlantic Ocean – and no matter how tightly she bunched the duvet around her, she was still bitterly cold. Her mug of tea sat untouched on the bedside table, and downstairs in the kitchen her tart with its fresh cream and berry filling would slowly be turning sour. Della lay still and quiet, convinced that she would never be able to sleep, not ever – at least, not until Mark came home. But she must have drifted off somehow as next thing she knew, it was 10.37 a.m. – she had slept solidly for something like eleven hours – and someone was rapping sharply on the front door.

Chapter Twenty-Three

As she tumbled out of bed, Della was already formulating what she was going to say. *It's okay, let's just put it behind us. We all feel a bit weird sometimes and, yes, of course I was upset. But let's forget it. You're here now and that's all that matters . . .* She grabbed her keys from the shelf, stabbed the Yale into the lock and flung the door open.

'Oh, Della! Sorry to disturb you. I thought you'd be up by now.'

Della pulled her dressing gown – which she'd slept in – tighter around herself as she stared at Norma from next door. 'I, erm, I *was* up. Just not dressed . . . you know. But it's fine.' She forced a tight smile. 'Is everything okay?'

Fine rain was falling steadily and, under normal circumstances Della wouldn't leave her neighbour standing outside. However, she couldn't face inviting anyone in right now. She wasn't up to casual chit-chat and, ridiculously, she was ashamed of the mess of burned pork and melted bin bag and incinerated potatoes lying in the sink.

'Well, I won't keep you,' Norma said briskly. 'I'm just

doing the rounds, seeing who's remembered Clean-up Day . . .'

Della peered at her, then glanced up and down the street in case Mark's car might have miraculously reappeared. 'Clean-up Day?'

'Yes, we talked about it at the meeting, remember?' Nora's mouth pursed. 'Oh, I don't think you were at that. Well, it was decided then, and Sunday seemed to suit everyone . . .'

'What for?' Della asked, uncomprehending.

Norma's small, pale grey eyes fixed on her. 'Picking up litter, Della. The situation's got worse, I'm sure you've noticed. I know you're busy but we all care around here, don't we? We all want safe, tidy streets . . .'

'Oh, yes, of course.'

Something caught Norma's eye: a lone, highly dangerous Kit-Kat wrapper, flapping on the pavement, as if planted there to illustrate her point. 'So we can count on your help tomorrow?'

'Tomorrow?' Della exclaimed.

'Well, yes, that *is* Sunday . . .'

Della laughed awkwardly. 'Of course it is. Yes.'

'And Mark too, if he's not busy? We could do with a big strong man.' *Yep, because crisp packets are heavy . . . but unfortunately we have a small problem there. You see, he seems to have left me.* 'We'll make it fun,' Norma added. 'We're planning to dress up, involve the kids. The theme's nursery rhymes but of course, fancy dress is optional.' Of course it wasn't. In Della's experience it never was. Yet she hoisted a smile – the effort made her feel quite sick – and took a step back into her hallway.

'Great, well, I suppose I'll see you then.'

'And Mark too?'

Della's chest tightened. 'Maybe. I'm not sure of his movements tomorrow.'

Norma nodded. 'Bright and early, then. Eight o'clock start. And don't forget to dress up!'

Back in the sanctuary of her home – although now it felt like anything but – Della tried Mark's mobile again. Never mind her vowing not to call. This was her marriage, not a who's-going-to-crack-first sort of game. She was greeted by his perky recorded message: *Hello, you've reached Mark Sturgess, please leave a message and I'll get straight back to you . . .*

'It's me,' she growled. 'Could you call me?' Then, without bothering to shower, she pulled on the nearest clothes to hand: old jeans, baggy T-shirt, Sophie's cast-off cardi. Mark wouldn't be acting like this, she decided. He'd be showered, all citrussy fresh and probably be on the golf course with his beloved Peter, as if this was just a regular Saturday morning. Actually, no, he couldn't be. He'd walked out with only the clothes he'd been wearing; no clubs were dragged out to his car. They would have hampered his speedy get-away. It didn't seem right, though, him leaving without so much as a change of underwear or even a toothbrush. It didn't seem very *Mark*.

In their bedroom now, she frowned and opened his underwear drawer. It had been ransacked; only one pair of boxers remained, the jokey reindeer ones Sophie had bought him last Christmas (Mark wasn't a novelty pants sort of man). His sock drawer, too, was depleted – so at some point he had smuggled these essentials out of the house. Della perched on the edge of the bed. Had he snuck them out bit by bit, the odd pair of socks stuffed up his sweater like contraband goods? Or had he packed a bag at some point, while she was out? Whatever he'd done,

213

it must have been before his jaunt to Weston-super-Mare. With a wave of unease she threw open his wardrobe and estimated that perhaps half of his shirts – all neatly pressed by the ironing lady, and shrouded in clear plastic – had gone, as had several sweaters.

Could they still be packed from the conference? It occurred to her that she didn't remember seeing a suitcase when he'd returned on Friday night. Must still be in his car, she decided. Yet even if it were, he wouldn't have taken something like ten shirts and half a dozen sweaters with him, not unless the conference had involved some kind of fashion show. Della stared at the plundered wardrobe, the empty hangers dangling there. Evidence suggested that, over some period of time, he had laid careful plans to leave her.

Della's hands trembled as she tried his number again: *Hello, you've reached Mark Sturgess, please leave a message* . . . No, she wouldn't leave a message, not again, like some cast-off teenage girlfriend. She would be the model of decorum and calm. 'Can I come over, please?' she sobbed on the phone to Freda, spilling out what had happened.

'God, of course,' Freda exclaimed, 'come right away.'

Like Della and Mark –– or, rather, just Della now, although she could hardly bear to allow that thought to lodge in her head – Freda lived in a Victorian terrace house. However, hers hadn't had every shred of character knocked out of it. Bill, her ex, had never been one for DIY, and Freda's approach to home decor was occasionally to add more interesting objects – a bright pink cushion, a fluffy fern-green rug – so the place was constantly, gently evolving. Della sank into the faded inky-blue velvet sofa and cradled a mug of tea.

'Sounds like he's having some kind of mid-life crisis,' Freda observed gently.

'But why? I mean, why have a crisis now?' As soon as she'd said it, Della realised how silly she was being. Crises weren't haircuts or dental appointments; they weren't booked in advance.

Freda shook her head. 'I don't know . . . everything piling up, getting too much for him? Work pressure, Sophie leaving, that conference looming . . .'

'That's the thing,' Della asserted. 'Before he went away he seemed totally normal.' She paused. 'Actually, he just seemed like Mark, you know? Distant, grumpy, as if he was there in body only and his mind was actually somewhere else . . .' It was true, she realised: at the goodbye gathering for Sophie and seeing her off to college, even at Kitty's funeral, he'd merely been going through the motions, doing what was expected of him as a husband and father. These past few months, he had acted as if their marriage – their whole family life, really – was just a job to him, something to be tolerated and got through until Saturday rolled around and he could join his new-found friends on the course. 'I think he just wanted to get away from me,' Della added.

'But why would he want to do that?'

'Well, all those months I was preoccupied, looking after Mum . . .'

'So what? He's a grown man, he can fend for himself. No decent man would resent his wife looking after her dying mother . . .'

'And then there's the books,' she went on, 'hundreds and hundreds piled up in the hall . . .'

'They've only been there a week,' Freda protested. 'This isn't about the books.'

'But it might be! The day Mum died, we all went to Rosemary Cottage and Jeff was going on about the clutter, how it can't be good for a person, virtually suggesting it might have been partly to blame for her cancer . . .'

Freda squeezed her friend's hand. 'That's crazy. Anyway, clutter doesn't make someone leave their wife, Dell.'

'Sometimes it does. You see those TV programmes about compulsive hoarders. I saw one the other day. Rooms piled high with bin bags and stuff spilling out, family driven mad. In the one I saw, they couldn't find a woman's cat for three days. It was hiding in one of three old cookers she'd been storing in a bedroom . . .'

'You're not one of those people!' Freda exclaimed. 'Come on, Dell, you're not even keeping the books. That was just a temporary thing. You keep saying it's about you – something you've done to annoy or upset him – and it's just not. Please stop blaming yourself.'

Della shrugged and drained her tea. On the coffee table sat a plate of Freda's speciality lemon cake, neatly sliced. Della hadn't touched it. She had never been so uninterested in food. 'Well,' she said quietly, 'there must be some reason, and he says there's no one else. I mean, he was adamant about that . . .' She caught Freda giving her a doubtful look. 'If there was, surely he'd just say? I mean, what would be the point of denying it? I'd be bound to find out at some point . . .' Her voice tailed off. 'Please don't mention any of this to Evie, will you?'

'Of course not,' Freda assured her.

'Because I'd prefer Sophie to hear about it from me.'

Freda nodded. 'I promise, I won't breathe a word.'

'It probably won't come to that, though,' Della added, pulling Sophie's cardigan tighter across herself, 'because we'll sort this out.'

'Of course you will,' Freda said firmly.

Della cleared her throat. 'But the bookshop . . . well, obviously I can't do that now.'

'Yes, you can. Why are you saying that? I'll help you, I'll do anything you need me to do. I'm good with a paintbrush, you know. Please, Dell, don't start thinking like that. And don't do anything rash.' Freda pushed back her fine fair hair. 'You know what I think? I think he's just having . . . a bit of a turn.'

'A bit of a turn,' Della repeated dryly. 'And when he's over this turn, what d'you reckon I should do then?'

Freda put am arm around her. 'That's for you to decide. But right now, instead of all this speculating, I think you need to sit down and talk to him and find out what the hell's going on.'

Despite Freda's suggestion that she should stay the night – 'I don't want you pacing about at home, going over and over things' – Della insisted that she'd be fine, that she was over the shock now, just about, and had things she needed to do. Of course she wasn't over it: Mark's abrupt departure still seemed like something she had glimpsed, briefly, whilst channel hopping, which actually had nothing to do with her at all. She made herself a mug of strong tea and carried it upstairs where she caught sight of herself in the mirror on the landing wall. Although she didn't intend to, she couldn't help but appraise her appearance in a cool, objective way – viewing herself as a stranger, or perhaps Mark, might see her. People had often told Della she had 'fabulous hair'; it was an asset, even Roxanne had said that – 'What I'd give for your hair, Dell, all thick and dark and glossy. The money I have to spend on mine!' She wouldn't say that today, Della reflected. Unwashed and oily, it hadn't even been brushed. She had walked halfway across Heathfield looking like that, and Freda had been too kind to tell her. Some greyness had appeared too, at the roots. Della usually coloured it herself, with Sophie helping to distribute it evenly at the back. With a pang, Della realised there was no one now to help her.

She stepped towards the mirror and checked her face. Pale, drawn and more aged than it had ever looked before – at least to her knowledge. Maybe she looked that way all the time? It would take more than a slick of *Impassioned* to perk that up. The T-shirt she had snatched from the pile on the chair could have belonged to a teenage boy or a sixty-year-old woman, and as for the buff-coloured cardi: hell, the thing was virtually welded to her body these days. A fisherman's cardi! Was that why Mark had left – because she had taken to dressing as if she had just stepped off a trawler? This wasn't the North Atlantic. It was a bustling and reasonably well-heeled North Yorkshire market town. Mark didn't slob about, even on weekends. To Della's knowledge he had never rummaged through a bag of cast-off clothes to see if there were any pickings to be had before it was sent to charity.

In the kitchen now, her hand twitched over her phone. To delay the business of leaving him yet another message, she decided she really must eat – something bland and comforting, like hospital food. She delved into one of the boxes of cookbooks, extracting *Meals For One*.

Was there ever a more tragic concept? Della had several single women friends – Freda, for one –– none of whom would dream of referring to such a sorry little volume in order to make themselves something to eat. She tossed it back into the box and knocked together a simple pasta dish with tomato and herbs. Having managed to eat

218

roughly a third, she shoved the bowl aside and, resisting the urge to pour herself a large glass of wine – she would *not* become Kitty, anaesthetising herself with booze – decided to give Mark's number one more try.

'Della. Hi.'

Her breath caught in her throat. His real voice, not a recorded message. 'Mark? Why haven't you been answering my calls?'

'It's been, er, difficult.' He sounded muffled, as if speaking from the inside of a cupboard.

'Where are you?'

'Um, I'm staying at Peter's, for the moment. On his sofa.'

'Yes, well, thanks for clarifying that. Just so I don't think you're lovers. So where does Peter live?'

'Just across town,' he said vaguely. How bizarre, she thought bitterly, that she hadn't met any of these new golfing friends. Mark knew all of hers: the mum crowd, a couple of old schoolmates, even the far-flung friends, like Jenny from her secretarial course and Shelley and Nicola from Belling & Doyle, with whom she still met up occasionally. He might not *like* them especially, but he knew them all. This new best friend Peter – who didn't even seem to have a surname – could have been anything, a brain surgeon or bus driver or a ruddy taxidermist for all she knew.

'Look, I need to see you. I know half of your clothes are gone, you've been planning this.'

'I'm . . . I'm sorry,' Mark mumbled.

'So, can we meet up at least? We need to talk. For goodness' sake, you've given me no explanation at all.'

'I know, I know,' he groaned like a scolded child.

'Is there something wrong? Are you depressed or having – I don't know – some kind of breakdown?'

'No!' he exclaimed.

'Well, I just don't . . . I mean, what are we going tell Sophie?'

'I don't know,' Mark said weakly, and the thought of going round in a never-ending 'I don't know' loop filled Della with rage.

'You'll have to do better than that.'

'Yep, I know.' For goodness' sake, she could slap him! She could rap him on the head with *Meals For One*. Still, anger was good, Della decided. If being left by one's husband involved going through various emotional states, then wanting to whack him with a cookbook had to be a step on from crying loudly as he drove away.

'Okay,' she said firmly, 'so how about you come round now?'

'Now?' He sounded horrified.

'Or are you too busy?' she asked, aware of the trace of meanness in her voice.

'No, I'm not busy . . . can we make it tomorrow, though? It's just, I'm not feeling too good . . .'

Neither am I, she thought bitterly. 'Okay, come round tomorrow then.'

'Erm . . . I'd rather meet somewhere . . . neutral.'

'Somewhere neutral? What are you talking about? I'm your wife, Mark, not a stranger you're meeting on a first date. I'm not planning to accost you.'

'I just . . .' He broke off. 'I think we should have lunch, that's all.'

'Well, we could have lunch here.'

She sensed his brain whirring as he dredged up a reason why he couldn't come home. Maybe he thought she would shout, cause a scene, or perhaps try to poison him. 'Let's meet at a restaurant,' he said. 'What's that Italian called – the one down that alley where no one goes?'

He meant down the cobbled lane that led past the gallery, the silversmith's and Iris, purveyor of ridiculously frivolous silk slips. The dismal little restaurant that sat right at the end, tucked away and long-forgotten. 'Nico's, I think. Is it even still open?'

'Not sure, but we could meet there anyway. Shall we say one o'clock?' As if he was booking her in for a foot appointment.

'Look forward to it,' Della replied dryly, and finished the call. Still, at least they were meeting, and a dreary Italian restaurant – where the pink napkins were set out in concertina shapes, as far as she recalled – was probably as good a venue as any. At least no one would be likely to see them in there. It felt as if she was having an illicit encounter with her own husband.

With contact established, Della stretched out on the sofa and surveyed the living room Mark had planned so carefully. Well, she could plan too. She knew he thought her impetuous but this time, in preparation for tomorrow's summit meeting, she would have a well-rehearsed script in her head.

If you're unhappy, it's best that you try to explain why, so we can figure out how to fix it.

I'm sorry if you feel I haven't been there for you. I haven't felt as if you've been there for me either. D'you think we could start being more open and honest with each other from now on?

The thing is, we still love each other, don't we? Shall we try some counselling, do you think? Talk to a neutral third party? Yes, I know you would rather prise out your eyeball with a teaspoon but that's what they're for, they're trained to help and they see couples like us all the time . . .

That's what Roxanne would suggest, Della felt certain – although she had no intention of turning to her sister for advice. She had long since given up on asking Rox for fashion advice even, as her suggestions had so often come out sounding like mild criticisms: *A dirndl skirt might work better with your hips; I think if you go for a dark, matt fabric, it might help to minimise things up top . . .*

The landline trilled and she leaped to answer it.

'Hello, Della. Is Mark back yet?' asked a familiar dreary voice.

'Er, no, Val,' she said, trying to sound pleasant and light.

'Really? I thought he was due back last night?' In any other circumstances Della might have found his mother's concern quite endearing.

'Oh, yes, he *was* back, and then he had to go out again.'

Small pause. 'Where is he today?'

At Peter's, Val, his new best buddy's – which appears to be his new home. 'Golfing, I think,' Della said vaguely. 'Is everything all right? I mean, is there anything I can help with?'

'Oh, no. Please don't make a big thing of it. I was just worried, after we spoke on Thursday, that it might have sounded as if we were upset . . .' Della frowned, uncomprehending '. . . about our anniversary,' Val added, almost in a whisper.

'You didn't sound upset,' Della said, riled now that she was having to lie on Mark's behalf.

'Right. Well. We thought we might pop over tomorrow, have a little walk around Heathfield, maybe visit the castle . . . could we pop in for coffee?'

222

'No!' It came out louder than Della had meant. 'I mean, we'd love to see you, of course we would, but we have, er, plans.' Damn him for landing her in this situation. 'We're having a day out ourselves,' she added, realising that if Mark really wanted out of their marriage – and this wasn't a blip or a mini-crisis – she would have to shake off the habit of saying *we-this, we-that*, as if they were inseparable.

'That's nice,' Val remarked. 'Not a special occasion, is it?'

'Not our anniversary, no,' Della replied with a tight laugh.

'Where are you going?'

She fixed her gaze on the books with their glossy jackets, untouched for years. 'Er, I can't divulge our plans, Val,' said Della, adopting a playful tone. 'You see, I'm taking him on a mystery trip.'

'A mystery trip!' A tinkly laugh. 'Oh, how lovely. What *fun*. I'm sure he'll enjoy that after working so hard lately. 'Bye, then.'

Della replaced the phone, having promised to visit soon, and ran a finger along the spines of his books. Her gaze dropped to the chess set on the shelf below. In fact, she had bought it for Mark, aware that he had played as a child and figuring that he might teach Sophie the rules. It had bored her, though. 'It takes too long,' she'd grumbled. 'It goes on and on and nothing happens.'

Mark had explained that that was the point: it was all about patience and strategy and planning ahead. Like golf, she realised. When you thought about it, golf and chess had a lot in common. But golf had an advantage in that it provided the perfect excuse for getting out of the house for entire Saturdays. Plus it had a social aspect too, which meant that yet more hours could be spent away from home. Of course, that's why Mark had been so keen to start playing when he and Peter had got chatting after a consultation. It wasn't the sport itself that appealed but the fact that it took virtually all day. Della stood still, her index finger resting on an onyx pawn, as she realised he had chosen golf as his 'thing' because it meant that roughly half of his weekend could be spent away from her.

Della paced around, trying – and failing – to resist slugging back wine, and by the time 10 p.m. rolled around there was only one thing for it: to totter, rather woozily, up to bed. Never mind the script, she decided. Never mind *I'm sorry if you feel I haven't been there for you.* Golf . . . that's what they would talk about tomorrow, and she would wrangle the truth out of him.

She shivered, standing naked now in the middle of their bedroom, and burrowed through her drawers for something to sleep in before realising that all of her PJs must be in the wash. From one of Mark's drawers she tugged an outsized blue and white stripy nightshirt – another unwanted gift, from his mother this time – and pulled it on over her head. It was quite pleasing in its hideousness, somehow befitting sleeping alone – forever, probably. She toyed with the possibility of letting her leg and underarm hair grow; with her strong brunette genes, she tended to keep on top of such duties, but now she could allow it to bush forth. Give it a couple of weeks and she'd look quite feral, all hairy and splayed diagonally across the bed in her ex-husband's hideous nightshirt.

All this might have seemed quite appealing if Della hadn't been overcome by a sharp pang of loneliness, so real and tangible it felt like a kick in her guts.

Chapter Twenty-Four

Rap-rap-rap. Della's eyes blinked open and she scrambled up in bed. More sharp rapping, then, 'Della, hello? Della, are you there?' Sounded like someone shouting through the letterbox. For goodness' sake, who could possibly need her at this hour? It was ten-past eight on a Sunday morning. Della cursed as her bare feet hit the floor.

She hurried downstairs, spying the fuzzy spectre of a short, stout person through the front door's frosted-glass panel. She stabbed her key in the lock and opened the door to find Norma, wearing a headscarf, an apron and a rather stoical expression.

'Norma, hello!' Della exclaimed.

'Morning, Della. All set, then?' She was brandishing a cardboard box containing rolls of bin liners and yellow rubber gloves. 'Clean-up Day,' she prompted.

'Oh, yes! Yes. Of course . . .' How could she have forgotten this, amidst the breakdown of her marriage? Della flattened down her bed-hair with her hand. 'I, er, overslept, I'm afraid.'

'That's okay, we're just getting started.' Norma's

large-featured, rather masculine-looking face broke into a semblance of a smile. 'At least you dressed up, though. Not everyone has. Good to see you've made the effort.'

With a frown, Della peered down at Mark's nightshirt. 'Wee Willie Winkie,' Norma added approvingly. '"Upstairs, downstairs, in his nightgown . . ."'

'Er, that's right,' she said quickly. 'And you're . . . er . . .' Her gaze skimmed Norma's scarf, which was tightly knotted under her chin. Apart from the white apron she was clad in a baggy navy blue sweater and a sack-like brown skirt that shrouded her short legs, finishing at her ankles.

'Guess,' Norma commanded.

'Er, Little Miss Muffet?' Della was sweating now, whether due to her mild hangover or the stress of the situation, she wasn't sure.

'Old Mother Hubbard,' her neighbour chuckled, turning to indicate several others who were already meandering along Pickering Street, stopping now and again to pick up litter.

'Oh, right. Of course.' Della forced a smile.

'I'd put a jumper on,' Norma added, 'if I were you. It's pretty chilly.'

'Yes, good idea,' Della said, realising how ridiculously obedient she was being, scampering back inside and grabbing the nearest sweater to hand, which happened to be Mark's: a burgundy crewneck that smelled of him. She allowed herself a deep inhalation of the knitwear, then regretted it as her vision started blurring again. Stop this, she chastised herself. She would *not* wander around sniffing his sweaters and pining for him. Glimpsing her bare feet, and remembering she had no knickers on either, Della rectified matters with a large, unfetching pair of washed-out pants, plus leggings and scuffed wellies, and hurried back outside to join her neighbours. Armed now with rubber gloves and a bin bag, Della started to scour the street for litter. The more she could find, her reasoning went, the quicker she could hand in her spoils and bolt her front door until it was time to meet Mark at the restaurant. Further down the street, the Richardsons were dressed in identical yellow tops, plus cropped red trousers held up with braces and accessorised with red baseball caps. Tweedledum and Tweedledee, she decided, with an impressive bulging bin liner each. 'Look at *this!*' cried Mrs Selby in the far distance, holding an empty wine bottle as if it contained nuggets of gold.

'Well done!' Dennis Richardson called over, not entirely sincerely. Spotting Della, he gave her a cheery wave. 'So what have you come as?'

'Wee Willie Winkie,' she called back.

'Ah. Sorry, didn't get it . . .'

'No, the sweater sort of spoils the effect.'

'Very good, though. Original! Anyway, better start collecting or there'll be nothing left.' As if this were a jumble sale, an urgent matter of grabbing the best stuff.

Kirsty Bingham was doing well, Della noted. Her bin liner was full already, and she beamed smugly as she dumped it at the collection point. 'Well done,' Norma said, presenting her with a fresh new bag like a winner's sash.

'Oh, it's just good to help,' trilled Kirsty. So what was she supposed to be in her polka-dot frock? Della's money was on Little Bo Peep who, to her mind, was virtually indistinguishable from Jill, out of Jack and Jill; generic nursery-rhyme girls with their bouncy pigtails and white ankle socks. It wasn't a look that suited many fifty-something women, although Della was aware that she hardly looked her best, clad in Mark's burgundy jumper, the nightshirt flapping below it, her sock-less feet clammy now in her wellies. She started to march briskly down Pickering Street, her radar gaze sweeping left and right. The pavements, and even the gutter, appeared to be entirely litter-free. So was Malton Street, which ran adjacent, because Jill and Kevin McNally had already swept along ahead of her, their bin bags impressively weighty-looking as they swung around the corner and out of sight.

All these couples, united in nursery rhyme jollity: the Mitchells, the Carpenters, the Rigbys, the Hamilton-Webbs. Norma was just Norma, of course, so what would Della be now? Just plain old Della, on her own. *Poor, abandoned Della. Did you hear he left her, out of the blue? Three days after Sophie left for college? He must have been hanging on, desperately counting the days!* She wasn't being paranoid. The inevitability of being gossiped about filled her with dread.

Della stopped and leaned against a rough brick wall. It was all wrong, being out here hunting for litter when she should be at home, *preparing*. It struck her that she had to take control, to stop being so obliging, so afraid of upsetting people. What was happening to her? It was only thirty-six hours since Mark had walked out, and already she was roaming the streets in particularly unfetching nightwear like a crazy person. Checking the street for Clean-up Day volunteers – there were none in sight – she spotted a litter bin attached to a lamp post, and beetled towards it. Bingo: it was full of rubbish and nothing too disgusting as far as she could make out. She opened up her bin liner and placed it at her feet. Quickly glancing around, as if about to steal a car, Della started to scoop up the bin's contents – cans, plastic bottles, newspapers and a child's sodden shoe – and dropped them into the bag. The lower reaches of the bin, where the remains of Chinese takeaways had begun to decay, were more unpleasant, and it struck her that, in life generally, she had plummeted to new depths too. But the bin was now empty and her bag pleasingly weighty as she knotted it up and started to march back to Pickering Street.

'Della?'

She swung around. Norma was standing a few metres away. 'Hi,' Della said brightly.

Norma frowned with concern. 'Er, how are you . . . getting on?'

'Oh, fine,' Della said briskly. 'In fact, I'm going to drop this off and finish up, if that's all right?' Why was she being so apologetic? Norma didn't have the authority to decide whether or not Della could go home. This wasn't the army; she didn't have to wait to be officially dismissed.

Norma stepped towards her. 'I mean, how are things generally?'

'Er . . . okay,' Della murmured, alarmed at the tingling sensation that was starting up at the back of her eyes.

'Because . . .' Norma had adopted a kinder tone now. 'Because I'm sure it must be difficult,' she added.

Della's heart seemed to stop. Norma must have seen her on Friday night, yelling after Mark as he walked out. 'It is quite,' she muttered, gripping her bin liner tightly.

Norma came right up to her now and patted her arm. She had never been married, and had no children; she had once briefly mentioned that the great love of her life had died in his thirties, and she simply hadn't been interested in anyone else after that. Della focused on the slightly frayed hem of Norma's baggy brown skirt. 'I thought it might be,' she added, 'when I saw you . . .' So she *had*

229

witnessed Della yelling like a banshee at her front door.

'I'm really sorry you saw that. It can't have been very pleasant for you.' She blinked rapidly and cleared her throat. She wouldn't cry, not here in Helmsley Street with the very real possibility that Tweedledee and Tweedledum might appear round the corner and see her.

'Oh, no need to apologise,' Norma said quickly. 'When big things happen we can act in the most peculiar ways.' Her gaze drifted down to Della's bin liner. 'And it *is* a big change for you, with Sophie leaving . . .'

'Sophie leaving?' she repeated.

'Yes. All the years I've seen the two of you playing in the garden, having a lovely time, all the picnics and games and painting, all the fun you used to have . . .' Della swiped at her eyes with her hand. 'So, if you're feeling out of sorts,' Norma went on, 'you should have just said, you know. As it's turned out, we have plenty of volunteers, so really there was no need to cheat.'

Della's cheeks blazed. 'You, um, saw me emptying the—'

'Let's not say another thing about it.' Norma pressed her thin lips together and smiled. 'Like I said, we can all do silly things when we're upset. Come on now, let's drop off your bag and you can go home and sort yourself out.'

Sort yourself out. Well, yes, she must at least acquire a veneer of coping marvellously, Della decided, letting herself back into her house. It was 9.15 on a Sunday morning and she didn't know what to do with herself. She could call Liam, who had failed to get back to her with a possible date in his crammed schedule, but the chances of him being awake at this hour were slim, she decided. Instead, she phoned the least cold-hearted house-clearance company she could find and left a message detailing her requirements. Then she fired off a text to Liam: *Could you call me please? Thanks D.*

Della curled up on the sofa and dozed fitfully, and when she woke there was nothing left for her to do other than to pull Sophie's treasured sari fabric from the washing machine – it had puckered in the wash, like seersucker – and set about getting ready for lunch. Della pulled off her hideous attire and showered quickly, before selecting the correct outfit with which to arm herself against her husband's ineffectual wafflings. No blow-dry or *Impassioned* lipstick today. The last thing she wanted was for Mark to assume she had made an effort for him, and was trying to 'win him back' with brazen lip colour.

Instead, she chose a rather stern ensemble of white shirt and narrow black skirt – an outfit she had worn numerous times to work – and tied back her hair in a ponytail that was so tight, it gave her an instant headache. Coupled with her pale, drawn face, Della looked as if she was ready for court.

The sky was clear blue, and there was an autumnal bite in the air as she strode towards the town centre. She crossed the market square, which had long ago ceased selling useful items and had now descended into a ragged selection of stalls offering cheap quilted leather handbags and replica models of Heathfield Castle cast in bronze-effect plastic. She passed the library, then the row of cottagey shops with their jaunty red-and-white-striped awnings: an old-fashioned butcher's, a bakery, and The Candy Box, where boiled sweets were dispensed from jars.

She snatched her phone from her bag as it rang.

'Hi, Mum.'

'Sophie, hi! How are you? Is everything okay?'

'Yes, of course it is. Don't sound so worried!'

231

Della laughed awkwardly. 'I'm not worried, love. I've just been wondering.' She paused. 'I've been thinking about you a lot . . .'

'Well, I'm fine, Mum. My flatmates are great, and the others across the hall too. They came over to ours and we had a bit of a night last night.' *Over to ours:* she was at home there already. And that was wonderful, of course it was.

'I'm so glad,' Della said. 'So, do your lectures start tomorrow?'

'Yeah. So we're going out tonight, a massive group of us . . .' Della stopped herself from saying, *You're going out the night before college starts?* 'Is Dad there?' Sophie asked.

'Er, no . . . I'll see him in a minute, though. We're going out for lunch.'

'Out for lunch on a Sunday?'

'Yes, I know.' Della forced a laugh. 'It's very unusual.'

'So, where is he?'

'Oh, he had, er, things to do. I'm meeting him at the restaurant.'

'That's nice,' Sophie said with a trace of surprise, and no wonder: Della couldn't remember the last time she and Mark had eaten out. 'You'll be going out all the time,' she added, 'now you've got rid of me.'

'No stopping us,' Della said, feeling as if there was a vice clamped around her heart.

'Ah, that's sweet, Mum. You're getting all romantic!' Sophie laughed. 'Well, say hi to Dad for me. Love you, Mum.'

'Love you too, darling,' Della said. She stopped outside a greetings card shop and took several deep breaths before striding onwards, turning into the narrow alley off the high street. She walked briskly down it to Nico's, the tucked-away Italian place that no one ever seemed to go to. *Be calm,* she instructed herself as she pushed the door open and stepped in. The place still called itself a trattoria. It had pink tablecloths and shelves crammed with wine bottles and rather beleaguered-looking plants. No Mark yet. Just an elderly couple peering bewilderedly at enormous laminated menus garishly embellished with Italian flags. 'D'you have a table for two please?' Della asked the waiter in an overly bright voice.

'Yes, where would you like?'

'That one, please, in the corner.' *As far away from the window as possible.* Della knew she was being unnecessarily cautious as no one was likely to walk by.

She was shown to a corner table where she took a seat and plucked a breadstick she didn't even want from the glass on the table. She nibbled its end, like a rodent; she might as well have been eating a twig. Her stomach was tight with nerves, and it struck her that the only other time she'd felt so edgy prior to meeting Mark was on their first date, after he'd called in at the florist's on pretence of wanting to thank her for putting together such a lovely bouquet for his mother.

The restaurant he'd chosen had seemed incredibly sophisticated then, the food presented all piled up in a neat little stack, like Jenga bricks. Della had never encountered a restaurant where they did that. They'd gone on to the pub afterwards, the Gordon Arms close to Heathfield Castle, which unbeknown to them happened to be hosting a fancy dress evening with a musical theme.

Della, who was wearing a figure-hugging black dress, murmured to Mark that they were the only people not dressed up. 'But *you* are,' he assured her. 'You look like

233

one of those gorgeous jazz singers from a smoky bar.' They'd laughed and downed their drinks quickly, then escaped the hordes of fancy dressers with joke punk hair and Beatles wigs. They'd dodged a drunk Mama Cass, who had tried to kiss Mark as they slipped out into the rain.

Then, standing under the butcher's awning, they had kissed and kissed, and Della Cartwright had known she was truly in *something* – if not love, then crazily in lust.

Now that felt like a hundred years ago, when they couldn't sit together without entangling themselves. So when had it all changed? Della had no idea. Perhaps when Sophie was born – but that was eighteen years ago. Could the deliciously thrilling part really have been so short?

She flinched as the restaurant door opened and Mark strode in, ten minutes late. Although he tried for a sort-of smile, he couldn't mask the fact that his eyes were filled with dread.

Chapter Twenty-Five

'Sorry, sorry,' he said, shrugging off his navy blue linen jacket and taking the seat opposite. He picked up a menu, then put it down again and twiddled with the vase containing an artificial red rose. He was thinner in the face, Della decided; more angular, a little starved-looking and definitely sleep-deprived. He'd only been gone forty-eight hours and already he looked different.

'It's okay,' she murmured. 'I just thought we should see each other. All those times I called you, and you were avoiding me . . .'

'Well, I'm here now.' His eyes were cold, his face set in a frown, and it occurred to her that his hair looked different too, sort of wet and stiff as if he'd put something on it, some kind of product like wax or gel – but surely not. Mark didn't put stuff on his hair. Maybe it was merely greasy and he was falling apart, forgetting to wash it, which had to be a good sign, she reasoned.

She breathed deeply. They hadn't got off to a good start. *Take it gently,* she decided. *Don't go on the attack.* Something else she'd probably picked up from Roxanne's magazine. 'So what d'you fancy?' Mark muttered, lowering his gaze.

Nothing, she wanted to say, *apart from forgetting this lunch and you coming home with me so we can get on with our lives and pretend this never happened.* 'I might have fish,' she replied flatly.

'Fine, me too.' They both ordered plaice. While Mark declined alcohol, requesting only a glass of tap water, Della ordered a large glass of house white which smelled faintly of bubblegum.

'So,' she started, sensing a twisting sensation in her gut, 'can you please tell me what's going on? Just be honest, Mark. It's awful, not knowing. I *really* have to know . . .'

He looked at her, and she saw a vein throb in his neck. 'Dell, I'm sorry. I'm . . .' He bit his lip and looked around distractedly. 'I'm just not happy, that's all.'

She glanced at the door, willing more people to come in, to fill the place with conversation and laughter so she didn't feel quite so conspicuous. 'Mark, I have to ask you,' she hissed, 'are you sure there's no one else? Because if there is, I'd rather know.'

'Dell, please. No, there's not. I've already told you.'

She glowered at him, unsure whether to believe him or not. She used to pride herself on being a pretty good judge of character, and now she realised she knew nothing at all. 'Let's just go,' she murmured. 'Come back home where we can talk properly.'

'But we've ordered food.'

'I don't want food,' she snapped, causing the waiter to glance over and frown at her. 'I'll pay for it anyway. God, Mark, as if I even care.'

He looked down at the table. 'I can't anyway.'

'You can't come to the house? Why not?'

'I told you, it feels better to meet on neutral ground.'

'Will you stop saying that? You're making it sound like I'll tie you up and hold you hostage.' Her voice had risen now, and the elderly couple kept glancing over with concerned faces but she didn't care, couldn't stop. She gulped her wine, half the glass gone already. 'I promise you, all I want to do is talk in private. You'll be free to go, I won't falsely imprison you . . .' She stopped abruptly as their plaice arrived, accompanied by slimy green beans and sautéed potatoes. The fish was so bony that eating it seemed like a terrible effort when you considered the reward, not that Della wanted it anyway. She grabbed a breadstick, and Mark flinched as if she might hit him with it. 'So, you're not happy,' she ventured. 'Can you at least tell me why?'

Mark pursed his lips. 'I'm sorry, Dell. I don't think we're good together anymore.'

Della blinked at him. 'Is this a recent thing, or have you felt like this for ages?'

'A while, I suppose.' They lapsed into a brief silence.

'But . . .' she lowered her voice to a murmur '. . . isn't that normal?'

'What, to feel that things aren't good?'

Della glanced at the waiter who was busily setting tables, pretending he wasn't listening in to their exchange. 'Yes. Well, no, not exactly – but to feel a bit . . . dissatisfied. It's what happens, isn't it, when you've been together this long? People get stale but we can fix it, Mark, especially now it's just the two of us. A sort of fresh start . . .'

She looked at him, knowing he was only listening – only sitting here in this dismal restaurant – because she had forced him to. He didn't think they could fix it. He didn't want to, she realised with a wave of dread. She had lost him already.

The coffee machine hissed into action and there was an outburst of banter in the kitchen. Della felt her eyes brimming with tears and dabbed at them with a napkin.

'Della . . .' Mark's hand touched hers. 'I'm sorry, but we can't fix this.'

Her mouth quivered. 'Why not?'

He dropped his gaze. 'It's too late.'

'But . . . why?' she hissed.

Mark shook his head and summonsed over the waiter with a nod. Although their plates were barely touched, it was clear that neither Mark nor Della was going to eat anything more. 'Bill, please,' he said, in an irritatingly normal voice.

'Of course, sir.'

Della sat with her teeth clenched as the waiter brought their bill on a little silver dish.

'I'll get it,' Mark said quickly, fumbling for his wallet.

'No, it's fine.' Della dumped three tenners into the dish. The elderly couple scrutinised them as they stepped out into the cool September air.

'Are you coming back to the house?' she ventured.

Mark shook his head. 'I will, but not now. Now while you're being like this.'

'*What* am I being like? What d'you expect me to be like?' She went to grab his hand but he tugged it away. 'Mark, please, you said you're not happy, that's fine . . . well, obviously it's *not* fine. I just want you – I want us – to be happy. Could we please just talk?'

'Okay,' he muttered.

'So, shall we go somewhere?'

'No, we can talk here.'

'What, in the street?'

'Stop shouting, Dell!'

She stepped back. Was she shouting? She had no idea. She seemed to have lost the ability to control the volume of her voice. 'I'd just like to know when we can see each other properly, to sort things out.'

He sniffed loudly, and a younger man approached whom they both knew by sight. A keen runner who lived in their street, he was pounding towards them in neon yellow trainers, with some kind of device strapped to his upper arm. 'Hi!' he bellowed.

'Hi!' they barked back as he cantered onwards, and only when he was out of sight did Mark turn to Della and say, 'Look, you know I'm staying at Peter's. And we can meet up soon, I promise. I'm just not sure when.'

'Why not? D'you need to check your diary, see when you can fit me in?'

'Della, *please.*'

She stared at him. Though not a violent person she had the urge, right now, to slap him hard. 'I'm not one of your patients,' she growled. 'I'm your wife and I think I have the right to know.' The words caught in her throat. 'I need to know, is this it? I mean, when you said we can't fix it, that it's too late . . .' Tears were rolling down her cheeks now. 'Does that mean it's the end of us?'

She saw Mark's Adam's apple bob as he swallowed. 'I'll call you,' he said, and something flickered in his eyes – a trace of warmth, perhaps, or kindness – and he reached a hand towards her. She held her breath, expecting him to do something tender like touch her cheek. But his hand hovered over her shoulder, and he patted it quickly before turning and walking away.

'Mark?' she called after him – not too loudly; she didn't want to be accused of 'shouting' again. 'Mark!' she yelled as he marched past Iris, the silversmith's and the gallery,

239

then turned the corner into the high street and disappeared from sight.

Della glared after him. What was the patting all about? You patted dogs, or small children when they were hurt – not *wives*. Patting meant pity; so he felt sorry for her, did he? Well, she wasn't having that. Fuelled by anger and bubblegum wine, she strode briskly after him and scanned the high street.

As most of the shops were open on Sundays, the town centre was bustling. It was the day visitors tended to come to Heathfield, for the castle and the prettier of the shops, and the pavements milled with family groups, chatting and exploring, seemingly in no particular hurry to go anywhere. People were eating ice creams, despite the chill in the air, and emerging from the deli with brown paper bags of posh loaves.

Della peered up and down the street, with no idea which way Mark had gone. It had, as lunches went, been a disaster – like the Tuscan meal she had so lovingly prepared. Food was starting to seem less like something to be enjoyed and celebrated and more a marker of terrible times.

She started walking, scanning both sides of the street for a tall, slim man in a navy blue linen jacket, who could hardly bear to sit in a restaurant with her. Anger was bubbling inside her again, and she wondered now if this would be her default state; permanently at a rolling boil, as she was now. She felt hollow and slightly dizzy, possibly due to that nasty wine or the fact that all she had eaten that day – at almost 2 p.m. – were a few flakes of over-cooked and possibly not especially fresh plaice.

'Dad, it's that lady!'

Although Della registered the child's voice, she reassured herself that she was not the lady being referred to.

'Oh yes, it is, isn't it?'

She glimpsed him as he approached – the boy from the castle shop, and the supermarket when she was trundling a trolley of booze – with his father. She willed them to march straight past her. After all, they had failed to recognise her by the fish counter.

The man stepped towards her, smiling. 'Hi, um, d'you remember us?'

'Er, yes, I *think* so.' Della felt her entire body stiffen. Of course they recognised her; she was wearing smart work clothes, and not the garb of a Norwegian fisherman she'd been showing a preference for of late.

'We met you in the castle shop?' he prompted her.

'Yes, yes, I remember . . .' Her gaze flicked past him across the street.

'We've been back three times,' the man went on. 'I think we should qualify for a loyalty card by now.' Della smiled vaguely. 'We haven't seen you, though,' he added. 'We wanted to thank you for the tip about the dungeon tour. Brilliant, wasn't it, Eddie?'

'Yeah, it was great! *Really* scary . . .'

The man turned back to her. 'Maybe you don't work on Sundays?'

'Oh, I've left actually,' Della said distractedly.

'Ah, right. So where, um . . .' His voice faded as Della scanned the street, aware that under any other circumstances she would have chatted happily and enjoyed Eddie's enthusiasm.

'Why don't you work there any more?' The child's voice cut through her thoughts.

'Er, I've decided to open a bookshop.'

'A bookshop?' his father exclaimed. 'Really? That's fantastic! Around here, you mean?'

'No, er, in Burley Bridge, you probably don't know it.'

'Oh, yes, we know Burley Bridge, don't we, Eddie? We stopped off for fish and chips that time, remember?' Someone caught her eye then, a man emerging from the newsagent's across the street, carrying a newspaper – no, *several* newspapers, by the look of it, a whole bunch of Sunday papers to relax over as if this were just an ordinary day.

'Sorry,' she blurted out, 'I've got to go.' And she hared off, darting across the road.

'Careful!' Eddie's father shouted, but Della was focused only on keeping Mark within sight as he marched off down the street. He had the air of a man on a mission, having ticked 'meet Della and let her rant at me' off his list. She considered catching up with him and forcing him to come home with her and sitting him down for a Big Talk. But that wouldn't work. Mark wasn't the sort of man you could force to do anything. He had an uncanny knack of stating how things would be, and the unwavering confidence that suggested that he really did know what was best for everyone.

The town centre was still busy and Della kept glimpsing him ahead of her, bobbing along with his neat, weirdly gelled hair, looking forward to reading the papers, no doubt. It incensed her, that he was able to act so normally after such a terrible meeting. She could no more sit down to read the newspaper right now than perform heart surgery on a baby. She'd follow him, she decided. Yes, it was precisely the kind of thing only a deranged, thwarted woman would do – but then she *was* a deranged, thwarted woman. She was a parent, too – they both were – and he

242

had given her precisely no guidance on how he thought they (or, more realistically, *she*) might tell Sophie that her parents had split up when she had barely got around to unpacking her toothbrush.

He had quickened his pace now – those long, strong legs were excellent for striding – and Della was having to scurry along in her silly low heels in order to keep up. She wished she'd gone for jeans and flat boots today. What had she been thinking, ironing a blouse and skirt as if she had been setting off for a job interview? 'Clothes are powerful,' Roxanne had announced once, when Della had asked her to explain fashion to her. 'They totally alter the way you carry yourself.' Well, Della's hopes that being smartly attired would make her feel powerful and in control had failed.

Mark was gaining headway now, and crossed the road. 'Excuse me!' snapped a woman in a thick tweed coat as Della collided with her. She darted into the road, causing a taxi driver to honk furiously and a cluster of young mothers with toddlers in buggies to stare at her in alarm. Della held up her hand in apology, her heart thumping as she stood in the middle of the road and waited for a gap in the traffic so she could cross. She must be more careful because, however much she cared about her marriage, she didn't want Mark to think she was so distraught as to fling herself under a car.

Della stopped and pushed back a strand of hair that had escaped its topknot and was dangling limply beside her simmering cheek. Mark had disappeared from view. She scanned the pavement, her shoes squeezing her toes, stinging fiercely. Could feet swell due to stress, she wondered? She knew the very man to ask.

Della scampered on, wincing in pain and peering down

each side street as she passed. No Mark. Perhaps he has hiding, she thought darkly, watching from a shop doorway and shaking his head at the pitiful sight of her trying to trot along in heels, like a deranged secretary. She stopped again and glanced along one of the smarter side roads that led away from the town centre to a posh, newly built estate. There he was, in the distance, strolling leisurely now with his newspapers tucked under his arm as if he didn't have a care in the world.

She licked her dry lips and tried to compose herself, then turned into the lane. She hadn't been up this road since Sophie was a toddler. There'd been a nursery here – Sophie had attended – but that had been demolished to make way for detached mock-Georgian houses with imposing doorways and windows consisting of numerous tiny panes.

The estate had a just-finished feel about it. Some of the houses looked unsold and empty, and there was still a show home with a limp plastic banner flapping in the light breeze, with Briar Copse Executive Development emblazoned on it. The gardens of the occupied houses were decorated with all manner of accessories – bird tables, sun dials, a miniature wishing well – as if to compensate for the fact that nothing had had the chance to grow yet. So this was where the famous Peter lived. Not for the first time, Della felt a twinge of annoyance that she had never had the opportunity to meet all these new friends of Mark's. She had started to feel like the lunatic wife he'd kept hidden away in the attic.

Mark was still climbing the steep hill, where the houses had become even larger and grander, with double or even in some cases *triple* garages for the small fleets of vehicles these families required. She was past caring now that he could turn around and see her. She wanted to find out where Peter lived and, more importantly, she needed some answers: like why her husband felt they couldn't fix things, and what specifically had made him start to feel this way. He was nearing the top of the hill now, still with a jaunty spring in his step while Della was breathing hard – whether from exertion or agitation, she couldn't be sure. The mild buzz from the cheap wine had worn off.

The houses at the top of the hill were the grandest of all, with ostentatious pillars flanking their grand, glossy doorways. Arranged in a curve around the end of the cul-de-sac, five prestigious homes seemed to be staring at her, like a stern panel of interviewers daring her to approach. Mark strolled towards the middle house and opened the front gate.

Della stood and watched, telling herself he was just going to Peter's, the friend who had generously helped him out in his hour of need. They were probably going to laze around and share out the sections of the Sunday papers whilst sipping freshly ground coffee. With a house this size, she assumed Peter had a wife and children and wasn't rattling around in his mock-Georgian pile all by himself.

She spotted Mark's black BWM in the small parking area, in between two similarly smart cars. The house looked immaculate, and the garden, which had yet to mature or do anything interesting, was dotted with what looked like ornamental animals. She focused hard and realised they all appeared to be hedgehogs. How very cute, she thought bitterly. Either Peter was a hedgehog fanatic or his wife was. Della switched her gaze from the moulded creatures back to her husband, who was walking briskly towards the front door.

Less confident now about how she'd handle herself if

245

spotted, Della positioned herself partially behind a silver people carrier and wondered how she had come to find herself spying on her husband like this. Just a few days ago she'd been going about her business, seeing their daughter off on a thrilling new stage of life and fretting about whether she should have bought her a cheese plant. She spotted movement at one of the windows of the house, as if someone had been watching and waiting. The front door opened before Mark had even reached it.

A woman stood there in a neat grey dress, her wavy red hair cascading over her bare shoulders like a shimmering, rust-coloured waterfall. Her delicate heart-shaped face broke into a beaming smile. She must be Peter's wife, Della reasoned: a generous woman who was happy for Mark to crash on their sofa until he got over whatever kind of mid-life crisis was happening to him. Only this didn't look like a sofa-crashing sort of house. They'd have a spare room, a guest annexe probably, and the red-head obviously wasn't Peter's wife – unless they had *that* kind of arrangement – because now she and Mark were kissing, full on the mouth, her arms flung around him, pulling him in tight.

Della's heart seemed to splinter as they tumbled inside, clearly delighted to be together, like a couple in a building society ad who had just been given the keys to their new home.

Chapter Twenty-Six

For a few moments, Della did nothing. She just stood and stared at the overblown house – someone would probably alert Neighbourhood Watch – and tried to figure out how to react to something she didn't yet fully understand. *I'm staying with Peter* . . . was there a Peter? And had Mark even been golfing all those Saturdays when he'd come home, murmuring about having had a 'great game'?

Della felt chilled as the realisation dawned on her that it was *here* he'd been, not at Heathfield or Cragham or any other golf courses for that matter.

He had gone out and spent an astronomical amount on a full set of clubs for a sport he didn't even play. He had bought little leather caps to keep the clubs protected when they were probably just transported around in the boot of his car. Golf was a decoy, that was all. Week after week, after buttering her up with perfect coffee in her favourite mug, he had lied to her. Which probably meant – and it wouldn't take a private detective to figure it out – that the conference in Weston-super-Mare hadn't happened either.

Although she needed to know for certain – Della had

to know *everything* now, like who that woman was and how long it had been going on – she also prided herself on being reasonably dignified. This meant that marching up the path and bashing on the swanky red-painted door was out of the question. She refused to be the kind of woman who made a scene, who screamed and yelled and broke things in a fit of rage. Although she wanted to, very much – she wanted to *club* him, actually – she couldn't bear to lower herself to being escorted off this sterile estate as if she were some random crazy, rather than the woman with whom Mark had shared a bed virtually every night for twenty-one years. She could call him on his mobile and summons him out of the house, but that would be just as humiliating. What if he refused to come out and just stared at her from that living-room window with the tiny twee panes? Instead, Della turned and walked slowly down the hill, heart thumping, feeling as if she might vomit right there outside the show home.

The afternoon had turned cooler and she shivered as she reached the high street and made her way past the shops. There was a golf store, where Mark had bought his clubs. She glanced in through the window at the array of diamond-pattered sweaters and the kind of trousers she supposed were called 'slacks'.

If Della had ever been inclined to have an affair – which she hadn't, the thought had never even occurred to her – she wouldn't have been able to stop herself from telling Mark. She wasn't a keeper of secrets, a sneaker-arounder capable of leading what was in effect a double life. She wouldn't have conjured up an imaginary friend and a whole sporting life to conceal her illicit activities. As she glared into the golf shop, in which a couple of middle-aged men were examining a pair of beige trousers with forensic interest, she wondered now if Mark had taken care to drag his clubs through muddy grass just to dirty them up a bit before heading home. She walked onwards, feeling nauseous and wretched, dreading to consider what he and that red-headed woman might be doing now.

Back home, Della caught sight of her anguished face in the small flower-shaped mirror on the fridge: the one Sophie had stuck there because, despite having the beautiful gilded mirror in her own room, 'the kitchen has the best light'. It was the reflection of a stupid, gullible woman who had taken on the rental of a shop which, if she was completely honest, she didn't have the first idea how to set up or run. To think she'd assumed it would miraculously fall into place with the help of a few amateurish drawings and a hapless nineteen year-old who didn't even seem to possess a tape measure! On top of Mark's activities – which hadn't even begun to sink in, not remotely – she now had to make a go of it alone. Not that her husband would have helped much but he'd have been *there,* dispensing sage advice from the sidelines. Even the thought of him grumbling and rolling his eyes about fondues and margarine seemed a more attractive prospect than his not being there at all.

The *lying,* that was the worst part. All he needed to have done was to tell her he didn't love her anymore. Della filled the kettle, suddenly picturing Sophie, oblivious to all of this and probably congregating with her new flatmates in a good-humoured hungover fuzz. Della's eyes brimmed with hot tears.

She couldn't bear to be here right now, trapped in the awful silence. So she hurried upstairs and pulled off her shoes, blouse and skirt. She had a mottled rash on her chest and a dense pounding in her head. Her whole body seemed to be reacting against the sight of Mark being fiercely kissed by the red-headed woman.

Shivering in her mismatched bra and pants, she considered calling him just to ask, rather tersely, if he wasn't a little too long in the tooth to have an imaginary friend. But she feared that her delivery might falter – in fact, that she would be incapable of speaking coherently – and the last thing she wanted was to be that sobbing woman on the phone while his girlfriend looked on in disdain. Instead, Della pulled on soft cotton socks followed by jeans and a sweater and her comfiest ankle boots. Then she grabbed her car keys, plus the keys to Sew 'n' Sew's – she had yet to stop thinking of the place as a haberdasher's – and the shoebox containing the pencils and sketchbook which she had purloined from Sophie's room.

In the front doorway, she paused to check her phone for missed calls in case Mark had rung to say he'd made a dreadful mistake. Of course he hadn't. In the absence of any heartfelt apology, she climbed into her car and set off for Burley Bridge. It was just gone four, and the clouds had gathered in angry swirls as she parked in front of the shop. Today she couldn't face checking on Rosemary Cottage. Instead, she let herself into the shop and switched on the harsh fluorescent strip, which buzzed in a sinister fashion above her head.

Della's heart sank as she looked around the dingy shop. What had seemed so full of promise when Freda was here – and even when she'd shown Liam around – now had all the allure of a long-forgotten municipal building. It felt like the side room of Heathfield Community Centre, where Della had taken Sophie to music and movement classes, dutifully bashing a tambourine and singing 'She'll Be Coming Round the Mountain' with a gang of exuberant mums. It could have been the back room of St Martin's Church, where she had volunteered as a Brownie helper and come home with a dusting of glitter on her clothes.

It occurred to Della that a large proportion of her life had been spent in the side and back rooms of community buildings, with their dusty floors and chipped mugs of Nescafe; but actually, these places had lifted her spirits and helped to chase away the new-mother loneliness she'd felt sometimes. For the most part, the other mums she'd befriended had turned out to be as interesting and entertaining as women in any other walk of life. Dads were a rare feature. Della loved the way women were when there were no men around: open, confiding, secrets and anecdotes all tumbling out amidst the poster paint and Duplo bricks. And now, as she hoisted herself up to sit on the dusty counter, a thought began to form that her bookshop could be just that kind of place. She didn't mean the chipped mugs of Nescafe; more the feeling of warmth and inclusiveness, where her customers would always feel welcome and might start chatting to a likeminded soul. It would be a place to relax and forget the pressures of the day, where anyone could browse for as long as they liked without any pressure to buy.

Browsing doesn't make money, Mark had pointed out. Yes, well, it was her shop, and they would be her customers, and they could browse all they wanted.

She flinched at the sight of a large spider crawling slowly across the ceiling. Of course, before browsing could happen she would have to scrub down the place thoroughly and, she realised now, get the lighting sorted because that buzzing fluorescent strip would have to go. Liam would have to kick into action too. Luckily, she had enough savings stashed away to pay him, and to cover

251

everything else – but she would need to open the shop, and start making a decent living, as quickly as possible. It wouldn't matter if it wasn't quite perfect, if the sign hadn't been painted or she still had little finishing touches to add. She would aim to open – with a party – in just two weeks' time. Dammit, she would prove to Mark that she was capable of pulling this off, all by herself. The thought of untangling her life from his made her head whirl, but all that could come later. Right now, she would focus only on the shop.

Freda would help her to fill the shelves, and she needed to pick up the cookbook collection from the Gumtree ad. She would need to source *hundreds* more books, Della estimated now, as she surveyed the bare walls. Although the shoebox of pencils and paper sat beside her, Della didn't feel the urge to draw. It was all there, vivid in her mind, and somehow, just being here in her shop – even in its dismal state – was bringing her a sense of calm.

Della jumped down from the counter, turned off the light and locked up the shop. She felt different as she climbed into her car: calmer – *eerily* calm, in fact. She jabbed the key into the ignition but instead of switching it on, she called Mark's mobile, expecting it to go to voicemail.

'Dell?' he answered.

'Hi, Mark. I, er . . . look, I just need to talk to you.'

He cleared his throat. 'But we did talk, at the restaurant.'

'We did,' she said firmly, 'but not honestly, did we? At least, *you* didn't.'

A small pause. 'What d'you mean?'

Della sighed. This was making her feel very tired, and now all she wanted was to be curled up on her sofa, spending the evening formulating plans, making lists, figuring out how to open her beautiful bookshop as quickly as possible. 'I know you lied to me about there not being anyone else.'

'What?' She sensed his heartrate quickening, even down the phone. 'What are you talking about?'

'Look, I followed you, okay? After our, er, chat.'

'You *followed* me? Why?'

'Because it didn't make sense,' she said levelly. 'I mean, okay, people leave for all kinds of reasons – they're bored, unhappy, whatever – but mostly it's because there's another person.'

'But Della—'

'So I followed you,' she cut in, 'all through town and up that road, the one where Sophie's nursery used to be.'

'Um, look,' Mark said, a tremor in his voice now. It was so unlike him not to sound one hundred per cent composed.

'And I saw you going to a house,' she continued, 'and a woman came to the door, and from what I saw she's not Peter's wife.'

Silence stretched in the air between them. 'Look, Dell.' He coughed, and she thought she heard a murmuring in the background. 'I was going to tell you,' he added.

'You didn't, though. You sat there and lied right to my face.'

'No, well, I . . . didn't want to hurt you.'

'You thought that would be better? To absolutely *insist* that there was no one else?'

'No, I don't. I really don't. Christ, I've messed up and I'm sorry . . .'

'You think I'd rather you spun some line about staying with a friend, with *Peter*.' Even now, although Della's chest was tight, she felt oddly composed. She glanced out of her car at the bleary Sew 'n' Sew's sign. A whole new start, that's what she needed; she would find a sign-writer and have it freshly painted as soon as possible.

253

'I didn't know,' Mark murmured. 'I just didn't know what to do.'

Poor love, she thought wryly, watching as Len emerged from his garage across the road and lit up a cigarette on the forecourt before striding away. Health and Safety clearly hadn't reached Burley Bridge. 'So who is she?' Della asked.

'I, um . . . just someone.'

'Could you be a bit more specific?'

'I met her through, er . . . work.'

'You mean she was a patient?'

'Er, sort of, yes.'

'You examined her *feet*?' Della wasn't sounding quite so calm now.

'Well, it is my job.'

'And it's also your job to sleep with your patients, is it? I mean, can't you get struck off for that?'

'Oh, don't be ridiculous, Dell.'

'You've been having an affair and you're calling *me* ridiculous?' Her voice had risen and she tried to rein herself back. She would *not* be accused of shouting. 'How long have been seeing her?'

'A few months,' he murmured.

'And what's her name?'

A hurried clearing of his throat. 'Um . . . Polly.'

'Polly,' Della repeated witheringly. 'And what's her surname?'

'Della, why are you doing this? You don't need to know.'

'Actually, I do. I *want* to know.'

'It's Polly Fisher. Look, Dell, I'm so sorry about this . . .' Sorry, as if he had forgotten to buy tickets to a play she had wanted to see. Only they never saw plays, or films for that matter – they never did anything because, she realised now, his head had been so full of Polly Fisher, there simply hadn't been room for anything else.

Della bit her lip. 'Are you in love with her, Mark?' Only now had a tremor crept into her voice.

'Please, this isn't going to help . . .'

I'll take that as a yes then, she decided, turning the key in the ignition.

'I'm sorry,' Mark added. 'I tried not to go there, but in the end . . .' He paused. 'Well, I couldn't help myself.'

And that's what did it, more than any 'sorrys': he'd lacked the willpower to stop it. Della was familiar with the problem – the allure of tempting treats she really shouldn't help herself to: a second helping of crunchy roast potatoes or a slab of oozing Brie. But they were hardly marriage-wrecking . . . or maybe they were, and if she'd been thinner, more athletic or whatever, well, perhaps then he'd still be with her and not Polly Fisher.

It didn't matter. It was done now. Yes, she felt foolish, and telling Sophie would be terrible, but Della no longer felt she was solely to blame. ''Bye, Mark,' she muttered, finishing the call before he could say anything else and jabbing her phone into her jeans pocket.

With the engine running, she took a moment to breathe in deeply.

I couldn't help myself . . .

As if he had been swept along, out of control. Let him get on with his life then, she decided as she drove home. Back at the house, she slipped off her wedding ring and placed it in an old earring box, then hid it at the bottom of her sock drawer. Now she knew the truth, Della could get on with her life too. This was her opportunity to shake Burley Bridge out of the doldrums and send her mother's cookbooks out all over the country, if not the world.

Chapter Twenty-Seven

Although she hadn't set her alarm, Della woke just after seven on Monday morning, as she had on every single morning of her working life. Only now she had no job to go to.

She sat up with a start. Okay . . . *don't panic*. To distract herself from the acres of emptiness stretching before her she grabbed her mobile and called Liam, then rang off quickly, remembering what time it was. She needed to call Nathan, too, to ask if it would be okay for her to get in an electrician to instal somewhat kinder lighting than the terrible fluorescent strip that buzzed in the shop. Yes, it would be a good, practical thing to do. Della needed to get things moving and make proper plans, rather than sitting around drawing and fantasising about lots of cerise paint.

Even more urgently she wanted to ring Sophie, although not to tell her about her father leaving – she would need to build up to that. No, she just wanted to hear her daughter's voice. But it was far too early to call any of them. *Why didn't people get up and start work at a reasonable hour?*

Downstairs, she pottered around, searching for more cookbook collections online – no joy this time – and just after 8.30 she returned Monica's call. *Hello, there's no one to take your call right now, please leave a message after the tone . . .* Monica's voice. Della wanted to speak to her in person rather than leaving a message. She put down the phone and wondered what on earth to do next to distract herself from wanting to Google the hell out of Polly Fisher.

Up in Sophie's room, trying to ignore the fact that so many of her daughter's personal possessions were missing, Della set about removing the little blobs of Blu-tack that dotted the walls. If ever there was a clichéd empty-nester task to be undertaken, this was it: the laborious peeling away of those little pale blue blobs. The landline trilled downstairs, and she raced to answer it. 'Hello, is that Della?' A gravelly, older woman's voice.

'Yes?'

'You called earlier. It's Monica Jones.'

Della's breath caught in her throat. Kitty's *recipe* friend. 'Oh . . . yes. Thanks for ringing me back. I hope I didn't disturb you, calling you so early?'

'No, not at all,' Monica said briskly. 'I was out running, that was all. Lovely morning. So, um . . . you're Kitty's daughter?'

'Yes, that's right.' She wondered now how to break it to her that Kitty had died. Hopefully the news wouldn't upset her too much, seeing as they hadn't been in contact in years.

'And I'm in her address book?' Monica added, with a note of surprise.

A dollop of Blu-tack had softened in Della's hand. 'Erm, yes. You see, I found a memo from something called the

257

Recipe Sharing Society when I was clearing out . . .' She paused. 'I'm sorry to say, Mum passed away nearly three weeks ago now.'

'Oh, I *am* sorry.'

'Thank you. Actually, I should really try and contact everyone in her address book.'

'I'm sure you've had a lot on your plate,' Monica said, her tone softer now.

'Well, yes, there's been a lot of sorting out to do.' Della cleared her throat as an awkward silence hung between them. 'So, er, I've inherited her books, her cookbooks – she had hundreds, maybe you knew?' She paused, waiting for Monica to say something, then ploughed on: 'I've decided to open a bookshop – a cookbook shop – and when I came across the memo, I noticed your name was on the list of members present . . .'

'Really?' Monica exclaimed. 'Well, I don't know what to make of that.'

Della frowned, deciding, as she had previously suspected, that there must have been some kind of squabble amongst the group, perhaps about the best method of making a suet pudding. 'It's all very mysterious,' she agreed, 'and I was sort of intrigued, you know, about what the society actually did, what happened at the meetings and who the people were. I mean, maybe I could start something similar in the bookshop, to get people involved and using it as a meeting place. I'd like it to be more than just a shop, you see.'

'Hmmm. And you're trying to track down the members of this . . . this *society*?' Monica had reverted to a rather brittle tone now.

'Well, yes, but you're the only person listed who's in Mum's address book.' Della licked her dry lips, craving coffee now.

'What are the other names?'

'Oh, I'll just check.' Della took the phone to the hallway where *Sugarcraft Delights* sat on top of one of the packed boxes. As she extracted the memo her mobile trilled from her bedroom. It could be Mark, calling to say he'd made a dreadful mistake. Too late, of course, but if he felt the urge to grovel and cry, then she wanted to hear it.

'Er, it says "members present",' Della explained, already halfway upstairs, 'Barbara Jackson, Kitty Cartwright, Monica Jones – that's you,' she said unnecessarily, grabbing her mobile from the bed: Liam, returning her call, amazingly, at not yet 9 a.m. She let it ring out. 'Celia Fassett, Moira Wallbank, Dorothy Nixon . . .'

'Mmmm,' Monica murmured.

Della's mobile stopped ringing. 'So I'm guessing you were all friends.'

'I wouldn't say that,' Monica said dryly.

'Oh. So was there some sort of – I don't know – falling out or something? I mean, I know Mum could be volatile . . .' Della stopped. Was it disloyal to say that to a stranger? It was true, though. She pictured the violent scribblings in Kitty's address book, the cheap Biro biting into the page.

'Not really a falling out,' Monica said, 'but you know, if you're thinking of doing this – a shop, maybe a society – well, perhaps you and I should meet.'

'Oh, I'd love to,' Della exclaimed, 'if you're sure that's okay. Could I come and see you sometime?'

'That would be fine,' Monica said coolly.

Della sat on the edge of her unmade bed and rolled the Blu-tack into a perfect sphere. 'Where do you live? I'm in Heathfield but I'm sort of free most days at the moment.' How limp and pathetic that sounded.

'I'm at Kinnet Cove. Do you know it?'

'I think so. I seem to remember Mum taking us all there when we were little.'

'Well, I live at Garnet Cottage. It's very easy to find – last one along the straight road that runs alongside the shore. So, shall we say tomorrow, around this time? About eight?'

'Er, that early?' Della exclaimed.

'Well, yes, if it suits you. I like to get the day started.'

Della smiled, intrigued now by this smart, feisty-sounding woman. 'That sounds perfect,' she said, her spirits rising as she finished the call. Tomorrow she would meet one of the members of the Recipe Sharing Society and, better still, for at least five minutes Polly Fisher hadn't entered her mind.

'Della, hello! How's it going? Got the place fitted out yet? I must drive over, check what you've done, maybe even buy a book, not that I'm any sort of cook. Christ, you could just about trust me to burn jelly . . .'

Della sipped coffee with her phone pressed to her ear, waiting for Nathan to pause for breath. 'Well, you'd be very welcome, of course, and I'm sure I'll have whole books about jelly, but I'm not quite ready to open yet.'

'Well, I'm sure you'll get things going soon,' he said eagerly.

'Yes, I intend to, which is why I'm calling.'

'You want that drink!' he exclaimed. 'I thought you'd never ask.'

She laughed. 'No, it's not quite that. It's about the shop's lighting, actually. I'd like to change it, if that's okay, to make it softer, more inviting.'

'Ooh, yes, make it lovely and cosy, sort of dark and

260

intimate . . . I can picture it now.' Eugh, it sounded as if he was actually drooling.

'So, is it okay if I call in an electrician?'

'Feel free! Do whatever you like. I mean, it's a wreck – no, I mean, it has great potential, we both know that. But my uncle's not even interested in it. Think he's losing his marbles, actually – he's probably forgotten he even owns it. Short of demolishing the place, you have free rein to do whatever you like.'

Free rein. She toyed with the phrase as they finished the call, and considered the fact that, if she wanted to go out for a drink with a man, then she would be perfectly at liberty to do so. She could do whatever she wanted now. While she would never have chosen this – to be lied to and left – at least now she could please herself. But still, she wanted to Google Polly Fisher, and now the spectre of Polly's feet had snuck back into her mind: pretty and petite, devoid of calluses, feet of such exquisite beauty they could feature in adverts for beaded flip-flops, or the latest colour for toenails.

She felt herself being drawn, as if by a powerful magnetic force, to her laptop for Googling purposes, and to stop herself she returned Liam's call. 'So,' she said brightly, 'I was just wondering, have you had any thoughts?'

'Oh, yeah . . . I think it's going to be fine,' he replied vaguely.

Della frowned. 'Really? You mean taking the shelves out of Mum's cottage, fitting them into the shop, all that?'

'Yeah, yeah. I think it's all fine.'

This worried her slightly. She knew what *fine* meant, when it came from the mouth of a teenager. Sophie had done 'fine' in her maths GCSE (in fact, she had failed spectacularly), and she'd felt 'fine' when she'd tottered in from Evie's eighteenth and thrown up all over her bedroom carpet, creating an orangey stain that had never completely gone away. 'So, um . . . d'you have a plan?' Della was conscious of tiptoeing around Liam, as if he might burst into tears if too many demands were made on him.

'Yeah, I'll drop it off for you.' Her heart sank. Would that mean in a few days, or actually – more realistically – never? 'I'll come over today,' he added, 'unless you're too busy?'

'Oh, no,' she said quickly, 'I'm not busy at all.'

While she waited for Liam, she called Irene Bagshott – pusher of unwanted chicken and leek pies – at her Burley Bridge general store and asked for her electrician brother's number. 'Sounds simple enough, Della,' Douglas said when she called him. 'I'm happy to come and take a look.' He paused. 'What a character she was, your mum. I remember her chasing me out of your garden when my football went in. Oh, and we hit her with a snowball. Jeez, it was Kevin Thornbank who threw it but your mum was convinced it was me . . .'

'Yes, ha-ha,' Della laughed dryly, thinking, *Okay, let's just get on with it, please*. 'Bit scary, if you don't mind me saying!' No, she didn't mind him saying. 'Great. So, see you later, then? About four-ish okay? Can't wait to see what you're planning to do to your shop.'

Her shop. The words still gave her a little flurry of joy. Plus, with all this phoning and sorting things out she had temporarily lost interest in Polly's feet. She would find out, in good time, who she was and what she was all about – but now she was calmer, having ticked all those tasks off her list, she allowed herself to phone Freda, who insisted on coming over right away.

'This happened yesterday?' she exclaimed as Della let

262

her in. 'You should have called, come round . . . why didn't you *phone* me?' She held her friend in a tight hug.

'I couldn't. I just had to be by myself.' They stepped into the kitchen where Della poured her a coffee and they sat, with Freda clearly stunned, opposite each other at the kitchen table.

'Oh, Dell, what the hell is he thinking? I could kill him! Did you suspect anything at all?'

'No, not a thing. I mean, when he said he wanted to leave, of course I asked him, it was the first thing I thought — but until then . . .' She shrugged. 'I honestly didn't think he ever would. I mean, there's no reason why not, I suppose, he's never been short of female attention . . .'

'So who is she?'

Della shrugged. 'Polly Fisher. A patient, apparently.'

'A patient? Is that even ethical? I'm sure that's not supposed to go on. Could you report him or something?'

'*Report* him? It's not actually a crime, is it? Lying, cheating, pretending to head off to golf every Saturday morning . . . I mean, it's not great. But it's not against the law either . . .'

'No, I mean the Board of Podiatrists or whoever they are, for getting involved with someone when he's meant to be in a position of trust.'

'That sounds as if he took advantage of her. She didn't look terribly exploited when she virtually dragged him inside her front door . . .'

'Yes, but it's still not right, is it? Doesn't he belong to some kind of regulatory body?'

Regulatory body. Della thought of Polly Fisher standing there on her doorstep in her neat grey shift dress, late-thirties maybe, slim legs, tiny waist, red hair rippling over her shoulders. 'It doesn't really matter how they met. I don't care. Well, I do, of course I do – I mean, we're going to have to tell Sophie when she's just started college, ruin the whole thing for her . . .'

'Oh, Dell. How d'you think she'll take it?'

'Honestly, I have no idea.'

They fell into silence for a few moments. 'Have you Googled her?' Freda ventured.

'I've resisted so far.' Della looked at her friend, and the urge to know all about Polly Fisher welled up inside her again. 'Just a minute,' she murmured, fetching her laptop. She pulled up a chair so she and Freda could pore over her findings together.

Polly Fisher . . . well, of course there were thousands. She tried Googling Polly Fisher Heathfield; nothing of note there. 'Hang on,' she murmured, her fingers clattering over the keys.

'What are you looking for?'

'That professional body thing. You're right, he has crossed some kind of professional line . . . Look, it's the ICP, I think that's who Mark belongs to. The Institute of Chiropodists and Podiatrists.'

Della peered at the screen. Surely something called an Institute wouldn't take kindly to one of its members having an affair with a patient. They had a code of ethics, she noted, but it was mostly about members being 'allowed to treat a patient's foot, and related structures, by surgical or mechanical means'.

'There's nothing about a podiatrist not being allowed to fall in love with a patent and totally screw up everything,' Della remarked. She flinched at the sound of a knock on the front door. 'That must be Liam. I'd forgotten he was coming over. He's going to fit out the shop for me . . .'

'Oh, that's great. And you're right, you know. All this Googling, it's not going to help.' Another gentle knock. Della smoothed back her tangled hair and hurried to let him in.

Liam shambled into the kitchen and mumbled hello to Freda. 'So, er,' he started without even sitting down, 'here's what I thought.' As if handing in homework he wasn't too sure about, he delved into his pocket and thrust a piece of lined A4 paper at Della.

She stared down at the plan he'd drawn, all marked out immaculately with measurements. He had even added a couple of armchairs. 'This is fantastic, Liam,' she exclaimed. 'It looks so . . .' She broke off and laughed. 'So orderly!'

'Yeah, well, I just thought, y'know, I'd show you what I could do.'

She looked back at his plan. On the other side of the paper he had detailed the cost of materials – which were negligible, as virtually everything would be recycled from Rosemary Cottage – and an estimate of man hours required. His handwriting was tiny and astoundingly neat.

'I, er, tried to keep the costs down,' he said, a little defensively.

'No, no, the quote's fine,' Della said quickly. 'It's really reasonable, in fact.' She glanced again at the plan. 'I like it that you put those armchairs there. That's a nice touch.'

'Yeah, well, drawing's not really my thing . . .' He broke off and shrugged. 'But I thought, well, people will want to sit about and read and that. I mean, I assume it's going to be that sort of place.'

She grinned. 'It'll be exactly that sort of place . . . so, you're sure you can do this?'

'Oh, yeah,' he said, brightening. 'Dad's fine with it too.'

'Really? I'd hate this to cause any trouble between you.'

'Nah, he said he's glad I'm working, getting out from under his feet.' Liam sniggered awkwardly. 'And he's working with a couple of mates for the next couple of weeks so I can even borrow his van.'

'Oh . . . that's great!' Della hadn't considered the transport aspect, and the thought of this lanky nineteen year-old in charge of a vehicle seemed quite alarming.

'I *can* drive you know,' he added, catching her expression. 'I passed my test two years ago.'

'Oh, yes, I'm sure you can . . . so when do you think you could start?'

'Tomorrow? Would that be okay?'

'Yes, of course, that would be fantastic!'

He grinned. 'D'you have a spare set of keys for your mum's house?'

'Yes, I do.' Della rummaged through the kitchen drawer and handed a keyring to Liam.

'Great. So, I reckon I should be finished by the end of the week.'

'Liam, that's so brilliant, thank you.'

He shrugged, flushing pink, and stared down at his trainers. 'It'll be good, I think. Y'know, I've never done a bookshop before.'

She caught Freda's eye and smiled. 'That's okay, Liam,' she said, resisting the urge to hug him, 'neither have I.'

Chapter Twenty-Eight

At 6.45 a.m. – far too early, but Monica struck her as someone who wouldn't appreciate lateness – Della set off for Kinnet Cove. Her stomach growled hollowly as she sped along the motorway. Apart from not having had breakfast, she hadn't eaten last night either. After Liam – then Freda – had left, she had nipped over to Burley Bridge to talk electricals with Douglas Bagshott. When she'd come home, she had been unable to face cooking anything for herself.

Having refuelled on a Danish and coffee at a service station, Della rejoined the motorway, a little nervous now. *It's okay,* she reassured herself. *This is no big deal at all. Monica's just one of Mum's friends from way back.* She felt the need to remind herself why she was heading for the coast on this pink-skied Tuesday morning instead of tackling the enormous task of sorting the cookbooks into categories. It just felt important to meet Monica and find out what the Recipe Sharing Society had been all about. Once that was done, she would crack on with ordering her cash register and buying her brushes and paint, and pull together a PR plan for her grand opening party as Charlotte had urged to do: writing a press release and mailing it to local papers and radio stations. She would then commence the mind-boggling task of pricing the books, and snap on a pair of Marigolds and scrub the place down – not to mention sprucing up Rosemary Cottage in preparation for the estate agent's valuation. Keep busy, busy, busy: that seemed to be the way in which she would avoid obsessing over Polly Fisher, or reporting her husband to the ICP.

Kinnet Cove was in view now, a string of whitewashed cottages dotted sparsely along the straight, narrow road that followed the coast. The sea was a glittering silver, dotted with bobbing dinghies and small fishing boats, the sky a wash of pale blue still daubed with pink. Della slowed down as she entered the village and passed the cottages, mostly holiday lets by the look of it, all facing the sea. There was a small general store, not even open yet, another shop selling wetsuits, and a tearoom with lacy net curtains, which looked as if they were long overdue a boil wash. There wasn't a single person in sight.

They *had* been here, Della remembered now: Kitty and the three children. As their father hadn't come, Kitty had had to drive. She had never seemed entirely comfortable behind the wheel, which might have explained her ill humour that day. She had seemed distracted, Della recalled now, as if somehow resenting the fact that she had found herself in a nondescript fishing village, even though it must have been her idea to come. Della vaguely recalled her mother setting off 'to find ice creams' and returning hours later, claiming that she'd got lost. Perhaps she had snuck off to see her old friend Monica, and hadn't wanted three damp, sandy children tagging along and spoiling her fun.

Della was aware of her arrival being noted as she pulled up outside Garnet Cottage. She assessed the place as she climbed out of her car: a well-kept house painted a pale buttermilk shade, its tidy front garden filled with neatly trimmed shrubs and ceramic pots. The short path to the faded green front door was made from sea-worn pebbles and broken shells. She pressed the bell, and the door was swiftly opened by a woman so tall and elegant – all cheekbones and piercing bright blue eyes – that Della was momentarily lost for words.

'Della, hello, do come in.'

'Thank you. It's good to meet you, Monica.' Della followed her into a small hall, its walls covered with so many framed paintings – no, not paintings but pieces of printed fabrics – that there were hardly any gaps in between. 'Let's sit in here and have some tea,' Monica added, padding bare-foot into the living room overlooking the sea. 'Do make yourself comfortable. I won't be a minute.'

'Thank you,' Della said, perching on a faded rust-coloured corduroy-covered couch as Monica swept out of the room. Could this vital, youthful-looking woman really be one of Kitty's friends from their recipe-sharing days? Della scanned the crammed bookshelves and the knick-knacks cluttering the carved wooden mantelpiece.

Monica reappeared with a tarnished metal tray bearing a mishmash of china, plus slices of cake. Her long, silvery hair was tied back in a ponytail, and she wore black leggings and some sort of sports top with a voluminous flecked grey cardigan thrown on top. A fisherman's cardi, Della decided, but on Monica's lithe frame it looked sort of bohemian, thrown on to warm herself after a run. Although Della supposed she was well into her sixties, it was tricky to pinpoint her age. She poured strong, dark tea into dainty flower-patterned cups and arranged herself in an armchair with her small feet tucked under her.

'So, Della,' she started, 'you found that memo. That must have been quite . . . a surprise.'

Della lifted a cup from the tray. 'It was, yes, because Mum had never mentioned it. But I suppose there's no reason why she should have, really. I mean, I was only a little girl then and she probably got up to all sorts of things that I was never aware of.'

A wry smile crossed Monica's fine-boned face. 'You haven't been able to contact anyone else from the list?'

'No, although I've only had a look through her address book. I haven't done any proper hunting around yet. I suppose I could Google the names, maybe try and arrange some kind of reunion . . .' Della smiled, and Monica laughed tightly.

'Why does it interest you, this society?'

Della sipped her tea, taken aback by the question. Monica was regarding her intently, her face tilted slightly upwards, her blue eyes fixed directly on Della's. 'Well, as I mentioned on the phone, I'm opening a bookshop. Mum's cookbooks sparked the whole idea really. I mean, I couldn't keep them in the house. There are nearly a thousand, they were driving everyone mad . . .'

'Everyone?'

'Well, my daughter Sophie wasn't too sure at first but she's off doing her own thing now. She'd just started at art college.'

'Really?' Monica's eyes gleamed with interest, and Della glanced around the living room which, like the hallway, was entirely decorated with framed fabrics in exuberant prints, some embroidered, others embellished

270

with wispy feathers and sparking beads. The effect was quite stunning.

'She's a very talented painter,' Della explained. 'But really, it was my husband who objected to the books.'

'Ah, I see.'

'We've just split up,' she added.

'I'm very sorry to hear that.' Monica leaned forward, her aloof expression softened by concern now.

'Well, I'm fine,' Della said briskly. 'Or at least, I will be. You know how it is. Well, you probably don't . . .'

'I'm sure it's been very difficult, Della.'

She nodded. 'Yes, it has, and I probably still don't know what to make of it. I mean, it hasn't really had time to sink in, you know? I'm not sure it ever will. So right now, I'm trying to focus on getting the shop together. You see, I've just left my job – I worked in Heathfield Castle gift shop – so I need to get things up and running as quickly as possible . . .' She stopped and delved into her bag for the memo, which she handed to Monica. 'This is what I found. Look, there's your name.'

Monica reached to the coffee table for a pair of tortoise-shell spectacles and slipped them on. Della watched as she scanned the list of names, then turned the memo over and read the hand-written note on the back. 'I don't know what that means,' Della said, with an awkward laugh.

'"Yours affectionately, R."'

'Yes. D'you have any idea who that could be?'

Monica placed the memo on the table between them and drank her tea. 'Well, I think that was probably Rafael.'

'Rafael? Who was that?'

She caught Monica glancing distractedly out of the window and followed her gaze to the expanse of silvery sea. She had done this all wrong, Della realised. Obviously, the Recipe Sharing Society was a delicate matter; she should have built up to it and chosen her moment with care, the way she planned to when she drove over to Leeds to take Sophie to lunch and tell her that her parents weren't together anymore. She should have taken time to get to know Monica first, asking her about the beautiful textiles in reds and pinks and golds that filled this welcoming cottage; it felt so different to Kitty's place, which had faded as the years had rolled by. Now, she could sense that Monica wanted her to go.

'I'm sorry,' Della ventured. 'I don't mean to pry. If it's something personal between you and Mum, and you really don't want to go into it . . . I mean, the first time I called, the man who answered said you weren't here.'

Monica cleared her throat. 'It's very difficult to explain, Della.'

She inhaled deeply. 'If you want to say something about Mum that's not exactly – well, not especially *complimentary*, then that's okay. I'm sort of used to it. I had all that at her funeral tea, you know. I mean, the locals, the people who'd known her for decades – they were affectionate enough. But there was also lots of, "Oh, wasn't she a character? Didn't like to get on Kitty's bad side!"' Della was babbling now, trying to fill the awkward silence.

'Yes, I do remember what Kitty was like.'

Della drained her cup and placed it back on the tray. 'Monica . . . I think I'll just go now. It was good of you to see me and I'm sorry if, well . . .' She picked up the memo and slipped it back into her bag. 'If this is stirring up something unpleasant for you.'

'No, no, it's fine,' she insisted as Della got up to leave. It wasn't fine, though. Monica made no move to persuade her visitor to stay.

'I'll see you out then,' she said coolly.

'Thank you again,' Della said. She felt Monica's eyes fixed on her from the doorway as she crunched her way back along the shell-and-pebble path and climbed into her car. She waved briefly and Monica flapped a hand in response, then disappeared back into the house. As Della turned the ignition key she wondered why she had agreed to see her in the first place.

She indicated, and as she started to pull away something caught her eye. Monica had reappeared and was waving – properly waving now – from her front door. Della stopped the car. And now Monica – no longer barefoot but in trainers – was striding along the path towards her. Phone, purse, bag? Della wondered what it was she'd forgotten. Hardly surprising she'd left something behind; she'd felt so *tense* in there.

'Della?' Monica bent at the driver's side window. Della turned off the ignition and opened the door.

'Is everything okay?'

'Yes, it's fine . . . well, actually, no, it's not. I've dragged you all the way here and been terribly rude and I'm *so* sorry.'

Della studied her face, the cheekbones high and pronounced, the eyes elongated and full of intelligence. 'You weren't rude, Monica, but I felt that perhaps you didn't want to rake over the past.'

She shook her head firmly. 'Please, park the car again and come back inside with me. No, in fact, it's a beautiful day – could we go for a walk, do you think? Would you like that? There are a few things I need to explain.'

As they set off along the roadside, Della decided just to listen this time, at least until it felt okay to ask a question.

She glanced at Monica, who was striding along at quite a pace, her legs long and slender, her ponytail flapping in the light breeze. 'It wasn't what I expected,' she ventured, 'seeing you.'

Della didn't know what to make of this. 'What did you expect?' *And who is – or was – Rafael?* she wanted to ask. She focused instead on the waves lapping at the pebbly beach to their right.

'It's probably easier to explain,' said Monica, a little hesitant now, 'if I tell you about your mother and me.'

'I'd really like that,' Della said.

'Well, you know Kitty was a seamstress? We both were.'

'Yes, I knew Mum was. She made all our clothes when we were little. Of course we would have preferred them to be bought from C&A or Miss Selfridge, like all the other kids' clothes.' She smiled at the memory and glanced at Monica. 'All we wanted were our clothes to have shop labels in. But we didn't dare say, of course.'

'No, I can imagine.' Monica chuckled, and Della started to relax. 'When we first started out, your mother and I worked for a theatre company. Did you know that too?'

'I didn't,' Della admitted. 'Mum never seemed particularly keen to talk about those days.'

'Well, we'd both have been nineteen or twenty. We did all the costumes, dressed the sets, took care of repairs and alterations – it was a lovely time.' Monica smiled.

'Had she met my dad then?' Della asked.

'Er, they were sort of seeing each other, you know. Kitty was a very popular girl in those days.' Della looked at Monica, thinking, *Bet you were too.* There was something ageless about Monica, she decided: rangy and shimmering with life. So she was Kitty's age – mid-seventies —yet had already been for a run that morning, and was now walking at a purposeful pace as if she could keep going all day. Despite the faded running top and leggings and that ratty old cardi, she exuded more glamour and style than any of the baby-complexioned models in Roxanne's magazine.

'We were close friends at that time,' Monica went on. 'Very close. Like sisters, really.'

'It seems such a shame you lost touch,' Della ventured. 'What happened after the theatre company?'

'Oh, I retrained as a teacher and taught art for many years, but then I wanted more time to do my own thing so I started on my textiles, took some classes, started to get the occasional commission . . .'

What happened with you and Mum? Della had meant, but now she was picturing the blaze of beautiful framed fabrics in Monica's cottage. 'They're lovely, the ones I saw in your house. So vibrant. Do you sell them?'

'Oh, I dabble a little,' Monica said, a trace of amusement in her voice. Della wondered how to swerve the conversation back to Kitty – or, more specifically, Kitty and Rafael. Cautious after getting off to a shaky start, she decided to proceed with care.

'So, er . . . you were still in touch with Mum when she got married?'

'Yes, I was one of the witnesses at her wedding.'

'Oh, that's you, in the photo! Outside the register office, I mean. It's the only picture I've ever seen of my parents' wedding.' *And who was the man you were with?* she wanted to ask, but Monica cut in.

'Maybe I shouldn't tell you this, but Kitty was already pregnant then with her first child.'

'With Jeff? Are you sure?'

'I'm *absolutely* sure.'

Della inhaled the sharp, salty air. 'I never knew that. I

suppose I could have worked it out, if I'd known their wedding date – but then, Mum was always pretty vague about it and it didn't seem important to know.' Della paused. 'That was quite scandalous in those days, wasn't it? A pregnant bride, I mean?'

'Not for us,' said Monica quickly. 'Not amongst the friends we associated with, the theatre people. It didn't matter a bit.'

'But they *did* get married,' Della pointed out.

'Yes, rather hurriedly, just a tiny service at Wood Green Register office, only two guests.'

'You and . . .'

'Me and Rafael, yes.'

Della gave her a quick look. Rafael – Mr-yours-affectionately-R – had been at her parents' wedding, as a witness presumably. Did that mean he had been Monica's partner back then? She strode on briskly, seeming not to have noticed that his name had slipped out. 'It was William who wanted to get married,' she added.

'To make an honest woman out of Kitty?'

Monica smoothed back her ponytail. 'Yes, something like that.'

'Well, Dad was pretty traditional,' Della remarked. 'But surely she must have wanted to marry him too? You know how strong-minded she was. I don't think I ever saw Mum doing something she didn't want to do.'

They walked in silence for a few moments, following the path away from the beach now and into the gently undulating hills behind the village. Della had no idea where they were going and it didn't feel important to know. 'Kitty did plenty of things she didn't want to do,' Monica murmured.

Della looked at her. 'D'you mean . . . marrying my

276

dad?' She pictured her mother in that photograph, standing close to William but with her attention clearly elsewhere.

'It was only because of the baby, Della.'

She nodded, wondering now if Kitty had resented that ceremony, even the baby growing inside her, and felt a twinge of pity for Jeff. 'You know, you can't tell Mum's pregnant in that picture. I assume it was quite early on . . .'

'Oh, she was showing by then, but her dress was made by an excellent dressmaker.' Monica smiled, and the atmosphere seemed to lighten.

'*You* made Mum's wedding dress?'

'Well, yes. It wasn't a wedding dress as such. Kitty hadn't wanted that.'

'Yes, I can picture it. White lace, a simple shift shape. I always wondered what happened to it.' Della paused and looked at Monica. 'Er, it was William's baby, wasn't it? I mean, William is Jeff's dad?'

'Yes, of course he is, darling!'

Darling. This felt as if they had moved on somehow, and now Della thought: To hell with it. She needed to know and, as she might never see Monica again, she might as well ask the question that was burning inside her. 'Monica, can I just ask . . .' She looked around at the sweeping hills and Kinnet Cove behind them, now bathed in bright morning sunshine. 'Even though Mum was pregnant then, was she really in love with someone else?' *And of course I mean Rafael, but I can't bring myself to say it . . .*

Monica looked at her as they stopped at a bench, and indicated for Della to sit beside her. 'I hope it's all right to tell you all of this. I know it's probably not what you came here for, but it's part of it all. I worry that you might find it rather shocking.'

277

Della looked past Monica at the hills dotted with farm-houses and swathes of dark forest. She wasn't a naturally shockable person, and now, a mere two days since she had seen her husband fall into another woman's arms, she wasn't sure that anything would ever shock her again. 'I'd rather you just told me everything . . . so, how d'you think my dad felt about all of that?'

She paused. 'Oh, William was utterly devoted to your mother, you know.'

'But . . . he left her, Monica. He left her for Jane, a woman he worked with, when I was about ten years old.'

Monica poked at the earth with the toe of her trainer. 'Maybe he'd had enough. You could hardly blame him, I suppose.'

'Enough of what?'

'Enough of Kitty being in love with Rafael.'

Della frowned. Was that why her father had run off with 'that woman', as she was forever known in Rosemary Cottage? The two women sat side by side, the sun warming their faces as the cool morning opened up into a beautiful autumn day. 'I hope you don't mind my asking,' Della said hesitantly, 'you and Rafael . . . were you together back then?'

'Oh, yes, we still are really.'

Della blinked at her. 'Is he your husband?' She held her breath, relaxing again as Monica chuckled and shook her head.

'No, dear, I've never have one of those. We're very fond of each other but I can't live with him. I tried it . . . ugh!' She shuddered dramatically. 'Couldn't be doing with him being around, hovering about, insisting on reading things to me from the newspaper . . .' It sounded lovely, Della thought. 'So we are sort of together . . . but not.' Monica's face softened and, almost as if she could read the question hovering on Della's lips – 'So, Kitty and Rafael were having an affair?' – answered it for her.

'You see the Recipe Sharing Society was an excuse your mother conjured up. Something to go to, you see, so she could be with him. It was easier for Raff – we each did our own thing, he had all the space and freedom he could have wished for, and so did I.' Della nodded, willing her to go on. 'But your mother . . . well, especially after the baby arrived – Kitty needed an alibi.'

Della focused ahead on the scattering of creamy stone cottages dotted sparingly around the hills. A plume of smoke rose slowly from a chimney, and the soft rolling Yorkshire landscape was bathed in bright autumn light. 'A kind of decoy activity,' she murmured. *Like Mark and his golf.* Something to go to, to make the affair possible – and with Kitty's collection of cookbooks it would have seemed quite plausible. *Just popping out to a Recipe Sharing Society Meeting, darling. I'll cook you something nice when I get home . . .*

'Very perceptive, Della,' Monica said with a wry smile. 'That's exactly what it was. Now, you see that old wrecked-looking farmhouse down in the valley there? The one with the red roof, looks like a gust of wind could blow the place down?'

Della peered in the direction Monica was pointing. 'Yes, I see it.'

'That's where Raff lives.'

'Really?' she exclaimed. 'Can we visit him?' She leaped up from the bench like an eager child.

'Not today, I'm afraid. He's away in Spain – that's where he's from. Grew up in Valencia, still has cousins there. He's away a few more days.'

'Another time then? I'd really love to meet him.' Della steeled herself for a brisk response and wondered again whether she had overstepped the mark.

'Oh, yes, you should do that,' Monica said. 'I think it's *very* important that you two meet.'

Chapter Twenty-Nine

On those rare coastal outings of her childhood, Della had loved to collect things: smooth pebbles, fragile shells, softly worn driftwood. She would insist on taking them home and arranging them on her bedroom shelf, a miniature museum of treasures. And now, as she and Monica strolled along the water's edge, it was facts she was gathering, each more precious to her than any cormorant's feather or nugget of sea glass. Rafael Avina, she learned, was a renowned landscape and portrait artist, having come over to London in the 1950s to study fine art at the Royal College of Art. He and Monica had met in some shady basement club in Soho; she had wanted to go to art college too: 'But my parents thought it was a ridiculous notion,' she explained. 'No money in it, they said. No prospects.'

'Sounds familiar,' Della remarked. 'Sophie's had all that from her uncle Jeff.'

'Well, I'm glad she didn't listen,' Monica said firmly.

'Oh, Sophie knows her own mind,' Della said, thinking, *And thank goodness for that*. The waves lapped around Monica's feet. She didn't seem remotely concerned about getting her trainers wet, or that the bottoms of her leggings were being splashed with spray. She picked up a shell – pearly pink, like a baby's ear – and thrust it into her cardigan pocket. 'You know, I should have guessed the Recipe Sharing Society wasn't real,' Della ventured. 'Mum wasn't a joining in kind of person. Occasionally she'd go along to something in the village – an embroidery group or a patchwork club – and come back muttering that it wasn't her thing, and she wouldn't be going again.'

Monica smirked. 'That hardly surprises me.'

'So . . . the other names on the memo. Who were they?'

'I've never heard of any of them. Just made up, probably.'

'Really?' Della shook her head in disbelief. 'All that effort to cover her tracks.'

'Well, she only typed out a memo, Della, and probably left it lying around for William to see. Kitty was a pretty nifty typist.'

Della nodded and wondered how to phrase the next question. 'So, um, Kitty and Rafael . . .' She glanced at Monica, gauging her expression. 'Was it, you know, I mean . . .'

'Look, Della,' she said firmly, 'I honestly think – and I'm not just saying this, I do know the man inside out – that it was infatuation on his part. Kitty was . . . a very difficult woman to reach. Men were drawn to her. It was a power thing, I think – she bored easily and enjoyed the attention.' Della nodded, unsure of how to respond. 'And what about Kitty and William? What were they like together?'

Monica shrugged. 'They just sort of . . . co-existed really.'

'And you and Mum? I guess it was impossible to be friends when all that was happening . . .'

'It . . . *became* more difficult,' she said hesitantly.

'I can imagine.' And now Mark and Polly Fisher crept into Della's mind; that ridiculous house, the menagerie of

282

hedgehogs, and how on earth she was going to break the news to Sophie. 'D'you have children, Monica?' she ventured.

'No, it wasn't to be,' she said blithely. 'I'd have liked them, and so, I think, would Rafael. But it didn't happen and, you know, maybe it was for the best.' As they approached Kinnet Cove, Monica turned to Della and smiled. 'We've both had plenty of space to do our own thing, so we've been very lucky, you know. I have never felt trapped or limited in any way, and neither has he. It seems churlish not to appreciate that.'

'Sounds ideal,' Della said, and it did: take away the Kitty affair and it was pretty much the perfect set-up.

'I'm sorry about the first time you called,' Monica added.

Della frowned. 'Was that Rafael who answered the phone?'

'Yes, it was, and I think it – well, you calling out of the blue . . . it had been a long time since he'd heard anything about Kitty, you know. It shook him up a little.'

'Did it shake you up too? Me calling, I mean?'

'No, Della. That's why I called you back when he wasn't there.' Monica looked at her. 'Do you want to know how I really felt about Rafael and Kitty?'

Della winced. 'I'm sorry, it feels so intrusive. It's just – Mark, my husband, is with someone else now. Sounds like it's been going on secretly for months. Actually, I have no idea but I do know that things haven't been right between him and me for a very long time.' Della's vision blurred and she quickly cleared her throat.

'It *is* hard, darling. When it happens that way, I mean – all the lies and deceit. But, you see, it wasn't like that for us.' Della stared at her, uncomprehending. 'Raff was a silly fool, the way it all panned out,' she added. 'Bit of a mess, really. But no, I wasn't jealous, if that's what you mean.'

Della pictured Mark, striding jauntily with a bundle of

283

Sunday papers towards Polly Fisher's house. 'I find that incredible,' she muttered. 'I hope you don't mind me saying, but I just do. I couldn't have handled that at all.'

'It's amazing what you *can* handle, when it comes to it.'

'You're stronger than I am, then.'

'Oh, no, I wouldn't say that. It seems to me that you have an awful lot of strength, Della.' Monica smiled kindly. 'But Raff and I – well, we were very young, you know. And I have to tell you, I was no angel either.'

As she drove back to Heathfield, Della chastised herself for not finding out more. Yet she couldn't have asked; at least, not on their first meeting. That really would have been overstepping the mark. Nevertheless, she sensed that some connection had been made today. Somehow, Della knew she would see Monica again, and she wanted to, very much. It was images of Monica's arty, quirky cottage that filled her mind as she drove home to Heathfield, and already the sense of dread she had felt at stepping into her empty house was beginning to recede.

Della let herself in, settled at the kitchen table with a plate of toast and opened her laptop. The compulsion to Google was a terrible thing, luring her like a slab of pungent Cheddar in the fridge or, her particular weak spot, cold roast potatoes: 'Still *at* those?' Mark had remarked once, finding her tucking into the remains of a roast. She had guiltily swallowed down the last spud, all pleasure gone. In fact, since Mark's abrupt departure her clothes had felt looser. Although she was tempted to think it was weight loss through grief, she had simply been too busy for idle snacking.

Della had sat down with the intention of finding out

at least *some* nuggets of info about Polly Fisher – what she did for a living, whether she was on any committees, perhaps the Hedgehog Preservation Society if there was such a thing. However, now she found herself typing in Monica Jones's name instead. There she was, presiding over a beautifully designed website. There was a small picture of her, all arresting blue eyes and sharp cheekbones and self-assured smile. She was wearing a baggy Aran sweater and jeans, arms folded, silver hair blowing in the breeze. It all looked incredibly professional and, although she knew she shouldn't think that way, Della couldn't help feeling surprised that a woman of her generation had a website like this when Val, her mother-in-law, nurtured a deep fear of answerphones, and Kitty had refused point blank to acquaint herself with her mobile phone.

Della clicked on the *Recent Projects* page and scrolled through the images. Again, it all looked incredibly professional. While the framed textiles in Garnet Cottage were lovely, they clearly represented just a tiny part of what Monica could do. Here were sumptuous designs created for upmarket department stores: wallpapers, upholstery fabrics, stationery ranges for leading hotels. Monica's designs featured on cushions, bed linen and even a range of ceramic kitchenware; almost anything that could be patterned, she had adorned in the most beautiful way. There were big, blowsy poppies, ladies dancing with umbrellas, and all kinds of other motifs linked by her bold use of colour: oranges, reds, the tones of a butterfly's wing. She was a one-person design business – and Della had rather patronisingly asked her 'Do you sell them?' as if she might occasionally set up a stall at coffee mornings.

She switched her attention to Rafael Avina, who wasn't quite as easy to find, clearly not being of the slick website

Well, that was wrong, Della decided: Monica couldn't abide him hanging around her all day long, insisting on reading to her from the newspaper . . .

There was more information, about his early years as a teacher, his numerous exhibitions and accolades, and a trust he had set up to fund art classes in underprivileged districts of Valencia – but it could have in Mandarin for all it was sinking in. Della's gaze kept being dragged back to the picture of a young man, startlingly handsome, with a sweep of black hair, a strong chin with pronounced dimple, and rather solemn eyes.

In the picture he looked to be in his early twenties, so would already have left his family in Spain to pursue his dream of studying art in London. At that age Della had merely flounced out of the tawdry offices of Belling & Doyle. Yet they were so clearly linked, she felt her whole world shift as she studied his face: the same dark eyes and strong nose. Same colouring. All at once, everything she thought she knew was thrown up into the air, yet seemed to make perfect sense. Everything seemed to freeze inside Della – her breath, her heart – as she stared at the striking young man gazing back at her.

Chapter Thirty

Della wouldn't freak out or jump to conclusions because whatever the truth was – whatever her genetic make-up – it was far too huge and unwieldy a matter to deal with now. She couldn't begin to consider the implications: not with the shop to set up and, more pressingly, deciding how to tell Sophie that her father had left. It felt like the wrong time, with her daughter barely having settled into her student life – yet Della knew that, if she happened to find out from someone else, Sophie would be livid about being kept in the dark.

She shuddered at the idea of dropping this terrible announcement on her, and needed input on how to handle it, just as she had needed input when Sophie had been briefly bullied in her last year of primary school ('What d'you think we should do, Mark?' 'Tell her to thump them!' was his considered advice). And now, on a rather wet Wednesday morning, Della had managed to force her way through Mark's security wall, getting past Brenda, his steely secretary, in order to gain similarly helpful advice on what she should say. 'I'll leave it up to you,' he murmured.

288

'Mark, this is a pretty big deal, you know. We're not talking about what sort of birthday cake she should have or whether we do party bags this year.'

'No, I know that,' he muttered.

'I really wish we could do this together, show her that we're still her parents.'

'Of course we're still her parents!'

'I mean, that we're still capable of being in a room together and, you know, being *civil* . . .'

'I'd rather see her on my own,' Mark said wearily. 'I just think it'll be . . . less dramatic.' Della was pacing the living room, clutching the phone, wondering if it was possible for blood to actually boil. 'Look, I'm sorry,' he added, 'but I have a patient due in four minutes.'

'They can wait, can't they? Or is their foot likely to fall off?'

'Don't be like this,' he said, in an infuriatingly calm tone that make Della want to send a hail of golf balls through the window of his consulting room.

'I'm not being like anything. I just think, like I said before, that we should tell her together, put on a united front.'

'Yes, but . . .' *We're not united,* was what he wanted to say, before mumbling a curt goodbye. And so Della was left to prepare herself for the terrible task of calling Sophie, and sounding all perky and bright, and just happening to mention that she was thinking of popping over to Leeds tomorrow, and did Sophie fancy a spot of lunch?

The very thought of it made her feel quite sick. Unable to settle to anything, Della started to gather up Mark's possessions: the chess set, the toiletries he'd left in the bathroom, the architectural books, their pages virtually

289

untouched by human hand – all the pieces of him she no longer wanted in her line of vision every time she entered a room. What about the golf clubs, still propped up in their leather bag in the hall? The very sight of them infuriated her so much, she'd have to stash them away under the stairs until she was less inclined to take a hacksaw to them. Meanwhile, she dumped all of his smaller items in a box and re-read the short profile about Rafael Avina on her laptop until she could have recited it by heart. When her eyes ached from staring at the screen she unpacked all the cookbooks from their boxes and set about categorising them, until she was entirely surrounded by teetering piles.

It was growing dark by the time she had lightly pencilled prices on the inside jackets of around 200 books. She had downed half a bottle of wine – not her smartest move, her pricing system would be all askew. At 10.37 p.m., urgently needing to hear a human voice that was less hostile than Mark's, she found herself calling her sister.

'Dell? Everything okay?' Roxanne sounded surprised – but pleased – to hear from her.

'Erm, I just wanted a chat really. Sorry it's so late.'

'No, it's not. I've just got in actually. Had a bit of a rubbish evening but . . . oh, I won't go into that.'

'A date?'

'Yes, sort of.'

'Oh, tell me how it went.' She wanted to hear all about it now. Roxanne rarely revealed anything significant about her love life – it seemed to ricochet between passion-filled highs and devastating lows – and at least hearing about someone else's woes would stop Della from forensically examining Rafael's face, or churning over how to break the news about Polly Fisher to Sophie.

'I've had better nights,' Roxanne said with a dry laugh. 'Anyway, what's happening with you? All ready to go with the shop?'

'I, er . . . not really, but getting there. I just wanted to tell you something.'

She could sense Roxanne's puzzlement radiating all the way from her tiny flat in Islington. 'What is it?'

'Mark's gone, Rox.'

'You mean . . . oh, God!'

'No, I don't mean he's dead. Nothing like that. I mean he's left me.'

'What? But I thought—'

'Oh, everyone thought that,' Della cut in. 'So did I, actually. I thought we were fine, just rattling along, you know, the way couples do . . .'

'You mean he's just gone? Did he say why?'

'No. Well, he didn't have to. He seems to be living with someone else.'

However flaky Roxanne had been in the past, she was saying all the right things now. And so Della spilled out all the details – the golf, the perfect coffee on weekend mornings as if in an attempt to assuage his guilt – and then not wanting to spend the day with his wife when they had dropped off Sophie at college. And when it was all done, and the bottle of Sauvignon was finished, Della looked around at the piles of cookbooks and suddenly – rather tipsily – felt a whole lot better. 'Thanks, Rox,' she murmured.

'Oh, I haven't done anything.' She paused. 'I feel bad, you know, not being there for you now, and when Mum was ill . . .'

'It's okay, it's just the way it was. I mean, I was on the doorstep, virtually. It was bound to fall to me.'

'It doesn't seem right, though. I was so wrapped up with stuff here, and now Sophie's gone and I feel like her childhood's just flown by and I've missed it.'

Della laughed dryly. 'Tell me about it.'

'D'you think she'd like to do an internship in the Christmas break? In our art department, I mean?'

Della thought of Jeff suggesting she should design jam jar labels and Sophie, ever the idealist, only wanting to paint. Although she would probably shun the idea of working on a magazine too, it was kind of Roxanne to suggest it. 'I'll mention it,' said Della. 'Actually, I think it'd be great for her.'

'She could stay with me, enjoy a blast of London life . . .'

'That would probably swing it for her,' Della said. They chatted on, about Rosemary Cottage and whether anyone in their right minds would ever buy it. Eventually – it was gone 11 o'clock now – they gossiped and giggled, and Della decided she couldn't tell her sister about Rafael tonight. It was too much to blurt out on the phone and she hadn't even figured out what it meant yet, although the implications had already hurtled through her mind: that if it was true, then Roxanne was her half-sister and Jeff her half-brother, and Sophie had acquired a grandfather she never knew existed, who had possibly passed his artistic genes down to her. But of course, Della might have got it all wrong and her dramatic dark colouring was nothing to do with a Spanish artist but just some genetic thing from way back, which had resurfaced in her.

She knew nothing for certain. It was only a *picture*. And so she simply said, 'Rox, it's been really helpful talking to you tonight.'

'Come on, Dell, I haven't said anything useful.'

'No, you have, really. And thank you.'

'Is there anything I can do? Anything at all?'

'Er, there is one thing actually. Would you mind telling Jeff about Mark leaving? I don't think I could face it right now.'

'Oh, I don't blame you. Of course I will. And, listen . . . you will tell me if there's anything I can do, won't you?'

'Of course, Rox. And thanks.' Della smiled as they finished the call, doubting if there was anything Roxanne could actually do to help – but appreciating the offer anyway. In fact, right now, she wanted to hug her sister more than anyone else in the world.

And now she knew she was capable of telling Sophie what had happened. It was late, but then Sophie seemed to be keeping to a fairly nocturnal schedule right now. Della called her mobile.

'Mum, hi! I'm just getting ready to go out . . .'

'Okay, love, I won't keep you. It's just, I was thinking of driving over to Leeds tomorrow, grab a bit of lunch with you, if that's okay?'

'Er . . . yeah. Yeah, I s'pose so.'

Della cleared her throat. 'Well, shall we meet at, say . . . one-ish? Are there some decent places near your halls?'

'Yeah, loads. Look, I'd better go.'

'And your room's comfy, is it? You've got it all set up?'

'It's looking great, Mum . . .'

'Have you put your mirror up yet?'

'No, not yet.'

'Want me to do it for you while I'm there?'

'No, thanks.' An audible sigh.

'It's no trouble, I can bring a hammer.'

293

'Mum, please! I don't need your hammer. Now, I really have to go. See you tomorrow, okay?'

'Yes, looking forward to it, darling.'

That went well, Della thought.

Chapter Thirty-One

Della was up with the lark and pulled on a wrap dress and her favourite jacket, because as Roxanne was always keen to remind her, clothes have a huge impact on how you feel inside. Would it work? Della wondered. Would her casual/dressy appearance enable her to explain what had happened without dissolving into tears in the restaurant? Her stomach fluttered with nerves as she drove first to Burley Bridge. At just gone 8 a.m. the morning felt fresh and bright, and she tried to reassure herself that this lunch would be the worst part and everything would feel better once it was all out in the open. In the meantime, rather than spending the morning pottering anxiously at home, she was on her way to check on progress at the bookshop.

To her surprise the shop was unlocked with Liam's dad's van parked outside. Even more startling, Liam's power drill was whining away. She stepped inside and, for a moment wondered if she had wandered into the wrong shop.

Liam nodded at the sight of her and turned off his drill. 'Hi . . . so what d'you think?'

295

She wandered around the shop, running a hand along the shelves that had lined her mother's kitchen and had now been cleverly reconfigured to fill almost every available space. Just one wall remained bare, awaiting paintings, and perhaps shelves on which she could display Kitty's favourite kitchen utensils to give a homely, retro feel to the shop. 'I think . . . it's wonderful, Liam. You've done an amazing job.'

'Well, it's all come together okay,' he said, sounding a little surprised, as if it had somehow happened by accident.

'Seriously, I'm so impressed.' Della took pictures with her phone so she could plan where to put the different categories of cookbooks. Entertaining, seasonal cookery, desserts, baking . . . it had gone from a crazy idea to something tangible which, she knew now, she was perfectly capable of pulling together in time for her opening party in nine days' time. Having thanked Liam profusely she strolled through the village to Rosemary Cottage, where she gathered up the mail before driving on to the retail park to buy paint. She enjoyed a frisson of rebellion as she selected the butterfly brights she had always been drawn to: a dazzling cerise for the bare interior wall, and a deep red for the woodwork. In her car, she called Nathan.

'Ah, lovely to hear from you . . . what can I do for you?'

'I'm changing the sign on the shop,' she explained, 'and I wondered if you knew of any sign-writers around here? I'd like a proper old-fashioned painted sign like Christine and Pattie had for the haberdasher's.'

'Um, I might know of someone . . .'

'I thought you might, with your, er, varied business interests.'

'Oh, yeah, I have plenty of contacts in this town.' Della

296

smiled. He made Heathfield sound like Chicago. 'I'll text you a number. Anything else you need?'

'Er, no, I think I'm almost sorted now.'

'I'd love to see your shop when it's finished. Could I pop round sometime?'

'Yes, of course. Why don't you come to my opening party a week on Saturday, if you're free? It kicks off at two. That's why I'm in a bit of a rush now. There's still so much to sort out . . .'

'Sure there's nothing else I can help with?' Della reassured him that she was fine, thank you, and her mobile trilled as soon as she'd finished the call.

'Mum?' It was Sophie, miraculously awake and alert before 10.30 a.m. 'Are you still coming today?'

'Yes, darling, if that's all right. I hope it is. I'm really looking forward—'

'It's just . . . can we meet somewhere else instead?' Sophie sounded cagey and agitated. Della hoped it wasn't an omen.

'It'll be easier if I just park at your halls, love, then we can walk somewhere.'

She could sense her daughter frowning, and pictured the little furrow that appeared between her dark brows. 'Er . . . okay then,' she mumbled.

'Look, I'm not going to embarrass you, you know. I'm not going to insist on hanging around and chatting to everyone, trying to *make conversation*.'

'Okay, just come here then,' Sophie said hotly, then, as if catching herself, added, 'it'll be really nice to go for lunch, Mum. See you soon.'

The drive was not a pleasant one. Della couldn't remember a time when she had dreaded seeing her daughter; in fact, there had never been one, until today.

Possible opening lines looped around in her head: *Darling, I'm really sorry to tell you this but Dad and I have split up . . . Sophie, I don't quite know how to say this but Dad has met someone else . . . Dad has been having an affair . . . He's gone and fallen in love with some woman whose feet he fiddled with . . .* no, no, no. She mustn't say anything negative about him, mustn't launch into how unethical it was to sleep with a patient, and how the lying swine had hauled out those wretched golf clubs every Saturday morning since God knows when.

She mustn't say how horrendously let down and stupid she felt, and how, although the blinding anger had faded a little, she was still seized with an urge to march round to that sterile estate with its hangar-sized garages and hurl one of those smug little concrete garden ornaments through the living-room window of Polly Fisher's house.

Della wouldn't say any of that, she decided, breathing slowly and deeply now in an attempt to calm herself, because it was none of Sophie's concern. She wouldn't foist the grubby details on her daughter. She would remain calm and controlled and, once the terrible business had been attended to, they might even be able to enjoy a pleasant mother-and-daughter lunch . . .

Della was a little early as she pulled into the car park of Sophie's student village. Her heart felt like a boulder as she tramped up the concrete stairs and knocked on the door to Sophie's flat. The door swung open. 'Hi, Mum,' Sophie said with an awkward smile.

'Hi, love. All set then? Anywhere you fancy going?'

'Um, I haven't really thought . . .'

'Well, I'm sure we'll find somewhere. Er, can I come in?' *Rather than being left standing at the door like someone selling dusters,* was what she meant.

298

'Oh, yeah! Yeah, of course . . .' Sophie backed into the hallway, allowing her mother just enough space to step in. Della glanced at the door to Sophie's room.

'Can I see how you've settled in?'

'Er, not right now, Mum.'

Della frowned. 'Why not?'

'It's just a bit of a mess at the moment . . .'

'Oh, I don't mind that,' Della said, turning to the door and deciding she would *enjoy* glimpsing a tumble of beer cans and Pot Noodle cartons and clothes strewn around. Wasn't that what being young was all about? Eating rubbishy food, drinking too much, having no regard for putting things away in drawers . . .

'No!' Sophie screeched as Della reached for the door handle. Now she was physically blocking the way.

Della stared at her. Sophie's hair was a tangle – she had been too uptight to notice this before – and her smoky eye make-up might possibly have been applied the previous night. She was wearing a matted brown sweater, ripped jeans, and her favourite Doc Martens, which were daubed with paint. 'I'm . . . I'm sorry, love. I didn't mean to intrude . . .' Della broke off as the realisation hit her: there was a *boy* in her daughter's bed. They'd slept in – despite Sophie insisting on packing that shrill alarm clock – and he was still lying there in a post-coital fug. 'Let's just go,' Della said quickly.

'Yeah, okay. Do I need anything?' Money, Sophie meant.

'No, darling, lunch is on me.'

A wave of awkwardness hit Della as they headed downstairs and out into the breezy afternoon. She had imagined the get-togethers they'd have, when Sophie had been offered her place at art college; long chats over lunch with much gossip and laughter, more like friends than mother

299

and daughter. Now Sophie was mooching along, looking rather pale and glum, Della noted. Despite the terrible news she had to break today, Della had to rescue things somehow.

Mexican, she decided. Sophie and her friends were crazy about guacamole, sour cream and refried beans. They turned the corner and marched past a row of dismal-looking shops. 'D'you know if there's a Mexican place around here?' Della ventured.

Sophie glanced at her. 'Oh, yeah, there is. We all went for Becca's birthday . . .'

'Becca?'

'She's in the flat opposite. It was great. Her dad sent her money and we all went out. Yeah, let's go there.' Five minutes later they found themselves in a chain restaurant thumping with salsa music and the shrieks of laughter from a large gathering of students at the next table. 'Like it?' Sophie asked, snatching the menu from the table.

'It's great,' Della managed, resting her elbows on the sticky table.

'D'you know what everything is?'

Of course she did – Kitty's cookbook collection included several guides to Mexican cooking – but she realised Sophie wanted to talk her through the myriad of dishes. 'I'm not sure,' Della murmured. 'What d'you think's best?'

'Okay, so tacos are, like, the crispy ones, a fajita has chicken and vegetables, rolled up, and burritos are like that but with everything wrapped up inside, you know?' Sophie paused. 'Nachos – well, you know nachos . . . and enchiladas are like all the others but with a sauce poured over and baked, I think.' Sophie looked up at her. 'Is it okay if I have a beer, Mum?'

'Don't you have lectures this afternoon?'

300

Whatever made Della say that? This was Breaking the News day. Della had no idea how Sophie would react; she could have one of those frothy cocktails that were being delivered to the clearly well-heeled students' table if she wanted.

'No, I'm free for the rest of the day,' Sophie said airily.

'Go on then. And I think I'll have . . .' In fact, nothing whatsoever appealed to Della, so she just picked the first dish her eyes landed upon.

'Great choices, guys,' enthused an exuberant young waitress in a short black dress with pom-poms stitched to the hem. She performed what Della assumed was a little salsa move as she shimmied her way to the kitchens.

Della turned back to Sophie. 'So . . . tell me what you've been doing.'

'Oh, er, just this and that.'

'I mean on your course . . .'

'Drawing mainly.'

'Oh, right!' Of course she had been drawing; she was at art college, for goodness' sake, what did Della expect her to say? Studying medieval poetry or the nervous system of the human eye?

'Bit of sketching and stuff,' Sophie added.

'Bet that's interesting . . .' Conversation faltered, and Sophie flicked her mother a quick look as if she were a tiresome distant relative foisted upon her at Christmas. She seemed hugely relieved when the waitress brought her beer, virtually snatching the bottle from her. Della dearly wished she could have something stronger than fizzy water. 'So! What are your lecturers like?' she ploughed on.

'Yeah, they're all right.'

'D'you have a favourite yet?'

'Mum!' Sophie widened her eyes in a rather alarming

301

fashion. 'They're fine. They're all great . . . *everything's great.*'

Della was starting to sweat, through nerves probably. She glanced at the students' table where everyone was having a marvellous time, shouting good-naturedly over each other and obviously celebrating a birthday. Or maybe it was just a normal thing, to gather for a Mexican feast with cocktails on a Thursday lunchtime? Della wanted to blurt it all out now, to get this over and done with as quickly as possible, but she would have to wait until their food arrived as it wouldn't do to be interrupted by the pom-pom girl.

And here, finally, came their burritos: bulging logs packed with rice and beans, resting on mounds of avocado and anaemic chopped tomato with a token scattering of coriander on top. 'Great, thank you,' Della enthused.

'Enjoy!' said the waitress, scuttling off to refuel the party table with more cocktails.

As Sophie sawed one end off her burrito, Della replayed her selection of openers with a couple of new additions thrown in: *There's no easy way to tell you this, darling, but I have some news for you* . . . News? That sounded as if she – or Mark – had just been diagnosed with a terminal illness. *Erm, before I say any more, I want you to know that we both love you – you mean the world to us – and nothing will ever change that* . . . Was Sophie too grown-up for that kind of talk, and would she find it patronising? Della had over-thought it, that was the problem, and now she had to say something because, although Sophie had severed the burrito into two fat chunks, she had placed her cutlery on her plate and was staring at her mother across the table.

'Sophie . . .' Della cleared her throat.

302

'Mum . . .'

'Look, darling, there's a reason why I wanted to see you today.'

'Yes, I know.'

'I mean, of course I wanted to see you, we should do this regularly – not like this, I mean, just a regular lunch to catch up . . .'

'Mum, I *know*,' Sophie cut in.

Della placed her own cutlery beside her untouched plate. 'Er . . . *what* do you know, darling?' A moment ago Della was stifling hot. Now she felt chilled.

'About Dad,' Sophie said calmly.

'You mean—'

'Yeah, he called me last night.'

Della stared at her. She was aware of the pink birthday balloons bobbing above the party table and someone, presumably the birthday girl, having a sombrero plonked on her head. 'He told you . . . on the phone?'

'Yeah, he said he thought it was better that way rather than getting together, making a big event of it . . .' It all came out in a rush.

Della was momentarily lost for words. *But it is a big event,* she wanted to say. After nineteen years of marriage her husband had left her for someone else. She would struggle to think of anything bigger than that. 'So . . . what did he say?'

'Mum, I don't really want to go into it,' Sophie muttered, eyes cast down to her dissected burrito now.

'No, I don't mean tell me exactly what he said. Of course I don't. I just mean . . . did he tell you . . . what his situation is now?'

Sophie nodded.

'That he's living with someone else?'

303

She cleared her throat. 'Yes, Mum, he did.'

'And how do you . . .' Della broke off as an enormous cake, ablaze with candles and sparklers, was carried past them to the students' table. A rowdy rendition of 'Happy Birthday' broke out and Della wanted to cry. At Sophie's eighteenth, in a country hotel just outside Heathfield, Mark had been there. They'd still been a proper family and Della had had no idea of what was about to happen. Sophie's mouth had started to move but Della couldn't make our her words over the whoops and cheers that followed the song. *Hip, hip, hoorah! Hip, hip, hoorah! Hip, hip, hoorah . . .*

'Sorry,' she said, 'I can't hear—'

'I said it's a shock, of course it is,' Sophie repeated, more loudly this time. 'I'd never imagined that happening to you two . . . I mean, I had no idea . . . but it's okay, I'm not a child anymore and it's happened to loads of my friends. You just deal with it . . .' Then Sophie was up and out of her seat and hugging her mother, saying, 'Sorry, Mum, this was totally the wrong place for us, can we just go?'

'Yes, of course,' Della said, filled with relief. And before their waitress could waltz over and ask why they hadn't eaten their meals, she quickly calculated how much it had cost, added an extra tenner just to be sure, and the two of them hurried towards the door.

'Oh, are you leaving?' Della turned as the pom-pom girl called after them. 'Sorry, I didn't realise you were in such a hurry. I'll get a take-home box for you.' Della stood, bewildered, her head too full of Sophie's heartfelt speech to be able to figure out what that meant. The waitress disappeared to the kitchens, returned with a garish cardboard box emblazoned with cacti and proceeded to pack their burritos into it.

'Here you go.' She marched up to Sophie and handed it to her.

'No, no, it's okay . . .' She teetered back in alarm.

'Come on, you've hardly touched them . . .'

'Yes, but . . .' She shot Della a *help-me* look.

'Waste not, want not,' the waitress chirped, which seemed like a ridiculously aged thing for a girl of something like eighteen years old to come out with.

Della forced a grateful smile. 'That's what I always say. Thank you very much.'

'No trouble at all,' the girl trilled as they left the restaurant. 'Enjoy!'

Della hadn't imagined that laughter would feature today but once out on the pavement, they caught each other's eye and spluttered. 'I'm not carrying this, Mum,' Sophie exclaimed, thrusting the gaudy box at her.

'And what am I supposed to do with it?' Della countered.

'I don't know. Have it tonight? I know you hate waste . . .'

'Actually, you're right.'

'So do I now,' Sophie admitted. 'Mum, I had no idea how much food actually costs!'

Della smiled. Her daughter had only been gone for just over a week and had already learned one of life's hardest lessons: that food didn't appear, as if by magic, in the fridge. 'Shall we pick up some groceries for you now?'

'Oh, no, I'm fine.' Sophie hesitated, obviously wrestling with her pride. 'Actually, yes, would you mind?'

Of course Della didn't mind; in fact, it felt companionable, strolling around Sainsbury's together on what could have been a terrible day. Sophie didn't look remotely traumatised by her parents' break-up as she browsed the many varieties of hummus, and if Della was annoyed with Mark for not telling her that he had planned to call their daughter – to be the one to break the news – then she was also grateful that he had in effect done the most difficult part for her.

As they were laden with shopping now, it seemed perfectly natural for Della to walk back to Sophie's halls with her, to lug the groceries upstairs and be admitted into her actual flat. They packed away the provisions in the kitchen. 'Actually, Mum,' Sophie murmured, 'would you still like to see my room?'

'No, it's fine, darling. It's your private space.' *Of course I would. I'm desperate to!*

'Come on, there's something I want to show you . . .' So perhaps it wasn't a boy left languishing in her bed after all. And maybe not even a load of booze bottles or take-away cartons. Della's heart quickened with anticipation as Sophie led them along the corridor and pushed open her bedroom door.

Della stepped in and looked around her, not knowing quite what to say. 'It's . . . so tidy!' was what sprang out of her mouth.

'You thought I'd be living in squalor,' Sophie remarked with a smirk.

'Yes. Well, no. I didn't know what to expect . . .' She took in the single bed with its duvet smoothed over and Sophie's owl cushion propped on the pillow, the art books neatly lined up on the shelf. The gilt-framed mirror was propped up on the desk, and Sophie's shoes were arranged – neatly, in pairs – along one edge of the room. But never mind all that, because now all Della could see was Sophie's easel in the corner, and a painting propped up on it: of a shop, a beautiful *bookshop*, its window filled with dashes

306

of vibrant colour. Although the display had been suggested with quick, sweeping strokes, Della could still identify the covers of *A Guide to Tuscan Cookery* – painted in bold strokes of red and blue – and the shimmering yellow of *The Margarine Bible*. The shop itself was bright white, the door vivid green. Orangey light glowed from the window, and there was a sign that said Open.

'Sophie, it's just beautiful.' She tore her gaze from the painting and looked at her daughter.

'It's not finished,' Sophie said quickly. 'That's why I didn't want you to see it. I wanted to keep it for your opening day, but you know when you have a present for someone that you can't wait to give?' She grinned like a ten year old.

'Yes, I do know that feeling.' Della smiled. 'It looks finished to me, though.'

'No, see the sign? It's still blank.' Sophie indicated the strip of red woodwork above the window. 'I don't know what you're going to call it,' she added.

Della examined the painting more closely now, wondering how Sophie would react when she learned about her artist grandfather; Della would tell her soon, but not today. 'I'm calling it The Bookshop on Rosemary Lane.'

'Oh, that's perfect. I'll paint it in . . . so when are you actually opening?'

'A week on Saturday. I'm having an opening party. D'you think you can make it?'

''Course I can! God, d'you think I'd miss that?'

'Well . . . I wasn't sure. But I'm so glad, darling.'

'I'm really proud of you, Mum, doing this with everything else that's happened . . .' Sophie's voice trailed off and she flushed. 'You know what I mean.'

Della nodded. 'Yes, I do.'

Sophie smiled crookedly, and they hugged. 'Oh, and don't forget these.' She handed her mother the box of burritos.

Della took it from her, feeling oddly relieved as they said their goodbyes. She made her way back outside to her car, placing the box on the passenger seat. The feeling of relief remained, combined with a sense of excitement at what was to come, as she drove back to Heathfield. And when she pulled up outside her own house, it didn't seem to matter that the burrito box had leaked orangey oil all over the passenger seat. Della no longer felt like the colossal fool who had believed Mark's lies. She felt free.

Chapter Thirty-Two

Della's life was now being run by to-do lists. She had lists of people to call and numerous errands to run, plus the publicising of her bookshop to attend to. So next day, egged on by Charlotte – who was gratifyingly furious with Mark – she designed and printed out a simple poster to advertise the opening party, plus a press release with the heading: *The First Specialist Cookbook Shop in Yorkshire* . . . She stopped and glanced at her friend. 'I don't know what to put,' she admitted.

'Well, how did it start?' Charlotte asked, whose confidence knew no bounds when it came to getting something talked about. She pulled her chair closer to Della's at the kitchen table.

Della bit her lip. 'Well, I inherited Mum's cookbooks, of course, and at first it felt as if I was just giving them a temporary home, saving them from being dumped at a charity shop or, even worse, flung away.'

'So what changed your mind?' Charlotte asked.

Della considered this. Perhaps she had known, even then, that she needed to make a drastic change in her life.

'Well, the cookbooks – they're part of my childhood really . . . at least, the happiest part, when I felt close to Mum, just working away together, chopping and stirring in her kitchen . . .' Della's voice cracked.

'Hey.' Charlotte smiled and touched her arm. 'It's more than just a shop, isn't it? It's your life, Dell. You're putting your life into this shop. So that's what you should write.'

Della looked at her friend, always so neat and pulled together with her blonde crop and red lips, her black-rimmed spectacles lending her an air of quiet authority. She remained silent as Della's fingers flew over her laptop keys. When it was done, Charlotte checked it over and rattled off a list of newspaper and radio contacts whom Della should send it off to. 'Think anyone'll be interested?' she asked.

'Interested? Of course they will be! When does anything like this happen in a little place like Burley Bridge?'

Della laughed. 'When does *anything* happen in Burley Bridge?'

After Charlotte had left, Della did the rounds of all the shops in Heathfield that would allow her to pin up a poster, then she drove over to Burley Bridge where the owners of *all* the shops – plus Len's garage, and even Nicola Crowther's hair salon – put them up immediately for her. She knew now that it would work, because Charlotte was right: it was more than just a shop. It was something Burley Bridge – in fact, the whole of Yorkshire – had never seen before. Perhaps she really could help to bring the village back to life.

At Rosemary Cottage Della loaded up as many paintings and small pieces of furniture as her car could accommodate and deposited them at the Heathfield auction house and charity shops, having reserved a small collection of her favourite pots and utensils from Kitty's kitchen. There were fluted glass pie dishes, hefty burnt orange enamel casseroles and top-quality knives (Kitty's frugal streak hadn't seemed to apply when it came to kitchen kit).

Next day, Della drove to a hamlet on the East Yorkshire coast to pick up the unwanted collection of cookbooks from the Gumtree ad. 'I'm just happy they're going to a good home,' said Mr Wheeler, the elderly man who had advertised them. 'They were my wife's, you see, and I've never cooked. Wouldn't know where to start so they're just wasted, sitting here.' He smiled wryly as Della loaded the boxes into the boot of her car.

'Perhaps you should keep a couple of them,' she suggested, 'just to help you to get started?'

Mr Wheeler tweaked his neat silvery moustache. 'No, dear, I'm too old for that. There's a perfectly good chip shop here. And I'll say one thing for Margaret – before she took off, she at least had the decency to leave me a whole pile of frozen dinners.'

Della laughed involuntarily, still shocked as she thanked Mr Wheeler profusely and drove home. His slight frame and mild manner reminded her a little of William, and now she wondered whether she had jumped to conclusions when she had seen Rafael Avina's photograph: would Kitty have lied all those years about who her real father was? But then, no one had really lied. They had just never talked about anything real.

As the weekend came around, Della was grateful that she had no time to think about anything else, apart from being ready for her opening day. With Morna's assistance – Kitty's neighbour had spotted her cleaning the shop's window and offered to help – she'd scrubbed the place from top to bottom. 'It's going to be wonderful,' Morna enthused as they sipped take-away coffees from the chip shop. 'This is just what we need, you know. Something new, to get the village talked about. This place has wilted over the years . . . d'you remember there used to be three pubs here once, and a tearoom?'

'I vaguely remember,' Della replied.

'What about Rosemary Cottage? Still planning to sell?'

'Yes, as soon as possible . . .'

Morna hesitated. 'I could rally some people together to help you get the place ready, if you like, if it doesn't feel like interfering? We could paint the outside, tidy up the garden . . .'

Della smiled. 'That's very kind and, yes, I know it's a terrible mess at the moment.'

'Well, you've had enough on your plate with the shop,' Morna remarked.

'Yes, but it feels important to deal with Mum's place too. In fact, the house-clearance guys are coming on Monday.'

'Really? That soon?'

Della nodded. 'Yes, I thought it was better to get it over and done with.'

Morna squeezed her hand. 'What a lot you've had to deal with, Della love. Everyone's been saying so. Kitty would be very proud.'

Although thoughts of Mark and Polly Fisher – and Rafael Avina – hovered in the back of her mind, Della strictly forbade herself to obsess. She spent Sunday with Freda and Charlotte, pricing up the rest of the books, and on Monday morning the three of them loaded a hired van with Kitty's entire archive, plus Mr Wheeler's wife's collection. As arranged, Della picked up Liam, who had agreed to help her

312

to unload at the shop as well as tackling the last remaining pernickety jobs while she dealt with the house-clearance men. So much was happening, yet it all seemed doable. She felt determined and ready to witness the emptying of her childhood home as she strode down the lane, leaving Liam at the shop, to meet the clearance men.

Stewart and Mac were burly types with arms like truncheons. They worked fast, having politely declined Della's offer of coffee or tea. Without stopping for a break they hauled enormous wardrobes and rolls of well-worn carpet out to their van. As Rosemary Cottage emptied, so the van filled. Della was astounded by the way a home – which had evolved slowly over decades – could be cleared in less than three hours. As she watched the men carry out the wobbly old dining table, her phone pinged with an incoming text: *Hope you're OK, Mum. Love you xx*. It was as if Sophie knew she was standing here watching the sideboard being loaded, plus the old faded curtains and the rugs which, in some places, had no pile left at all. But of course, Sophie was referring to Mark and not the emptying of Della's childhood home. *I'm fine thanks darling,* she replied, grateful for her daughter's thoughtfulness.

'Putting the place up for sale then?' asked Mac as he slammed the van door shut.

'Yes, it was my mum's place. I grew up here actually.'

'Right.' He smiled benignly, omitting to comment. They were used to this: the disassembling of homes after someone had died. Still, it was done now. She thanked them profusely and, on the journey home with Liam in the passenger seat, the silence that settled around them felt anything but awkward. In fact, it seemed just right.

*

By Tuesday afternoon the Sew 'n' Sew's sign, with its scattering of haberdashery items, had been painted over in a rich, glossy red and by the following day new lettering had taken its place. Della gazed up at Jerry's handiwork while the unassuming sign-writer packed up his ladder and paints. It was perfect. It fitted exactly into the space. Well, of course it did; Jerry had painstakingly measured it all out, in the simple lettering Della had chosen, gold against red. Inside, the red theme had continued as she and Freda had painted the exposed wall, then filled the shelves, and Della – who was no stranger to a cash register – got to grips with the smart new machine, which had just been delivered. It was neither vintage nor beautiful; the antique ones Della had pored over online, whilst more in keeping with an archive of cookbooks, were mainly sold as 'for display only', for collectors rather than a bona fide businesswoman like herself.

From the row of brass hooks that Liam had put up for her, Della hung Kitty's collection of aprons: checks, polka dots and floral prints, all gently faded with age. Enamel pie dishes were displayed on the shelf, along with an earthenware jug filled with her mother's vintage steel ladles and slotted spoons. Here was the potato masher Della had used when painstakingly cooking that first dinner all by herself while Kitty was away in a world of her own, nursing her gin. Here was the burnt orange oval Le Creuset pot in which she had placed the chicken to roast. With the buzzing fluorescent strip now gone, the shop glowed in the light of several yellow lamps.

Still speckled with paint, Della enlisted Liam's help to pick up the squashy red velvet sofa, plus the sage green armchair, which she had spotted on Gumtree. She and

Freda worked through the days, and as the bookshop took shape – they were on to finishing touches now, scouring charity shops for cushions, and setting out Kitty's vintage cups and tea plates – the spectre of Mark and Polly Fisher began to fade, just a little. Naturally, Della couldn't bear to think of him there in Polly's executive home, having a life with her. But just a week ago she couldn't imagine how she would ever manage alone, and now she knew she would do more than manage; she would *thrive*.

After locking up the shop for the day, Della strolled through the village, glimpsing her posters in every shop window:

**Grand Opening of The Bookshop on
Rosemary Lane
A haven for cookbook fans and recipe lovers
Read, relax and browse in a delightful new shop
filled with delicious surprises
2 p.m., Saturday October 10
All welcome**

It was happening. It was real. And in just three days The Bookshop on Rosemary Lane would be open to all. But before that could happen, she had an important appointment to keep.

He was already waiting outside Rosemary Cottage: a short, brick-shaped man with a shock of jet black hair which seemed to grow upwards from his head, and who knew 'just the types' who would be itching to buy Rosemary Cottage. 'It's got character,' enthused Tony Nicholas of Nicholas & Stone estate agents. 'They don't often come on the market, you see, and some people – well, they don't want the flimsy new build with the garden that hasn't even started to mature yet. They're not after the show home, Mrs Sturgess.'

'I'm glad you think so,' she said, showing him from room to room and pausing to admire Liam's immaculate plasterwork where he had whipped out the shelves.

'I like this house very much,' Tony said firmly. 'Oh, I know it needs a bit of an upgrade but that's what people want – to put their own stamp on a place and start afresh.'

Della smiled, reaching into her bag as her mobile rang. 'Excuse me, I'd better take this.' Tony nodded and wandered off to take measurements of the rooms.

'Hi, Della, is this a good time?'

'Hi, Jeff. I'm just at Mum's, actually. The estate agent's here . . .'

'Oh, that was quick! Good for you, getting everything sorted.'

It hasn't been easy, she wanted to say. Never mind the physical work; the clearing out, the seeing Kitty's wardrobes being flung into a van . . . the emotional side was far harder. But she didn't say this because Jeff was rattling on now: 'Look, Dell, I'm sorry I can't make your opening night—'

'It's an afternoon do actually, next Saturday.'

'Yes, well, that makes it even worse. I can't get away. It's mayhem here with the conservatory happening . . .'

'Oh, what's going on with that?'

'Didn't I tell you? We're finally getting rid of that hideous old thing – ' the perfectly serviceable conservatory attached to their five-bedroomed house, he meant ' – and having it replaced with a purpose-built garden room to Tamsin's own design.'

'Lovely,' she remarked, glimpsing Tony as he bounded upstairs.

316

'So there's all *that* happening. It's living hell.'

'Hmm, must be. But listen, it's okay. There'll be plenty of people there. Roxanne's driving up on Saturday morning and I think – I *hope* – all the locals will turn up.'

'Yeah, I bet it's worrying, though.'

'Well, no, not exactly.'

'Stressful,' he butted in, clearly not even hearing her, 'throwing a party when you've no idea if anyone's actually going to come.'

'Jeff, I've sent out a pile of press releases and distributed about fifty posters—'

'But then, on the plus side, it's a tiny shop, isn't it? No room to swing a cat really. So even if there's only a handful of people wandering in it'll still look, er, quite busy. Anyway, hats off to you, Della. You've been a dab hand at getting things moving. Mum always said that, didn't she? That if you need something to happen, then just ask Della.'

Her back teeth had taken on that tin-foil feeling. 'I think what she actually said was, "She might not be the brightest bulb in the box, but she certainly gets things done."'

'Ha-ha! Well, you *are* quite bright, really. Qualifications aren't everything, Dell!' Then, just as her tolerance plummeted to critically low levels, the twins kicked up some sort of commotion in the background. Bless those boys, she mused, as Jeff abruptly ended the call. And at least he hadn't made any knowing remarks about her marriage falling apart. Roxanne mustn't have told him yet, so Della still had that pleasure to look forward to.

Back home in Heathfield, there was, however, someone she *did* want to talk to. 'Hello?' Monica answered her phone after two rings. It was as if she had been waiting for Della's call.

'Monica, it's Della.'

'Oh, I was hoping you'd get in touch. I very much enjoyed meeting you.'

'Me too.' Della perched on the sofa arm, picturing her barefoot and in leggings, with the waves rushing onto the shore outside Garnet Cottage. 'I sort of wanted to apologise,' she added, 'in case I offended you.'

'Why on earth would I have been offended?' Monica sounded genuinely astonished.

Della bit her lip. 'All the work you've done – your textiles. I had no idea, you see. I just thought, well . . .'

'It was a little hobby of mine?' Monica cut in, and Della could tell she was smiling.

'Yes. And I looked you up – I was curious, you know – and you've designed special edition wallpaper for Liberty!'

'Oh, that was just a pattern from my archives,' said Monica, laughing throatily. 'Someone happened to see my website and it all took off from there.'

'Well, I think it's amazing,' Della marvelled.

'Hmm. Well, it keeps me out of mischief, you know. So, how's the bookshop coming along?'

'It's just about there. I can hardly believe it's actually happening.'

'I have a very good feeling about it,' Monica remarked.

'Thank you. I do too. Erm . . . would you like to come to my opening party, Monica? I know it's an awfully long way.'

'It's not Siberia,' she chuckled. 'Of course. I'd love to come.'

'Great. It's on Saturday at two, and, er . . .' Della paused.

'I'd really like to meet Rafael at some point – if he's okay with that? I mean, I don't want to foist myself on him. I'd, um, just like . . .' *To be sure,* she wanted to add, *or at least, as sure as I ever can be.* But she couldn't quite manage the words.

'I thought you would, darling. Don't be put off by him not wanting to talk to you that first time you called. I've told him you were here, what a wonderful person you are . . .'

Della's heartbeat quickened. 'Thank you.'

'Would you like me to come with you?'

'Sometime perhaps. But the first time, you know . . .'

'You'd rather go alone,' Monica said gently. 'Well, I can understand that.'

'Yes, I think it might be easier somehow. Could I have his number, please?'

Monica chuckled dryly. 'Believe it or not, he doesn't have a phone. He did have a mobile – I insisted on it but he claimed it was broken or lost. I suspect he hid it, actually, and I gave up. Honestly, he's like a child sometimes.'

Della frowned. 'Could I email him, then? Does he use a computer at all?'

'After a fashion, but your message could languish there for weeks.'

'What about Facebook?'

'You *are* joking. The man's a Luddite. Look, he's coming over tonight. I still cook for him, you see. Terrible, isn't it, but God knows how he'd survive if I didn't. Shall I tell him you'd like to visit him tomorrow?'

'Tomorrow?' exclaimed Della. No, tomorrow was too soon. This was something to build up to, like that lunch with Sophie.

'Well, yes, I think that's probably best,' Monica said

319

briskly, before Della had a chance to protest. 'He's heading off on a jaunt with his friends on Saturday. It's a yearly thing, an autumn trip to the Lake District – they rent a cottage for a month, supposedly to paint, to observe the changing season – ' Della sensed Monica rolling her eyes ' – but it's actually a thinly disguised boys' holiday.'

Della paused. 'So, if I don't see him tomorrow, I'll have to wait until next month?' That is, if he agreed to see her at all.

'Yes. Tell you what, Della. I'll mention it tonight and if it's a problem I'll call you back. And if you don't hear from me, well, you can assume . . .'

'. . . that's he's okay about seeing me?'

'He'll be more than okay, trust me.'

Would he, though? Della wondered, having thanked Monica and rung off, still buzzing with questions she wanted to ask. He hadn't even wanted to acknowledge her, that first time she'd called, so how could Monica be so sure now? Della was just a 'thing' from his past – a mistake, the result of an infatuation – and she couldn't imagine him being exactly delighted by it all being dragged out of the closet fifty years later. It was intrusive, she decided; a reminder of a part of his life he would probably prefer to leave buried. Also, was there really any point? Although a distant and shadowy figure, William had been her real father and there was no pressing need to find another one. She still didn't know for sure, either. A slight resemblance detected in an old black-and-white photograph . . . what did that actually tell her? It was like horoscopes, Della decided. If you looked hard enough, you could always find what you wanted to find.

In the hallway now, she glared at Mark's golf clubs wearing their silly hats. They too were a reminder – of

320

the lies that had spouted from the mouth of her jaunty, Sunday-papers-carrying husband. They were heavy, too, she realised, as she lifted the bag experimentally. Would the charity shop want such a bulky item? She'd try them first and, if they didn't, she'd have to dispose of them some other way. She lugged them out to her car and slammed the boot shut, wishing it felt more satisfying. As an act of revenge it was hardly on a par with chopping up his favourite suit – the one he'd worn to 'the conference at Weston-super-Mare' – because they had never meant anything to him in the first place. Still, at least the darned things would be out of her way.

She parked as close as possible to the charity shop and hauled in the clubs. 'Just leave them in the back room, please,' trilled the elderly assistant, rather mechanically, as she rang up a purchase at the till. Della carried them through the shop, greeting a younger woman in the back room who was steam-cleaning trousers on a clothes horse.

'Thank you,' she said, giving the clubs a quizzical look. 'Oh, those again!'

Della frowned. 'No, these aren't from here. My husband bought them from the golf shop on the high street . . .'

The woman switched off the steamer and gave them a closer look. 'Are you sure? No, I remember the bag quite clearly – the yellow and green.' She smiled briskly. 'So nice when a customer gets good use out of something and then, when they've had enough, they re-donate it to the shop. Keeps everyone happy, doesn't it?'

Della forced a big smile. 'Yes, it does.' *Everyone is absolutely over the moon . . .*

'I hate to think of things lying about unused, cluttering up the house, don't you? They should have another life really, be enjoyed all over again . . .' *The bookshop, just*

think about the bookshop, that's what matters now.
'. . . So your husband got tired of golf,' the woman laughed, her crystal beads jangling, 'just like mine did. But at least he didn't spend too much on the equipment!'

'Hmm, yes, that's a good thing,' Della managed.

The woman draped a swirly-patterned skirt over the clothes horse. 'I was more annoyed when my Barry spent over two hundred quid on waterskis he used once.' Della smiled sympathetically, then squeezed between the rails of clothing and made her escape. It all made sense, she realised, as she drove home: Mark wouldn't have wanted to spend too much with them only being *decoy* clubs. Yet another lie he'd chalked up.

As she turned the corner into Pickering Street, Della had a fleeting urge to drive on to that new estate with the show home and triple garages – just for a look, not to damage the property – but what would be the point? It was over now, and she had a bookshop to open and, as long as Monica didn't call tonight, a very important person to meet.

Chapter Thirty-Three

Roxanne always knew how to dress for any occasion. It was an instinct, she said; you always knew when an outfit was right. Perhaps Della didn't possess this instinct because, today of all days, she was utterly stumped as to what to wear to meet Rafael Avina for the very first time. Did she want to impress him by appearing smart, pulled together? Did she want to look *arty*? She was wary of dressing to play a part. In the end, she had gone for a simple grey knitted dress and opaque tights, which had felt satisfyingly understated: *it's just a visit, no big deal at all*. She was simply driving to the coast to have a cup of tea with an elderly man.

He's fine about me coming, she reminded herself, realising her knuckles were white as she gripped the steering wheel along the twisty narrow roads. At least, she assumed it was okay as she'd had no call from Monica, warning her off. She wished now that Monica would be there too, being brisk and no-nonsense and glamorously barefooted. As Rafael's house appeared in the distance Della's stomach swirled, and she slowed down to thirty miles per hour, then twenty-five, slow enough to madden anyone driving behind her on the narrow road. When her speed dipped to a twenty-miles-per-hour crawl, she knew she was delaying the business of meeting him.

Della pulled up on the patch of weed-strewn gravel outside the house. Perhaps the woollen dress had been a poor choice as she was now bathed in a slick layer of sweat. She smoothed back her hair unnecessarily – she was wearing it up, in a tidyish bun – and quickly checked her teeth in the rear-view mirror. Then she stepped out of the car and turned towards the open door where Rafael was already waiting for her.

'Hi, Rafael.' She tried to exude calm as she strode towards him.

'Hello, Della.' He pressed his lips together. 'Come in.'

He looked young for his age, she decided; plenty of hair still, a kind of pewter grey colour, and barely a line on his face. Strong jaw, dark eyes, and still handsome and reasonably trim: he was entirely recognisable from that old photograph. She followed him along a dark, narrow hallway and into a small, low-ceilinged lounge, which happened to be the most cluttered room she had ever seen. Jam jars filled with brushes were crammed onto a wobbly-looking sideboard. Reams of paperwork were stacked messily on a shelf, and a side table at the small grubby window was laden with sketchbooks and papers and packets of rolling tobacco. In the corner, a black cat lay snoozing on a faded rug. 'Thank you for seeing me,' Della ventured.

'That's okay?' He phrased it as a question, as if wanting to add, *And why precisely are you here?* He sank onto the low, cracked leather sofa and motioned for her to sit. She perched on an unyielding armchair opposite him, which was upholstered in a bright, splashy abstract fabric. She suspected it might be Monica's work.

Silence settled around them like dust, and Della tugged her dress down over her knees and cleared her throat. *I'm just here to have a cup of tea with an elderly man.* Only there wasn't any tea – not that she wanted any really, but she would have been grateful for a small gesture of welcome.

'Erm . . .' She pulled at her dress again. 'I know this is a little strange for both of us.' Rafael nodded, regarding her with indifference as if she had arrived to inform him of a planning application for building work on a nearby field. He would hear her out, his look seemed to say, and then she could go. 'The reason I'm here,' she lurched on, 'is because of something I found in a book, in a cookbook of Mum's . . .' She stopped. 'Do you know I'm Kitty's daughter?'

'Yes, I do.' Those dark eyes were fixed upon her unswervingly.

'Well,' she started, 'Mum passed away a few weeks ago and I found a note, which I think – at least, Monica thinks – was from you.' Was this too much, too soon? He was regarding her levelly. She took this as a signal that he wasn't going to be appalled by what she had to say, or manhandle her out of his house. 'Just a short, affectionate note,' she went on, feeling marginally calmer now, 'and it set me wondering . . .'

'Who I was.'

'Yes, exactly.' She raised a small smile. 'D'you mind telling me a little bit about yourself?'

Rafael shifted on the sofa. He was wearing a checked shirt in sludgy colours, bark-brown corduroys and a pair of rather smart, perhaps even recently polished, black lace-up shoes. She wondered if he had in fact made an effort for her. 'I was born in Majorca,' he started, 'but we left for Valencia when my father's photography business was faltering . . .'

'Your father was a photographer?'

Rafael nodded. 'Just portraits really – weddings, babies, family occasions – and there wasn't enough work where we lived. He heard through a contact about a job as staff photographer on a newspaper.'

'And your mum? What did she do?'

Rafael frowned. 'She raised us, of course – my brother Carlos and me. Did a little book keeping . . .' Della watched Rafael as he spoke, his accent still detectable, sunk deep in the sofa as if he might easily disappear altogether. Perhaps she should offer to make tea? No, that would feel wrong. She didn't come here to start looking after him. She ran her tongue over her teeth and wondered how she might work the conversation around to the startling resemblance between them, because the longer she sat facing him, the more obvious it became.

It was his long, straight nose she had inherited – and his full mouth – as if Rafael's genes had almost entirely obliterated Kitty's. 'You're so like your mum!' neighbours would tell Roxanne on a regular basis, then they would look at Della and nothing more would be said.

'And you moved to London to go to art college,' Della prompted, deciding to stick with the interview format for now.

'Yes, against my parents' wishes, I have to say.' A flicker of a smile curved the corners of his mouth.

'That must have been an amazing time,' she suggested. Rafael nodded, and Della ploughed on, still skirting the real reason she was here. 'My daughter's just started at

326

art college. She's studying fine art. My brother Jeff thinks it's a terrible idea.'

A small frown. 'But why?'

Della smiled. 'Oh, because she can't possible make a decent living out of it, he reckons. He tried to persuade her to go into websites, or designing washing-powder cartons or marmalade labels.'

'Pfff!'

'Did anyone suggest you should do that instead?'

He shrugged. 'There were no websites then.'

'No, of course not.' Ah, so now he was being awkward. 'I mean, not follow the path you wanted to take.'

'Yes, but I didn't listen and she shouldn't either.' Della looked at him, wondering if he would ask her daughter's name. It was highly probably that she was his grand-daughter, for goodness' sake.

'She's called Sophie,' Della said, trying to erase the trace of frustration that was creeping into her voice. 'She's my only child. Her father and I have just split up, actually.' *Seeing as you haven't asked a single thing about me.* No reaction there, though. She caught him glancing distract-edly at the bookshelf as if he really should start sorting out that paperwork as soon as she'd gone. 'Can I ask you about Kitty?' she blurted out. Hell, might as well just go for it.

Rafael frowned. 'Well, I suppose so, yes. What do you want to know?'

'Well, erm . . .' A wave of hotness surged over her. 'Only what you want to tell me, I suppose. I'm not going to pry. Well, maybe I am, but I don't mean to. There are just certain things I need to know for it all to make sense.' He sat there, impassive, which she took as a cue to continue. 'You and Mum had a sort of a . . . thing, didn't you?'

'A sort of a thing?' he repeated, raising an eyebrow.

Oh, for goodness' sake. Irritation rose in Della again but she had to remain calm or Rafael might ask her to leave, and she didn't want to, not yet. 'I think, from what I can gather, that when it started – when you first met, I mean – she was pregnant with my brother.'

'Yes, that's right.'

'And then after that, when Jeff was born, you and Mum started a . . .' Della broke off. Why was he making this so difficult for her? *Are you my father?* she wanted to ask. *Please stop being so damned difficult.* 'You had a relationship with her,' she murmured, to which Rafael merely nodded. Della stood up and smoothed down the front of her dress, which now dipped weirdly at the front from all the tugging on it.

She felt him studying her as she wandered towards the window and looked out. The view was of a scrubby field. In the distance a disused mobile blood bank was being used as accommodation for a horse, whose head was visible, peering out of it.

She turned back to Rafael. Might as well get this over with, she decided. She had seen her daughter leave home and been left by her husband, so she could darned well ask this difficult old man a direct question. 'Are you my father, Rafael?'

Now, finally, he looked fully alert. He cleared his throat before mumbling something inaudible, as a teenager might.

'Sorry,' she said, 'I didn't catch—'

'I said, we never really knew for certain,' he said sharply.

Della stared at him, then perched awkwardly beside him on the dilapidated sofa. Outside, gulls squawked shrilly. 'You mean . . . Kitty didn't know who my father was?'

328

'Not with absolutely certainty, no.' His hands made a rasping sound as he rubbed them together.

'But . . . don't you think she must have done, when I was born, when I started to grow up?' Ridiculously, Della's eyes filled with tears. 'I mean, we look so alike, you and I, Rafael. Can't you see that?'

'We didn't talk about it,' he said gruffly, 'but yes, you're right, we certainly do.'

Della blinked rapidly. She hadn't expected to feel so upset, and now she was horrified at the thought of crying in front of him. 'Did you ever see me when I was little?'

'Of course I did,' he exclaimed, looking put out that she had the audacity to question his commitment as a father. 'I saw you lots of times, but then – well, it was for the best, really. Kitty had to focus on her own family and I had my work. You would have been, I don't know . . . around a year old when we stopped seeing each other.' She realised he would no longer meet her gaze.

Della shook her head in disbelief. 'So what you're saying is, William and Kitty carried on as if I was theirs and everything was completely normal.'

'Yes. What else would they have done?'

'Been honest, maybe?' Della exhaled loudly. 'I don't know. It just seems bizarre, that's all.' She glared at the cluster of jam jars filled with brushes soaking in murky water.

'Why did you come here, Della?'

His question felt like a punch. 'I have absolutely no idea,' she said bitterly.

'No, come on. I'm interested to know what you hoped to find.'

'Oh, I don't know,' she said irritably. 'Just a definite answer, I suppose.'

329

'Well . . .' He tone had softened now. 'Don't you see? There isn't one.' They lapsed into silence again and she considered telling him that Kitty had had another child after Della, and that William had left her eventually and she had spent the rest of her life resolutely single, sipping gin. But what would be the point? Della stood up and looked down at the man whom she had hoped – ridiculously now, she realised – would be perhaps a little shell-shocked, but also quietly thrilled to meet her. She should have known, of course, from that first time she had called Monica Jones. *There's no one of that name here* . . . 'Thank you for seeing me,' she said, as if he were a solicitor who had advised her on a legal matter.

'That's quite all right.'

She glanced at the living-room door. 'So, um . . . I have a lot to do to get my shop ready. I'm opening a bookshop, it's actually filled with Kitty's cookbook collection . . .' *Do you remember those books?* she wanted to ask. *Did you ever come round for romantic trysts at Rosemary Cottage, when William was out at work?*

'I'll see you out then,' was all he said. There was no hug or even a handshake as they said a brief goodbye on his doorstep and Della climbed into her car. By the time she glanced back at the saggy old farmhouse, he had already disappeared inside.

Well, at least I know, she told herself as she turned the key in the ignition. At least it's clear that my real father – and now there was no doubt in her mind – is a curmudgeonly old man with no interest in anyone. It was always better to know, wasn't it, that your husband was now having to negotiate fifteen concrete hedgehogs every time he stepped out of the house, and that your own father had probably never given you a second thought in forty-odd years? He hadn't divulged a single piece of information about himself apart from the small slivers she had managed to extract, like tweezing a splinter out of a thumb. He hadn't even shown her his paintings.

She glanced back at his house with its untended garden and dilapidated garage, and sat there for at least five minutes with the engine running, willing him to hurry out and say sorry, and could they talk? Perhaps he'd suggest a walk, just as Monica had done. But something told her that, no matter how long she sat there, a Proper Talk with Rafael was not in the offing. She dallied some more, checking her phone, pulling the band out of her hair and retying it, and then she started to move away from the gravel and onto the single-track lane.

If this were a film, he'd have come running out now and . . . okay, perhaps a Big Talk *was* too much to hope for. Tea would have been nice, and a chat, so they could have got to know each other a little. But this wasn't a film. It was an ordinary wet Friday morning in Yorkshire and tears trickled down Della's cheeks as she drove home.

Chapter Thirty-Four

The to-do list was done. *Paint shop, order cash register, have sign painted, fix lighting, clear out Rosemary Cottage, pick up Gumtree sofa, meet my real father.* She had ticked off the lot and although the last task had felt less than satisfactory, Della felt ready to move on. There would be other, equally difficult things to do – how to disentangle her life from Mark's, all the legal gubbins – but that would come later. Right now, more pressingly, The Bookshop on Rosemary Lane was ready to open for business and Della had her lipstick on.

'Sophie, where are you, love?' She had been up and pacing around since 7 a.m. and now, at almost 11, she had been unable to resist calling her daughter.

'Stop worrying,' Sophie said cheerfully. 'We'll be there in plenty of time.'

'We? Are you bringing a friend?' There was much chatter and laughter in the background.

'Yeah, hope that's okay?'

'Yes, of course it is, darling, the more the merrier. Uncle Jeff said I'll be lucky if a handful of people turn up.'

'That was nice of him!'

'Yes, that's what I thought.' Della chuckled. 'So, when are you due at the station?'

'Oh, we're not getting the train. We're getting a lift so we'll see you at the shop, okay? Is everything all right? Are you nervous?'

'No. Well, yes, of course I am. I'm completely petrified . . .'

'You'll be fine, Mum. You'll be great! Phone's almost out of charge, see you soon, okay?' And with that, she rang off.

Della would have preferred to pick up Sophie from Heathfield station, and to have her comforting presence – in lieu of a husband's – before setting off for Burley Bridge. She wanted *someone* sitting in the passenger seat with her, but Freda had arranged to head over with Angie and Meg from the castle, bringing with them a great pile of cakes, sandwiches and vol au vents that the tearoom staff had prepared for the party. So Della set off alone, her hair freshly blow dried, wearing the dazzling cobalt blue dress that had been tossed aside in a fit of annoyance prior to her fiftieth birthday. It now fitted her perfectly. Just for the hell of it, she was wearing the siren slip underneath; no one else would know, of course, but *she* would. And as the road dipped down to Burley Bridge Della's nervousness ebbed into a kind of anticipation, and she decided that yesterday didn't matter; she had tried, at least. She had managed perfectly well for fifty years without having Rafael Avina in her life, and now she had a shop to open up to the general public.

She lifted the case of wine from the back seat and let herself in, clicked on the lights and took a moment to absorb the transformation that had taken place. The lamps cast a honeyed glow over the shop, and the shelves, crammed with treasures, looked perfect. She straightened books' spines unnecessarily and made herself a coffee from the percolator that sat on a shelf behind the counter. She fiddled with the till and stacked the wine in the small fridge, wondering now whether Jeff had been right that few people would deign to visit a bookshop – especially a specialist bookshop – on what had turned into a rather damp and drizzly October afternoon. But suddenly she didn't have time to fret any more because Freda and Angie and Meg had swept in, laden with trays of party food, followed by Sophie together with an incredibly tall girl with choppy bleached hair.

'Mum, this is Becca! The one I told you about? She lives across the hall . . .'

'Hi, Becca, lovely to meet you. How did you two get here?'

'My dad gave us a lift,' Becca explained.

Della's attention was caught by the painting, which Sophie must have brought with her, the stunning picture of a bookshop in dazzling colours and flecked with gold.

'It's incredible! We must put it up right now. Where d'you want it to go, Dell?' asked Freda, already grappling with it.

'Er . . . there, please.' Della indicated the bare cerise wall.

'D'you have a hammer?'

'Not here, no.' As they ummed and ahhed over how to hang the painting, Liam arrived and gave Sophie a brief, rather awkward hug, and everyone else started setting out food and unpacking boxes of glasses and plumping up cushions in readiness for the shop's very first customers.

'*You* did this place?' Della heard Sophie exclaim. 'You mean, you built the shelves?'

'Yeah, 'course,' Liam replied. 'Told you I was working here.'

'But I never thought, you know . . . you'd really manage to *do* it. And it's actually quite good!'

'Thanks,' he said with a snigger.

'No, I mean it. It's amazing. So, um . . . have you been all right?'

While Della was trying not to eavesdrop, she couldn't help hearing snatches of conversation. 'Yeah, I've been fine. Busy, y'know, with this place.'

'Yeah. So, um . . . we're okay, then? We're friends?'

''Course we are,' Liam blustered, before scuttling out of the shop to fetch a hammer from his father's van. Just as the painting had been hung the villagers began to arrive: Len from the garage and Irene Bagshott, laden with a tray of tiny pies. 'Is this okay, Della? Just a small contribution. Your mum said how much she enjoyed hers, how crisp my pastry was . . .'

'Of course it's okay, it's wonderful,' Della said, hugging her.

Nicola Crowther the hairdresser strode in, with a startling new blonde do, followed by Nathan, who swooped on her immediately. 'Hi, I'm Nathan Sanderson, I let Della this place. And you are . . . ?'

'Er . . . Nicola.'

'She wasn't sure, you know, but I always reckoned it had huge potential . . .' Nathan grabbed two glasses of wine from the tray that Angie was offering around and handed one to Nicola. And now here was Georgia, who manned the castle ticket office, and Harry who tended the grounds, plus Charlotte, accompanied by a woman Della had never met. 'This is Jessie from the *Heathfield Gazette*.'

'From the paper?' Della exclaimed.

'Yes,' Jessie said – she looked barely old enough to have a job at all – 'we received your press release.' Amidst all the activity Della had forgotten she had sent it out. 'I'd like to do a feature on you, just a quick interview, the photographer should be here any minute . . .'

'Yes, of course,' Della said, her attention caught now by Roxanne, who flew in apologising volubly. 'Sorry I'm late, Dell. Traffic was awful, totally jammed up on the M1. I wanted to come early, help you get ready . . .'

'It's fine, don't worry, I'm so thrilled you're here.' Roxanne caught Sophie's eye and kissed her, and Della glanced at her sister as she greeted everyone else. This time, though, it was the books that entranced them, rather than the glamorous fashion journalist from London. 'Look at this,' Nicola marvelled, selecting *Fear of Frying* from a shelf. 'These are amazing. I don't cook, you know. D'you have any books for people like me?'

Della laughed and handed her *What to Cook Today* and was just about to select other possibilities when she was whisked off to a corner by Jessie from the *Gazette*, to be interviewed about how the shop came to be.

'Why did your mum collect so many books?' Jessie wanted to know.

The Recipe Sharing Society – Kitty's alibi – flickered into Della's mind. 'I'm not sure how it started but once it had, it sort of kept going, you know? She just kept buying more and more until they took over the whole house.'

'This is when you were a little girl?'

Della smiled. 'Oh, yes, she already had a pretty serious habit by then. She never stopped. It's as if she was looking for, you know, the *one* . . .'

The shop door opened again and Della's stomach

lurched. Val, her mother-in-law, had wandered in, wearing that frozen expression that usually suggests a horror of walking into a party alone.

'I wonder if she ever found it,' Jessie mused. 'The one, I mean.'

But Val wasn't alone because Terry had shuffled in behind her, reminding Della of the teenagers who would sometimes be hauled along by a parent on a tour of Heathfield Castle when they would dearly have loved to have been anywhere else. And then Della was no long registering Jessie's questions because Mark had just walked in.

'Della?' Jessie prompted her.

'Oh, sorry, it's just, I should really chat to everyone. '

'Yes, I realise this isn't the best time. Could I possibly email you some questions?'

'Yes, of course.' She smiled apologetically, her heart thudding as she made her way through the crowd. '*Cooking With Crisps*!' someone exclaimed, waving a faded old book in the air. 'Did anyone actually ever do that?' Della flashed a quick smile but it felt tight and awkward. She caught Sophie throwing her an anxious look as she strode towards Mark and his parents.

'Hi,' Della said flatly.

Mark formed a pained little smile and swept back his hair. 'Hi, Dell. Er, hope you don't mind us gatecrashing your party?'

'No, of course not.' *No, I'm delighted to see my cheating husband making a surprise appearance just as I'm being interviewed for a newspaper.* She turned to Val and smiled rigidly. 'I'm really glad you're here, Val. I did want to invite you personally, but—'

'Oh, no, I understand,' her mother-in-law whispered, as if cancer was being discussed.

337

'It's just, er, you know – things are a bit tricky right now.' Della was aware of a twitching sensation beneath her left eye.

'Yes,' Val whispered, 'we're terribly sad about the whole situation.' She threw Terry an imploring look. He just stared ahead as if watching an uneventful football game.

'So,' Mark boomed, far too loudly, 'shall we just have a look around, Mum? Oh, Dad, look – there's Sophie.' And the three of them beetled off, leaving Della wondering what had possessed her husband to think it might be a good idea to show up.

Freda hurried over to her, clutching a glass of wine. 'Here, you look like you need this.'

'No, it's fine, I'm driving home later.'

Freda sipped from the glass and threw Mark a sour look. 'What are *they* doing here anyway?'

'Honestly, I haven't a clue.' She watched him, chatting awkwardly to Sophie while Liam and Becca hovered close by, helping themselves to Meg's cakes with the enthusiasm of children at a birthday party.

'He just couldn't keep away, could he?' Freda went on. 'This is *your* day, you've worked so hard for this.'

'It's okay, Della said quickly. 'I'm not going to let him spoil it.' And she fixed on a smile as the photographer from the *Gazette* arrived, introducing himself as Darren and taking her photo while she still looked a little shell-shocked after Mark's appearance. Her husband had likened Kitty's legacy to scurvy and smallpox. So was he just here to gloat, to remind her that a cookbook shop wasn't *viable*?

Della kept glancing at him as she went around topping up glasses and managing to enthuse over various books her guests had plucked from the shelves. Cooking with

Lard, *yes, amazing! Oh, yes, that fondue guide is one of my favourites too* . . . Over by the counter, which was being manned by Freda, Nathan seemed to have cornered Nicola Crowther. 'Look, if you're interested in a new heating system for your salon, electric radiators are the way forward now. Zero maintenance, no fiddly bleeding to do, instant heat whenever and wherever you want it, I can do you a special deal . . .'

She noticed Mark and his parents standing together, looking a little isolated amidst the throng. The teenagers had moved over to a small table bearing an opened bottle of wine and were casually topping up their glasses. Sophie looked beautiful, Della thought, in a simple vintage black lace dress and Kitty's delicate gold chain. The three of them were locked in intense conversation, and she saw Liam burst out laughing at something Becca had said. How relaxed they seemed, Sophie and Liam and Becca, who was now waving towards the door.

Della followed her gaze as a man walked in, tall and brown-haired and casually dressed in a white shirt and dark jeans. 'We're here!' Becca called out with a wave, and his face broke into a grin. Della looked at the man again. It was *him:* Eddie's dad, whom she'd left standing on the pavement when she ran off in pursuit of Mark. He made his way towards her. 'Hi,' he said. 'Hope it's okay to just drop in like this . . .'

'Yes, of course it is. What a lovely surprise. It was an open invitation, you know.'

'I hoped it was. I was intrigued, you see, when Becca mentioned your shop. I mean, I knew it *had* to be yours.'

Della smiled. 'Yes, there's only one bookshop in Burley Bridge. So . . . you're Becca's dad?'

He nodded. 'That's right. Oh, I know what you're

thinking. There's quite a gap between her and Eddie. Ten years, in fact.'

'That *is* quite a gap.'

'Keeps me on my toes.' He chuckled. 'You know, I saw you that day they moved into halls. I hope that doesn't sound stalkery . . .'

'Of course not,' Della laughed. 'You should have come over and said hi.' She took in his wide smile and kind blue eyes, and willed Mark and his parents to tire of browsing the books and leave. This felt better: getting to know the parent of one of Sophie's new friends, the two of them in the same boat. She wanted to ask how he had felt that day, and how it was now with Becca gone. Plus, he was attractive, she happened to note – and there was no wedding ring. While she wasn't sure if she would ever be ready to meet anyone else, she wasn't entirely against the idea of befriending the handsome father of one of Sophie's new college mates.

'. . . Oh, I wasn't terribly together that day,' he said. 'You know, I'd hoped we might might spend some time together, Becca and me. But she virtually marched me off the premises . . .'

Della laughed. 'So much for the tearful parting. So, um, you drove the girls over today? That was good of you.'

'Ah, I had an ulterior motive,' he explained. 'You see, I'm a bit of a keen amateur cook . . .' His voice tailed off as Mark appeared at his side, clearly curious as to who this stranger might be.

Della cleared her throat. 'Mark, this, is, er . . . I'm sorry, I don't even know your name.'

'Frank,' the man said.

'This is Mark, Sophie's dad . . .' *Who really should be thinking about leaving now.*

340

'Good to meet you, Mark.' Frank smiled brightly. 'Anyway, I'm just going to have a browse, if that's okay?'

'Of course,' Della told him. Frank wandered off to the baking section, leaving Della and Mark hovering in awkward silence. 'Can I just ask what you're doing here?' she muttered.

'Nothing! I just wanted to show my support.'

She stared at the man who had wooed her, she supposed, in the old-fashioned way, all those years ago by festooning her with gifts and dinners and attention. How she had loved him, and how she wanted him to be very far away now. 'I don't need your support, Mark.'

His face – which she'd once thought the most handsome she had ever seen – seemed to crumple. 'I can understand why you'd feel that way. Look, I'm sorry, Dell. Maybe I should have called you first instead of just bowling up like this . . .'

'With your mum and dad,' she cut in.

'Okay, okay. It was a mistake, I can see that now. But I just, well . . .' He raked back his hair again. 'Can we talk somewhere private, just for a moment?'

'Do we have to? This is my party, you know. I'm kind of *busy*.'

He gave her a pained look. 'I'd really appreciate it if we could, Dell.'

'Oh, come on then.' She pursed her lips and led him through the throng to the tiny store room at the back. 'What's this about?'

He looked around distractedly, not that there was much to see: just an old Belfast sink, plus boxes of overspill books that hadn't fitted onto the shelves and a wicker basket of light bulbs. Mark cleared his throat. 'It's true, I wanted to support you, but more than that . . .' He tailed off.

341

'You wanted to unnerve me on my opening day?'

'No! Honestly, of course I didn't, what kind of monster do you think I am?'

She glowered at him. 'It's a wonder you didn't bring Polly. Would she have enjoyed this? A free glass of wine and some cake?'

'Della, please . . .'

'I mean,' she snapped, 'if you were planning to shake me up on a day I've worked so hard towards, then that would have been a good way to—'

'It's over!' he barked.

Della stared at him. 'I know. You've made that pretty clear.'

'No, no, not *us*. I mean Polly and me.'

'What d'you mean, it's over?'

He groaned, as if in actual pain, and rubbed at his face with his hands. 'It was a total mess-up, Dell. I think I went slightly mad. Well, not slightly. Completely, really. I don't know what happened. It just kind of started up, and then sort of escalated and ran completely out of control . . .'

She regarded him coolly. 'You're making it sound like a train.'

'Yes, well, it sort of was.'

'As if you had nothing to do with it at all?'

'Exactly!' Relief was flickering in Mark's greeny-blue eyes as if he was off the hook, having merely lost control of his faculties temporarily and been unable to prevent the marital catastrophe that had ensued. 'Honestly,' he ploughed on, 'I didn't mean to hurt you and upset Sophie and mess up our whole family like that. D'you believe me, darling? We have a life together, a family and a house, and I think you're incredible. I suppose I'd started to take all of that for granted . . .' Della stared at the face she had once thought she would never tire of looking at. Sometimes, in their early months together, she had lain awake in the bed they shared and simply watched him sleep. '. . . what you've done here is amazing,' he added, a crack in his voice now as if he might actually cry. 'I know I was against you opening a shop and, to be honest, I probably felt a bit threatened . . .'

'Threatened, by *cookbooks*?'

'Yes . . . no – I mean, by you moving on, being so determined to do your own thing and make it work. Imagine what your mum would think, Dell. She'd be so proud.'

'I don't know about that,' she said tartly.

'And you . . . look at you now, in your stunning dress. You look sensational. Have you lost weight?'

Della's mouth was hanging open. Not an attractive look, she was aware of that, but she didn't care. She stared at her husband, realising she no longer felt angry or bitter towards him; in fact, she felt nothing at all. 'Mark,' she started, 'I have to say, all those lies you told – well, they were just incredible.'

His face sagged. 'What d'you—'

'The golf clubs, for one thing,' she cut in sharply. 'Going to the lengths of buying them and setting out cheerfully every Saturday morning when you were seeing *her*. And lying about having to move to a different course! You actually sat next to me and told me all about the problems with moles.'

'The moles are true!' he protested. 'You saw on the website . . .'

'And getting drunk on Peter's birthday . . . does Peter even exist?'

Mark dropped his gaze. 'Uh, look, Dell, I know I behaved abominably but I'm trying to apologise . . .'

'It's too late,' she said firmly, breaking off because Angie had appeared and was grimacing apologetically.

'Sorry to interrupt.' She glanced from Mark to Della, widening her eyes in a *you-need-to-come-with-me-now* sort of way. 'It's just, some people have arrived, Dell, and they were wondering where you were.'

'Oh, who's that?' She stepped gratefully away from Mark, leaving him looking stranded amidst the lightbulbs and boxes of books.

'I'm not sure, they're an older couple.' Della followed her and scanned the still bustling shop. 'Look, they're over there, by the till.'

Della's heart seemed to stop as she saw Monica . . . and Rafael, who was gazing around with open curiosity. Della scurried towards them. 'Hello! Oh, I'm so glad you could come.' She kissed Monica's cheek, then, not knowing how to great Rafael, she took hold of his hand and shook it, which seemed to startle him. He glanced at Monica as if awaiting instructions on what to do next.

'This place is wonderful, Della,' she enthused, turning to Rafael. 'So beautiful and creative. We must buy something. It's time you learned to cook, Raff.'

'It's a little late for that,' he said, and Della saw his mouth curl into a hesitant smile.

She looked at the rather shambolic elderly man from whom, perhaps not entirely reasonably, she had expected so much. But the next thing she knew, he had leaned towards her and was mumbling something into her hair that sounded like, *I'm sorry.*

She frowned and studied his face. 'Why are you sorry?'

Rafael shrugged. He was wearing the same brown

corduroys and even the same checked shirt as the first time she had met him. 'For yesterday,' he said.

Della glanced at Monica who raised an eyebrow and subtly – tenderly, Della thought – touched Rafael's arm. 'It's okay,' Della said gently. 'And, you know . . . it's never too late.'

He looked up, and she saw his gaze flicker across a shelf crammed with books: the treasures she had loved as a child. 'To learn to cook, you mean?' he asked hopefully.

'Yes, that,' she said, smiling, 'but anything, really. It's never too late for anything at all.'

Chapter Thirty-Five

Della introduced Monica and Rafael to Sophie – simply as Monica and Rafael, all the rest could come later – and then, rather bizarrely, to Frank, because he strolled right by them with a whopping a pile of books. 'You're my first customer,' she said, taking over from Freda at the till, her heart soaring as she deposited his purchases in a Rosemary Lane brown paper bag.

'I'm honoured,' he said.

'Well, I hope you'll be a regular here.' She glimpsed Mark, who had finally emerged from the store room – perhaps he'd needed to take a few moments to compose himself – and had now resumed the bland expression he reserved for conversing with his parents. He was so out of place, Della decided, in a bookshop. In fact, books seemed to agitate him. When she was little, Sophie had reached up to the shelf in the living room for his enormous tome about Bauhaus architecture – it weighed about the same as a small refrigerator – probably attracted by its bright yellow spine. 'That's not for you!' Mark had exclaimed, and she had dropped it with a thud. The corner had dented, the dust cover torn. Of course, he wasn't a bad father. He loved their daughter to distraction; he was admiring her painting now, and loudly telling anyone who'd listen that it was Sophie's work. His parents stared blankly at it as if it were any old Debenham's print.

Beside them, Nathan was still trying to charm Nicola Crowther, who was tactfully moving the conversation away from radiators now. 'D'you like teddy bears, Nicola? That's another sideline I have, beautifully made – real glass eyes – heirlooms really, rather than toys.' Della smiled and caught Frank's eye across the shop. He seemed in no hurry to leave, she noticed, but then, she assumed he would be taking Sophie and Becca back to their halls. Whatever, she couldn't quite understand why it made her so happy to see him here.

'Erm, we're heading off now,' Mark muttered, appearing at her side. 'Mum's got a bit of a tummy upset, thinks she's had too much of all that rich food.'

Della gave the plundered plates of sandwiches, cakes and vol au vents a cursory glance. 'Sorry to hear that.'

He grimaced at her. 'So we'll talk, yes?'

She nodded. 'I suppose it'll be necessary at some point.'

Mark nodded, rather sadly it seemed, then ushered his parents towards the door. It wouldn't be so bad, being single, reflected Della as she watched them leave; it was hardly unusual, after all. Freda was divorced, and roughly half of Sophie's friends' parents were no longer together. It happened, and sometimes it was for the best. After all, she had felt alone for a very long time and now she could simply be herself – and *please* herself – without constantly worrying that someone was finding her lacking in some way. Della had lost any desire to whack Mark with a golf club. She didn't even want to report him to the Institute

347

of Chiropodists and Podiatrists any more. She just wanted to throw herself into her bookshop and amass yet more lovely vintage cookbooks; she pictured baking classes here . . . perhaps she could hire Freda to lead those? A temporary worktop could be installed in the shop, and the store room could be remodelled to accommodate an oven.

Her mind raced as she looked around with pride. Freda was back on the till, which rang constantly. Despite Mark's insistence that there wouldn't be any passing trade, several people had wandered in, fuelled by curiosity, having seen the busy shop from the street.

'This is the most comforting bookshop I've ever been in,' enthused Irene, landing heavily in the armchair with a large glass of wine in one hand and a slab of coffee and walnut cake in the other.

'She's right, it's absolutely wonderful,' Rafael remarked to Monica, who was flicking through a book on Turkish cookery with rapt interest. He turned to Della, busy offering glasses of wine to the new arrivals. 'And what are all those hanging there?' He indicated the row of hooks where Kitty's aprons hung, next to the jar of her favourite utensils.

'They're Kitty's things,' she said. 'I thought they belonged here with her books.'

'Oh, I see.' A moment of awkwardness passed between them.

'We *can* talk about Kitty, can't we?' she ventured as Monica wandered away to investigate the baking section.

'Yes, of course we can. We probably should, I suppose.'

'Not now, though,' she added, and he smiled.

'Perhaps not, Della.'

A comfortable pause settled between them. 'I'd love to meet up again,' she added, 'if you'd like to.'

'Yes . . . yes, of course.'

She paused. 'Weren't you supposed to be going away to the Lake District today? It's just, Monica said—'

'Oh, I'm joining them tomorrow,' Rafael said with a chuckle. 'I didn't want to miss this. I wanted to, you know, see you *properly*, rather than going away on my trip and worrying that I'd made a bad impression on you.'

'Well, thank you, Rafael. It's meant a lot to me today, you being here.' It was true. Yesterday she had felt pretty certain that they would never have any kind of relationship, and now she knew that wasn't the case.

'Ah, never mind that,' he dismissed her thanks. 'Now off you go and look after your guests.'

She smiled, and found Charlotte and a rather tipsy Irene agreeing that online recipes were fine, but what you really wanted was to turn the pages, to hold a cookbook in your hands.

And so the party went on, with more wine brought out as the day tipped into evening. There were now just a dozen or so people in the shop, still browsing the shelves or lolling on the red velvet sofa. Frank was chatting to Len from the garage, and had assumed a patient expression while being instructed on how to consume minimal fuel while driving. 'Obviously, don't drive with extra weight, like a roof box on or golf clubs stashed in the boot . . .' Della winced and tuned into a conversation between the two older, immaculately turned out women who worked in Nicola's salon. There was much talk of childhood picnics, of Christmas dinners and outrageous birthday cakes. It was the only party Della had ever been to where goose fat and dripping were discussed. 'Of course, it has to be goose fat for roast potatoes,' Nicola declared, adding, 'Nathan, would you like to come over for Sunday lunch sometime?'

'Oh, I'd love to, thank you.'

'Tomorrow, then?'

'Um, yes! Why not?'

Della smiled, taking it all in for a moment and thinking: well, here is it, it's real now. Just a few weeks ago she had wondered if a vague intention of selling books about fondues and suet puddings indicated that she was going quite mad. And now it was clear that she wasn't.

Gradually, clutching brown paper bags of books, Della's guests started to drift away. Sophie, Becca and Liam had gone on to 'a bit of a party' at his place, and Monica hugged Della goodbye. 'We've had the most lovely time,' she exclaimed, clearly a little merry and still clutching her wine glass. 'Thank you, Della. Raff's driving,' she added, patting his arm as if were her chauffeur.

'See you soon, Della,' Rafael said, giving her a brief, rather awkward hug.

'Yes, definitely, and enjoy your trip.' She watched them leave, conscious that Frank was still here, with just a few of Della's friends who were beginning to tidy up. He looked as if he didn't quite know where to put himself.

'Can I help?' he asked.

'Oh, we're fine, thanks,' said Charlotte, gathering up plates and glasses and stashing half-empty wine bottles back in the fridge.

'No need to rush off, though,' Della added, surprised by her boldness. In fact, Frank seemed eager to linger, replacing on shelves books that had been left scattered around, and sweeping up crumbs from the floor. When that was done, he and Freda washed up, while Meg dried and Della found herself feeling quite redundant. 'D'you need a lift anywhere, Frank?' Angie asked as she pulled on her coat.

'No, thanks, my car's just down the road.'

She smiled at him then hugged Della, exclaiming, 'You should be incredibly proud of yourself.'

'D'you know,' she said, feeling oddly tearful, 'I really am.'

Della's friends left in a flurry, leaving her and Frank alone in the shop together. Della sank into the sofa and motioned for him to join her. 'Exhausted?' he asked.

'It's funny, but no, not at all. I'm just relieved it went so well.' She looked at him, wondering if he had stayed on out of politeness; perhaps he was one of those types who liked to be busy, to feel useful.

'It was a perfect day,' he said. 'I hope I haven't outstayed my welcome. Do say, if you want to lock up and go home now.'

'No, not at all.' They sat for a moment, and the silence that settled around them felt anything but awkward. She got up and wandered towards the door, where she turned the sign to 'Closed'. Then, hoping he wasn't about to leave, she sat back beside him and started to tell him – for no other reason than that he was there, and she felt able to – about what had happened to her during the past few weeks.

Frank listened, and after a while Della grew embarrassed. 'Sorry, I don't know why I'm telling you all this.'

He touched her arm, and she looked at the man who already felt like a friend. 'I'm glad you have,' he said.

'So, what about you? Are you married?'

He shook his head. 'I'm divorced. Jill left when Eddie was two. There was no one else, though – she just needed to leave, she said. Left the kids with me. We hadn't planned to have Eddie and I don't think she could face going through the whole thing again.'

'How was it for them?' Della asked.

Frank shrugged. 'Harder on Becca, really. She was twelve – needed her mum around. But we got there. Over the years Jill decided she'd changed her mind, that she wanted custody, but then at the last minute – when it was about to become legally messy – she backed down and said they could stay with me.'

Della frowned. 'That sounds pretty harrowing.'

'Yes, well, all's calm at the moment, but who knows?' He smiled, and her heart turned over. 'Becca's very taken with Sophie, you know. Non-stop chatter in the car all the way from Leeds. She said it feels like they've always known each other.'

Della looked at him. *I know that feeling,* she thought. 'Are you sure you don't want me to go?' he added.

'No, of course I don't.' They were sitting closer together now; Della wasn't sure how that had happened. 'Tell me more about you,' she prompted him.

And so he told her about working at an architectural practice, and then latterly setting up on his own, working from home, a few miles out of Heathfield. He wasn't flooded with work but there was always enough to keep things ticking along. 'It's been better for Eddie,' he explained. 'More flexible, and I can be my own person, spend more time with him.'

Della nodded. 'It was quite a brave thing to do, though.'

'I suppose so. Like opening this place.'

'Well, I sort of had to do that,' she said with a smile. 'I mean, as soon as the idea came to me, I just knew it was right.'

'You'll make a big success of it,' Frank remarked.

'I'll give it my best shot anyway. The party went well, didn't it?'

He grinned. 'Yes, the place was packed! There was a cookbook stampede.'

'Hardly,' she said, laughing, but knowing what he meant: the place had whipped up enthusiasm for food, for recipes, for sharing. She knew now that one of her very first tasks when she opened on Monday morning would be to set up a Recipe Sharing Society of her own.

How natural it seemed to Della, being here with Frank as they exchanged life stories. 'No one will ever want to leave,' Irene had said, and she was right. And when sleepiness finally started to creep over her, Della glanced towards the window and gasped. 'It's getting light out there!'

Frank laughed. 'God, yes. We've sat here talking all night. I don't think I've done that since university.'

'I don't think I *ever* have,' laughed Della, resting her head on his shoulder. 'So, are we done, then? D'you think we know all about each other now?'

He wound an arm around her and she edged a little closer. 'I don't know about that. In fact, you know what I'd like to do now?'

She glanced at him. 'No, what?'

'I'd like to ask you one more question, if that's okay.'

'Of course it's okay,' she said, closing her eyes for a moment. She sensed him hesitate, and when she opened her eyes and turned to look at him, she knew what that question would be.

'Can I kiss you, Della?'

She looked at the man who had strolled into her shop – and her life – and answered him, not with words but a kiss. Her head spun as they kissed gently, surrounded by her mother's legacy. It felt like a very promising start to The Bookshop on Rosemary Lane.

Chapter Thirty-Six

Five Months Later

'I'm not sure about you on these roads,' he said.

'It's fine, don't worry.'

'These bends are awfully tight.'

'Yes, I can see that. It's okay. Please stop worrying . . .' *I'm fifty years old,* she wanted to add. *I passed my driving test thirty-one years ago.* She shot him a quick look, then focused on the frankly perilous bend ahead.

'You're too far in the middle of the road. Get further over to the edge . . .'

'Please, can you just pipe down and let me drive?'

'Move over! Christ, Della . . .'

'Please don't touch the steering wheel!'

A petulant sigh. 'Okay, if you say so. Just drive how you like. Dither about all over the roads. I won't say another word.' He stared moodily out of the passenger window. Della glanced to her right, where his hot breath was misting the glass. What had possessed her to think this would be a good idea? She could see his chest rising and falling agitatedly, and his hands clenched into fists on his lap. 'Are you sure about this trip?' Sophie had asked.

Yes, of course she was. 'Well, good luck then,' her daughter had added, and she'd sensed exasperation radiating down the phone.

In fact, Della *was* a little uncertain about using a left-hand drive car – Mark had always done the driving on rare holidays to France or Spain – not to mention the roads which zig-zagged up the mountainside, although there was no way she was prepared to admit that. She had booked their accommodation and flights, plus the hire car; she had researched enticing restaurants in the hills, plus quiet coves where they could enjoy a swim. She had figured out the local food markets and had even packed a cook-book, for goodness' sake. She was in charge of the trip.

'Can't you just look out at the scenery and enjoy it?' she remarked, remembering saying something similar to Sophie as a child after her parents had had the bright idea of taking her on a scintillating drive to see some stalagmite caves. The journey had taken way longer than she and Mark had anticipated, and Sophie had huffed and sighed in the back. *Are we nearly there yet? Will I like it? How long do we have to stay?*

As her daughter's whining had reached critical levels, Della had handed her a mini carton of apple juice, which she had squirted through the straw onto the back of her mother's head. Thankfully, this hadn't happened so far today. She looked at Rafael, who now appeared to be trying to relax, albeit in a rather self-conscious way, by gazing out at the scenery, as directed.

It was just the two of them, for now: Della and Rafael, getting to know each other at last. She'd been surprised that he had agreed to come on the trip. Monica had been all for it. 'It's just what he needs, the grumpy old fool, after spending far too much time with his cynical friends. Go on – show him how to enjoy himself, for goodness' sake.'

Was he enjoying himself now? Della wasn't so sure. They had met several times; she had even spent a night in a lumpy single bed at his place, shortly after he had returned from his Lake District jaunt. But she didn't know him – at least, not yet – and she had the uneasy sensation of having found herself in sole charge of a rather unpredictable child who wasn't hers.

One minute he was looking out at the roughly chiselled mountains with rapt interest; the next he was fiddling with the air conditioning. Perhaps he was nervous, she reflected. The villa she had booked was just outside the village where he'd grown up. She'd hoped this might help to make things more comfortable between them; that, once they had settled in, he might offer to show her around. 'Rafael,' she ventured, 'I was thinking, shall we just spend the afternoon in the garden today, and maybe you could show me around tomorrow?'

'That sounds okay,' he said non-committally. *Maybe you're tired after the flight?* she wanted to suggest. However, wary of sounding patronising, she decided to leave it.

'When was the last time you were here?' she asked.

Rafael shrugged. 'When I was a child.'

'You mean . . . a small child? Didn't you ever come back after your family left for Valencia?'

'No, I never got around to it,' he said, rather gruffly, and they lapsed into silence again, although at least he was no longer grumbling about her driving. And he was right about one thing: Majorca was beautiful in spring. The sky was a bright wash of blue, the air warm with a light breeze, the hillsides green and lush and yet to be parched by the hot summer sun.

Della could understand why Pattie and Christine had

356

upped sticks from Burley Bridge to live here. It was stunning. She had already had a text from Freda, who was manning the bookshop, to tell her that back home it was tipping with rain, and that a young woman – early thirties, in a sort of smock top – had sunk gratefully into the red velvet sofa that morning and chatted about her new home, Rosemary Cottage. She and her husband had two young children with a third on the way and she had completely run out of ideas about what to cook.

All three of the Cartwright siblings had been surprised by how quickly Rosemary Cottage had sold. Della had expected to feel a wrench the first time she saw the new owners' curtains at the windows, their car parked outside. But it had felt fine. They had already attacked the garden with gusto, and all through the winter she had noticed new additions to the lawn: a swing, followed by a sandpit, then a trampoline. She had often glimpsed small children bouncing perilously close to its edge.

'Rafael, would you check the directions for me, please?' He looked around distractedly as if he had no idea what she was talking about. 'To the villa. I printed out the directions – they're in the glove compartment.'

He made a big thing about rummaging about, even though there was only the car's handbook and a sheet of typed A4 in there. He unfolded it and peered at it. 'I'm not very good with maps.'

'Oh, come on,' Della cajoled him. 'This is your homeland, Rafael. It's in your blood.'

He smirked, and she glimpsed a hint of amusement in his dark eyes. 'Okay, keep following the road until you see a right-hand turn, then take that for, uh, five kilometres or so. We'll pass a farm, a small village – I do remember a very nice little restaurant there.'

They reached the village, and Della was taken aback by its weathered beauty. 'It's lovely here, Rafael.'

'Yes – that's my old house, just down that lane.'

'Really?' She glanced at it quickly, wary of letting her attention wander when he clearly didn't believe that she was capable of driving a car safely.

'Oh, yes, that's the place I grew up.'

'Shall we stop? Do you want to see?'

'No, no, just drive on,' he commanded, and she smiled, thinking now of her childhood in her own sleepy village. She told him about cycling along the leaf-strewn lanes of Burley Bridge, and the long, long days that turned her skin honey-brown, before Kitty called them all in for tea.

They found the villa easily, and she opened the shutters to let sunshine stream in. While Rafael prowled around the small garden she prepared a simple lunch of bread, ham and cheese, which she carried outside. 'Isn't this lovely?' she said. Rafael conceded that it was. As conversation faltered, Della fetched the bottle of wine she'd bought and poured them two large tumblersful to drink on the terracotta-tiled terrace. She had thought that, with a little wine inside them, they might while away their first afternoon talking about Rafael and Kitty and what really happened all those years ago. But instead, still wearing those corduroys which were surely too hot for the weather, he disappeared into the villa.

She waited, and dozed, and an hour or so later glimpsed Rafael bringing something out to the terrace. 'I found this in my bedroom,' he explained.

'Oh, I'm sorry, I don't play chess.'

'It's very easy, Della.'

She watched as he set out the worn wooden pieces. 'Honestly, it's not really my sort of thing.'

'Why do you say that? Didn't you have a chess set at home?'

'Not as a child, no. There is one in my house, though – it's Mark's. I bought it for him in the hope that'd he'd teach Sophie.' So they'd have something they could do together, she reflected, which was perhaps Rafael's reasoning now. So she listened as he explained all the moves, and enjoyed the scent of the thyme wafting from the garden as they began to play. The game drifted on, taking hours, it seemed – just like golf. Only, she found herself enjoying the steady pace, and the fact that Rafael clearly had no intention of letting her win. Of course he didn't. She wasn't a child. 'You've just thrashed me, Rafael,' she laughed when they'd finished.

'You'll learn,' he said wryly. 'By the end of the week you'll be winning, you'll see.'

Della very much doubted that, but what she could do was take charge of provisions. Next day they explored the local market, returning home with gnarly loaves and paper bags of plump tomatoes, great bunches of heady basil and oozing cheeses. Della couldn't remember being so content for a very long time. 'You must let me pay,' Rafael kept saying, delving into the pockets of his cords whenever they stopped off at a bar.

'Not this time,' she insisted. 'Next trip you can, but this is my treat.' In fact, she was enjoying spoiling him, and seeing his face light up with pleasure when she'd driven into the nearest town alone and returned with a cake or a chocolate tart. For once she could afford a holiday, so why shouldn't she spoil him a little?

It had taken ten weeks for Kitty's will to be settled, even though it was pretty simple: everything to be split three ways. Jeff was using his share to add yet another extension to his house, building on to the kitchen so it would gobble up pretty much all of the garden. A vast island workspace would be installed in the middle of the sparkling new area, with a super-sized American-style fridge to house all that leftover pecorino and kale. 'I've always wanted an ice maker,' Tamsin had enthused.

Less forthcoming about what she would do with her share, Roxanne eventually admitted, 'Oh, there's a stunning coat I have my eye on.'

'You're spending it all on a coat?' Della exclaimed, before catching herself: she sounded like Kitty.

'No, not *all*. But I want to have fun with it. That's what you should do too.' Roxanne was right, and what had Della done but booked this holiday, and successfully bid on three more cookbook collections on eBay, which would be arriving shortly after she arrived home? She still had some of her inheritance left over – at least enough to provide a sort of safety net, should the bookshop fail. But in fact, it was already thriving. She loved being there so much, she had started to think about selling 57 Pickering Street and approaching Nathan about possibly buying the shop outright, along with the flat above it. The house in Heathfield was far too big for one person. It belonged to her former life, not the one she was living now.

By the third day of their holiday Della and Rafael had settled into a comfortable pattern of enjoying a morning walk before settling at the poolside. 'Are you sure you're okay about them coming?' she asked, leaning over to top up his glass from their jug of iced water.

'Of course,' he said, 'why do you ask?'

'Well, it's your holiday too.' She watched as he stood

up and stretched tall, then strode to the pool's edge and proceeded to dive in.

All the talk about Kitty could wait, she decided, in awe of his power and strength as he ploughed up and down the pool. She had already surmised that he had simply chosen a life with Monica over one with Kitty – and who could blame him, really? He had been guided by his heart, she supposed. It was hard to criticise that.

Rafael emerged from the pool and dried himself vigorously before perching on the sun lounger beside Della's. 'I think you'll like Eddie,' she ventured, checking his expression. 'He's very clever,' she added. 'I bet he'd love it if you taught him to play chess.'

'I might be busy,' Rafael murmured. 'I was thinking of painting tomorrow, going for a hike in the hills.'

'In the evening, then?' she suggested, scrutinising his face. 'You won't want to be hanging around here with me.'

Della frowned, understanding now: while they were here, Rafael wanted her to himself. He was feeling a little possessive. 'Oh, come on, where will we go around here at night? We're in the middle of nowhere! Anyway,' she added, touching his arm, a small gesture that caused his face to soften, 'I'd like to be here with you. And Frank – well, he's important to me too. I'd like you to get to know him.'

'Well, if that's what you want,' Rafael murmured.

'We did talk about it before we came away, didn't we? And you said it would be okay?'

Rafael caught her gaze and nodded. 'Of course it will be. It's just . . . I'm enjoying this.'

So am I, Della decided as she wandered into the cool kitchen and started to prepare dinner, making a simple roast chicken with mashed potatoes and green beans. They ate, sipped wine and played another game of chess before, both sleepy from the sun-filled day, going to bed early.

When she padded out of her small, sun-filled room in the morning, Della was surprised to find Rafael already showered and dressed. 'I'd better leave now,' she said. 'Their flight arrives at nine. Would you mind getting some breakfast together? There's eggs, ham, plenty of fruit.'

'Oh, you know I don't cook,' he said.

Slicing up figs and oranges is hardly cooking, she thought with a smile. 'Coffee, then. Coffee would be good.'

He smiled, and she knew he was teasing because even before she left he was already lifting the cheeses from the fridge: 'They shouldn't be refrigerated, Della. Chills all the taste out of them.' She also knew, as she sped along the motorway, that he would be pottering around, setting the table, a little nervous perhaps, just as she was.

She parked as close as she could to the terminal and strode, in her loose flowery cotton dress and flat sandals, to the arrivals gate. No blow dry, no make-up and certainly no siren slip today. But she felt healthy and tanned and filled with sunshine. She spotted Eddie waving at her. 'The plane was great!' he enthused, running towards her.

'It was his first time,' Frank added, kissing her cheek.

'First time abroad?' she asked.

'Yeah,' Eddie said. 'So, what are we gonna do?'

'Oh, I have a few ideas,' Della replied as Frank's hand wound around hers. He turned and caught her smile, and her heart flipped over as they wandered across the air-conditioned concourse and out through the glass doors into a wall of Majorcan heat. 'Wow, it's so hot!' Eddie exclaimed.

Della laughed and turned to Frank. 'Ready, then?'

'Yes, I'm ready.' He squeezed her hand.

'Come on then,' she said. 'Come and meet my dad.'

Chapter Thirty-Seven

The Bookshop's First Birthday

Sometimes, even though it had been open for a year now, Della still couldn't quite believe she had a shop of her own. Business was brisk, and there were always a hundred tasks on her to-do list, yet at the same time she never felt pressured. Occasionally, it baffled her how everything had fallen into place so easily.

Of course, she had been right in her hunch that people would love such an unusual, specialist shop. However, she hadn't foreseen that she would be featured in glossy magazines – without any involvement from Roxanne – or that her Recipe Sharing Society would fill the shop with excitable chatter and laughter on the first Thursday evening of every month. Monica turned up sometimes. Della tended to see Rafael on the odd Sunday afternoon when they would stroll for hours along the coast, getting to know each other more and slowly filling in all the years they'd missed together. While Jeff seemed nonplussed about the whole situation, Roxanne seemed almost thrilled by their mother's dalliance, and the fact that the Cartwright family set-up was rather more exotic than anyone had known.

363

'I still don't think of Raff as my dad, you know,' Della told Frank, who had come round to help her redecorate the flat above the shop.

'That's natural enough,' he conceded. 'I mean, he didn't raise you or know you as a child. I'm not surprised you can't just switch into a daughter-dad sort of thing with him.'

Della smiled. He just got it, that's what she'd noticed first about Frank; right from the off, he seemed to have understood what she was all about. He was there for her, yet he knew, instinctively, when she needed her own space. They had fallen into a pattern of spending a couple of nights – plus weekends – together, and she couldn't remember ever feeling happier.

'And I had William,' she added, tearing the cellophane off a newly bought paint tray. 'He wasn't involved especially, but he was there, you know, still being my dad? Even when he met Jane and moved away, I always knew that.'

Frank nodded. He, like Della, had grown up with an absent father; perhaps that was why he was so keen to be as committed a dad as he could possibly be. She loved that about him too, the way he never seemed to run out of ideas to make Eddie's life fun. The little drawings and jokey notes slipped in his lunchbox: Della's heart had melted when she'd first seen them. He had a way with teenagers, too. After fitting out Della's shop so beautifully, Liam had been offered enough work to keep him going all year, and now he was busily holed up in Frank's garden, building a summerhouse. She had heard Frank bantering with Liam in a way that she never could.

Frank said he had always wanted a summerhouse but

Della suspected he planned it as a place for them to escape to together, to watch the sun setting over the moors once Eddie was in bed. She loved being at their place out in the country, but she loved her new flat above the shop even more. At least, she would when they had painted the dingy mustard walls and taken down the gloomy curtains to let the sunshine stream in. Together, they began to paint, not in butterfly brights but the clear, pale blue Della had chosen to brighten her tiny home.

They worked quickly, until the light faded, then Della and Frank headed downstairs to the shop to make sure everything was perfect for its first birthday party the next day. Roxanne was arriving from London, and even Jeff said he would put in an appearance. 'It's looking great,' Frank said, 'but we should restock the shelves tonight, there are a few gaps.'

Together, they unpacked a new collection of cookbooks, which they had heard about from a regular customer. 'These are amazing,' Della enthused, sitting cross-legged on the floor beside him. 'So many original fifties ones and they're in great condition.' She pored over a book of elaborate cake recipes, while Frank handed another slim volume to her.

'Look at this, Della.' He nudged her. 'Don't you have this already?'

She turned and peered at an old faded copy of *What to Cook Today:* the first cookbook she had ever turned to, and which had offered such comfort to her as a child. She took it from Frank and flipped through its pages. 'Potato soup. Roast chicken. Semolina pudding. Oh, I remember all this so well . . .'

'Comfort food,' he said with a smile, squeezing her hand.

She nodded, then closed the book and kissed him lightly on the lips. 'D'you think tomorrow will be okay?'

Frank chuckled. 'What d'you mean? Of course it will. You'll be fantastic Dell. You're a natural – you know that.'

She shook her head and laughed. 'I don't mind cooking in front of people. That's okay. It's the other part, *you* know . . .'

'Hey.' Frank smiled and took her in his arms, kissing the top of her head. 'You'll be amazing, darling. Just be yourself.'

After Frank had left to collect Eddie from his mother's, Della ran over and over what she needed to do tomorrow, until she could hardly bear to think about it anymore. It was 8 p.m. and she'd been unable to face any dinner. 'You'll be fine,' Irene said when she dropped off a huge bunch of late-summer blooms from her garden, as promised, to decorate the shop. 'Just relax and be yourself.'

'That's what Frank said,' Della laughed, and together they ran through the recipes again, in order to soothe her nerves.

In fact, Irene had become an important part of the bookshop's success. While Kitty had taken exception to being given a home-baked chicken and leek pie, Irene's reputation as a pastry guru had led to her giving regular demonstrations in the shop, and she and Della had become firm friends. 'The place looks lovely,' Irene remarked, as they arranged the flowers in jars and gave the bookshop a final glance.

'Well, I hope Gemma and the crew think so too.'

'Come on, you know they love it already! They wouldn't be filming here otherwise. I really think this'll lead to your own series, you know.'

'Let's just see,' Della said, hugging Irene as she left, then switching off the lamps before making her way back upstairs to her flat.

Although she didn't expect to sleep that night, soon she drifted off and woke with a start at 5.40 a.m. Far too early to be up, of course, but she slipped out of bed and padded to the kitchen to make a pot of coffee. She didn't have fancy ground beans these days but as she sat at the window and sipped from her mug, it tasted as good as any coffee she had ever had. Della glanced around her freshly painted kitchen. She loved the simplicity and compactness of the flat; it felt like a holiday home. The smaller bedroom was always made up for Sophie, who stayed over more often than Della had anticipated. 'Just fancy chilling for a night,' she'd explain, and Della knew she enjoyed the calm and stillness of her little bedroom overlooking the rolling hills. She stayed over at Mark's too, of course, in their old family house, which he had moved back into, having bought Della out. She was happy for him to have it. She had never felt truly at home there.

She felt utterly at home here, though, and although the kitchen was the smallest she had ever had – it made the one in Pickering Street seem hangar-like in comparison – wonderful dishes were created in it. She was running cookery classes now, inspiring by her meagre facilities: if a whole book could be written about cooking without a kitchen, then this hardly seemed like a challenge at all. And so, Della's regular classes – *Recipes from a Tiny Kitchen* – were born, with word spreading to the point at which a TV production company had heard about them. 'It's an amazing story,' Gemma had said, the first time she'd called. 'Can I come along one evening and watch your class?' Of course she could, Della said – although she hadn't expected anything to come of it. Now here she was, showering and blow drying her hair, even though Gemma had told her that a make-up and hair person would be arriving in plenty of time before shooting began.

She stepped out of the shower, wrapped herself in a huge towel and surveyed her reflection. She, Della Sturgess, was being filmed for TV. The crew would be arriving in a couple of hours on this, the bookshop's first birthday. They would film her demonstrating some simple dishes before an audience, and they would return for three successive weeks after that, then edit it all into a programme just about her. No, not about her, she reminded herself, as panic fluttered in her chest; it was about the shop, a quirky emporium in a previously forgotten Yorkshire village. The bookshop would be the real star of the show. She checked her watch and, when she glanced out and saw Frank's car pull up, hurried downstairs to greet him.

'Wow, you look sensational!' He kissed her cheek, and Eddie sauntered straight to his favourite section where the children's cookbooks were arranged.

'Thanks.' Della grinned and looked down at the new red dress, which fitted her perfectly. 'You don't think it's too much?'

'Of course not. You're going to be on TV, darling. Nothing's too much!' She laughed, aware of a surge of nervousness again, which faded away as Gemma and the TV crew arrived: a cameraman, a sound guy, a couple of assistants plus Andy, the hair and make-up man, who positioned Della in a chair facing the window – 'For natural light, darling' – while he attended to her face.

Her demonstration table was set up already. Gemma and the crew flitted around rearranging things, neatening books on the shelves and placing a jug of pink stocks within view. One of the assistants was marking the spot where Della should stand when demonstrating the recipes, with a cross of blue tape. She had been introduced to the crew but, apart from Gemma, couldn't remember a single person's name.

Andy's blusher brush skimmed Della's cheeks. Mascara was applied, then lipstick – in a vivid red, she was happy to note. She hoped she looked okay, but now everything was out of her hands and she was happy to sit there, being primped, while everyone else milled around her. In the corner of the shop, Frank and Eddie looked on with interest. 'Wow, is that me?' Della laughed as Andy held up a mirror for her to see her reflection.

'It's the TV you,' he said with a grin as the door opened and villagers started to wander in: Morna, Nicola and Irene, and the girls from the chip shop, and Len from the garage, plus his daughter Lucy, who helped out in the bookshop from time to time. Sophie arrived with Becca, having driven them here; she had passed her test, and Della and Mark had clubbed together to buy her a little second-hand Fiat for her birthday. 'Good luck, Mum!' she exclaimed, hugging Della tightly.

'Thank you, sweetheart,' she replied, her heart hammering now.

The shop began to fill, and Gemma motioned for everyone to settle down and Della to take her position at the table. She inhaled deeply and glanced down at the bowls of ingredients for her first dish: a creamy and warming potato soup. She looked up again, and across the shop caught Frank's eye. He smiled encouragingly, and her heart leapt. Then, taking another deep breath, she fixed on a bright smile as a sense of calm settled over her.

She could *do* this. Frank was right; she should just be

herself and everything would be fine. Della skimmed her gaze briefly over the friends and neighbours who had helped and supported her more than she could ever have imagined. She would do this for them, for Kitty, for Sophie and for the village where she had grown up.

And herself, of course. She would do this for the new Della whose life was now very much her own.

The camera was rolling and she ran through the greeting Gemma had asked her to prepare. 'Hello,' Della said warmly, with a big, bright smile, 'and welcome to The Bookshop on Rosemary Lane.'

Loved *The Bookshop on Rosemary Lane?*

Then join Della and friends, and curl up with the rest of the Rosemary Lane series . . .

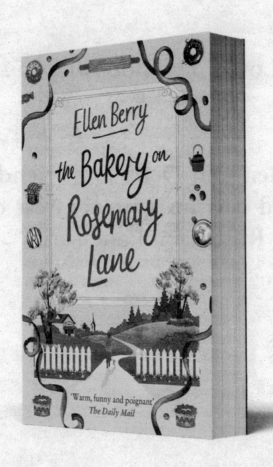

Ellen Berry

the Bakery on Rosemary Lane

'Warm, funny and poignant'
The Daily Mail

Coming in July 2017

Ellen Berry

the Bistro on Rosemary Lane

'Warm, funny and poignant'
The Daily Mail

Coming in July 2018

Looking for more? Then get your hands on Ellen's other books, writing as Fiona Gibson.

Midlife crisis? WHAT midlife crisis?!

A warm, funny read for fans of Carole Matthews and Catherine Alliott, Fiona writes about life as it really is.

Have you ever wanted to escape from it all?

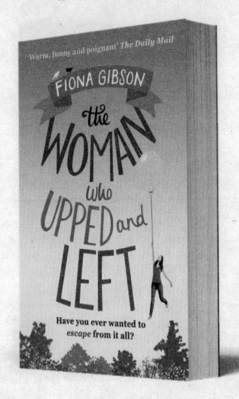

A warm, funny read for fans of Carole Matthews and Catherine Alliott, Fiona writes about life as it really is.